DARK SKY FULL OF STARS

An M/M romance

Roman Schreiber

Umbra Infigure

"I would recognise you in total darkness, were you mute and I deaf. I would recognise you in another lifetime entirely, in different bodies, different times. And I would love you in all of this, until the very last star in the sky burnt out into oblivion."

Song of Achilles (Almost)

MADELEINE MILLER (I MEAN, KINDA SORT OF)

CONTENT WARNING

This book includes a gay character in a long-term (platonic but performative) relationship with a woman, reflecting a very real way many gay people tried to survive in less accepting contexts. It's not a cheating trope fantasy; it's about the messy, painful process of trying to live honestly after years of hiding.

This book ends on a very slight cliffhanger. The series contains detailed and intense themes of survivorship, suicide, and PTSD. Contains explicit language and on-page explicit content. Depictions of mental illness, eating disorders, violence, trauma and sexual assault. Absolutely not suitable for minors. Full open door sex scenes.

1 AUSTEN

"Shut the fuck up or I'll choke you out and leave you behind this dumpster."

His arm is almost suffocating me. I feel around beside me for something to hit him with, but it's so narrow back here, I can hardly move. In the only rational moment of the evening, I press the panic button on my bracelet. I sit still and wait for my brother and the cavalry to arrive. There's a lot of shouting in the lobby, and outside. It's getting louder.

Mischa's arm loosens a little. He smells like cinnamon. He always smells like cinnamon, and something else sweet and warm and comforting. Aniseed?

It all happened so fast. I was walking in front of him, going down the stairwell of the hotel. I was looking at the carpet, and he must have been looking over my shoulder to the door in the main foyer. Then he puts his hand over my mouth, grabs me from behind, and lifts me up. We're not exactly sober, and I'm over six foot so that's an achievement. I jerk up in surprise and whack the back of my head on his temple and we crash into the wall. He lets go of my mouth but squeezes my waist harder and charges through to the parking garage. For a second I see the men in the lobby, but before I can think about it he has me in a sleeper hold, dragging me into the shadows like a fucking serial killer.

Now he's looking through the narrow slot to the view of the door and breathing hot air on my earlobe. That familiar *beep-beep-beep* is coming closer. William bursts through the door in full King Kong mode. His green eyes are black holes in the stark garage light. He's in his boxers, shirtless, and murderous. His sandy brown hair is wet from the shower.

The grip around my neck tightens a little, maybe as a warning to stay still, or maybe automatically. I tense again.

"Mischa you *motherfucker!* You're fucking *dead!*" He listens for us and then screams "*BEE!*"

It's raw and guttural, like an animal in pain. He's a raging bull, pacing between the cars.

My heart sinks. He's unraveling again, and so am I.

Mischa lets out a tiny noise that almost sounds like *"Huh?"*

It is so quiet, but William hears it and pivots to our corner. As he walks our way, the commotion outside bursts in. Ten drunk guys have broken off from the rabble on the street to answer William's war cry.

They fan out. One has a knife and three others are packing heavy blunt-force trauma. Poor bastards. That won't save them for what's coming. They're about to be hit by a comet.

William puffs up like one of those kangaroos around here that look like they're on steroids. My hands go to Mischa's big warm forearms and I lean back into him, like he's a therapist's couch.

We watch as William neutralizes each threat one by one. Knife goes first by a knockout, headbutts baseball bat next and uses it to hit crowbar and… is that a fucking copper pipe? God is all of this country insane? One last roundhouse kick and all ten are flat on the concrete, and William growls like a monster.

Mischa makes an involuntary, but thankfully silent giggle that I feel against my back.

"God damn, can you do that too?" he whispers. "That's *hot.*"

I bristle at the comment, and push him off me. He doesn't fight it, because William is coming our way, scraping the copper pipe along the ground. I crawl out and pop to my feet. We face each other like two sides of a mirror, except my reflection has blood splattered on his face, and he's panting with his whole body.

"I'm here," I say. "I'm okay."

He is not coming down from his psychotic energy. I can feel myself shaking like a leaf. Our bodyguards Hayden and Kane come in and tell him the lobby is contained.

"Upstairs!" William bellows.

I run back to the door and William marches behind me. I

don't dare cast a glance back to the dumpster.

I knew tonight would end in blood. Again. I didn't even make it out of the hotel this time.

2 MISCHA

The best part of my week is my job. It's only one hour, but it's honest work. Only, not really.

Tuesday nights I sling dough, literally and figuratively, at a pizzeria from nine thirty till half past ten when it closes, to cover for the waiters while they are having dinner next door.

It's a tiny old building next to our family restaurant. Running it is a crash course in laundering money. That's why we bought it. Training wheels for me and my brothers to learn the ropes one after the other.

It's an extremely inefficient way to legitimize criminal money, but our father insisted. I explained all the better, more cost-effective options, like a company in the Caribbean, Delaware, or Liechtenstein, but he was hell-bent on having the two best Italian restaurants in some quaint little college town in Middle America. What kills me about it is that we already own restaurants in Boston and Jersey, and we'd all much rather be there. We're not even Italian. The whole thing makes no sense.

The servers take the sales money for their silence, and go next door to eat good Russian food with my brothers while I hold down the fort here, and crunch all the numbers. There are only two small tables and it's very intimate and candle-lit. The food is excellent. It's popular with hipsters, but Tuesdays are usually dead by nine.

After a year, I've banged anyone in this town worth banging, and some people that were not. As a result, I bump into people I've slept with EVERY DAY. Some are obsessed, because I'm unfairly hot for such a small place. Thank God tonight's too cold for even the diehard stalkers. It's never *not* awkward. I really need to get out of here.

I am putting in purchases for next week at the counter when the bell at the door chimes. I look up from my order form to see a tall guy with sandy hair and emerald eyes. William Blazey is brushing snow off the hood of his parka.

He inhales sharply when he sees me.

"Oh *wow*," he says.

Oh wow what? I think.

Wait a minute, did I just take his breath away?

That's fine. I have that effect on people. I'm gorgeous. I've been told so a thousand times. It's not even the first 'Oh-wow' I have had this week and it's only Tuesday. I'm tall, muscular, and handsome in the extreme. Curly black hair and the body of Adonis. Covered in tattoos but you can't tell with the waiter's uniform on. I'm not arrogant or loud about it either, just extremely thankful. My beauty is the reason my father adopted me and my little sister Sofie, but the gun is still to my head, so I work at my looks and body slavishly. It's also how I make money to support Sofie, so I thank God every day for giving me the face of an angel, and saving our lives. No apologies here; everyone can get absolutely cactus-fucked if they try to humble me.

So William Blazey thinks I'm hot? Seeing him now, he's not so bad either; certified hunk if I'm honest; tall and built, half inch taller than me, which is such a rarity, cute too. More than cute; chiseled, handsome. Really handsome. Teen heartthrob vibes. Only... that guy is a hateful asshole who usually looks at me like I am dirt under his shoe.

I frown in surprise. He knows I caught his reaction, and he winces, dipping his head before shyly looking up with his big green eyes.

"I mean, *hi*," he says and clears his throat. "Hello."

The sound of his voice, and his adorable British accent hits me like an arrow to the chest and I gasp. The way he talks is usually so contemptuous and now it's so sweet. Now he's taking my breath away.

For a split second, his eyebrows flash, and mine do too. *What is happening?*

Is William Blazey really this gorgeous? How did I never notice this? This cannot be him.

"Wow," I blink. "Hi. Wow," I blink again. "Who are *you*?"

An involuntary smile breaks out over both our faces.

The door chimes again and *another* William Blazey comes inside.

"I'm Austen," he says.

There's two of them. The recluse is not just his *brother* but his fucking identical twin. They are both dressed like rich white boys but Austen wears it better. Cooler. Less uptight. William definitely has a stick up his ass. He steps forward, and the clouds come over his double, until he's surrounded by sadness. What would have been the start of something special freezes, and Austen steps away from the counter. But that moment before he arrived is proof that if William wasn't such a dick, he might actually acknowledge my god-like beauty.

Funny.

William looks at me with a sneer. "Don't I know you?"

Are you actually kidding me?

We've taken the same classes for a fucking year now, and go to the same gym and hangout spots around town. This is not the first introduction we've had.

Why does he look at everything he sees with contempt? Why is this guy so hateful about everything?

"Yeah, I think so," I shrug. "You're at Amherst? You fight too? Study business... with me. It's... um... *William* right?"

"Whatever," he bristles.

Ding-ding. Two bouncer types enter and William nods to them.

Man... He really takes them everywhere now? Bodyguards for pizza? What a coward. I would never. Sooner die than look like a wimp.

"Two pepperonis and four colas," William says and turns to Austen. "I'm going to the washroom."

William leaves, and his gorgeous brother comes back to the counter.

"You know him?" Austen asks me.

"Me and Will? We *totally* know each other. We spent all yesterday afternoon in the same room, and he asks me if he knows me *every* time we meet outside of class," my brow furrows. "What's his problem?"

"It's nothing personal."

"You know him too then? Tell me he knows *your* name?"

"Yeah, we're related," Austen says quizzically.

"Sorry for you."

"People say we look alike."

"No, you're way cuter," I smile. "You want to order something else?"

"Yeah, um, do you have anything a little lighter?" he asks. "Like a salad?"

"We have the Al Gore," I say.

"What's that?"

"It's just a regular pepperoni pizza hidden underneath salad greens."

He throws back his head and laughs, "Okay, but like, anything *without* cheese?"

"In a pizzeria?" I frown.

He blushes. "Yeah sorry I'm kinda lactose intolerant, but it's a stupid question. Never mind."

I nod toward the bathrooms. "Why isn't William also lactose intolerant? Doesn't he have matching DNA?"

"Oh he almost certainly is, but he's not in tune with himself enough to realize something that simple," he sighs.

"He doesn't even know if he should drink milk?" I laugh.

He shakes his head. "No."

"We have proper food in the restaurant next door. We eat there after it closes. I could grab you something?"

"No, I can't take your dinner," he smiles sweetly. "I will survive."

Then I see his *dimples*, ugh. Perfectly *round*. Adorable. He's completely charmed me. If he was the love of my life, I'd die happy. His twin returns, and a wall comes up between us as they both take their seats.

I get the feeling Austen is scared of William.

I go to the kitchen and feed two pepperonis into the oven, and then dash out the back, and into the back of our restaurant next door where my eight brothers are kicking it with the rest of the staff.

I nod to Yuri, one of the teenage waiters who is on tonight.

"I need you to give the guys next door their colas," I tell him. "Now."

He gets up and leaves without question.

"Dinner's going to be a little late tonight, sorry guys," I say.

I grab a salad, a plate of chicken Kiev and a clay pot of pelmeni dumplings. Then just to be cheeky, I grab two large meat shish that have just been perfectly grilled over charcoal. I know it is Grigor who will protest first. He's always the one to put a stop to any shenanigans. That's how he got the name Green Pepper.

"Lemon," he says, "you better not be walking out of here with that."

Ivan is the second oldest, and my most dangerous looking brother, sees the two skewers of meat leaving and bleats like a goat, "I will stab both of those swords through your heart."

Even in a suit Ivan screams Russian mafia. We call him "Chamomile" because he's always on edge, and you know, could do with a cup of herbal tea. It's awkward when he makes death threats like that, because the moment you look at him you think, *"Oh man, he looks like he's killed people."*

People think Russians are cold and hard but they are hopeless romantics when it comes to food. They love it passionately and wash it down with its mistress; alcohol.

"You fuckers are going to have to wait another twenty minutes, you *all* owe me a bunch of favors."

I head into the back of the pizzeria and point my face to the pizza oven.

"Yuri," I say, "give one pizza to each table."

I follow behind and place the plates of my favorite dishes in front of the boy with the sparkly eyes and he lights up in surprise. William looks confused and his brother tells him he ordered it while he was in the bathroom.

"Jesus, you said you were really hungry," William tells his twin, "but when was the last time you ate?"

Austen tries the salad and closes his eyes and smiles. He turns to me back at the counter and mouths a silent *"thank you,"* and I nod.

I return to my paperwork and put my headphones over one ear but leave the other a little open to listen to their conversation. I have had Kayne West's new album *Graduation* on high rotation lately. He won me over when he got on national television and said the president didn't care about black people. That was epic, and he was just saying what everyone was thinking.

At the table, Austen takes a skewer and looks at it like it's Excalibur.

"How are you going to eat it?" William asks.

Austen shrugs and puts the sword to his mouth and sinks his teeth into the succulent meat.

"Mmm," he says, as he chews with his eyes closed and his shoulders go up in pure joy at the taste.

He sits back and a little bit of juice runs down the side of his mouth to his chin and he laughs and catches it with his thumb and licks his fingers.

Instant erection. I am completely at this guy's attention. Usually people have to work a little to give me one like this but the guy wasn't even *trying.* Pretty sure my mouth is open too.

What the fuck?

This has never happened to me before, and I am freaking out. I go out back and take a breath. I need to pull myself together, and get my dick down. I think about chess behind the ovens but it stays rock hard. What is happening? I have no choice but to pull it into my waist-belt and tie an apron around it.

I have to fuck that guy, or I have to stop thinking about fucking that guy. Can we just remember that he's William Blazey's brother? I hate that guy. That should be enough to kill this thing dead...

Out front the waiters and busboys are in the street passing

by the window one by one, and sneaking a look at the guy eating their dinner.

Oh god, my brothers will be out soon. They'll play it cool, having a drink until replacement dishes arrive from the chef, but curiosity will get them eventually.

"Are you sure you want to do this?" William asks Austen.

"Of course, Billy Bee, come on!" Austen says, "It's gonna be great."

Outside Anatoly is now smiling over the scene, and raises an eyebrow to me. He has his hands in his suit pockets with his feet slightly apart and looks like a billboard for Hugo Boss.

"Fuck off, Chili," I mouth at him in Russian.

He has very good luck, so he's the chili pepper.

He turns and leaves and Dimitri takes his place.

"Fuck off, Spud."

It's still only my younger brothers. Soon it will be Maxim, Aleksandr, Arkady... one after another, almost a version of the same guy, only older and more intimidating each time. Eventually Konstantin or Ivan will come out and that will definitely scare him off.

Austen wipes his mouth with a napkin. "I haven't been up this late in forever," he says.

Really? The clock just turned ten.

They call it a day and William tells one of his goons to get the car.

That was quick. I put that food down maybe five minutes ago.

Austen comes to the counter to pay, and the others head outside. He picks up my scruffy old paperback lying on the counter and turns it over.

"What's your name?" he asks me.

"Mischa," I say. "I mean, Mikhail. My mom used to call me Mischa, but most people just call me Lemon."

"Lemon?" he says, all posh and British. "But you are so sweet. I like Mischa. Dinner was amazing."

"It was nothing," I say, and feel my cheeks get hot.

"Not true, it was incredible."

"Thanks. You should never eat pizza here again."

Austen laughs. "Yes, I definitely won't."

God, what a smile. His dimples are *killing* me. I'm very hard again, and cannot wait to close this place up for the night and have a very vigorous conversation with myself. I just have to drink up as much of him as I can while he's here.

He gestures to the Godfather and Scarface movie posters on the wall.

"Great movies."

"Yeah, we're real film buffs around here."

"You know there's a film festival soon? They are playing *Santa Sangre* next week too."

"Really?" I say. I've never heard of it. "I've heard it's good."

His face goes all gooey looking at me. The space between his eyebrows pulls them up together again.

He wanted me to see that one. Holy shit, he's about to ask me out.

"Hey, I don't suppose you would..." he starts.

I see William through the window, coming back.

"Yes!" I tell Austen, and nod my head emphatically. "Yes, yes I would love to. Absolutely. Tomorrow is good, or the weekend."

The dimples say hello. Ding-ding. William is behind him again. Austen's eyes flicker a little, the dimples disappear. Definitely scared of that asshole. I wait for him to finish his question.

"Um..."

"Yeah...?" I say, encouragingly, and leaning forward on the counter.

He thinks for a moment and then seems to change tact. "You should volunteer."

"What?"

"For the film festival, if you're interested. They need volunteers."

He was definitely not going to ask me that before William came back in. Cockblocking motherfucker.

"Oh…" I say. "Yeah, that could be cool."

William is drilling his eyes into the back of Austen's head, and Austen knows it. My hot little dumpling is deflating with his brother's frigid presence. He puts down the book, and I grab a menu.

"We deliver," I say, and hand it to him. "From the restaurant too. Our phone number is at the bottom. If you call tomorrow, or the weekend, we'll deliver, anytime."

He takes the pamphlet from me, and I use the moment to stroke his fingers with mine secretly. His eyes dart from his hand up to my face.

He turns, William shoots me a nasty look, and they leave. I stare into space for a few seconds, and then look down at the bill.

He left an enormous tip.

※　※　※

Everyone has almost finished dinner by the time I return. They're all bemused by the night's events.

"Are you back to steal dessert?" Dimitri asks.

"You fucks got lucky tonight," I tell the staff. "You all get two-hundred and fifty each."

"He left you a *grand*?" Yuri gasps.

Yuri is the sole English speaker and breadwinner in his family. The other waiter, Danni, was homeless before I met him. He was too young and scared and too much like my younger self not to take him in.

"Yeah," I say casually.

"Oh my God," Danni says, taking his cut. "You can steal dinner anytime."

"Yeah, suck his dick," Yuri says.

"Hey!" Gregor says in a warning tone.

The two scamper away with their wads of cash.

"That was a very attractive young man, *Mikhail*," Konstantin says pointedly. "Or was it both of them?"

"The one on the right."

"What difference does it make?" Anatoly frowns.

"The one on the left is an asshole and scared the nice one off. So disappointing." I shake my head. "The shop phone is mine this week," I say, and hold up the flip-top phone charging by the till. "I gave him a menu with the number. I'm going to sleep with this thing in case he calls."

"I will bet any of you a thousand bucks he never calls," Anatoly smirks.

"So do you only like guys now?" Maxim asks.

"Well," I shrug, "sixty-forty."

"Sixty percent men or women?"

"Women," I lie. "Or maybe I'm just a sex addict? I don't

know. I really need to have a fuck soon or I'm gonna go crazy."

Gregor shakes his head. "Then you have to fuck someone before you come here next week because I'm not waiting till after ten to eat again."

"I think Dimitri is at least seventy percent men," Maxim smiles. "He's lucky we're not Italian," he gestures like his hand is a gun that fires at Dimitri, who stares him down. "And I don't even want to think about *Anatoly*." The boys all start laughing.

"Ninety-nine percent?"

"He's a sharp dresser!" Arkady chimes in and Anatoly reaches over and thumps him in the arm.

"I'm five percent gay," Ivan says, and the room goes quiet. "Maybe a little more. It is a comfort to me when I think about the Gulag. If I have to spend a few years in jail, I am getting some meat."

The others laugh.

"Prison is different. It's all just holes, isn't it?" Dimitri says. "We can fuck anything. I mean I am not going to tattoo a whore on my stomach and open for business, but I'd go either way in a pinch."

"Do tell, jailbird," Anatoly says.

"Yeah Melon," Maxim says. "Weren't you in prison?"

All the boys start to jeer.

"Shut up," Dimitri says. "For your information, I was cellmates with a beautiful... person... of indeterminate... affiliation... who I'm still trying to work out... named Ivanna Krotchlickmehoff. I remember our time together fondly. We changed positions every night. Sometimes it was the top bunk and sometimes the bottom. Sometimes in her peepka and sometimes my poopka. I promised to marry her but she's got forty years to go, and I'm still a young man... but I do miss the foot massages. I mean she had enormous feet, but she was a nice lady. Matter of fact, I think the big feet were one of the things that made her... unforgettable."

Dimitri survived prison with his self-effacing sense of humor, and the terror Dad wields inside.

I stare out the window with a bewitched look on my face. I can tell the Green Pepper is about to nip any tender feelings in the bud.

"You are smitten?" Gregor asks. "You're feeling something?"

"Your dick, perhaps?" Dimitri says.

A wild rumpus of hoots erupts.

"He has charmed you?"

I don't want to dampen the atmosphere so I perform for my brothers.

"What if he has?" I gesture theatrically. "He's truly majestic. It's almost like he's some sort of rare woodland creature that has appeared in a forest clearing," I stand on my tippy-toes, and dance a little from *Swan Lake*. The boys laugh. "His handsome eyes glinting in a shaft of light through the trees. A bird sings a sweet song of spring and he turns to listen to it. A beast like me would only step on a twig and watch as the echoing *snap* scares him away forever."

Applause comes up from the group.

"Lemon is the winner tonight! Give him a drink."

I take a shot of Russian Standard and they cheer. A flash of sadness crosses over me but I push it back down.

"What's with the security and expensive car?" Ivan asks.

"They are the Blazey brothers," I say. "Vincent Blazey's two grandsons. Their grandfather is a billionaire."

"Is that so?" he looks over to Konstantin.

"They would have been heirs to an enormous fortune but the old man disowned them after they stole an airplane in Switzerland and crashed it into a ski field. The old man said they were dead to him."

"Womp-womp," Dimitri takes a shot of vodka.

Strange though. They must be burning through the last of their trust fund, because they don't seem to deny themselves anything. They have a huge mansion out of town as well.

After dinner the Green Pepper comes to extinguish the last of my embers for the beautiful British dandy.

"Don't even consider it, Lemon," Gregor says. "Everybody

falls for someone at least once in their lives, but please try to choose carefully. This is a delicate time and we need to be focused. Spoilt little rich kids are a pain in the ass. He's already a public figure as well. Most romances end in pain anyway, and if you fell for him you wouldn't be one of few lucky ones that don't."

My parents were lucky. Tragic maybe, but lucky in love.

"You're probably right," I say, and pat the shop phone in my pocket. "But I have never in my life felt so pulled towards someone. One more push could tip me over the edge. He was going to ask me out and I already said yes."

Konstantin sighs. "You don't have the luxury of being powerless to someone's charms like you were tonight. I can't even imagine you fixated on someone. It's a little terrifying if I'm honest. We have a duty, a place in a chain of command."

"Of course," I say. "The family comes first always. What should I do? Fuck him and get it out of my system?"

"No!" Anatoly whips around. "You're not in his power yet. Do you want to be?"

I absolutely want to be.

"Of course not."

"Then stay away."

"You're circling the drain, baby brother," Maxim puts his arm around my shoulders. "Take it from me and Chili, we know the pain. Get out while you still can."

"You can't see him again," Anatoly nods.

"You *really* can't see him again," Alexandr shakes his head.

They're being dramatic. We'll meet at a third location to have sex on the regular. I don't do relationships. I'll never be boyfriend material.

"Right," I nod. "It should be easy. I never saw him this whole year. I just need to avoid him for a few weeks and then we're done here."

"Let's not risk it," Anatoly says. "Me and Gregor will go to Boston with you tomorrow. We need to dodge this arrow."

He'll call. He'll call me tonight.

"Okay," I say.

"Find someone casual," Maxim says. "Try to avoid the shot from cupid's bow until you at least find someone more... easy."

"Have you ever been in love?" I ask him.

"No," he shakes his head. "I hope when I do fall in love it will be short and painless or long and beautiful. Pain is more likely with people like us."

"I have also not yet been in love," Dimitri says. "I wonder if it's real."

"What about Ivanna?" Maxim jokes.

Dimitri smiles. "That was a marriage of convenience. I imagine real love will be like a pig being eaten by a python.

Hopefully I'm the python. I will fall, and I will think it will be too much, that it is enormous, insurmountable, and incredibly satisfying, but then slowly I will digest their soul and deflate over a few weeks or months. I will come down from the cloud and will regain my senses. I'll have a lot of sex with them and get bored and move on. At least I hope that's how it will happen. I can't imagine aching for someone."

Austen seems nice. I wouldn't be doing him any favors by eating his soul like a greedy snake. I should let him go before the cage comes down.

3 AUSTEN

Tuesday, December 4, 2007, 10.06 pm.

I don't leave the house, unless I have to. We have everything we need here; a pool, a gym, a shooting range. It's literally a mansion. We converted it from an old Catholic Girls' school, and made some new additions. It's lovely, with ivy growing up the stonework.

Our lives outside our home are bizarre and complicated. Nothing's ever easy, and I hate it.

Thanks to our insane parents, my brother's name is not actually William, or Billy either, and neither is mine, but we try to keep things simple, so that's what he goes by.

I go by *'Austen'*. It's not my name either.

Believe me, it's better this way.

We have two bodyguards, Hayden and Kane. Hayden is the light-haired, olive-skinned one that looks like a golden retriever and Kane is the dark-haired, tanned one that looks like an enormous puppy. I don't understand why my brother hired them and what they are doing here. Don't get me wrong, they're great guys, they are just a little too much. Kane worked on our estate when we were younger and came back to work for us after a few years in the army, and he recommended Hayden after they did a few tours together. They live in the guest houses, and they'll kill anyone who tries to get in, which is good, I guess. I just hate how my brother makes them go to school with me.

I read a lot, study, play music and walk the dogs. Some days are so quiet I feel like I'm the last man on Earth.

I have classes most days. My brother and I are both in our freshman year at the local college, after a gap year. Given that college was never in question for us and always a *heavy expectation*, in a line of *heavy expectations*, I think we are doing okay. I don't hate it, but I do sometimes wish I could feel more than this deep, yawning apathy to the whole thing. I study law because I have to, and history, because in another life, it's a subject I might have loved. William picked business. Well, he had business picked for him.

We were missing for high school. By design. Nobody knew where we were. Even our famous, rich, piece-of-work birth-father. He pretended he did to save face, but we were in the fucking wind, with only our trusted inner circle knowing where we were.

Last year, we were lured by an old classmate to a superyacht for an afternoon. It was a setup. Paparazzi shots of one of us (me, but who can tell?) pushed us back into the spotlight. Once the French tabloids figured out we were James Blazey's sons, the photos went to the British tabloids, and sent lusty social-ites into a frenzy.

James tried to contact us after that. Yuck. A few weeks later my brother moved us here, but the house was almost com-pletely remodeled by the time we arrived, so I think he was planning it for a while.

After a year back in society, people are waking up to the fact that William Blazey has returned a man, and quite an impos-ing one. My brother is heir to an aristocratic title and the perks that go with it. I don't think many people know I exist, and I like it like that. My future is still up in the air.

I play drums and guitar. I joined a rock band a few months ago, and we have practice twice a week. I also train every day with my brother, and we talk to our foster parents almost every day too. Then maybe once a week I call my Grandpa, and that's as much socializing as I can bear.

We live in a university town in Massachusetts. I realized when we first came here, there was no point making friends. Eventually I'd have to lie to anyone getting to know me. Most people who want to know rich boys are sleazy anyway. I'm not looking for a mean girl to be nice to me in exchange for gifts. I don't have time for it. William, on the other hand, is a woman-izer who screws like his dick is about to fall off. He also likes cage-fighting. Very red-blooded. I sometimes wonder, if things were different, would I be too?

The thing is, I'm completely, absolutely, and irrevocably, totally fucked up. Unfixable. I usually feel like I'm just under the still water of a deep pond. Like I'm tied down and can't reach the surface, so I have to breathe through a reed straw. I try to ignore all these hopeless feelings, but it's getting worse and worse. And you know what they say about drowning men. They tend to drown others with them. I don't want anyone to get hurt except myself.

My solitude has not been easy for William. I'm dragging him down too. I tell him I am focusing on study but I don't think he believes it. He feels me pulling away.

I make exceptions for low-key parties on special occasions. We had fireworks for the Fourth of July, and a bonfire for the Fifth of November. Seeing the leaves fall and the jack-o-lanterns at Halloween was amazing. I dressed as a Tolkien elf, and he was Beetlejuice. I gave candy to trick-or-treaters. We went to Thanksgiving a few days ago with some friends of his. I really enjoyed it, until one of the girls said she wanted to see me again.

Now it's almost Christmas, and we have this lovely snow just before break. I'm trying to get as far from everywhere as I possibly can. When I saw a note pinned to the history bulletin board advertising a "cultural exchange trip" to Australia,

I knew we had to go. Yeah, it's a school thing, but we all know that it's basically a glorified holiday with a school credit attached, so win-win. When I told my brother's girlfriend Isobelle, and Sabrina, my fiancé, (don't ask, it's complicated) who both still live in France, they insisted we tack on a trip to New Zealand at the end and go on a boat journey around Fiordland. I love the idea.

We won't be back for the first few days of school, but I talked to each of our professors about it beforehand, got our syllabi and assigned readings and promised to study on the trip. None of William's professors realized they were talking to me and not him, but it had to be done. Billy is already signed up, and I already paid for it before I talked to him. I just have to persuade him to go.

We make a rare visit to the pizzeria everyone raves about. I tell William what I have done, and how a holiday Downunder would be a good thing.

"I don't know," he says.

"It's gonna be *great*."

"Do you really want to?"

"Of course," I chuckle. "Come on Hon... argh, shit, sorry," I roll my eyes, "I haven't been out in public for *ages*. I mean *bro*... Billy Bee... *William*..."

He gags in disgust. "Don't call me *William*, it makes my skin crawl."

"But *Will* is okay?" I giggle more. "Because it's that, or everyone knowing what a sweetiepie you *really* are..."

"Why are you happy?" his brow furrows. "Why are you smiling? What's this about?"

"Nothing!"

"Oh God. Do you have an ulterior motive?"

My brother puts his hand on mine and I push it away. "No."

"You're not planning to do anything, are you? I'm not going to have to sing *You Are My Sunshine* all night, am I?"

I scoff. "It's okay..."

"Remember our deal..."

"I swear it's not like that. It's just a holiday."

"No secret agenda?"

"No," I say.

My brother stares at me like I'm abstract art.

"Not all relaxed and happy because you're going to take me on a trip to say goodbye, then kill yourself like a fucking asshole?"

He's seeing the signs. Ugh.

I lean back, frustrated. "No."

"You'll tell me if you're struggling?"

"Yes," I lie.

"Good, because I love you, and I will kill myself and track

you the fuck down in Hell and kill you for real. You don't get to quit, Baby."

I don't want to hear this.

"Understood."

"I love you," he says.

I roll my eyes. "I know that, Honey Bee."

"So much."

It's not enough.

"This is what I mean by *'smothering me'*."

"Please don't kill yourself."

"Please stop."

He huffs, and thinks about it. "Australia?"

"Yes."

"Why do you want to go?"

I shrug. "I want to go somewhere *warm.* I want to live a little."

"You could just start dating," he smiles. "It can be a lot of fun. Some of those religious girls are so gorgeous, and they'd never push you to do anything you didn't want to..."

"I don't want to *socialize*," I tell him. "You promised me koalas, and I promised to stay alive, remember? It's time."

"True..." he thinks about it. "But you can't die after, because your fucked-up logic is that we've seen the wombats and koalas and all the Ozzy shit now as promised, and so now you can skip out on me, right?"

He knows me too well.

"Of course not."

"We don't have to go on a school program, we could just go by ourselves? I'll get us a private plane, five-star tropical beaches..."

He wants to control the variables. All inclusive resorts. Lots of cameras. Nobody leaves the island easily. Can't slip away on a helicopter. Can't hitch a ride out of there with a stranger.

"It's worth a credit," I tell him.

"Alright. But with Kane. And Hayden."

"Of course. The school is willing to accommodate them, yeah," I nod. "Not that I'm happy about it."

"And the girls can babysit you too."

"Babysit? Accurate."

"Not *babysit.*" He rolls his eyes. "*Baby...* sit."

"I think you mean *'accompany'* me, Billy Bee."

"You know what I mean."

This is our monthly cheat day. Billy usually measures every bite of food, and only lets it pass our mouths after a grueling daily workout at five in the bloody morning. We're never alone, because hunger is always with us. Even so, he's horrified because we've ordered way too much food, and it arrives all at once, and fills the table.

I eat a whole dumpling and smile. I eat some meat and giggle. It only makes him more suspicious of my good mood. It's stressing him out. He pretends to sip his drink. He won't even have a slice of pizza. He's gonna make us leave soon.

I offer him the chicken Kiev.

"You have to try this, Bee."

"I'm good," he says, and passes it over, along with the dumplings, to our bodyguards at the next table.

He has to eat *something*, so I negotiate that we can both have half the salad, a hunk of meat, and nothing else. He agrees.

"I got a gig next week," I tell him.

"That's great," he says. "Where? When?"

"Next Saturday. In Boston."

"We should..."

"Take Hayden and Kane," I interrupt. "Yeah, I figured."

4 MISCHA

Boston always feels like home. Gregor has a place in Back Bay. The area looks more like Europe than any other part of America. I have been here a week and I think I want to stay.

I have tried finding some new hook-ups, but I just haven't felt that *'click'* of their puzzle piece and mine falling into place. I don't mean sex feels weird. I mean I don't vibe with them enough to get that far. It's the same with my old hook-ups too. I'm starting to feel bad, because they all want to jump me the moment we meet and I have to disappoint them.

I've been walking around just hoping to bump into someone that doesn't bore me to tears. I did get as far as a cute model's bedroom, but my dick did not want to join the conversation. Anatoly and Maxim have been stuffing me full of oysters every day in the hope of restoring my once legendary libido, but it's not working. I've decided to join a sex addict help group, because I am not coping without lots of sex.

Today Ivan and Konstantin have asked us to meet them at a Russian bathhouse for a shvitz. They have business to discuss. There's a secluded one with a good reputation. I have never heard a word of English in the place. I love pretending I'm home there. Really home. Like I could shower and walk out the door and see my mother again.

Gangsters have always used bathhouses – Italian, Russian, Asian. You can't wear a wire when you steam because you're naked and it's wet. The masseuses here are deaf so they can't overhear anything. There's also a restaurant upstairs that's insanely good. There's only one table up there.

My brothers are probably already in the banya whipping each other with oak leaves. I reach the changing rooms and can't muster any energy to go in. When I'm down like this I know it's time to call my sister Sofie. She's sixteen. I'm in Massachusetts partly to be near her boarding school. My eight other brothers and older sister come and go, but Sofie is my heart. She's also my only blood too.

"Are you up or down?" she asks when I call.

"I'm just…"

"Good. I can't deal with you when you're up. Have you practiced today?"

Three hours of piano and three hours of ballet every day since we could walk, now I can play most instruments by ear. Every morning I have to get up and practice. My mind wants to stop but my body won't let me.

"Always."

"Have you heard from Mom and Dad?"

"They got a message to me," I say. "They are proud of you."

"Are they proud of you too?"

I sigh. "I hope so."

"That was a joke, Mischa."

She sounds like Mom.

"Yeah," I say. "It's almost Christmas. What do you want?"

"I want you. None of the others. Just you."

"Not even Natasha?"

"No."

"She'll get jealous."

Sofie laughs a little. "I know. Just give me Christmas Eve."

"Okay, My Heart."

"See you soon."

After the call I look at my shoes. I think I can take them off now.

I get into my robe, and someone enters from the baths. Mid twenties, handsome, tanned, gym body. He has a towel around his waist and is drying off his hair and panting. He goes to his locker and grabs an electrolyte drink. His skin is red and blotchy from the sauna and he's dripping with sweat. As he drinks, the towel comes off his face. He seems familiar. He's a little older. I like older. Tall, attractive, dark hair. Golden-coloring. Sexy.

Haven't I seen him before? Who cares. Maybe he'll do.

He nods at me. "Man, it's so hot, I'm dying in there."

He has that British accent too.

"Do you have a hat?" I ask, and hand him one. "You wet it and they keep your head cool."

"Thanks," he says.

He smiles as he takes it slowly and purposefully from my hand, looking in my eyes. Then he checks out the rest of my body. I know he likes what he sees.

He's hot. I should like him. I'm usually down for this sort of thing, but there's only the tiniest spark. Not enough to get me in a situation. Fuck. Something's wrong with me. I need to get out of my head again.

Maxim comes in from the baths and looks at me from behind the guy. I rise to my feet at his silent command, and I follow him to the sauna.

"See you out there," I say, as I pass.

The place is empty. Almost.

I pass the door to the spa where another guy is bathing. He's totally relaxed in the water, with his eyes closed. What's unusual is he's wearing a swimming top that covers his body in a place where casual nudity is the norm. Even so, his body is insane. My glass heart jumps a little and the electricity runs down my middle. He's the one I want.

And then I recognize him.

No.

God no.

How?

Here?

No.

That's impossible.

Austen?

I'm losing it.

Austen is here with me. Cupid's arrow hits its mark. BAM. I feel the direct hit, square in the chest, knocking the air from my lungs. *Oh holy God.* In a split second, my emotional inner world changes into something unrecognizable. Austen has stolen my heart, and it feels incredible.

Reality starts to transform around me. I almost feel like I have been drugged. Chemicals are charging through my bloodstream, past my bones and flooding my soul.

He didn't see me. That guy is his bodyguard. I knew I'd seen him before. This is bad. Bad bad bad. And really really really great. I don't feel in control right now.

I head towards the sauna and try not to think about Austen being here. I only saw him for a moment. This cannot be real.

I feel euphoric. Delusional thoughts invade me. I sense a greater purpose to our chance meeting here; it is all to deliver him to me.

He's mine, a gift from Fate, from the Universe. Mine.

Every priority in my life is abandoned, in favor of the single goal of being with him. It all makes sense now; it's my life's purpose.

Hold on. This has to stop. This will get you killed.

I think of all the ways I'm going to hide this from everyone.

I'll probably just skip town with him. He's from Europe, we can just hide in a cabin in the Alps or something.

My mind is whirring around and around. I need to get it together. I need to go from jittery to relaxed right now, get this meeting over with, and go meet my destiny with Austen.

Gregor is in the steam room with Anatoly. Konstantin comes in and sits down too. Ivan is on his way or something.

I stand in the door and stare at the three of them. I see my life from a distance and wonder how someone else might see it. With our shirts on my brothers look threatening, but without them, they look deadly. Gregor's intricate stick-poke tattoos of demons and saints and onion dome cathedrals un-furl over his chest. Anatoly's network of signs and symbols, cards, dice, naked women, and Madonnas. Konstantin's growl-ing lions, tigers, and bears, oh my. My moon and stars across my collarbone, my sacred heart on my chest with an eye in the middle, and my portrait of Sofie on my shoulder. In my head I'm a kid, but outside I'm a big scary fucking man covered in Russian hooligan tattoos.

One look and he'll wonder why he ever thought I was a nice guy. I can't let him see, but I can't hide my ink in front of my brothers.

"Are you going in?" Maxim grunts behind me.

I think to myself how to hide without hiding. *I could go for a massage... Perfect; Westerners don't go for scrubs like we do. Cover me in foam and whack me with leaves.*

I stand in the door holding it open. "Have you had a scrub yet?" I ask, and don't wait for an answer. I gesture with my head.

"We need to talk," Gregor says.

"Soon," I say. "I need to clear my head. Let's go upstairs and scrub, then talk, then eat."

This is the first time I've ever told the others what to do, maybe ever. They are all lethargic from the heat but move slowly out the door. They throw cold water on themselves, and we make our way to the massage room.

We find Ivan along the way. We all take our tables. Konstantin puts his face down and his masseuse starts working him over, everyone else follows. They cover us with thick creamy soap. They grab bunches of oak leaves and start hitting us with them.

I can feel the love pouring in like honey, filling up every part of me. I thought love was just some sort of extreme lust but this is light and warm and fluffy. When it has permeated all

DARK STARS IN THE SKY

through me, the feeling of pure desire lifts me out of my body. It's my only thought. I have never experienced anything like this.

We're almost done when someone arrives. He takes the table between me and Konstantin. I lift my head, It's not Austen. It's the apparently-gay bodyguard from the locker room.

Go away.

The masseuse throws a bucket of cold water on me, but it's too late for anything that simplistic. My brothers and I head back to the sauna. Dimitri is waiting inside.

"Dad wants us to finish things off here before heading to New York. Can you hold things down at home while we're in Boston?" Anatoly asks me.

"Of course," I say.

I'm not needed for the rest of it. They go over everything to keep me in the loop, but my mind is miles away. He's my *everything*—every tender bond a human being can have—mother, father, my newborn *baby* even. He's my other half, and *mine* completely. Austen. My love. My heart.

"Are you even listening?" Gregor asks.

I break out of my daydream. "What?" I say.

"Obviously not," Maxim smirks.

They look at me curiously.

The family comes first. This will get Sofie killed.

I forgot about Sofie. I can't put her in danger. I love her. Fuck. What am I thinking? I should reach out for help before this ocean of feelings drowns me.

"He's here," I say. "I don't know what to do."

"Who?" Ivan asks. "Who is here?"

"The guy I gave your dinner to the other week. The one I liked. Oh God, it's happening. I can't fight it. I feel like I'm possessed."

Anatoly rolls his eyes so hard he could give his face an injury.

"Oh for the love of..." he says, throwing his head back.

"This is kismet," I say. "This must be fate."

Konstantin flicks his eyes between me and Gregor. "He shows up at the restaurant, and now here?"

Anatoly runs his hand through his hair. "He's FBI or something."

"He's British," I say. "He cannot be FBI."

"He can be something," Ivan says.

Konstantin shakes his head. "Billionaire's kids don't do dirty work."

"We do!" Maxim protests.

"We're not Sivishni's real kids, Max," Gregor says, in a measured tone.

"I have to devour every inch of him," I say.

"Hey, hey. Lemon? Look at me." Anatoly clicks his fingers at me and shakes my shoulders while I grin at him. "Hey! Look at me! Snap out of it. We can salvage this. Lemon, you need to leave, now."

A quick shower in the changing room and I am ready to go when Austen enters, towel over his shoulders, still with the wet swimming top clinging to him. We lock eyes and the wind is knocked out of me. There is nothing but him, looking at me. I forget where I am. I forget *who* I am. I definitely forget my duty. The hole in my heart closes for the first time in forever. He looks stunned to see me.

"Oh wow... hi, hi... hello. Mischa, right?" he says. "I never thought I'd see anyone *here*... you..." his voice cracks from nerves and he coughs, "you're in Boston?"

I have to look away. It HURTS to look away. He's beautiful. I have had a lot of sex with a lot of hotties, but GOD DAMN. He's a marble statue. And that FACE. I CANNOT THINK.

"Austen. What are you doing here?"

"Yeah it's... very private here. Someone told me about the review in the paper, and I thought as long as I'm here... There's an eighties rock cover thing tonight downtown... it's stupid. You know, I've been to the pizzeria a few times but didn't see you this week. I was hoping to *not* eat pizza there again."

I feel timid. Jesus Christ. I am not fucking timid.

I smile. "I've been in Boston."

"Do Italians also like saunas?" he asks.

"I guess so," I say, confused.

"You're Italian, right?"

"No."

"Oh sorry I assumed you were," he looks at his feet, and flicks his eyes up to me in that shy, boner-inducing way.

It's hard to maintain any self-awareness. I'm totally fucking infatuated. I put my sports bag in front of my cock, just in case it spontaneously inflates again.

This is what love feels like? Holy *shit*.

I clear my throat and try to compose myself. "Because of the pizzeria, I get it."

"Wait, are you Russian?" he smiles.

"No. I mean, kind of," I wince a little. "What did you want to ask me?"

"What?" he searches my face.

"At the pizzeria? I felt like you were going to ask something."

"Oh, um..." he thinks about it and shakes his head, and looks at me sheepishly. "Since you work out, maybe you wanted to spar with William or something? My shoulder's hurting, and that's actually why I'm here..."

"I don't believe you," I say, before I realize I'm saying it.

"What?" he says, confused.

"I felt like you were going to ask me out when you mentioned the film festival."

Austen looks right at me and his mouth drops open, which could be discouraging, but I no longer feel shame, or any other emotion apart from the one making my body tingle.

"I didn't mean to come across that way," he says. "Sorry, I don't talk to people much and apparently I'm not good at it."

My superpower tells me he's lying.

The yearning for him possesses me completely. I need to scratch this itch.

I have to.

I have to have him.

I have to look at him all the time, because nothing in life could feel better, except for touching him.

I have to touch him.

"Can I ask you out?" I ask.

There is a pause so long, it feels like we'll be married between question and answer.

"Ask me...?"

He thinks for a moment before he understands. Then weighs it up in his mind until the fear forms on his face.

"I'm not interested, I'm taken—by a woman—sorry," he says, but his eyebrows flash, again.

I should be deterred, telling me he's straight, and falling for a straight boy, a straight "taken" boy for that matter, is a one way ticket to getting your heart ripped out, but I just can't buy into this farce. He thinks words can convince me, but how can they when his eyes, and beautiful face, are telling the real story? I have seen enough people interested in me before to know he is too. I cannot be alone in feeling this way.

He can't just slip through my fingers like this. We love each other too much.

"I don't believe you," I blurt out again before I realize, "You went *back* to the pizzeria, without William, everyday, all week? Nobody does that for pepperoni, or potato dumplings either. You wanted to ask me *something*. I already said yes. *Yes yes yes.*"

"No..." he stutters. "Please don't read into it. I actually wanted to ask if you could give us jobs in your restaurant as, well... as line cooks?"

"After you tipped three grand?"

"I'm a big tipper."

"Why does a big tipper want to be a fry cook, exactly?"

His eyes drop to his feet again. "I... I just... like cooking."

"Why didn't you call?"

He shakes his head. "The restaurant number doesn't actually work."

"Really?" I gasp in surprise.

Because it's a front for money laundering you stupid asshole there's not a chance in hell we'd be out there delivering food in the freezing cold all night and that's why Anatoly bet me a grand Austen would never call me because that fucking motherfucker knew all along it was wrong oh my god I am such an idiot I'm going to kill him...

"I just wanted something to do," he insists. "Just a job, not to lead you on."

Lies.

"Listen..."

My brothers enter, and silence descends over the changing room. They move in front of the person I am talking to. They see that it is indeed the object of my affection. They stare at Austen in a way that I understand can be quite intimidating to be on the other end of.

Maxim looks furious, and drops his robe to show his intimidating tattoos and even more intimidating monster cock. He moves to me, putting his hand on the small of my back and whispering for me to leave with a gentle push.

I move to the door.

"Don't hurt him," I say in Russian, and leave.

5 AUSTEN

That was, hands down, one of the strangest interactions I have ever experienced. I'm not sure what the fuck happened. I know Mischa's gay, saw me again, and now he's a little smitten. I'm pretty sure that is all it was.

I just can't believe he walked out without a word, and it wasn't exactly charming the way his friends—or whatever they were—were staring me down like they wanted to rip me apart. His boyfriend looks like a pit bull that has spent a few years in the pound terrifying all the other dogs. I got out of there fast.

And yet I keep thinking about him...

"Stop," I say, out loud.

"Stop what?" William asks.

"Nothing," I say, snapping out of my daydream.

The bar is having a tribute night to beer, and the eighties, so I'm dressed like Slash, with a wig of long curly black hair and top hat, and my brother is dressed as Axl with the long red hair and bandanna, but he's not performing tonight. I persuaded him to get in the spirit of it. I love disguises. I feel a lot more outgoing when you can't tell who I am. William is adding another portrait to his sketchbook. He's finishing a drawing of me while I look ridiculous.

"Do anything today?" he asks.

"No," I shake my head.

"You alright Baby?" he asks, concerned. "You're in your head?"

"Yeah, but don't worry about it," I tell him. "Let's have fun."

I'm a few minutes from showtime and I see Mischa for the second time today. That's probably not a coincidence.

This could be awkward, but it doesn't look like he's staying. He walks in and scans the room with those big eyes. It looks like he's come here to collect someone, but he's probably looking for me.

He's a very handsome guy, I guess. I'm not sure if it's right to call a guy pretty, but he's the type of profound beauty that looks like it's made from ivory and marble and gold flakes. He could be a model easily. Maybe he is. He has this piercing, smoky gaze. His luscious, curly black hair shines like dragonfly wings in the light. Pretty majestic all round really... I suppose I should be flattered that he asked me out.

I decide to dip backstage before he sees me. I peek from behind the curtain. He's about as big as me, so he's an absolute Sasquatch. He's taller than the rest of the crowd starting to form for the show. They are all milling about, drinking and chatting, but he's stony, like a statue. We're about to start, and I remember I'm in a costume. He might not even recognize me.

My cover band is called Empty V and I'm on drums. The lead guitarist, Jade, is a very attractive girl who wears almost nothing and posts a lot of sexy pictures of herself. She's probably the reason why our audience is getting bigger. She breaks into the first notes of *Welcome to the Jungle* and the crowd is pumped, and I know it's going to be a great night. I spin my drumstick in the air, catch it again and get into the beat of the music. Halfway through our set, the wig is trapping a lot of heat, adding to the stage lights, and my head is starting to boil. I hesitate before getting the hairdo off me, because Mischa is here and I don't know if I want him to see me. Maybe I'm not the reason, and if I am it doesn't matter; he doesn't realize how many walls he would have to jump over to get to me. I guess when he figures that out, he'll give up. I rip off the wig and my sweat-drenched head instantly starts to cool. I look over and Mischa's demeanor has changed. I have his complete attention, and he has found what he's looking for.

I'm wiping the sweat off my brow backstage when one of the bar staff brings us drinks. A great advantage of being in the band is you don't buy drinks, so you don't get carded. I'm parched and grab a cold stein. We were up there for an hour and played our hearts out, and I look like I could win a wet t-shirt competition.

I'm allowed thirty minutes back here, and one beer, but Mischa interrupts what precious little normal time I have.

I can see his silhouette in shadow from the door of the green room. I know he's looking at me, and for a moment it feels like we are the only two people in the world. When the light catches his eyes, I don't say that stupid "Oh wow," that popped out the first time I saw him, but I think of it and cringe internally that I ever said it at all. It probably gave him the wrong impression. It's time to stop this before it starts.

Everyone is talking excitedly and don't see me slip out the door.

"Can I buy you a drink?" Mischa asks.

"I'm good, thanks." I hold up my beer. "Why are you here?"

"To see the show," Mischa says.

"You're coming on a little strong, Mischa."

"I know, I'm sorry, but there's something between us; a fucking amazing thing. Love strikes like lightning; it's amazing! Do you feel it? It feels really nice."

Mischa seems more and more like a bad idea. More like a liability. Total loose cannon. This was not my intention. I have to let him down easy.

It's too late anyway.

"I am so sorry, but you've got the wrong idea. It's my fault, it seems I have accidentally misled you."

"We're meant to be. We are! I'm on fire; it's all warm in my chest. Meant to be. We are. Meant to be."

This guy is wired. Not mentally sound. Possibly on drugs. And way too late.

I hesitate. "You don't even know me."

"I feel like I do. I feel like I've found you, finally."

Crazy people can be a lot of fun. And he is ridiculously good-looking.

But too late.

"It seems like you are determined to force something to happen, but it won't," I sigh. "It won't end well. You need to forget about whatever you think this is."

He shakes his head. "I can't, it's an unstoppable force."

Why not though? At this point, what do I have to lose?

No. Too late. It would be cruel to do that to him.

"It isn't," I say, "but I am an immovable object. I already told you I'm straight, and um... taken, and I promise you I-I-I am not interested in experimenting."

What was THAT? God, did that sound as fucking fake and shaky as I think it did? What the fuck am I doing?

Mischa won't stop *staring.*

"What happens when an unstoppable force meets an immovable object?" he asks. "They're two incompatible premises —that there are such things as unstoppable forces, and immovable objects."

"Okay," I shrug. "So, you are brainy."

"Not really. My father was a scientist, so I learnt a couple of things."

"You can't science your way out of a firm rejection."

"Assuming both are real," Mischa continues, "the answer would be an impossible event."

He moves so close to me that I can feel his heat warming my damp, cold body.

My breath is stressed and shallow. "The fact that I won't budge won't change just because you want me to."

But god, what would it be like if... No. It would be evil for me to do that. It's too late.

"I understand that. The immovable object and the unstoppable force are indestructible. But it's also assumed that they are two different entities. I don't think we are. I think we're supposed to be one thing."

His mouth is so close to my mouth. My breath stutters in my chest. Some long dormant part of me is pulling the rest of me in a direction I can't go.

"You think we're one?" my voice is pitched unnaturally high.

"We're one," he says. "I feel it."

Too fucking late.

"It was nice to meet you, but I'm not interested, and I'm literally leaving the country in a few days."

That seems to break him out of the trance. "What?"

"I'm going to Australia."

"On that study program thing?"

"Yeah," I nod. "And I'm meeting my girlfriend *of five years* there, and we're going to New Zealand at the end. I'm not coming back here after that."

Mischa looks crestfallen. He slumps into the barstool by the door. Whatever he's feeling is obviously very real for him.

"We've never even touched before," he says, looking at me.

We have. I could feel his fingers touching mine all bloody week.

"We have," I glower at him. "We don't need to do it again."

He takes my hand in both of his and gently pulls me towards him. I feel strangely drawn in, maybe from curiosity, maybe surprise, and I go with it as he brings my arm up to his face and looks at the skin on my inner elbow.

"How the fuck are you doing that?" I ask, watching him.

"You feel it too?" he says.

"No."

"I want you."

"This isn't about me."

"I do."

"I don't care."

"I love you."

"No."

"So much."

Our eyes lock and I am speechless. He strokes his cheek into my hand, before kissing me on the wrist, and I can feel all the tiny translucent hair stand up. He kisses a little further up my arm, wet with sweat, where an old scar is. A scar I don't like.

"What was that from?" he whispers.

I recoil from him and pull my sleeve down.

"I'm really sweaty; sorry," I say. "I don't want to inflict my soaking wet body on you."

He gets up and leans into the wall I'm against, standing entirely too close to me. I'm trapped by his arms. He smells really good. He has this comforting scent that I want to roll myself in. It's warm and sweet like amber or caramel, but not sickly and more spicy and woody, almost like cinnamon.

Get it together. Straight. Fiancé. Normal. No weak points. No vulnerabilities. United front. My life is already over. I've written the letters, I've booked the holiday. It's not fair or rational, but I just don't want to do this anymore. It's too fucking late for this bullshit.

The reasons why we can't roll to the tip of my brain, but I can't try to invoke them, when they feel as flimsy as my self-control.

"Don't apologize," Mischa says. "Your body is exactly what I want you to inflict on me. Preferably soaking wet." He licks my sweat from his lips. "I like how you taste."

His knee touches my leg as he gets even closer.

By this point I am terrified. I gulp and it hurts from the lump in my throat. I'm frozen to the spot and there's nowhere to go anyway. I could shrink down the wall and crawl out but that would be as pathetic as I feel. Luckily, I don't need to, because Kane, my bodyguard, clears his throat from behind us and breaks whatever weird spell I have momentarily fallen under.

Kane and Hayden are young, and blend in with college students. Both also get attention from college girls, because they are ex-army and well built.

Hayden was my bodyguard until Kane asked to switch a week ago. Kane said he needed the swap because he couldn't *"deal with Will anymore."*

Fair enough, neither can I, but I had managed to work Hayden into a position of keeping away from me most of the time. Kane is a little too proactive for my liking, but that's suddenly a good thing, because I can escape from this madman.

"Is everything okay back here?" Kane asks.

"Yeah," I say, and chug the last of my drink, "we're leaving." I turn to Mischa as I get behind Kane, and extend my hand around him to offer another handshake. "Have a nice life," I tell

Mischa.

"You're funny," he says. "I'll see you soon."

6 MISCHA

Each of my brothers are deep in contemplation, having silenced them one by one by my giddy obsession. Anatoly is the last to concede that I need to pursue this white-hot love.

"Fight it!" he begs.

"I can't!" I say.

"Fuck!" Anatoly yells, and kicks a chair across the empty restaurant. "We need you in New York, we are under the gun, literally!"

"I just need the Christmas break. I'll work every day for the next year, I *promise*."

"I don't even know if we're allowed to date guys," Grigor shakes his head. "It's never come up. I'm guessing we're not."

"He's a *public figure*," Anatoly says. You gotta let this go, or else we gotta tell Sivishni and you don't want that..."

"I don't care!"

"Chili Pepper," Maxim reasons, "Look at his eyes."

Anatoly looks in my face and inspects my pupils.

"Wow, his eyes are as big as plates," he frowns. "He's on something?"

Demitri shakes his head. "No, but he may be in some sort of mania. Lemon, are you taking your medication?"

"Yes."

"Maybe you are taking too much? How do you feel right now? Good?"

"No, not at all," I say. "I can't stop smiling, and feeling bubbly, but I am also in excruciating pain."

"Look," Maxim says.

He grabs my forearm, pinching my skin as hard as he can, twisting it while rubbing against his finger until it becomes a hot burning sensation. I watch indifferently, making no effort to stop him or have any reaction to the pain, which seems perfectly tolerable.

"Pain?" he asks.

"Oh yes," I nod. "My heart hurts. What if he never feels the same way? But it's not like you have to be gay to want to fuck me, right? I mean who would throw the sexiest man alive out of their bed?"

"I mean, it's *pretty* gay," Dimitri says.

"God help us," Aleksandr looks at the others. "He thinks he's the sexiest man alive."

Maxim laughs. "He's just in love."

Anatoly frowns at me. "But your bedroom has been an orgy since the day you discovered your dick. How are you going to give all that up?"

"My dick is now reserved for Austen."

"That's that then," Konstantin says. "His fate is sealed. These things can't be helped."

"Goddamn it," Anatoly sighs.

Dimitri looks around the room. "Lemon, I'm sorry if this is a little hard to swallow. We all really thought Anatoly was the one who would go full gay. I've just lost a hundred dollars."

The joke lands in the middle of a silent room and nobody laughs, because it is so true.

"You need to come up with twenty grand a month," Gregor says. "You get ten from your speciality. I always supposed you got the other ten from fucking rich ladies, and maybe rich men too, correct?"

"I'll figure something out."

"It's maybe time we all started taking care of Sofie," Konstantin says, and everyone looks at him quizzically. "Or I could."

What a strange thing for Konstantin, usually the strong and silent type, to say. My stomach lurches, thinking he has more than just a soft spot for my little, *teenage* sister. He looks around and we all fucking know he has admitted something big.

"I've got it," I say firmly, and stare him down.

Ah shit I'm going to have to kill Konstantin and I've never killed anyone and I bet he's killed a bunch of people I bet he'll see me com-

ing a mile away oh this is gonna be stressful I can't think about this bullshit right now it will just make me spiral...

Arkady clears his throat, and breaks the uncomfortable silence.

"Lemon's carrying twice as much as us," he says. "I'll chip in a few grand, if it means he can pursue true love."

Maxim barely knows where to look. "Of course."

"Or Lemon could just be a little patient, go to New York and help some more there," Gregor says. "He'd make a lot of money..."

I tune everyone out as my thoughts get louder.

"I can't wait much longer. Austen lives out of town," I say to myself. "I gotta go drive past his house."

"You mean his mansion?" Gregor raises an eyebrow. "On his private estate? How are you going to drive past it? You gonna bust through the gates? Casually roll through the private driveway with a pair of dark glasses? Ask him all nonchalant *'what brings you here?'* Lemon, I don't think he'll assume it's a coincidence."

"Yeah," I say. "Maybe not."

"This boy," Anatoly winces, "this fucking little rich brat, already told you that he's not interested in you, and likely men in general, and for some reason that doesn't signal that you are going to get hurt?"

Maxim nods. "And what about when he finds out you're a street kid, a refugee, and... well... all the other things?"

"I'm not expecting this to work out," I say. "I tried avoiding him and now it's the pig and the python. I have to swallow every delicious bite of him until my hunger is finally satisfied."

Dimitri shakes his head. "His snake is going nowhere near your mouth and therefore you will never be satisfied."

"I can be very persuasive."

"I don't know who to feel sorry for, him or you," Anatoly says.

"Don't be too persuasive," Gregor tells me.

I am offended. "I'm not desperate, or like that."

Anatoly nods. "Not desperate; not usually, but now you're acting like you haven't bedded half of America."

"It's like I've never felt desire till now."

"For a straight boy?" Arkady asks.

"WE GOTTA START A BETTING POOL!" Dimitri exclaims, and claps his hands together.

"I'm sure he's straight," Anatoly scowls. "I'm putting twenty on it."

Maxim considers it. "Lemon has conquered many straight men. That Justin guy is still questioning his sexuality. I'll go one hundred he falls for you."

I shrug. "I think the best I can hope for is a holiday tryst."

DARK STARS IN THE SKY

Arkady smiles at me. "So put your money where your mouth wants to be."

"Holiday?" Ivan turns from staring out the window.

"He's doing one of the college travel abroad programs, the fuzzy-duck study ones. Like the bullshit one Arkady wanted to do in Italy about Renaissance art? Austen's going on the Australian cave-painting one where everyone goes clubbing in Sydney."

"It was worth a credit," Arkady insists.

Gregor and Ivan share a conspiratorial grin.

"Tour group?" Gregor asks.

"Yeah. Australia. Can I go?"

"How many people?"

"Over thirty kids, one or two chaperones."

"Thirty five?"

I nod.

He looks to Maxim, who hides the hint of a smile.

"You can go." Ivan says.

"That's unfair," Arkady whinges.

Ivan ignores him. "And I'm in for two hundred, because I *believe* in you. Make him fall in love. Squeeze the life out of your sweetheart, devour his soul, and come home like it never happened."

"What's the catch?" I ask.

Ivan shrugs. "I suppose this is a silver lining. Funny thing about package tours, they wrap all the suitcases together in plastic and stick them on a forklift straight to the plane. No conveyor belt through the x-ray for the old ladies heading to Malaga."

"And whose bag is whose anyway?" Gregor continues. "Point the finger at the other thirty kids and slip back into the crowd."

"You want me to smuggle something?"

"We need to get your gorgeous product to the Romanians. You can have your little holiday while Nicolai and Aleksandr are away, but after that, we need you focused."

"What do you want me to do?" I ask.

"Nothing. Maxim's the donkey but it's a big trade and he'll probably need the support."

"I'll do it," I beam. "Kismet."

"For the love of God," Anatoly rolls his eyes. "Please stop saying that."

7 AUSTEN

Friday, December 21, 2007, 5.39 pm.

My brother and I are waiting to board our plane. The airport is bustling. A cacophony of noises permeate the air from constant loudspeaker announcements to the wails of newborns. I am trying to stand as still as possible so my body doesn't convey the fact that I am on a razor thin edge and every tiny noise is liable to make me homicidal. All week, my mind hasn't belonged to me, but has instead been commandeered by a certain pushy behemoth who... what? Believes we are meant to be? It's ridiculous and yet...

God you're pathetic, my brain hisses. *Delusional. You're nothing special. He'll forget about you in two minutes. Kill yourself. Fucking die.*

I grab the long cord on Billy's jacket and follow along like a dog on a leash. He looks back and smiles at me. I think that leaving on this trip will be good for him. I hope it will also be the antidote to these irritating kisses that burrowed themselves into my arm after Mischa's lips were forced on me.

I can still feel them. All warm and soft.

I have never been so relieved to clear security. We're flying first-class, and are offered the opportunity to settle in early. I can't help feeling self-conscious for flaunting our money like this, but Billy insisted, and I can't deny that I am looking forward to the extra leg room.

Of course, our bodyguards, Hayden and Kane, are a constant shadow as we move through the airport, at the behest of my suddenly and weirdly overprotective brother. We shouldn't even have them. It just makes people notice us more. It's awkward walking past the rest of the students in the seating area.

I look back as we head into the plane and see a sight that stops me in my tracks. I can see a passenger walking past the gates carrying a small backpack. I can't know from this distance who it is, but my instincts are screaming at me that I know exactly who the fuck that is. It is either that, or I have officially cracked and am hallucinating. Because I swear, that the far away figure is Mischa. Certain. But am I that much of a narcissist to think that person walking in my direction is coming towards *me?*

The guy is so far away. I can't tell with my eyes but some other part of me knows it's him. I could just wait. Maybe the person will stop at another gate, and I'll realize just how conceited I am. I watch their stride and think how lovely it is. Good posture, but probably just my imagination. I mean, it's not like my mental health is good. I really am pathetic. And delusional.

The person gets closer and looks more and more like Mischa, until he really is Mischa, right in front of me, standing way too close again, and slightly breathless.

"What the actual fuck?" I say.

"I'm good friends with some of the admin girls. They agreed I should have a cultural experience, as long as I was prepared to do all my bookings myself and make a rather large donation to the school."

"No. You can't come."

He smiles smugly. "It's already been decided. I'm on the list."

The frustrations of the past week are boiling up, scalding my insides, and I'm suddenly furious beyond all rational belief. This trip is vitally important to me, and Mischa is just crashing it like it's nothing, like he hasn't... this whole thing hasn't... been bothering me this whole time.

Kane and I look at each other in bewilderment. This is new territory for both of us. There's nothing for it without causing a scene. I take some steadying breaths.

What do I care if he comes or doesn't come? He's nothing to me.

"Whatever," I grit out. "See you in Melbourne."

"See you on the plane."

"We're sitting in first class."

"Oh well..."

"Enjoy Coach," I snarl, and go onto the jet bridge.

I try to think what to do about this chaos vortex following

me to Australia. A solution isn't obvious. Should I just do nothing? I can ignore him, act like he doesn't exist. After all, the problem is only that he likes me a little *too* much. He just needs to accept that I'm not interested and move on.

William is up front with his headphones on and drawing when I arrive in the upstairs cabin. Hayden is sitting behind him.

"Can I sit with Will?" Kane asks, flicking his hazel eyes up to mine. "I need to talk to him about a couple things."

"Sure," I say.

He starts to walk away and I grab his arm.

"Wait..."

"Yeah?" Kane stops.

"Please don't mention this..."

"Oh, of course not," he pats my shoulder like he's my big brother, because we've known each other since we were little, and he is allowed to touch me. "I won't say anything to Will. It's just, you know, that guy is the kind of thing you really *should* use me for."

"I don't want it to sabotage the trip."

"You seem alright with him." Kane's golden features light up with a smile, and the old scar from the hit that split his lip becomes white and noticeable. "Maybe a holiday fling would be good for you? He's good-looking..."

I bristle at the thought. "But he's so fucking out of line."

"Alright," he agrees. "I can scare him off... or let you deal with him, you know, until you ask for my help, if that's what you want?"

"I don't know."

"What if I called you *Baby* in front of him?" Kane raises an eyebrow. "Show him how *close* we really are?"

"Oh my god," I snigger. "That could work, but it's risky. Maybe if he keeps bothering me after we get there. And if it looks like I'm starting to like him, slap me. Seriously, slap me."

He pats me again. "Okay Baby, we'll play it by ear."

Before I have much time to think, the curtain opens and Mischa comes in. He practically jumps into the chair next to me.

"I think you're in the wrong place," I tell him.

Mischa leans far back in the chair. "Nope, I just bought an upgrade."

I can't deal with this, I won't. I get up and go back down the stairs to speak to a flight attendant.

"You can't buy out his seat now that he's bought it," she says.

"Can I buy out all of first class?" I ask.

"Only the empty seats," she explains.

I admit defeat. I'm really mad, but I can't let it show. I need to get control of this situation.

I go back upstairs and wait for the plane to take off. William and our bodyguards are already watching films, and Mischa is staring at me with a beguiled look on his face.

"Alright," I tell him, "I don't want any bullshit from you."

"Of course not," Mischa says, trying to fake innocence. "I will show you that I'm a perfect gentleman."

I shake my head. "I don't want you to show me anything. I'm not trying to be rude, but I don't want to deal with... you, with this... I'm *really* unhappy with this situation. Please stay the fuck away from me. Don't talk to me, don't try and sit next to me again, and *please*, don't ever touch me, ever."

"You seemed to enjoy it the last time."

"I did not. I hate being touched, and now I hate you too."

"Why so combative? That was really bitchy what you said about sitting in Coach. Normally I don't like snobs with a chip on their shoulder."

"Normally I don't have conversations with my stalkers."

"Hey!" he says. "Don't be that way. Look, I can tell you're really angry inside..."

"And I can tell you're an idiot."

"There's no need to be *mean*."

"Yes there is," I explain. "You can't just mess with me like you do your other playthings."

"I don't have any other playthings, you're not a plaything..."

I tilt my head to Kane and Hayden. "Those two men could kill you in a second if you try to pull something. And my brother is crazy. He might go berserk if you even *look* at me funny."

Mischa throws his hands up in mock-surrender. "Woah there; we all have a couple psycho brothers; it's not a good idea to turn it into a competition. You don't need to sic your attack dogs on me. I'll behave."

"I just wanted to make myself clear. "

"Crystal clear."

"It's never going to happen, just so you know. We clear?"

He doesn't say anything. The plane starts to move and makes a thunderous roar as it speeds down the runway. Mischa turns himself towards me and begins singing very quietly in my ear.

"I'm sticking with you…"

"Knock it off," I say.

"Cause I'm made out of glue," he continues.

"I know you're high," I say. "Your eyes are like the moon."

"Oh no," Mischa says. "It's just the love, it does this weird thing to your eyes." He pulls down his eyelid. "Cool, right? Apparently it only happens for the first couple of weeks at most. So you're kind of right; love is the drug and it's wonderful."

I look in his pupils. He goes quiet as he looks back at me. The plane lifts into the air. It seems like looking at him is the key to making him shut up. He has really pretty eyes. After a while we get above the clouds in sunshine, and a grin stretches across his face.

"Your eyes are getting all moony too."

I break off from the stupid staring competition, and put on a movie. He puts on the same movie. It's really bad. Every so often I can no longer fight the urge to look over at him.

* * *

As the sun sets flying thousands of feet above the Earth, Mischa's smile disappears, and he looks more and more miserable. By dinner time he is gloomy.

"Are you coming down from the cloud?" I ask.

"A little, yeah."

"You understand how fucked up this is, right?"

"I know," he winces. "I *know*, okay? I'm not usually like this. It's the crazy love chemicals in my brain. It's usually people doing this kind of shit to me, a lot, because I'm, you know, so... well... *I mean*... look at me," he throws his hands up, and I want to laugh, "and I *hate* it. I never thought I'd be *that* person, but reality is hitting me hard right now. I'm actually doubting myself and this whole thing. I'm worried you'll be put off by how fucking desperate I'm being."

"I am."

He deflates even more. "And the past couple hours have been so awkward..."

"So awkward..." I roll my eyes. "You're such an ass. So immature."

He frowns in confusion. "I don't know why, but I felt like if I didn't come with you I'd lose you forever. Like it was my one and only shot in this life."

He's not wrong. Poor bastard.

"You can't lose me. You never had me."

"I feel possessed, and this is a lucid moment, like the eye of the storm or something. I just didn't think it all the way through, but I'm not crazy. If you knew what my life has been, you'd understand why I leave nothing to chance."

I laugh at him. Really laugh. "This bullshit ruins even a snowball's chance in *Hell*. This is a perfect way to make someone hate you."

"Maybe, but at least I can say I tried."

"I'll be sure to carve that on your tombstone."

"So I'm delusional? *Ugh*."

"You do seem kind of... manic?"

He steals a furtive glance at me. "Maybe..."

"Oh shit, you are?"

"Well..."

"Medicated?"

"Yeah," he sighs.

That makes me feel a lot less guilty.

"Okay," I say, trying to not freak out. "Please take some of your pills, and try to calm your thoughts."

"I don't think I'm *actually* manic though..."

"You absolutely are."

"I mean, it's time to take them anyway," he huffs, and gets a bottle of pills from his bag, and knocks on back without water.

"Thank you."

"Fuck," he says, after staring into space for a few moments. "Now I'm stuck on some stupid trip and hate myself right now. Reality plus fantasy usually equals nightmare. I literally want the earth to swallow me, I'm so horrified with myself."

He buries his head in his hands. I look at him with pity. I think of the journey ahead, and know I need to keep this guy under control, and to do that, I have to be nice.

"Well, this trip is very very very important to me," I tell him, "so let's just have a truce, alright? I hate you, but I really don't like conflict, and I need things to go well for my brother. I need to give him this. Once we get off this plane, we'll never have to talk again, but we can at least be civil for now."

"Okay," he agrees, but still looks sad.

An uneasy peace settles over us. For the rest of the night we talk about movies and books, all the while dancing around our uncomfortable situation. He's funny. He makes me laugh. Asshole. Time feels different around him. Faster and slower. Oh God, I think I might be a little in trouble here. The flight attendant brings us sparkling wine and it gives us the giggles. Kane walks past and is surprised to see Mischa, and presses his lips together, trying not to smile. This has to stop. Mischa's pinkie finger returns gently on the side of my arm. He watches me like a hawk until they dim the lights to sleep. I see him when I wake up, still watching.

8 MISCHA

Australia isn't like I imagined. Melbourne is hot, but cloudy every day, and colder in the evening than I expected. I also don't fall straight into a hotel room with Austen and stay there for the duration like I planned, so I have to figure out what I'm going to do instead.

Austen made me doubt myself. Made me think I was manic rather than in love. They are pretty similar, but this is love. Spending an evening with him in first class was like a date. The best one I ever had. I watched him sleeping. He looked at me when he stretched awake again, and yeah, I'm very in love.

The more I know him the more I want him, but he loses me when we get off the plane and I can't get near him again. William is always glued to his side. The heavies disappear into the background, but are always around, even when I forget. The golden-tanned, dark haired, very gay one who totally wanted to fuck me at the bathhouse is always warning me off with his eyes.

Austen never looks in my direction, and acts as if I don't exist. But I'm not special in that. He never looks at anyone. Every girl tries to talk to him and he's very stand-offish. He tells them he's *engaged* to be *married* if they ask. It's definitely a lie. It sounds painfully awkward every time he says it. William overcompensates by talking to all the girls, acting like he wants to fuck them but I'm not sure he does. It feels theatrical somehow.

We are a big bustling group as we arrive in Melbourne. I watch one of the taller guys trying to get Austen's attention, and pulling him aside, yanking him by his elbow.

The moment he touches Austen, it gets weird. William doesn't like it, but tries not to let it show. The gay bodyguard pops up and goes to Austen. Will steps in to speak to the guy, as Austen takes back his arm, and politely backs away.

"No," William says, "that's me. I'm Austen."

The guy apologizes, and asks if they can swap rooms.

The not-gay blonde bodyguard approaches William after, and gives him a juice pack.

"Will's epilepsy is acting up," he tells Will. "Probably the jet lag."

Jesus. Even their bodyguards can't tell them apart.

I go into the men's bathroom. Austen is sitting on the floor leaning against the wall with his eyes closed, holding his elbow like it's broken. The gay bodyguard is with him, looking concerned, holding a bag of candy and an inhaler. Austen looks drunk.

"You okay?" I ask.

"Fuck off," Austen says.

I see him a half hour later, drinking coffee in the lobby, sober again.

Our chaperone is a young lady named Athena who looks Mediterranean but sounds Californian. She pulls me, Austen, William, and a few other students aside to speak to us in a café next to our hotel. Some of the other kids who are known as bratty boys and party girls. One organizes dance parties on the side, another is the son of a famous footballer.

"I observed most of you on the plane," Athena tells us. "I also looked at your profiles online. You all seem like fun-loving people. You are also the most likely to pull something."

A fraternity-type jock named Kai, with a stupid backwards hat, laughs at the idea.

"Where's the lie?" he shrugs.

Athena sighs. "This is my last tour for this company, and I wanna make this trip a little easier on myself."

The group is quiet. I look at Austen but he looks firmly at Athena.

One of the girls looks confused. "Okay?" she says. "So you're asking us to behave like, *better* or something?"

Athena shakes her head. "I already asked you all to do that at the start of the trip."

"She's asking us to cut a deal," a pretty, British student, explains.

I think her name is Amelia.

"Within reason," she says. "You can't leave for the whole thing, alright? But if you get arrested for having sex in a bus-stop toilet, I may quietly post your bail and not feel the need to report you to the university. The only catch is you have to behave in Alice Springs on New Year's Eve. If you fuck up there, you're on your own."

The group are thrilled, and start talking amongst themselves about the possibilities this opens up. I roll my eyes, as nobody seems to fully understand what's happening.

"So *how much* is bail around here?" I ask over the top of everyone talking. "Around *nine-hundred*? I suppose you'd need that in *advance*, just in case, right?"

Athena looks relieved and nods with a wry smile on her lips. The kids look a little uncomfortable with the dawning realization that this is a shakedown.

"That's bullshit," one of the girls says. "I'm not paying you."

Athena sighs without a hint of concern. "If you're the girl that doesn't want to pay, but thinks she can scream at me to bail her out later, I promise you, I won't help you. Make a fuss and I will have you sent home this afternoon for all the shit that I can make up. You will be kicked out of school too, so don't even think about trying to ruin it for everyone else."

"I'll report you."

"To my ex-employer? The one who grabbed me between my legs? You have fun with that, Hannah. Your curfew is ten. Not a moment later. By that time, everyone in this room will be in a club talking about how much of a bitch you are."

Hannah is offended, brimming with tears, but is also the first one to pay. One by one the others agree to get the money to Athena, or pony up the cash right there. After a while it is only Austen and William left.

"We don't need it," William says, and stares at Austen "We're not going to have any problems."

William gets up to leave and the second he turns, Austen hands her a wad of cash under the table and leaves.

"Have you done this on every trip?" I ask Athena.

"Only after I realized the certainty of bullshit," she says. "Now every time they pull something, they'll think it's all bought and paid for."

"Isn't that a bad idea?"

"Weirdly, no," she smiles. "People think harder about the things they pay for than things that are free. It's had the strange effect of making these trips a lot *less* crazy."

We giggle together at the absurdity. I pull out my bribe and hand it to her. Three wads of folded notes tied with rubber bands. More than everyone else.

She pulls at the bands and snaps them back. "No pin then?"

she says, looking at the money. "Greek, Cuban… or Russian?"

"Greek," I lie.

"Lots of Greeks here, but also Lebanese and Italian too."

"I'll behave," I explain, "I'm only buying your *eyelids*."

She shakes my hand. "Consider them closed."

* * *

For the last stop on Christmas Eve we visit the State Library of Victoria. It's built around a six-story octagonal reading room. It has a large glass dome which makes it quite light and airy.

All the UMass students line up at the viewing balconies to take photos. All except for Austen and William, because William is nowhere to be seen, and Austen just walks around the octagon taking it in.

I watch him from a lower window. He goes back down the stairs, past the others to the bottom floor. There he goes all the way around again, trying to find the way out, but only finds himself back with me. He gives me a hard look and tries again and comes right back to the same spot next to me.

The elevator has a large group of geriatric women waiting for it. It seems to be hovering around the third floor and not moving anyway.

I follow him up the spiral staircase and try to find an exit on the next level. Up there it's the same problem, so Austen gets his sexy gay bodyguard to help. It seems like a few of the other students are also now finding themselves walking in circles around the octagon, with no obvious way outside.

We go back down a floor and do another lap around the perimeter but the stairs from the gallery are nowhere to be found. The bodyguard scratches his head.

"I mean we came in on the elevator, but there must be another staircase," he says.

The lowest balcony is one story above the reading room floor. A jump may not be high enough to kill someone, but it would be enough to cause a scene amongst the readers below. Austen looks down as if he's contemplating the same thing. The bodyguard heads off to make another dash around the internal balcony.

"You want to find the way out together?" I ask.

"Thanks but no," Austen says.

He returns looking frantic, and is about to head around again. He'll probably become even more panicked, so I grab his arm. He flinches.

"I don't bite," I smile. "You okay?"

Austen shakes his head. "I'm being hypersensitive. I got trapped somewhere when I was younger, and it's a bit of a phobia. We're obviously jet-lagged and disoriented, but *seriously*, where's the exit?"

"Look," I tell him quietly, "the elevator is moving again. Maybe it's the only way in or out."

He watches number three light up above the doors.

"We'll be stuck here forever," he huffs.

I go behind him and whisper in his ear, "Here's the plan, I'm going to knock over those little old ladies and charge through when the doors open. Then you press 'close' as fast as you can, so we can ride alone. If any of them try to wedge their walking-frames to keep it from shutting, I'll kick them out from under them."

Austen tries not to laugh. "Are you crazy? Don't answer that."

"I would kill everyone here to make you happy."

"You don't need to do that."

I put my hands on his shoulders. "Are you sure you don't want me to beat Doris's head in with her walking stick?"

"No. I mean, yes. Don't."

"Very well," I sigh. "I guess we'll just have to wait."

He turns to face me. "I don't think we should wait together," he says. "I don't want to encourage the incorrigible."

"You think that now, but we're going to look back on these three weeks and wish we hadn't played cat and mouse. Please, can we just get to the courtship already?"

"You really want to skip everything and get to the *'I love yous'*?"

"That is my suggestion. Or maybe just the waking-up-tangled-together bit?"

Austen raises his eyebrows. "Or... how about we jump over the honeymoon and go straight to the restraining order?"

"You could never do anything to make me want a restraining order."

Austen shakes his head, and tries not to laugh. "I'm... I'm not attracted to you."

Lies.

"Let's be friends then."

"I've never had friends."

"Well," I shrug, and run my hands down the sides of his arms to his elbows. "Better late than never."

"Honestly, how do you do that?" he asks, looking at the gap between us, and my hands on his forearms.

"Always look on the bright side," I shrug.

"No, I mean..." He smiles and searches my face, his eyes stopping at my Adam's apple. "We can get on the elevator from any floor," Austen suggests. "We might as well go see the top."

We ascend the spiral stairs right up to the dome viewing deck. From there it's another dead end, and we find ourselves alone looking down on all reading desks and remaining students at windows taking photos. I push the button for the lift. He looks over the ledge down the six stories, and so do I from the next balcony along. His phone rings and he takes the call, explaining that he is fine.

"Your bodyguard calling?"

"It's pretty overbearing," he sighs. "But they mostly know to leave me alone."

I zone out watching the view, with all the whispering library echoes and creaks, until I feel Austen's eyes looking over at me. I stay still, and let him look.

The elevator arrives. The sound for the door chimes. We get in, and stare at each other in the steel doors when they close.

"Thank you," he says. "You saved me from a crippling panic attack."

"It was nothing," I say.

On the next floor Austen's golden-tanned, hot, gay, body-guard gets in, and shoots me an almost jealous look. He stands too close to Austen, touching his arms and searching his eyes, and with that, I worry there's something between them. It all feels very tender and intimate. I feel so uncomfortable as he pats Austen's cheek.

"You okay, baby?" he asks, in a barely audible whisper.

What THE FUCK did he just call Austen? I feel like my insides are being ripped out of me. Austen's smile reaches all the way to his eyes as they look at each other, and he nods and touches the bodyguard's elbows like they want to hug but can't. Austen noiselessly assures him he's fine, then looks past him, and the golden hottie goes back into gay-bodyguard mode, turns to face the door in front, like they don't know each other, only Austen's hands are at his waist. One more stop and more people get in until the elevator is packed full. Austen is squished right in the corner. He makes the tip of his nose touch the back of his bodyguard's head and it makes them both smile.

We reach the bottom, and everyone gets out slowly, as Austen and I wait at the back. There's a momentary pause when it's our turn. I don't know if he's waiting for me to go first like a gentleman, or for another reason, but it makes my heart pump incredibly fast. We turn to look at each other, and his face is trying to figure out how I feel while I do the same.

I press the door-close button. He frowns in confusion, and I realize in horror what I've done. We both leap to catch the doors, and his gay-bodyguard-possible-lover turns around, but they close on us.

"Sorry," I say. "Accident." His eyes narrow at me, not believing my excuse. I flush with embarrassment. "We can just ride back down," I shrug.

We find ourselves back up where we started. We reach the second floor and a group of old ladies wait for us to get out so they can get in. Reluctantly, we step back onto the viewing balcony, and the elevator again departs. We both start to smile, but it's cut short by Austen's phone ringing. He tells the caller he's fine, again, only more exasperated.

"No," he huffs into the phone. "Kane, do not call William for this."

He grins as he listens to Kane talk, turning a deeper and deeper red, pressing his lips together like he is telling Austen something naughty.

The gay bodyguard I'm now planning to murder, Kane, appears on the floor of the reading desks one floor below, and talks into his phone loud enough that I can hear all of it. Austen hangs back, out of view, while I look at Kane from a balcony. Some of the readers on the table nearby watch too.

"You want to tell him how much you mean to me?" Kane asks, all dewy-eyed, looking up at me. "How I *love* you, how I've *loved you* for years? How I would *die* for you? I'd fucking *kill* for you..."

"My love, I think he can hear you," Austen says, and I turn to see him equally moonstruck.

I start watching them like tennis.

"This past month," Kane looks at the floor. "I... we... you... *you* mean *everything* to me..."

He actually wipes away a fucking *tear*. Ugh. Kill me.

Austen's eyes are welling too.

"Yeah," he sighs. "We said all the things. We got it out of the way. We're not tender people. We never have to be sentimental like this again."

"Maybe Christmas and birthdays," Kane agrees. "Although Christmas *is* tomorrow."

"See you in a minute, Kane."

"Sorry baby, what's my name again?"

"*Kane...*" Austen whines, becoming bashful, and twists uncomfortably. "That's too much... no... *please* no..."

"It's *Christmas*," Kane insists.

"Okay..." Austen whispers. "Bye... *Buttercup.* Love you."

"That's exactly right," Kane hangs up, looking fucking smug about it.

I want to fucking crawl under a rock.

"Buttercup?" I shake my head, pushing down all the murderous thoughts, trying to seem unbothered. "I feel like *Sugar-Kane* was right there."

"Sugar-Kane?" Austen cackles. "Love that."

This is the closest I've come to crying in a very long time. I know I won't, that it will turn into rage at a more appropriate time and place, but even so, the next few minutes will be fucking painful.

"You guys are adorable," I admit, and hold the back of my

neck. "How long have you been together? He was in the bath-house with you, right?"

They both tried it on with me. It's not a good omen for their own relationship.

Austen won't look at me. He furrows his brow and shakes his head a little.

"Yeah, he's only been my um... my bodyguard for a few weeks," he says. "The 1980's gig was the first time he... body-guarded me properly."

"Oh," I nod. "Right, yeah, *that* night."

I lit the fuse. I came on strong and threw Austen into the arms of his protector. I am amazed that my heart actually hurts. I feel pain. Real pain. I wonder if I'm having an actual heart attack. Although that would be good, because I want to die.

"We've known him since we were kids," Austen explains. "He's been on-and-off with Lord Tyrannus for a couple years now—as a bodyguard. He's driven him away then begged him to come back a couple times, but they had a fight last month and Kane walked out for good."

"He seemed very cosy with William on the plane."

"Yeah, they sorted it out," Austen sighs.

"Does Will know?"

"He knows he's my *bodyguard*," Austen says after a pause.

"It would not be good for him to find out that I really am..." he trails off. "It's all been very awkward."

"I'll bet. I didn't believe it, but you really are taken."

"Oh," Austen frowns. "Yeah."

"What?"

"I'm still marrying my girlfriend."

"Oh fuck *off*."

"What?"

"Girlfriend?" I wince. "It gives me more hope to know you go with guys."

"I don't... I just go with... Kane, I guess."

"But you're marrying someone else?"

"Kane is not my *boyfriend*, he's my bodyguard. That sorta comes with a physical and emotional component." He hesitates, and shakes his head. "I'm just good with him, you know, touching me and stuff because he's my bodyguard and he cares about me. Like my girlfriend."

"Can I be your bodyguard for free then?"

He chuckles. "I'll stick with Kane."

"But not monogamous?" I blink a few times. "So there's still a chance?"

He gapes at me, then rolls his eyes so hard he throws his head back. "Christ, I'm unsure if anything will scare you off."

"Probably not."

The crowds are gone, so we call the elevator. Kane arrives with it and we get in with him. He glowers like a fierce predator guarding its cub. He's fuming mad and gets in my face to menace me.

"I will fucking murder you…" he growls.

Austen puts his arm around Kane. "Hey, stop," he says, pulling him away. "I'm okay. He didn't do anything."

He pulls Kane by the jaw to make him look in his eyes.

"Baby this fucking guy…" Kane huffs, all worked up.

Austen kisses him, briefly, on the lips, trying to diffuse the tension. Kane snaps out of his anger in surprise, and smiles, mesmerized by Austen.

"I'm sorry," I tell them. "I didn't know."

"Thank you, Mischa, for being so kind to me today," Austen says.

His eyes fix on Kane, the electricity from their sexual chemistry zapping between them, while I watch in the reflecting door.

"It's all good," I tell them.

The lift has gone up, and people get in as it starts going back down. We three look at the floor like strangers. The door opens and we are in the basement gallery. I get out and they don't move. I turn as they emerge with caution, watching me like an escaped zoo animal.

I think it's time for me to return to America.

"Sorry again," I say, and I offer Kane my hand to shake. "I'll leave you two alone. He deserves someone like you," I smile, but it's not a real smile. "If it were me, I'd be getting the better deal, and he'd always have the raw end of it."

Kane looks at my hand then my face, and gives me another hard look before he shakes my hand, and my superpower goes off *hard*. So hard, my eyeballs tremor, and I gasp. It could be mistaken for divine intervention. His handshake isn't firm, it's *rigid*, and so is he. The moments flash in my mind like strobe lights. Glances. Movements. Frowns. A blink. A kiss. Smiles.

Kane says. "Are you okay?"

I look at the two of them, and compare it to the montage in my mind. My mouth drops open. I can see the slight-of-hand now. I put the pieces together fast. They aren't together. They almost fooled me. That kiss in the elevator was their first. Kane gave the game away with his face. Calling Austen "Baby" was planned; a performance for my benefit. *Motherfuckers.* Their phone call rammed it home. I believed all of it because they do love each other. They're just not *in* love. Scratch that; Kane is a little in love with Austen, and Austen tolerates it quietly. Something deep happened recently... I'd wager they dropped molly together, and they grew molly-levels of closeness, but they've never fucked. And they never will. Not sure how William fits in this picture, but it's something to do with not letting anyone near Austen. Kane included. Austen also truly loves me. Probably. I might have just started something between him and Kane. Ugh.

If Austen's going to fight this hard then I have to work harder. I can't call their bluff right to their faces, but I can work with it.

"It's just stress," I explain. "I just don't think it's fair."

They look at each other apprehensively.

"What?" Kane frowns.

I look at Austen. "You don't have to be happy with me, but you do have to be happy."

"Huh?" he frowns.

"Don't marry someone you're not in love with. Stay with Kane. Be comfortable in your own skin."

They look at each other and think about it. Kane raises his eyes to Austen, like I have a point.

Austen smiles and looks away. "That's not your concern."

I should drop the issue, so I don't risk really throwing Austen into the path of the hot gay bodyguard, another "straight" man who's half in love with him already.

"Better than some dumb girl at least," I sigh. "Alright, see ya, I guess."

"Do you want to get a drink?" Austen asks, walking after

me, and Kane follows up the stairs.

"What?"

"If you wanted, just for tonight?"

Kane looks at Austen, shakes his head, and mutters, "Should I slap you?"

"William and I have to be guarded," Austen explains. "We've had some difficulties, and Billy has become a little paranoid lately. You wouldn't have had the opportunity to be kind to me today if he was here. It's Christmas…"

"It's a full moon," I add.

"That too. Now that you know I'm not the one, I'll give you this evening to just… get to know us for real? The drinking age here is eighteen, so we're heading to one of the rooftop bars later, if you'd like to join us?"

An alarm goes off in my head, and I feel a sudden panic.

"Absolutely, but I'm supposed to meet Max for dinner," I say. "We're going to Stalactites."

Shit. Shouldn't have said that. Austen's smile disappears. The opening closes shut.

"Never mind," he says. "See you later Mischa—and thanks for showing me the way out."

He moves to the gallery entrance, and I grab his arm. He turns and I grab his other hand too.

"Come with us," I say. "It's not far."

"Thanks," he says, "but I don't want to meet your boyfriend for a romantic dinner."

"He's not my boyfriend."

"And I'm not either."

"Tomorrow?"

"William's in bed with a headache today. He might not be tomorrow."

I frown. "So?"

"So… I don't want to watch him kill you."

"But I really want to spend more time with you…"

"No, it was just a passing idea, and now you'll probably try to get it in with Kane too."

Austen really hates pressure.

"No I'm not interested in that… but you two are right under Will's nose… I kind of want to see how you do it."

That didn't help.

"What? No… my brother's not my *jailer*."

"I didn't mean it like that."

"Mischa, don't misinterpret this. I'm not leaving some window open. I don't like you. I hate you. I hate the whole situation in a way you can't even believe. You've been a total fucking creep, and I'm just trying to be polite. I was only offering because you might finally be moving on. My life," he spits with disgust, "such as it is, is fine without you. I'm being friendly because this trip is important to me, and I don't want you to ruin it."

"I'm not going to..."

"You already have been since the beginning. And if it goes wrong I don't know what I'll do, but probably something very rash and unfortunate."

I search his face. "Are you serious?"

Kane is suddenly very concerned, so I guess this isn't an idle threat.

"Please leave me alone," Austen says with his mouth, but his face and body are saying a lot of conflicting things.

Austen carefully pulls his arm away, and lets go of my other hand, and takes off down the steps with Kane. I watch them go, and then run off in the other direction up to the Greek eatery a block away. It is not even six o'clock, but the place is already packed. I head upstairs to the bathrooms and Maxim is waiting, and as pale as a sheet.

"Late," he says. "You missed it."

"Go okay?" I ask.

Maxim nods. "I... I *really* need a drink."

"Maybe we could check out some of the rooftop bars?"

I visit almost every bar in the city, but can't find Austen again.

The phrase, "My life... *Such as it is... such as it is... such as it is...*" rattles round my head for days.

9 AUSTEN

Tuesday, December 25, 2007 1.39 pm (Christmas Day).

Everyone goes to Hosier Lane, in downtown Melbourne, to look at the street art. Nearby, at one of the few open cafés, we hold a secret Santa to celebrate Christmas. Everyone exchanges crappy tourist gifts with each other. It's fun, but Mischa looks so sad.

"I hope you're not sad because of me," I tell him, down the end of one of the narrow alleyways.

"That's part of it. It's also Christmas Eve in America now. I promised my little sister I'd be with her. I'm her only family and I'm standing her up for a lame trip and a crushing three-week long rejection from a guy who fucking *hates* me."

"Oh dear. That's like exchanging gold for brass."

"It's starting to seem like it," he says. "Where's Will?"

"Headache."

"Where is your bodyguard-boyfriend?"

I hate that lie. The cure feels worse than the disease, but I have to think about Will too.

"I don't know, he has the day off. Things are a bit more relaxed now. My brother thinks it's safer here."

"William thinks Melbourne is safer than *Amherst*?"

"Look," I sigh, "I'm not going to argue if it means I'm left alone for once."

"I wanted to say goodbye to Kane. I'm going to the hotel to pack. I might see you guys next time you're at the pizzeria. Here's my number if anything changes."

He hands me a piece of paper.

"You're leaving?" I ask, and I feel my insides getting colder. "You don't want to do the rest of the tour?"

"No," he shrugs. "You made yourself pretty clear. I don't want you doing anything rash. I want to leave here in one piece. I'll maybe see you guys later. You know, you two can marry in Massachusetts. Or don't. Just please choose each other and not some random girl to make everyone else happy."

I hate lying. It's always such a balancing act. All just to manipulate someone who likes me.

"That's not why..."

"Look, Austen; I don't think this is mania. I'm actually pretty low in energy right now. I just love you, and fumbled the ball, badly. I wish you looked at me the way you looked at your *buttercup*, and that whole cute thing in the reading gallery made me believe in true love and broke my heart at the same time. All I want is for you to be happy because I love you, and want what's best for you. I have to leave now and chalk all of this up to experience."

"But you're here already. You might really enjoy the trip.

You could meet someone else."

Mischa shakes his head emphatically. "I don't actually want to meet anyone else. It was nice to get to know you a little, but I'm a little scared I might try to hurt myself if I keep punishing my heart like this. It's time for me to go. Have a good holiday."

"Hold on."

"It's cool, Austen. I gotta go."

"Wait, I want to give you something," I say, and hand Mischa a small box. "Merry Christmas."

He opens it.

"Oh wow," he says, as he looks at the silver pendant.

"It's a blackbird, like the song," I explain. "Please don't read into it. I just wanted to thank you for yesterday, and say sorry for being so nasty, but I still hate you."

"Thank you," he smiles and puts it on. "It's lovely. I'll keep it forever."

"Great, but don't leave because of me. I'd feel guilty if you left."

"I'm leaving because of Kane. I'm happy for you, I just can't watch it anymore. Take care."

All Mischa's emotions are bubbling just under the surface. I can see the pain and I want to comfort him, I just can't.

"Okay then, I guess. Bye Mischa."

"I'm Eastern European, do I kiss you goodbye or not? You

hate being touched so I don't know..."

I can deal with physical pleasantries when I know they are coming. A handshake, pat on the back, being kissed three times hello when we lived in France. I am always cautious, but can take it.

"Yes," I nod. "That's okay."

"Have a good holiday."

He pecks my cheek, and looks at me after pulling away, and his eyes judder around again like yesterday. I think it's that zing you get after embracing someone you have chemistry with. He seems to find it amusing, like he's trying not to laugh.

"What?" I ask.

"Nothing," he says, and kisses my other cheek, then slows for a third kiss, and whispers, "See ya."

He goes to leave and I step in his path.

"Wait," I put my hand to his chest to block him.

He looks down at my hand holding him back. "Yeah?"

"I'm not with him."

"What?" he says, crossing his arms.

I scowl at the ground.

"Kane," I say finally. "We're not. Never have been or will be. Our friendship was forged in Hell, and now he's very protective. He would kill you if I asked him to. He loves me but not in love, and he's not gay."

"Kane's not gay? What about you?"

I shake the thought off. "I'm just a mess."

Mischa frowns at some graffiti on the wall. "If you are prepared to fake all that just to get rid of me, then I should *definitely* go."

"Please don't leave."

"You want me to stay?"

"Stay. It seems only right."

"You don't really hate me, you love me?"

"No," I scoff. "I didn't say that. I *do* hate you, and I really don't want to fuck you either, but feeling hate is better than feeling guilt. I just want you to be around for me to hate... a little *longer*."

He admires the bird in the pendant, very amused. "Hmm, I don't know... this is very nice..." he narrows his eyes at me, and cracks into laughter. "Can we drop the act?"

"What do you mean?"

"We're just gonna pretend you aren't crazy about me while I burn alive, huh?" he gasps between laughs, "Austen... my love... my baby... you're so *cruel*... to both of us... seeing you try to fight it just makes you more endearing..."

I suddenly regret my choice, and put my palm to my forehead.

"*Ma caille...*" I whisper to myself, frustrated.

MA CAILLE?

DID I JUST SAY MY DARLING?.

WHAT THE HELL?

"The fuck you just call me?" Mischa stops, surprised. "*Mikhail?*"

I'm surprised at myself and let it show. My cheeks flush.

"Everybody calls you... um... *Mikhail.*"

"Not you. *You* call me Mischa. That was my name before everything was taken from me. Nobody's called me that since I was little, but you chose that for me, and I like hearing you say it. I won't make you sleep with me, care about me or treat me like you love me even though you do and pretend not to, and I know you'll probably never give yourself permission to show your feelings for me, even if I can tell how much deep they are, but please, give me this one little ray of sunshine, otherwise my life is all a nightmare."

He's really agitated. I am stunned into silence. The idea that everything was taken from him, and his life is a nightmare like mine, moves me a little.

"Sorry..."

"Don't say sorry, just don't call me that."

I grab his hand. "I love calling you... I mean I *love* the *name* Mischa."

"Yeah," he sighs, "yeah good..." He flashes a wicked smile.

"You'll love screaming it one day."

I turn on my heel. "Alright, you made it weird. See ya, pervert."

* * *

We go to the Dandenong Mountains a few days later. I am seated next to him on the historic train that runs through the old-growth forest. He brightens immediately.

"My sister thanked me for the incredible Christmas gift," he says. "It made her cry."

"Did you get her something good this year?" I ask.

"I did not, but some anonymous person remembered for me."

I give him a confused look. "Not me!"

"It's a beautiful car, Austen."

My mouth drops open. "I have *no idea* what you're talking about."

I ignore him the rest of the day, and he smiles out at the tall trees passing by the old train. The side of his pinkie finger touches the side of my arm again, and his fingertip lightly pats me an undetectable amount. If he were a puppy, his tail would be wagging violently.

10 MISCHA

Monday, December 31, 2007, 8.30 a.m (New Year's Eve).

The enormous rock that rises up from the flat red desert is visible for hundreds of miles. The landscape looks like Mars, until we reach Alice Springs, a little oasis in a small green valley.

"Things here are different," Athena tells us. "This is a dangerous town. The most dangerous in the country. Anything you think you can get away with, you can't get away with it *tonight*."

"But it's New Year's Eve!" Kai, one of the jocks who paid off Athena, with the stupid backwards hat, yells.

"Fucken oath it is," the darkly tanned old man next to Athena says. "And the most dangerous night of the fucken year. The powers that be, in all their superior wisdom, have lifted the fucken alcohol ban so shit's gonna kick off the moment that bottle-o opens. You cheeky ratbags try lair it up I'll crack the shits and send you back to Seppoland tout suite."

There is a pause while the group tries to decode the man's interruption.

"What?" one of the students says.

"Who are you?" the British girl says.

Her name is… Amelia? Pretty sure. Cute girl I would already be talking to if things were different.

"This is Johnno," Athena explains. "He will act as a local guide here."

Johnno adjusts his slouchy hat and sniffs. "Alright," he says, as if that's a greeting.

"Due to the unique social aspects of this town, you can all celebrate the new year festivities from inside the hotel. You can go out in groups, but you can't go anywhere alone, and you must be back before sundown."

I feel mildly amused at the idea of behaving like a cautious little schoolboy. Being locked in a hotel with Austen? Perfect.

"We'll be good," I say, speaking for the group.

❋ ❋ ❋

This whole thing has not been going anywhere good the last few days. Austen's always keeping an eye out for me, to leave rooms as I enter, but now I'm walking away, and paying him no mind either.

The girls on the tour, and even a few guys, are hitting on me, but I won't take the bait. That's only making them more persistent. I can't stand the idea of anybody else but him. He is my first, and most painful heartbreak. I take on every excruciating second with everything I have, in the hopes that it will toughen my emotional walls for the next time I become this irrational.

In the Alice "downtown" we meet some local indigenous artists at a gallery. William sticks around to talk with them, and sketch their portraits at the end. It seems like Will is not only intelligent, but creative and talented, and has a rich inner life. It fascinates all the girls to no end, and annoys me a lot. Austen waits around outside for him.

Groups of students peel off for lunch at nearby spots. I follow a group to a convenience store across the road. We all buy refreshments. I get a fruit-shaped popsicle.

"It is quite phallic, isn't it?" Amelia, the Brit, asks.

I frown. "What?"

"The watermelon at the top especially makes a perfect head shape."

I play along, licking from the base, before gently wrapping my lips around the tip and gently sucking at it.

"Seems like you have some experience."

I start laughing. "I'm very observant."

I like this girl, and she is attracted to me. A month ago, I might have propositioned her. Maybe I should. I can't believe how hung up on Austen I am. It can't be healthy.

Some students walk past and I follow them with my eyes, until I land on him, watching from across the street. I am always aware of him, but looking right at him thumps me hard. I freeze, unsure whether to keep eating in that suspiciously sensual way or not. It wasn't a performance for his benefit, but I got his attention.

There's just something about him. Maybe he's actually my soulmate, if there is such a thing. It feels like there is.

"Do you know who that is?" Amelia asks, as she looks over at Austen.

"Yeah, why? You're British so you probably know more. What's the deal?"

"Oh, I don't want to gossip."

"Sure you don't, but go on."

"Well I mean, literally everyone back in the U.K. knows their family. They have a bit of a reputation, I guess. William's a playboy, Austen was too until he got engaged recently, we all know they stole an aeroplane..." she frowns. "Between then and now, they have been dead silent. They seem to be doing okay, but they're disowned... and we're talking unbelievable wealth. American and European fortunes joined over and over again for decades, centuries maybe. That also makes them the least inbred aristocrats in Europe too. Their mother keeps a low profile, their father runs one of the family companies, and their grandfather owns several billion-dollar companies, and their grandfather's *brother* is probably the richest aristocrat in England, and *childless*. William's the older twin, so he's the heir. No matter what he does, he's destined to be a billionaire. Even if they don't get anything from their own grandfather, they'll be richer than the bloody Queen."

"So stealing the plane really wasn't the end of the road?"

"Yeah. I don't know what happened there. Everybody has heard little things; not that it was in the tabloids. Usually the papers are savage in England—they should be all over a story like that—but there was only one article in an independent newspaper. It was like someone told the British media to shut the fuck up."

"I wonder why?"

"Their grandfather is friends with all the newspaper monopoly men, so I figure he made the phone call."

"But he disowned them?"

"Yeah," she scrunches her nose. "I think there's a lot more to it.

I look over at him, all alone. It is almost like discrimination, for everyone to have opinions on him, before ever knowing him.

"Back in a sec," I tell Amelia. "Gotta go stir the pot."

I walk back in the store and emerge with another frozen treat. I cross the street and offer it to Austen.

"You seemed to want one," I explain.

"Oh I..."

He doesn't know what to say. Not taking it would make him

look petty or afraid, but taking it might make me think I won another chess piece. Because I would have.

"You still haven't given up on chasing me?" he asks, opening my gift. "I'm starting to pity you."

"That's okay," I shrug. "The chase is the most erotic part."

It's a chocolate covered ice-cream, but I have not forgotten that he's lactose intolerant, and can only have a bite.

"You don't really have to eat it," I tell him. "I know you don't eat dairy. I just bought it as a joke."

I turn over the wrapper and show him the name of it. *Golden Gaytime.*

He hands it back to me. "That's funny, but I think it's more for you."

I hold out my own popsicle. "Then we should swap."

A drop of red juice slowly makes its way down to my fingers.

"I..." he takes it awkwardly.

He looks at me and I wait. He doesn't understand why he's letting this happen. Maybe it's the melting ice causing Austen more anxiety than imagining the implications of sharing cooties with me. A drop of sticky cold liquid hits his finger and he reflexively licks the melt.

I breathe in sharply. "I love watching you eat."

My eyes flick half closed, savoring the sight of him. I feel like I just smoked something illegal.

He pauses, midway through his second lick, uncertain what to do. He presses his lips together and tries to discreetly remove the sticky syrup from his lips with his tongue. He's in way too deep again and he knows it, he just can't let me see.

Goddamn, my superpower is on *fire* today. It's almost as if, I don't know, he really is my soulmate?

Unfortunately, William comes out soon enough.

"Hi," he says, and smiles at us both.

I bite into the Golden Gaytime ice-cream with indifference.

"Sup?" I ask.

"Don't I know you from somewhere?" William asks me.

My stomach lurches.

Yes Will, you have spent ten days on vacation with me. You even went out to dinner with me and a group of other students, yesterday. We both have photos to prove this.

"Not sure." I shrug. "Gym maybe?"

William frowns. "You deliver pizza, right?"

Austen slaps his hand to his head.

"Yup," I say, popping the *P.* "I think I saw you fight a Russian guy... Gregor? You lost that, right?"

"I lost on points," William shrugs. "And I had the flu. You like the trip so far?"

It's as if William is trying to befriend me. He's terrible at it.

"Today is pretty neat," I say. "The Dandenongs and Melbourne library were also highlights."

Every time I had a moment with Austen.

Austen doesn't like this turn of events. He doesn't want me talking to his brother. I smirk, and then he looks at me defiantly, and hands William the popsicle to share with him. I watch in alarm, as Will takes it and sucks on it. Austen's eyes drill into me and I feel more and more revulsion. It's the first time he's knocked me off balance, and he can barely suppress a laugh bubbling up inside him.

"Are you doing anything later?" William asks, taking another lick.

I'm completely thrown, and it shows. Austen is thrown too. He shakes his head furiously at William, but Will ignores him.

"What do you mean?"

"We have till sundown to get a drink. That's like, ten o'clock at night around here. I need a very cold beer in a place like this. Do you want to ditch the girls and find a bar with us later?"

The playing field is shifting again. Now the alarm is back on Austen's face. William casually finishes the popsicle belonging to me and Austen. Austen frantically shakes his head behind William, trying to tell me to decline the offer, cutting his hand across his throat.

A grin breaks out over my face. "Sure."

"Back in a minute," William says, and leaves for the corner

store.

"That was evil," I tell Austen.

He shrugs. "There has never been a candy bar, lollipop, bon-bon, or drink I have ever been allowed to enjoy by myself. Billy also wants to eat what I eat because he's needy and annoying."

"So you'll be joining us for that drink?"

Austen glowers at me. "That's not a good idea. Billy's only suitable for controlled environments. The thing is, he's the *evil* twin."

"I already figured that out," I say. "That's actually why it might be fun. I think he likes me."

Austen raises an eyebrow. "He's straight too, but a total man-whore so you may have a better chance with him than me."

"I meant as a *friend*," I frown. "I only have eyes for you."

"What's the difference? We're exactly the same."

"You two are nothing alike, and I would never date someone like him. Nothing worse than the stench of ego," I scrunch my nose. "The show-ponying at fights, the expensive car, the fancy watches. That's what people are like with big egos. Tacky. And I'm from the Eastern Block so I'm an expert in tacky."

"Then why are you going for a drink with him?"

"Because I think he'll be my future brother-in-law one day."

Austen shakes his head. "I hate this so much."

11 AUSTEN

Monday, December 31, 2007, 4.55 p.m. (New Year's Eve).

Anzac Hill is a nice walk in the late afternoon. The panoramic views of the area are dazzling due to the electric blue of the sky out here. Johnno, our guide, smokes a cigarette and ignores us.

It's swelteringly hot, and Mischa has abandoned most of his clothes for just shorts and a black top that shows off his rounded, muscular sun-kissed shoulders and long legs.

He's already the most popular person on tour. He's relaxed, confident, and attentive, and it makes everyone melt. Every person he befriends feels like territory he's conquered. He's hanging around the other girls and guys. I stay in the shade and watch to see if somebody better catches his eye, so he can finally move on.

He's talking to the British girl again. Or rather she's talking to him. Talking and talking and talking. Her name is Amelia, I think. Pretty, but I didn't think he'd find her funny too.

Billy reminds Mischa about their drink, and he beckons me down the hill. I follow the bodyguards apprehensively. It's very out of character for my brother. I wonder what has got into him.

The dangers of the town seem overblown, until we reach the street our chosen bar is on. The ambiance has definitely deteriorated on the block before our destination. Dusty, weathered people in threadbare clothes mill around the street.

Mischa and my brother don't look like types to mess with, but I clearly seem weak. A basketball is launched at my head by some kids and my reflexes kick in. I catch it and start bouncing it from foot to foot. I smile at the buck-toothed kid with sun-bleached orange hair who threw it at me. He ducks as I send it back to him, and the boy behind him catches it laughing, and their game continues.

Mischa turns to watch, so I resume walking. There are several motorbikes outside the bar. Kane and Hayden stop William at the door.

"You think this is a biker pad?" Hayden asks.

Billy scoffs. "This isn't Reno, guys."

It doesn't look too intimidating, but just bad enough to be an extremely poor decision, considering we have a metaphorical grenade with us, ready to explode.

"Maybe we could try the nice bistro closer to the center of town?" I suggest.

"It doesn't look that bad," Mischa insists. "The other students are probably on their way here soon."

"I'm not looking for trouble," William rolls his eyes. "Non-aggressive de-escalation."

I look to Kane and Hayden, but they're only supposed to

help us live our lives, and stop us from getting killed while we do, not tell us what to do.

Kane winces. "Just let us deal with any issues if they appear."

The place has a rancid ambiance, and the stink of stale alcohol and daytime alcoholics. There are a couple of leather-clad bikers peppered around the place.

"My God," I say, as I lift my shoe and it unsticks from dried beer on the floor.

William is already ordering drinks.

"You study business?" he asks Mischa.

"Yeah, and some chemistry but it's not exactly a passion. I like more physical things, You know if you ever need a sparring partner, for training, we could work well together. I train all the time."

"We'd love that," my brother says, for both of us. "Maybe we could start tomorrow morning at the hotel gym?"

"Perfect."

If this was chess, I am losing my last bishop. Mischa has charmed even my asshole brother. My blood is starting to boil. Mischa is like a disease I can never be rid of, because Billy is an illness I am already lumped with.

An unwashed old man approaches us. You know the look, crazy-homeless, with bugging eyes that stick out. He pulls out a grimy pack of cards. It is an ancient tarot deck. The greasy, fat, mustached bartender watches the derelict like he wants an excuse to throw him out. As dreaded as such an encounter usually is, it is a thousand times better than watching my worst nightmare befriend my stalker.

"Read your fortune?" the man asks us. "Sing a tune? Clair de Lune?"

Hayden and Kane get closer but I raise my hand and tell them to back up.

"Oh yes," I say. "Absolutely. The tarot one."

I smile at Mischa and William. They look bewildered as the man pushes in beside me and clears away their drinks. The man smells like dirt and vinegar, and fumy vapors like industrial paint-stripper.

"Cross my palm with silver," the man instructs me.

I think for a moment, and hand him a wad of colorful Australian notes and the white-gold chain off my neck. The filthy man is thrilled. I'm also thrilled, but only because I'm temporarily distracted from the urge to smash Mischa's face into something.

I know William hates this, and I hope Mischa does too. The man hands me the dirty cards. They are old, hand-made, and foxed around the edges, and the pictures are mysterious. As I shuffle he mumbles to himself and looks around. Probably at things that aren't there.

"A big one," he says, when he gets the cards back. "My son. Run run run."

Mischa and William look at each other. Did they not guess this man was mad before?

The man lays four cards in a diamond formation, then places three more in a line along the middle. It makes a sort of cross and he places more cards at the end of the line above and below in a vertical line. Then he surrounds it with a circle of cards. Some cards slip out of the deck and he crosses them over other cards. Some are upside-down.

He points to the first card on the horizontal line. A tower with people falling from it.

"Fuck!" he gasps. "What happened to yous fellas?"

"What?" Mischa asks.

"Disaster has befallen your past, last, arm in a cast, run fast, everyone asked, wears a mask. Tick tick boom. Doom." the man taps his forehead and sighs, like he's trying to stop the flow of words from his mouth. He points to the next card, which is the Devil. "And you have already met the big bad. Big mad. Things will never be the same after the big sad, but did you want that?" He points to the queen of cups, upside-down, and a couple other cards. "Alone, at war. Your mum's not around. Your dad's a fuckwit. But there's a good man taking care of you anyway, paying for the holiday. The alliterate ones are your sword and shield."

"You mean me?" Mischa asks, and shakes his head. "Can you please stop rhyming?"

"I'll try…" The man laughs to himself and points to the cards placed on their sides. "The Wheel of Fortune, Clair de Lune. And all the threes. Three fates intertwined: three of cups, obviously… three of coins… all the money in the world…" he rolls his eyes. "Three wands—this adventure you are on, but—the three of swords?"

He shows us the card. It's a heart pierced by three swords.

"What does it mean?" I ask.

"Heartbreak," he says, and holds up the card placed before it, a man and a woman holding cups. "Young love… and then heartbreak. Terrible, horrific, heartbreak."

Mischa holds up the two naked lovers further along. "But what about these guys?"

"That doesn't mean what you think, think, think…" the man clears his throat, annoyed, like he's almost wrestling to not start rhyming again. "It's a fork in the road." He points to the flaming bush and the apple tree next to the nude lovers on the card. "Tree of Life and Tree of Knowledge. The choice between frivolity or responsibility, obligation or freedom, duty or desire, big liar. Where do decisions come from, louche aplomb? The head or heart? Wise or smart?"

"But does the romance work out?" Mischa asks.

He shows a card with a man on the ground with ten swords through his back. Then another card of a man in a black cape crying.

"Horrendous. Death is your only hope."

The man points to a few sword, pentacle, and wand cards, and then points to me and Billy.

"Poor boys," he says. "So many brothers without mothers. Fireworks. Networks. Cigarettes. Gingerbread. Moonshine. Valentine. Hungry boys hunting squirrels... Humble... Rebel. School is Hell. Let Doctor Feelgood help."

William and I are at his full attention.

"You're wrong," Mischa interrupts. "These two had a silver spoon in their mouth from the moment they were born..."

"Shut up," I tell him. "You don't know us."

The man turns his attention to Mischa. "You're from a world made out of cheese," he tells him. "Like on the moon. Can I have some more please? Wealth and privilege taste like ashes in your mouth."

"How'd you know that?" Mischa frowns.

"You're a fairy tale, Hansel and Gretel, Snow White, Red Riding Hood. Three little pigs. Pigs fly too. You'll get the happily ever after, after, after..." he holds up the death card, and flicks it at Mischa, and his face drops. Then he points to William and me. "You two; alone in the world. No home to go to. Big city, big smoke. You have a nice job until the old lady finds you. Fly away Peter, fly away Paul. Buzz buzz. Fly so far and so high the darkness tries to swallow you, but war is over, rover, bend-over, Mister Controller."

"Jesus *Christ*," I gasp.

The man points back to Mischa. "Now you have one another; a brother."

Mischa frowns. "Which one, Rumpelstiltskin? I have *eight* of them."

He points to William. "The one you are with."

"William's not my brother," he says. "William's his brother."

"Obviously," Billy's brow furrows. "We're fucking identical."

Mischa hands the old man the card with the skeleton on it.

"So… I will get my happy ever after, only when I kill someone? So who I gotta murder?"

The man holds up the Five of Swords that sat in the middle of all the other cards.

"I'll leave before the brawling, crawling, fighting, sure thing, diamond ring, on her finger, dad's a singer…"

The man keeps talking as he collects his cards, and leaves out the door, never stopping rhyming. We all stare at the door after he leaves, thinking about what just happened.

"Did he say alliterate or illiterate?" William asks.

"The *alliterate* ones," I look in his eyes.

He reads my mind.

"Austen, no," William says. "You're very silly."

I do feel a little silly.

Another man, this time much younger, bearded and very drunk, approaches the table.

"If you're gonna give him money, then give me some money too, ya cunts," he says.

"No," Mischa says.

Hayden and Kane move closer to me.

"It's okay," William says, and hands the man a twenty.

"That's not enough," the man says, looking at the note.

"Well give it back then," Mischa says, annoyed.

Kane pulls gently on the back of my belt from behind.

"You should probably wash your hands," he says. "Those cards were dirty."

I get off my stool and back away. Mischa's eyes get big at the sight of us leaving. Hayden walks in front of me and Kane walks behind. I lock myself in the washroom, Hayden and Kane guard the door.

I clean my hands, and try not to get frustrated or claustrophobic. More than a minute or two in here feels very uncomfortable. We are away from the action, and I am safe on this side of the bar, so it should be okay to step back out.

I stand behind Hayden and Kane, who are shoulder to shoulder, watching everything unfold. The man asking for money is becoming irate. Mischa is losing his cool. I feel a sudden twitch of alarm. William reaches for his wallet to give the man more money, but Mischa is not having it.

"Don't let this son of a bitch stand over you," Mischa tells him.

"*Son of a bitch?*" the man says to Mischa. "You calling my mum a *bitch*?"

"No, no, not at all... I was just calling *your dad* a bitch."

The man grabs Billy's wallet and punches Mischa in the face. Mischa pops up, and smashes his bottle over his head like we're in the Wild West. Jesus. What a way to escalate the whole thing. As soon as he does, the man's friends jump in and our corner explodes into a brawl. Mischa punches his way through bikers like a maniac—he's a good fighter—but he's in far more danger than he realizes.

"Hayden!" I say, as William and I lock eyes.

I know my brother is about to rip everyone in this bar limb from limb. I shake my head, my eyes pleading with him not to. He looks at me, and nods. He is still with it. Mischa knocks someone out. William holds another back. I get behind the bathroom door and hold it open a crack to watch. A man hurls a beer bottle and hits Kane. I watch Billy's eyes go black and he erupts from the his corner. Nobody even fucking touched me yet, but he's hitting guys left and right as he bulldozes his way over, smashing one into the bar.

I close the bathroom door and lock it. Then it's quiet.

"Bee!" Kane yells to me, sounding scared, calling for help.

I open the door. All bikers are down, but my brother is still in kill mode. Hayden and Kane back away to guard themselves, and fan out to try to tackle him. Mischa hasn't turned around yet, and we all scream for him not to move. Wild-eyed, Billy grabs Mischa's broken bottle and wields it as a weapon, grabbing the closest person to him, putting it to their throat. To Mischa's throat.

"Mischa!" I yell. "Stay still."

Hayden and Kane have their hands in the air. Mischa is confused, and my brother does not know where he is.

"I'm not..." Mischa starts, the sharp glass drawing a trickle of blood from his neck.

"Just shut up," Kane tells Mischa. "Don't move. Honey, you're okay."

I zero in on William. "Don't hurt him. I'm okay, Bee. Listen to my voice. Look at me. You're having a flashback. I'm okay, Honey. We're okay. Look at me. Listen to me. He's just a kid, Bee. Breath in and hold it. Don't hurt the little boy, Bee. He's just a kid. Breathe and hold. Give me the bottle, Honey. Look at me. Come back to me. Bee? Bee?"

I feel the moment I catch his eye. It's like a spell breaking. He releases Mischa, who drops to the ground and backs right out from him. I take the bottle and Billy grabs a pool cue and wields it like a rifle, pushing me behind him. Mischa looks at him like he's fucking insane, which is a fair assessment of the situation. I reach for the syringe in my pocket, but some of the bikers are getting a second wind. Can't knock him out now. Billy aims his imaginary rifle at them. I pull him out the door into the street.

On the street, I rub my hands through his hair and press his forehead to my forehead.

"Breathe," I whisper. "I'm okay. We're out. We're okay. You got us out Honey Bee. Hayden and Kane are here. Look where we are! We're in Australia. You're taking me to..."

Mischa turns to Hayden. "What the fuck is going on?"

"Who is that?" William points his stick at Mischa's head.

"He's my friend," I tell him. "He's just a kid. Look at me."

He drops his stick and starts babbling in a language only I understand. He says he wants to go home. I hug and kiss him and we sink to the ground. He is shaking all over. The monster is back, and we both need to run.

"It's time to go," I tell Kane.

Hayden shoves some candy in Billy's mouth.

Kane hands me candy too.

"Focus, Baby," he tells me.

They both put William's arms over their shoulders and move him. As we are almost at the corner, one of the maimed bikers comes out and starts yelling. We have knocked out his front teeth so his Australian accent sounds impenetrable. Despite this, Mischa turns back towards the man and flips him off. Another one comes out and tells us we're dead. Mischa throws a rock and hits him. I want to punch Mischa out, but I'm swaying a little and getting disoriented. He sees it, throws my arm over his shoulder and moves me. A few blocks later we reach the hotel. Johnno and Athena cast a wary eye on us as we enter.

"Sun's not down yet," Mischa tells them.

We get up to the room and they pull us into the shower. They slump me down next to Billy as the water pours over us and Kane. Mischa looks at my saturated clothes.

"Thank you for your help," Kane tells him, "but it's time you left."

Hayden escorts Mischa out.

"Sorry," Billy says.

"He says he's sorry," I translate for Kane.

"It's okay," Kane tells him. "You're not to blame, Honey."

We don't say anything for a long time as the water rains over us. I don't know how long. When I can move again and I'm sure he's stable, I leave him with Kane. It's dark outside.

When I exit, I find Mischa sitting against the door, and he falls back into the room when I open it.

"Hey," he says, looking up at me from the floor.

I look down on him, consider saying hello back, but only say, "Excuse me."

"Is William okay?" he asks.

I step over him and cross the hallway. Water drips off my clothes onto him.

"He's still in the shower. He'll be there a while."

"You want to tell me what happened?" Mischa asks.

"He's not all there."

"That's for sure," Mischa raises an eyebrow.

"I'm sorry about it."

"You saved my life," he says.

"I hope I won't ever need repayment."

"I know," he says, choosing his words very carefully. "I know what shell-shock looks like."

"Yeah, well then you know there's nothing for it."

"You did everything right, Austen."

I can feel my emotions welling.

"I should go," I say.

"You want to have a drink with me?"

"I don't want to talk about it, and I don't want to encourage you."

"Like you said, you hate me," he nods. "No talking. Just vodka. And maybe some Doctor Grinspoon to take the edge off?"

"If we leave this hotel it's going to end terribly. Either you'll try something and I'll beat you to death, or my brother will go spare and do it for me. Let's not tempt fate."

"Let's just go to the smoking patio; it's probably empty."

"Alright. Whatever."

12 MISCHA

Monday, December 31, 2007, 10.30 p.m (New Year's Eve).

I'm an expert at having only one shot at getting something important. I fled a war-torn country, and got out with a series of one-in-a-million chances. One of those shots was actually a one-in-twenty-four-million. Not to mention Sivishni adopting me and Sofie. Ending up with Austen would be one in seven billion, so every move I make is crucial.

The moment we start walking to the patio, time slows down. The thoughts going through my head start with how to win him over, but soon become close to marriage vows. *We are at the start of a beautiful adventure. We can figure it all out together. I will do everything to make him love me. I will do everything to deserve his love. I will never hurt him. I'm his bodyguard now. I'll always protect him. I want to lick his chest, his navel, his inner thigh.*

Okay, maybe that last one wouldn't sound good at an altar.

Austen's clothes are still wet from the shower, but they're drying quickly in the arid heat. His spirit remains dampened. He drinks a little vodka from my hipflask and sits awkwardly in the peacock-shaped wicker chair. I roll the joint on the coffee table.

"I like your t-shirt," he says. "As a drummer, I mean. Laibach, right? They're good."

I look down. It's a tight black shirt with a wide square grey cross in the middle of it. Nobody's ever recognized the symbol before.

"Thanks," I nod. "They saved my life."

I put the joint to my lips.

"How did you even get that?" Austen asks.

"You know that British girl Amelia? Sort of blonde and funny?"

"Not really."

I light the joint and inhale. "Well, she bought some in Melbourne and convinced some of the girlies to put it up their asses to bring it here for New Year's Eve."

I pass it to him.

Austen looks at it. "This has been in Amelia's butthole?"

"Yep," I laugh. "I would have done it too but she didn't ask me."

Austen smokes it and looks at me looking at him. I just noticed his medical bracelet and weird plastic dongle.

"You clearly want to ask me something," he says after handing the joint back.

"What is that?" I grab his wrist and read it. "You have hypoglycemia and epilepsy?"

"That's what it says," he looks away.

Austen does not have epilepsy, and definitely not hypogly-cemia. *Hmm.*

"Can I ask another question?"

"Sure," he says.

"Favorite food?"

He lights up. "Anything Italian."

"Favorite book, movie, band?"

He squints his eyes. "I read a lot, so my favorite book is a hard one." He thinks about it. "There are too many books, but my favorite Russian novel is *Doctor Zhivago*."

"What a hopeless romantic."

He smiles. "Runner up is *Master and Margarita*, my favorite film is *Withnail and I*, and I have at least ten favorite bands. My favorite play is *Under Milk Wood*, by the way."

"You want to know mine?"

"I really don't care, don't want to get to know you, or any-thing about you, but I'd wager *The Art of War*, *The Matrix*, and… Laibach?"

I chuckle. "You think I'm so obvious. You got Laibach right, but it's *The Leopard* and *Queen Margot*."

"Shit, my brother's is *Queen Margot* too, film and book, but his other favorite is the Gadfly."

I shake my head. "I'm shocked Will reads books. Especially those ones."

"I don't know if you like plays."

"I'm training to become a ballet étoile, so I guess it could be the ballet of *Romeo and Juliet*."

"Ballet? Really?"

"Yeah, my birth mother was a ballerina. My adoptive sister is going pro and I've been her dance partner for every style since I was young. I'm really good, I kind of like it, and she wants me to join her. She usually gets what she wants."

"What do *you* want?"

"What do I want?" I think about it. "I just want to spend the rest of my life with you."

Austen scoffs. "That's an *unpaid* kind of gig."

The New Year's Eve revelry has started. He takes another toke and we listen to the night sounds coming in from outside.

"About earlier," I say, and hear him huff. "I'm sorry, but I have to ask; it's not just fights, is it? William doesn't like people touching you at all, does he?"

"He does not."

"Would he react badly if I touched you in front of him?"

"It depends, but maybe. The bodyguards are not here for his protection, they're here for yours. And I don't like being touched either, and he hates seeing me agitated. I never imagined codependency could be this bad. It doesn't always happen, and it never used to, but it's been happening more often lately, especially when we're tired or stressed. I seem to be at my worst around very *tall* men too, ironically. It flared up when we moved away from our foster-parents last year. It was a real shock to realize that we were in a negative spiral because of each other. I've been getting worse, so he's getting worse too. He doesn't deserve this burden, but I can't fix it, and I've sort of given up trying to."

"Foster-parents? What about your real parents?"

He shakes his head. "They aren't around. They kinda... lost custody."

"But they're rich?"

"And they're unfit."

"How long?"

"Eleven was the last time I saw my father."

"Damn. Me too. That's crazy."

"But we love our foster parents."

"Do you still have money?" I ask.

"Some," he shrugs. "Our grandma left us enough to get by, but it wasn't easy to access. Getting cash injections always meant coming out into the open. We wanted to stay hidden, so we got jobs mopping floors at restaurants and working on vineyards and stuff. Our dad's child support stopped two years ago. As long as we had food and shelter, we didn't worry."

"And Will's been in a firefight?"

"I said I wasn't going to talk about it."

"Well, if you ever want to..."

"Nope."

"Okay."

"I want to trust you," he says, running his fingers through his hair. "But the wise thing to do is probably beat your head in with a crowbar and burn your body in the desert."

"Jesus," I say. "You'd sooner kill me than take a walk on the wild side?"

"It's nothing personal. My mother said stalking is murder in slow motion. That's why she killed her stalker."

"I'm not a *stalker*," I insist. "People fall over themselves to be with me. I'm honestly surprised my charms aren't working on you, I don't see why that's a death sentence."

Austen shrugs. "For one, I'm taken, also I don't like being touched, I don't like sudden movements, and I don't like yelling, and I can't upset Billy for obvious reasons."

I roll my eyes, "Oh yeah, *taken*. We are still running with that lie?"

"I need you to understand this Mischa; you *cannot* get attached to me. You will get hurt."

"Too late. I knew I loved you the moment I met you, maybe before."

Austen casts a look that is hard to interpret. "Mischa, I don't want to hurt you. It's not a lie that I am taken, but it is complicated, and you know if we ever had anything, you know, physical, that would be all it was. It could never be anything more, you know? It'd be wiser if we didn't. If we did, you won't get to have me for more than a week or two. The end would be very abrupt, very painful, and very final. You'll need to get over this sooner or later, the easy way or the hard way."

"Noted. I'll take whatever scraps you want to give me. You want to ask me anything?"

"Why did you ask me who I was, when you already knew William?"

"Because I had never seen you before and didn't know who you were."

"But you'd seen William before?"

"Of course, but you two are nothing alike."

The ugly sounds of fighting and banging from the street below interrupt our conversation. We watch over the scene. Two staggering groups of drunk men start a scuffle.

"This town is bad," I say.

"Dystopian," Austen agrees.

The rabble moves off down the road and a man starts harassing a woman at the crosswalk. He has a beard and a biker jacket and I'm pretty sure he attacked us and I gave him his black eye at the bar earlier.

"Didn't he steal the wallet?" Austen asks.

"Yeah," I agree.

Then he lunges to grab the woman and she shrieks.

"Hey!" Austen barks at the man below. "Back off her."

"Mind your own fucking business!" he yells back.

The woman, now free from his grip, runs off down the road.

I pick up a stone from the planter and present it to Austen.

"Do you think I can hit him?" I ask.

"No," he shakes his head. "We can't get away with anything tonight, remember?"

The man is still standing in the middle of the street, staring up at us.

"Aren't you the fuckers from this afternoon?" he asks.

"Huh?" Mischa shrugs. "Not us!"

"Yeah ya are, ya stupid fucken *wogs*."

I look at Austen. "What the hell does that mean?"

"I think it's a rude name for Italians," he says.

"Italian? Okay, I am offended."

I hurl the pebble and hit him in his already black eye and he recoils. Austen gasps, drops out of sight below the railing, and cackling with laughter.

"We're gonna fucking get ya!" the man howls.

He limps off, holding his eye.

Austen and I are both doubled over laughing, until he

catches his breath and says, "I'm really hungry."

"You have the munchies," I tell him. "Let's get refreshments."

* * *

Austen gets one of everything from the vending machine on the next floor. His red eyes stare intently to concentrate on purchasing it all correctly. He puts the money in for the first item, a candy bar, and watches it fall to the bottom. Then he buys the next and watches the wire turning to push it out, then the next, and the next, and the next. Soon the bottom of the machine is full of snacks and I'm howling with laughter. He realizes he's being ridiculous and laughs too. He reaches down and grabs two packets of potato chips for us to eat in the stairwell nearby.

I watch him savor the first bite and lick the salt off his lips.

His glazed eyes turn to me. "Are you watching me eat?"

I laugh. "Maybe."

He looks bashful and eats another one, his eyes flicking away and his cheeks flushing pink. His dimples make a cameo. I am completely fascinated.

He places the packet down and wipes his hands on his jeans. "I should stop..."

My breath hitches. "Please don't," I say. "It's literally my favorite activity."

Austen shakes his head. "Too nervous." He grabs another chip, and holds it up to me. "You have one."

I eat it out of his hand. He laughs and grabs a few more, so I eat them too. He gets another one and I hold his wrist as I chomp on his offering. Then I lick a little salt off his extended fingers as he watches my face. I suck one, then both of his fingers, then his thumb. When I am done he looks at his hand.

"I don't know how you do that," he says. "If anyone else I barely knew did that I'd be having a seizure on the floor, but you somehow bypass my defenses. Like a kind of magnetism my body has that pulls it that makes me feel possessed. It makes my whole body tingle."

"Maybe you like it?"

"Nope," he says. "I hate that my body never does what I tell it to. You're actually the one person I really should be bothered by."

I hold a chip up to him and he snaps it from my fingers. His glassy eyes are looking into mine. He crunches the chip and is content. He swallows and wipes his mouth with his damp sleeve.

My need for control is at a fever pitch. I make a little whimper of pain.

"You are driving me *so insane*," I tell him. "You have no idea."

ARK STARS IN THE SKY

He raises an eyebrow. "But isn't that the most erotic part?"

It feels like the right moment. I hook my pinkie finger on his. He doesn't pull away, he's letting me get closer and closer. *Oh shit.* He looks at my lips then my eyes. Jesus, he's biting his lip. *He wants me to kiss him.* I fixate on his mouth. He lifts his face to mine and I reach for his collar. The smoke-stop door down the hallway creaks open, and it fucks my fucking shit up and the spell is fucking broken and Austen fucking shifts away from me FUCK. That motherfucker Kai and the Stupid Fucking Backwards Hat walks towards us, and whispers loud enough for it to echo in the empty fucking hallway.

"Wow—you guys are so *blazed* right now!" he says. "The girls have made a giant three-pronged joint. It's so fucking cool. I call it Sea King's Fork—you know, like Ariel's dad? We're going to that garden in the back of the hotel bar at midnight to smoke that bad boy. You guys should come!"

"Count me in," Austen says, after a breath.

"I'm down," I agree.

"Oh shit—this thing is broken!" Kai says, looking at all the packets of food still at the bottom of the vending machine. "Fuck yeah!" He scoops up all our snacks and throws a couple chocolate bars at us. "I'ma bring these to the girls' rooms. See you soon."

Kai leaves with our snacks.

"You were going to kiss me," I say.

"Nuh-uh," Austen says.

"Ya-huh. My hands are shaking," I hold my palms up. "My body already knows you and needs you, *desperately*. How is that even possible?"

Austen giggles. "Crazy."

He gets up and goes to the vending machine.

"Come back," I say, "We can try again."

"Try what?" he asks.

He scratches his chest under his top and I see his ripped stomach. Brad-Pitt-Fight-Club abs. Torture. His body is always covered, neck to foot, like his brother, but underneath the long sleeves he's built like a god. I want to kiss him just above his belly-button. Then below it. He selects two colas and gives one to me. I'm very thirsty so the syrupy drink feels good going down. I pour in some vodka from my flask, and do the same for Austen.

"You keep trying to deny it, and it could fuck up your life, your future."

"What life?" Austen asks. "What future?"

Then it's quiet. I look at my trembling hands, and remember the last time they shook this bad. It storms into my mind like a deluge. I start talking out of nowhere.

"I've been in a firefight too, and my town was bombed when

I was younger," I say. "I saw a lot of death."

"Bombed in a war?"

"Yeah. I'm a refugee."

"Is your family alive?" Austen asks.

"My sister's with me. My parents survived, but we got separated. I haven't heard from them in a while."

"Shit," he says, and looks in my eyes. "How are you doing?"

"How am I doing?" I frown. "That's not the usual question people ask me."

"Sorry."

"No, you're the first person to not ask me *where* I'm from, *which* side, *which* war."

He shrugs. "All wars suck."

With that, he takes my breath away.

"I love you," I say.

"I know," he laughs. "In a gay way."

"Not just in a... I love that you said that. I'm doing good. And it's okay, you can ask me which war."

He shakes his head. "I couldn't take it if it was the Balkans."

"Well," I point to my top. "I did buy the t-shirt..."

"Oh *God*," he looks stricken. "That didn't occur to me."

I reach into the back pocket and hand him a small booklet inside my wallet that looks just like a passport. He opens it and sees a photo of me as a little kid looking back at him. He breaks into a smile and looks back to compare me to my younger self. He begins to leaf through the pages and stops on one with a stamp that says *'Österreich'*. Austria.

"This is the passport you escaped on?"

"I escaped on it, but it's not a passport; Laibach made them. Fake passports. It was an art project thing. My dad got me and my sister one and they ended up coming in handy. That's why I'm always wearing Laibach shirts. When I said they saved my life, I don't mean some emo shit. I mean *they saved my fucking life.*"

"That's amazing," he says, and curves the photo page to see the light catch the embossed logo, fascinated. "It looks so real."

"They saved thousands of people." I shrug. "So yeah, Sarajevo and all that."

"I think I just found my favorite band," Austen says.

"I think we have the same one."

He looks off into the distance for a while, then covers his eyes.

"*Of course* you're from Yugoslavia."

"Is that so bad?"

Austen makes a frustrated, guttural sound. "I promised myself if I ever met any of those kids, I'd look after them, be their friend."

"Pleased to meet you."

"Fuck off."

"It's so sweet. You going to keep that promise to little Austen?"

He scoffs. "Christ. I need to call a priest to drive you out."

"You can't get rid of me. We're part of each other; I feel it."

"No we're not. Me and my dickhead brother are a part of each other. You and I are strangers."

"He's not a dickhead; he's just a little messed up."

He smiles involuntarily again, and I feel my heart flutter.

"Maybe being so charming wouldn't work as well, if you weren't so good looking too."

I'm confused. "You think I'm attractive and my charms are working?"

Austen snorts with laughter. "I just feel bad about our situation. You deserve to seduce someone. Anyone except me, that is."

"You're right, I don't deserve you."

"No, you do. I mean, no..." Austen gets tongue tied. "You... do... deserve to be... loved."

"I'll survive," I shrug. "I'll try not to hit on you again, if you don't want?"

"Thanks, because I'll have to crack your head open if you do."

"Your threat seems a little empty, but please don't do that.

You love me, so it would hurt you just as much."

Austen shifts uncomfortably. "So... you left when NATO bombed?"

"Yeah."

"You must have been ten or eleven?"

"Yep."

"I watched it on the television for years, but when the bombing started, I'd watch the jets fly over all Summer..."

"Me too."

"You could see them so high in the sky when..."

"When the sky was really blue."

"Yeah," Austen says.

We look over the balcony. On the street two floors below, a rough crowd of revelers are getting into an argument.

"We're way too stoned for this conversation," he says.

"We'd never have it otherwise. You can't ignore things when you're stoned. Everything you're running from appears the moment you're finally relaxed to demand your attention. Things that are important that you don't want to think about usually."

"I'm only fighting to ignore one particular thing," Austen sighs. "Fight of my life and I'm losing completely."

"What are you trying to run from?" I ask.

"You."

Time stops as we watch one another.

"You know, I actually get it," I tell him. "I get that it's not a question of whether you want me or not. You just don't want to pull me into your problems. I can tell they're big ones. You were gonna ask me out one time, then disappear to Australia, and hopefully never see me again. The thing is, I usually roll like that too. I'm right there with my own bullshit, and mine is really bad, *believe me*. Your brother might slit my throat? My brother might slit yours. You got some baggage? I have a whole lot too."

"Maybe my problems aren't as big as yours," Austen shrugs, "but you don't know, they could be bigger. Maybe it's too much for you, for anybody."

"My father gave me up to a scary Russian when I was twelve to be a dancing monkey and I have post-traumatic stress disorder from watching members of my family being blown up in front of me, amongst other things. Big enough for you?"

"Okay yeah," Austen sighs. "Our problems actually compliment each other quite nicely, then."

I laugh. "But we don't have to be each other's person. Don't have to commit. We can be all cloak-and-daggers. That's usually the gay way anyway. And you don't have to make up your mind now. I'll never stop chasing."

"Where I'm going after this, you can't chase me there."

"What if I just asked you for this vacation then?" I suggest. "I'll promise to never talk to you again. Maybe we try just once. Only once?"

"You're not doing this because I'm wealthy, are you?"

"I am wealthy!" I laugh. "My adoptive parents are freaking loaded, and they like to show it. You're *disowned* too, and running out of cash, so it looks like I'm the sugar daddy here."

"What about the terrible, horrific, heartbreak thing?"

"You mean *the tarot cards?* I'm already having the heartbreak!"

"Far worse is coming, Mischa. I can give you everything in the world, except happiness. You have to find that without me. When you hear gossip about me, you'll hate me."

"I won't listen."

"But you *will*. And you'll believe it, because it's true. Then you'll know, and hate me, and be extremely hurt and so will I, and I'll never speak to you again."

I tilt my head. "I could never hate you."

"Don't be so sure."

"Well what is it?"

"I can't talk about it," he sighs. "The gossip's not even as bad as the truth, by the way. I wish it was."

I level my eyes at him. "Whatever it is, I don't give a fuck. Life is fleeting; try me as a holiday wild-card. I'm excellent in bed. Like, one of the all-time greats. Nobody does it better. Give me a *whirl*."

"I'm not sure that's a good idea, but I really do admire your honesty."

"Thanks. You should try it sometime."

Austen shakes his head. "That's a dangerous idea."

"Go on, try it. Tell me something true about you, seeing as I told you something about me, and you won't tell me what the bad thing is."

"Well," he sighs, and thinks for a while. "We ran away a lot, me and my brother. I've been thinking about it a lot lately."

"Why did you run away?"

"It's just a lot of pressure, I guess. The first time we ran away with Mom. She was a Rhodes scholar and Dad's English upper-crust. They married young and were pretty crazy for each other, until we were about eight, when Mom went on the run from Dad. I'm not actually sure why. All I know is my mother airlifted us from our life with no explanation. We were supposed to be going to Hong Kong Disney that day, while my father was in a meeting. She took us to the roof of the hotel and packed us into a helicopter to the airport."

"Where did you go?" I ask.

"America. She threw away our passports and credit cards and kept a stack of hundred dollar bills in a hollowed out bible.

We made this bizarre journey until we were deep in Appalachia, where Mom's mother lived. Meemaw is the best person on the planet."

"I'd love to meet her."

"They hadn't talked since she left for Oxford. She didn't even know about us and she was only about forty herself. We thought we had a normal life, but it had been gilded, and this was not that. It was dirty and cold and scary, at first. There was a lot of hillbilly deprivation everywhere. People's carpets were always so old and musty. I always wondered why they didn't just rip it up and burn it. So many feet had been over it. Now carpet is this thing I don't like because I know how bad it can get."

"They put carpet on the walls in Russia, like it's a painting," I say. "It never gets stepped on."

"That feels very correct to me," Austen agrees. "At first. Mom's accent changed and we stopped talking until we sounded right too. Sounded American."

"I can't imagine you sounding American."

"Looks can be deceiving," he says in a hillbilly drawl. "I can always sound like I'm from the hill country."

I gasp. "No way!"

"Yessir," he grins. "I was in the woods a long time."

"My god your voice is sexy in any accent," I say, and take a drink.

"Thanks," he shrugs. "But a year later my parents were back together like it never happened, and not back to the little cottage we were born in. Now we were in a castle. It wasn't normal anymore, it was privileged and extraordinary, and it took months for everyone to understand a word we were saying again. High society is difficult to get accustomed to, it requires so much of people. I call it the *'soul tax'*. The free life we had in America was honestly like a drug. Americans are so kind too."

"Real sweethearts," I agree.

"For nearly a year there, we had just been children, without the mountain of responsibility and obligation to prepare for a life of obscene wealth and power. We had nothing but the other kids to go shoot squirrels with so we could eat. We were deprived in every way, and it was fine. That's why we live in Massachusetts now, why we have a cabin in the woods."

"You make so much more sense now."

"I've never told anybody about that. I don't usually talk to people like this. I know that if I tell people about everything that has happened to us, they'll never believe it. I worry that even my therapist doesn't believe most of the things I tell her. Please don't tell anyone anything I've said. My sister was a newborn when that happened so she doesn't even remember."

"I believe you, and your secret's safe with me," I say.

Austen raises an eyebrow. "Well, one of them."

We can hear the revelry out on the street getting louder. It sounds like people having a lot of fun; shouts and hoops were coming from all directions.

"It's almost midnight," he says.

I get up and take his hand to pull him up too. "Time to head down."

＊　＊　＊

When I was eleven, in Austria, life was not easy. Because Sofie and I were seeking asylum without our parents, we were not able to stay at the Traiskirchen refugee center, and we were put in a group home. I fought viciously to protect my sister, and was planning to take her further north as soon as possible.

There were a lot of other kids from Yugoslavia around, and they brought the war with them. They would travel in groups. Albanians with Albanians, Serbs with Serbs, Croats with Croats... on and on. While all the languages are slightly different, they can mainly be mutually understood because they are very similar. Almost every day they would rumble with one another on the way home from school. Sofie was too young for that, so I hid our identity. We had learned American from television, and we called it Cartoon Language. I made Sofie use it on trams and buses so we wouldn't have any trouble.

The day we packed our bags to leave for Scandinavia, there was a mix of all the groups going home from school on a tram. I knew shit would pop off so I sat at the back with Sofie and waited. A Serb girl was getting really lippy with a Croat boy and he snapped back at her a blistering line that made me crack up with laughter. Suddenly all eyes were on me, and every kid was asking where I was from, who my little sister was. This or that? Those people or them. Where? What were we, exactly?

Sofie was terrified, and the tram had stopped near the Sacher Hotel in downtown Vienna. I grabbed her hand to run. The Croat boy stopped me and I punched him, so the Croats assumed I wasn't one of them. A Serb tried me too, and I hit him just as hard. The Albanians beckoned me but as one stepped forward I pushed him into the road. I ditched my heavy backpack, grabbed Sofie's arm and we bolted down the street to the Secession Building. There we hid in the empty basement gallery, surrounded by the Beethoven Frieze.

Sofie cried against the back wall. I hugged her, and battled my bubbling rage.

"You like this painting," I reminded her. "It's from the Ode to Joy. Remember when we would dance to it with Mom?"

She wiped away her tears. "It's very beautiful."

The large white basement was bigger than a dance studio. Our mom was a dance teacher. We started learning in the womb, and nothing makes my sister happier than dancing. We stepped out into the middle of the floor and started performing our ballet steps. Soon we were both spinning on one foot, in a competition to see who could twirl the longest. Sofie's laughs echoed against the lofty plaster ceiling, and I felt free.

When we stopped I noticed a man was watching us, holding my bag. He must have had velvet on the bottom of his shoes, because he came down the stairs so quietly, we didn't hear him. He had a fine suit and was carrying an ivory cane, although he didn't seem old or frail.

"Joy, the lovely spark of heaven's fire, an embrace for all the world," he said, in a thick Russian accent, and pointed to the frieze with his cane.

He did not apologize for staring, or try to explain. I took my bag silently and went to leave. His eyes followed us up the stairs.

Outside the Serbs were nearby.

"Look what we got!" an older boy yelled when he saw us.

There was nowhere to go from here. The man had followed us, and looked out at the scene from the top of the stairs. I told Sofie to wait and I stepped out to fight them. The first boy came and I pushed him past me. He came again and I hit him. The man came down and stepped in between me and the next one. The boy came for me anyway, and I grabbed the man's cane and gave the kid a hard whack. The boy may have been a bully, but he was still a boy, and couldn't take a hit like that without letting it show. He rubbed the top of his head where I hit him and stepped back.

"Leave my children alone," the man said in that strong accent.

Once he said it, I realized that these boys now thought I was actually *Russian*, and not Yugoslavian at all.

"*Da!*" I said, in the most Russian-sounding way I could muster.

The man was amused. The boys backed right off. Not their circus, not their monkeys, as the saying goes.

I turned to the man when they left.

"Thank you, sir," I said.

"Yes," Sofie said, and curtsied. "Thank you very much."

"You could have really hurt him, hitting him like that," he said.

"I wasn't trying to."

"Why are they making trouble?"

"They thought we were on the other side."

"Were you?" the man asked.

"We're only on our own side."

He nodded, seemingly impressed. "Do you have anyone taking care of you?"

"Yes," I lied.

"You do not," he said. "What's with all the candy in your bag?"

"I steal it, and sell it at school."

I realised he had looked in my bag, and I ripped it open to check the man hadn't taken anything.

"You're going somewhere?"

I turned to him, holding out our fake passports. I lunged and handed them to me, then I gave him back his cane.

"Norway," I said.

"How will you get there?"

"I'm stealing a car."

"You know how?" he laughed.

"Yes," I nodded, matter-of-factly.

"How old are you?"

"Nearly twelve."

"So tall for nearly twelve! You're a smart boy, also a very beautiful boy. I like you. Your sister is beautiful too. My daughter will like her."

"Please don't rape me or my sister," I told him.

The word *rape* is a long, hard to say word in German. Before I had even finished my sentence the man was bellowing with laughter.

"Straight to the point! I won't, don't worry."

"Put your hands up and swear it," I told him.

He held his arms up in the air like he was surrendering.

His hands gestured softly. "I am not going to hurt or kill you. No matter what."

I saw he was honest, because I can always tell if people are lying. It's my superpower.

"You're telling the truth."

"You can tell?"

"Yeah. I still don't trust you."

"This is a business relationship. A job. It doesn't require trust. Just a contract."

"What do you want from us?"

"First, I have some questions for you. Do you think people are good or bad?"

"Well... no," I shrug, not really understanding.

"Neither?"

"Not all good or all bad. Most people try to be good, unless they're pushed. Some people don't try, and then there's the crazy people."

"And in your heart, you are, in some way, better than those boys that tried to fight you?"

"Better how? Stronger or nicer? Or smarter?"

"Or all of those things?"

"How would I know?"

"In your heart?"

I searched my feelings. "No. Not the worst, or the best, if that's what you're looking for?"

"I am looking for you. You could go far. I want to train you to work for me. Ride motorbikes. Fly helicopters. Shoot guns. Blow stuff up. I will teach you to be deadly, and you will give me your loyalty."

"I want to blow stuff up!" Sofie said.

"You, little one, will learn to break hearts," he said. "You will be put in a school to study ballet, and my little daughter will dress you up like a doll."

"Who are you?" I asked him.

"My name is Victor, but you will call me Father, or *Sivishni.*"

I sounded the word out on my tongue. "Sivishni?"

"It means king in Russian. It also means God in Russian. And that is what I will be to you. Your father, your king, and your God. If you do what I say, we can run the world together. If you don't act right, you're on your own."

❋ ❋ ❋

Australia is as far away from Sivishni as I've been since the day I met him and his wife Koro. Most days he feels more like a father to me than my own. I miss being under his protection. I miss his approval. I even miss my stupid brothers. But to be honest, I don't miss blowing stuff up all that much.

I was cautious before I met him. He just taught me to always be hyper-aware of my surroundings and present in the moment. Just in case someone tries something. And now I assume trouble is always ahead, because it always is.

My protective instincts are in overdrive near Austen. It's like a different state of consciousness. A state of pure hypervigilance.

I can hear the shouts from the crowd outside, and that hoodrat Taylor B egging them on, calling them "kangaroo fuckers" while they call her a "Yank" or "wank". Austen is in front of me, and I realize there might be trouble brewing between the locals and Kai's group down at the bar.

Soon I hear a bottle smash. Probably Kai or Taylor throwing something at them. Then more bottles hit the building in return. As we descend the staircase, I hear barking shouts.

We reach the ground floor and Austen, as always, is walking with his head down. I can see past him to the lobby. There are bikers at the entrance, friends of those we crossed earlier, no doubt. It's a small town so it's not a surprise they figured out where we're staying.

We always assume opponents are armed, and we always assume their weapons are loaded. I am not armed. I am stoned too. With precious cargo in tow as well. This is not good.

If you can avoid a fight you should always try to. I grab Austen and move him. I have that strength that mothers get when they need to lift a car off their baby. Austen is as light as a feather as I pick him up and get him to the parking area. He's fighting me like a toddler the whole time.

I get my hands around his neck. "Shut the fuck up or I'll choke you out and leave you behind this dumpster."

I regret that the moment I say it. Physical force is the most rudimentary form of control, but sometimes it is not only effective, but necessary. He stops fighting me.

It's dark, and we are pretty well hidden. Then I realize Austen's sitting in my lap and I drink it in. He always smells so fresh and sugary. It reminds me of peaches, with an earthiness underneath. I put my nose to the back of his neck and breathe his scent. He yields to me and leans back and it's just us in the stillness. My arms hugging his neck, his on the sides of my hips. It's a moment of Zen in the middle of the hurricane.

I can hear a weird beep coming towards us but instead of the bikers it's William, and he's out for blood.

"Bee!" Will screams.

That's confusing, I don't get it; Austen calls William 'Bee'. William calls Austen 'Oz.' Why is he calling out to himself? I am not holding William am I? No. I'm just really fucking stoned. Maybe it will be obvious when I'm not stoned. Oh shit that beep is telling William where Austen is and he's about to find me and kill me.

The guys from the lobby come in and surround William. Thank GOD. He's going to get whipped and I can come in and save him at the end, and Austen will think I'm a hero. Only William's a robotic beast. Worse than at the bar. It's fucking cool actually. He takes each one of these douche canoes out in quick succession. Of course he's a great fighter. He's also terrifying. I know I can take him, but I think we would both be worse off by the end of it. I try to laugh it off but it's the first time my confidence in my physical prowess has trembled. I won't let it get to me.

"That's hot," I tease Austen, when all the others are on the ground, my lips on his ear. "Can you do that?"

William turns toward the dark corner behind the dumpster we are hiding in. There's not a lot of ways this can turn out well, so I have to let Austen go without me. It feels like I am letting a piece of myself go as I release him. I can still feel his body in my lap after he leaves.

The men on the ground get up and start lurching away. I move past them like a ghost. I'm furious, and almost daring them to fight me, so I can punish them for fucking up my opportunity to spend time with Austen, but William knocked the wind out of all of them, so they can barely get up. When I go out to the lobby, Johnno has a drunk pinned down.

"Go back to your room, mate," he tells me.

Two more men come in and I know they will scuffle with him to get their friend back. So I pummel one, then the other like punching bags until both are back on the street and laid out on the pavement.

The maimed bikers come out behind me and limp away. Johnno sees the damage inflicted on the others I get his drunk off the floor and push him away with the others. We close the doors behind them, and the steel security trellis locks us inside.

Johnno nods in admiration, and slaps me on the back. "Good man."

My chance has slipped through my fingers.

Austen's right. It'll never end well. He has a venomous, jealous demon shadowing him. There seems to be no way around it. At least not one that's obvious.

But I do love a challenge.

13 AUSTEN

Tuesday, January 1, 2008, 10.09 a.m (New Year's Day).

At first, things are quiet during our visit to Uluru, the massive sandstone monolith. The place is sacred to the people of the land. The tour guide Johnno is particularly passionate on this point.

"If you fuckers try and climb that mountain or take anything from here, then you're walking to the camp site."

Kai with the Stupid Backwards Cap rolls his eyes with his whole body. "You wouldn't let us party on New Year's Eve, and now you won't let us climb the mountain?"

"Too right I won't. It's for your own good. Firstly, it's steep and dangerous to climb, and people have fallen and died. Secondly, that place will curse you if it doesn't kill you. I don't want the bus flipping on me because some stupid Yank took a bloody souvenir. This has been around for millions of years, but you think a piece of it might look good as a doorstop? Where's your sense of *reverence?*"

The already bow-legged man is crouched at the waist as he gives his short monologue.

We drive a long way to get there, and intend to walk the track around the base of the mountain. Afterwards, we will be camping within Uluru-Kata Tjuta National Park for two nights. There we'll join a tribal meeting known as a *corroboree*. After that we're going to the red-rock formations known as "The Olgas".

The walk is unbelievably hot. Mischa has a very large back-pack. He's also carrying two bottles of water. One of which he pours on himself so his shorts and top cling to his perfect body. All the girls stare at him. Pathetic.

As the walk progresses, the different paces stretch the group into a long line. Some try to walk together but the heat makes some want to speed up and some slow down. My brother is at the very front. I am further back. Mischa is behind me for most of it but catches up to me halfway through.

"Hey, about last night..." he begins.

I cut him off. "I could have had a seizure, and my brother would have found us and killed you, moron. I can't risk this trip going badly again. I can defend myself by the way. I'm a better fighter than he is, or you, or those fucking idiots last night, and I would enjoy it. If anyone else did what you did they would have regretted it."

"It was wrong of me to grab you like that. I'm sorry. I won't do it again," he says. "How is William?"

"Awful. We had a rough night."

He reaches for my hand and it brushes his. I flinch and hold my hand like I scorched it on a hot iron.

"What are you doing?" I ask.

"I was trying to hold your hand," he says.

"Why?" I frown.

"I wanted... I don't know... to comfort you."

So many emotions flash through me. "Please don't touch me."

"Sorry."

"No it's not you... it's just not a good idea... please don't touch me."

"You want to stop for a snack?" he asks.

"Jesus, I couldn't eat," I say. "Although, you could have your way with me for a bloody popsicle. I'd fellate you for an ice-cold drink too. I'm boiling out here."

He frantically takes off his backpack and rips off the tape around the sides. His bag is a cooler. Inside are berries and fruit, drinks and water. He pushes back a layer of ice to reveal a range of frozen treats.

"I saw you liked strawberries at breakfast so I got some for you."

The air inside starts to form a cloudy vapor.

"What's that?" I ask, fanning it with my hand.

"There's dry ice at the bottom," he explains.

He holds out a punnet of berries and a popsicle. My jaw drops and I feel my heart melt a little. Checkmate. He's won over every piece on the board, even me. He hands me a huge strawberry with his wicked smile taking over his face. I sit down with him on the secluded rocky outcrop. I look at him and consider the fruit. I take a bite out of it. It's the most incredible experience. I close my eyes and moan. I give him the second bite and he takes it enthusiastically. I take a can of drink and roll it over my neck and feel the chill go down my spine. When I open my eyes Mischa is watching me. Of course.

"Thank you," I tell him.

He lowers his sunglasses. "So, can I get that fellatio now or...?"

✻ ✻ ✻

At the end of the walk, Billy is lying in the shade. He's dehydrated and red, his hat over his face. I give him one of Mischa's cold sodas and he inhales it. Then he flops back down and pours a bottle of water over himself. I give him a popsicle. He doesn't ask where it's from because he's too hot to care. He thanks me by doing the peace sign. Seeing him enjoy something unplanned makes me so incredibly happy. He's in a good place. I don't have to worry about him right now.

Mischa offers the rest to the other students. A couple other guys also joke they will suck his dick too. He has officially conquered the whole kingdom.

* * *

Our campsite is in the park, but it's still an hour or two by bus. The *corroboree* is at a historic Aboriginal campsite in the evening. After a meal there's a bonfire and traditional dancing and music.

Mischa seems to like everything more than the other students. The old ladies *love* him. The children *adore* him. They all try grab his hand and pull him this way and that. He's so *touchable*. He's so *touchy*. Everyone is so happy they get a pat from him. *Pat pat pat.* He drips with energy and sweetness and everyone is enthralled.

Johnno seems very comfortable in this environment too. He's making his way to everyone in the indigenous group and talking with them like they're old friends.

Hayden has the next four days off. We don't need Kane either, but he's here, looking awkward. The thing about bodyguards is they're mostly not needed, until they are. Billy really can't cope anymore without at least one around at all times.

An old woman of the tribe makes her way over William and I after lunch the next day. She's tiny and bent over and old. William is very polite, and I am very quiet. She uses a word that's probably not English that sounds like '*a-kon-ye*'. Neither of us can understand her accent and so she beckons Johnno.

"Japaljarri!" she calls to him, with his tribal name.

Soon Johnno approaches us and they confer with each other.

"This lovely lady is Madge," he says. "Well it's hard to explain. She can't talk to the translator because he's married to her daughter and there's tradition."

"What does she want?" I ask.

"She's a healer, and a bloody good one. She can see more than just the body. She can see spiritual sickness. They've been healing in an unbroken chain for fifty-thousand years. They know what the fuck they're doing. When my father was crook, she pulled the cancer right out of him. She got him walking to boot. Anyway, she thinks you have a spiritual thing that might be bothering you."

"Me?" William asks.

"Both of you. She can help a little, but you might need more than one visit."

Without hesitation Billy says, "Okay."

"Okay?" Johnno asks.

"We actually do have a spiritual thing," I explain. "We'll do whatever she asks."

For the next two hours, Madge works on my spirit under a shady tree and Johnno translates. She sings and plucks imagined spirits from my body and kneads the knots out of my shoulder and back. From time to time she blows onto the top of my head through a tunnel in her hands and after a while I start zoning out. When I zone back in I feel very relaxed and present. More time has passed than I realize. She says she's done with me and starts on my brother.

The sun is going down. Johnno pats me on the shoulder. I walk back to camp, taking in the colors of the desert with clear eyes. I'm not preoccupied, or sad, or just treading water in a sea of anxiety. I'm a human existing on Earth and there's nothing contaminating that experience.

Mischa is sitting on a log in a quiet spot at sunset, scowling, and reading a dictionary, of all things. I go to him. He's mildly alarmed, which I find mildly amusing.

"Hi," he says, and offers me a spritzer.

I take it from him.

"Hi," I giggle. "You're alone for once?"

"I'm in a bad mood," he says. "Ten days playing come-here-go-away and I'm fucking sick of it."

"You poor thing," I say "But life has no meaning without someone to torture you. Metaphorically, I mean."

Mischa frowns. "Are you high right now?"

I shake my head. "I'm just in a *good* mood for once."

I squint, and touch the tip of my tongue to my right canine.

"You're not holding out on me?" he asks.

"No."

"Or flirting with me?"

"No. Have you ever seen anything as beautiful as this sunset?" I ask.

"Yes. I think you know what I'm going to say."

I turn to him and smile. "You look beautiful in the golden light too."

His eyebrows shoot up. "You *are* flirting."

"Just paying you a compliment."

He stands and kicks the dirt hard. "THIS *IS* FUCKING *TORTURE!*"

Some of the other students at the picnic tables and bonfire turn to see the commotion. Mischa is fuming. I grab his arm and laugh.

"Sorry!" I say, pulling him back down.

"What's got into you?"

"I just had an old lady massaging me for hours and I can't remember what my damage is. You should seize the opportunity while it lasts. I'm usually morbidly depressed. I am quite enjoying the feeling of enjoying life."

Mischa can't follow. "You... what?"

"I feel less awful than I've felt in years. I'm so *happy*. I want you to feel happy."

He thinks about it. "Hang out with me then."

"Okay," I say.

He looks around. "Not here, I'm sick of being around all the featherweights."

Mischa takes my hand through the trees, and leads me to a small campfire far away from the others. We sit and he touches the side of my leg with his pinkie finger and it doesn't bother me. It's even slightly comforting.

There's a middle-aged woman in a long layered skirt and tie-dyed silk tunic at the fire with us. She's smoking a joint and watching the embers. After a while she introduces herself as Sharon.

"I'm just dropping acid and connecting to my indigenous roots," she explains. "You're here with Johnno?"

"He's our guide," Mischa says.

Sharon nods. "Johnno is what Australians call a *'great cunt.'* *Cunt* is Australian for *'person'*. Johnno is a really good *person*."

"A beautiful cunt," Mischa says, and I laugh.

"So what about yous?" she asks, and passes me the joint.

Mischa pushes his big toe in the red sand. "Well I'm in love with Austen here, and he thinks he's not in love with me, not even sure he's gay, so I'm trying to fall out of love with him. I have been unsuccessful so far, so I'm just trying to accept it for what it is."

"Well," Sharon frowns, "that's more honesty than I expected."

"We've both been through some shit, and don't fuck around," Mischa shrugs. "Life's too short."

"Have you kissed?"

"Absolutely not," I say.

"See what I'm working with?" Mischa shakes his head.

"See what I've got to deal with!"

"Look, Austen, just tell me no. I won't be angry. I won't be hurt. You're just being honest. I'll say thanks. I promise. I won't try to change your mind. I'll just move on. Just tell me. Will you have a little holiday fling with me? It's a yes or no question."

I'm not sure what to tell him. "I don't know..."

Mischa groans and falls face-first on the dirt in front of him for dramatic effect.

"That's a hard case," Sharon chuckles.

"Any pearls of wisdom from your trip?" he asks her, and dusts himself off.

"Three beers," she says. "You both need three beers."

"We only have seltzer," Mischa says and hands her one.

"Four then," she says, and cracks her can open. "Where are yous two from?"

"Massachusetts," we both say in unison, and look at each other.

"Neither of yous sound American," Sharon says, and points

to Mischa. "Well you do, but you don't seem like a Yank."

"I'm a refugee," Mischa says, as I hand him the joint. "From Yugoslavia."

"I'm really from Appalachia," I shrug. "I just sound British. That's the place that feels most like me. My town's a poor, rough, decrepit backwater, but I'd take it over any palace in the world."

Mischa stares at me. "We have more in common than you realize."

"I'm pleased. I do like you a lot, even though you tried to sabotage my holiday and I hate your guts."

"Don't hate me; we're both alone in the world," he tells me. "We should at least be *friends*."

"No. Wait. Maybe. I mean..." I think about it. "Okay."

"Can I also be your lover?"

"No."

"Oh well," he sighs. "That's okay."

"Really?" I ask.

"I told you it was fine, and it is. I'm sick of feeling like Pepé Le Pew. I always thought the opposite of love was hate, but it's indifference. Maybe it's the cure too. Maybe we could try being indifferent?"

"Okay."

Mischa smiles. "It's just nice, you know, having you here

tonight. You're *really* here. It's the first time you're here and not screaming at the top of your lungs since I met you."

My eyes squint. "I don't think I ever *screamed* at you, have I?"

"Your screams are silent, like drowning, but I hear them through my whole body, and there's nothing I can do to help you."

He hits me somewhere I thought was hidden. It's just a moment, but in this moment, all possible moments exist, if only for a moment. I try to let it pass, tell myself no, get back control but I can't. I just sit there, stunned.

Sharon hands me another joint so now we have two.

"Soulmates always see more of you than others," she says. "But that's my cue to turn in for the night. Thank you for the memory."

We sit, watching her flashlight disappear, then see another bobbing along the track towards us. It's Kane.

"There you are," he says, when he finds me. "William wants to tell you he's going to bed early and to leave him the fuck alone for the night. His words, not mine."

I'm confused. "We're sharing a tent."

"Don't shoot the messenger," he says and turns to leave.

"Fuck that," I yell after him. "He's sleeping and I'm not?"

"You can share with me, if you want," Kane calls back. "Unless you have a *better offer*."

"Oh my God," Mischa gasps, "did someone just win the lottery?"

"No, no, no," I laugh. "You did not."

"I didn't mean me; I meant *you*."

I scoff. "You think so highly of yourself."

"Austen, you're home free. You've got one night, and one night only, when he's not breathing down your neck. You can do anything, in complete seclusion and safety. How do you want to spend your golden ticket?"

He looks at me with hungry eyes, and takes my hands.

"It's not like I'm a prisoner," I say.

"I didn't say you were. I'm just inviting you to stay with me, without fear."

"Yeah, *right*," I say, and we sit in an uncomfortable silence.

"Can I just try something?" he says. "Can we just try the kiss? I mean, Sharon made a good point."

I glower at him. "Fine, whatever. Hope you're ready to press the button on my bracelet. Kane's gonna murder you, if Billy doesn't get here first."

Touch has a way of saying things best left unsaid. If I let him kiss me I can show him nothing will fix me, or shift me. I am committed to this stalemate we have. Him, adorable and love struck, and me cold and heartless. He sees me in a way that no one else does and makes me feel things I wasn't sure I could feel, but he doesn't understand that I don't have much to give. He's offering a fling on a golden platter, and I want to be the person that can take him up on such an offer, I'm just not.

He moves between me and the fire, crouching down, and takes my face in his hands and looks at me. I brace myself. He stares at my lips, and moves in closer. He tilts his head to the side and closes his eyes. He gives me a few gentle kisses. His lips are soft against mine. It feels good, and I'm not having a seizure.

I'm not having a seizure?

He pulls away, opens his eyes to look at my lips, then eyes.

"Don't read into this," I say.

Then I move in and return the kiss. Both our eyes close. His fingers race through my hair and caress my head. As his lips open against mine, my lips follow, and our tongues connect.

For reasons unrelated to Mischa, I want this kiss to be good. I let it go on longer, and pull him closer in a way that tells him I like it. That it feels right, and I want him. Maybe there's some truth in it, but I'm just screwing with his head. He makes a whimper of pleasure, and falls to his knees. He pulls away and looks at me in shock. The emotional knot inside me tightens.

"That's enough," I say, coldly.

First proper kiss. Probably the only kiss I'll ever have too. At least it was really good.

I take a swig of my drink, trying to appear blank and numb. He crawls back to his seat, breathless. He gets his spritzer. His hands are shaking as he drinks.

That moment was a bit too real, and I need to get back on an even keel, so I poke fun at him, as I tuck my own shaking hands under my thighs.

"You got it real bad, huh?"

"That wasn't for show," he says. "My legs are totally wobbly. I thought I might faint. It's ridiculous, and very embarrassing, to be *this* in love."

"Sorry," I say.

"Don't apologize. Until now I really thought I was above it all."

"Such *hubris*."

"Turns out I'm just as fucking lame as everyone else. If it was just some disgusting infatuation I could ignore you and fuck it away with other people but I love too fucking much. *FUCK!*" Mischa rips a tuft of straw from the ground and hurls it into the darkness, then huffs at his own powerlessness. "I'm going to be kind to all the people who fall in love with me from now on."

"No you won't."

"You know what's weird?" His brow furrows. "It doesn't even feel like we don't know each other. It feels like I've found you again, after a twenty-year search, and you're pretending not to know me anymore, and it's irritating."

"Interesting."

"We've done this before, haven't we? Sailed the oceans of time to meet again?"

I manage to light the new joint and hand it to him. "So now you know me from a past life then?"

"Yeah," he says. "I think so. I was always the one screwing everything up and you were always getting it right."

"Like buying tickets to the premier of *West Side Story* for your birthday and you forgetting mine?"

"Well, yeah," he frowns. "Just like that. That's oddly specific. Did that happen?"

I shake my head. "I was just speculating about what a relationship with you would be like. You're a little self-absorbed."

"Well, if I did forget your birthday fifty years ago, I'm sorry, and promise to never do it again."

"Never say never."

"No, really. I've already corrected my mistake."

"Are you saying you already got me a birthday gift?"

"Yep."

"Mischa... that's very sweet, but very sad..."

"By the way, I'm a little younger than you, so we can assume that I died a little *later* than you, and therefore you died before me and left me alone, you absolute bastard."

I laugh. "And we can also assume your mother outlived both of us."

Mischa guffaws. "And she's probably still alive today."

"Her natural sourness preserves her like a vinegar pickle."

He shakes his head. "I'm terrified of how true that feels."

"But we're only joking, please tell me we're only joking?"

"I've really missed you," he says, with big shiny puppy-dog eyes.

"Oh... I should probably stop indulging this stoned fantasy."

"Why? he asks. "It's fun."

"I'm worried you believe it."

"I'm worried you don't," he gazes at me with a coy smile. "Did you miss me too? Were you always lonely before we met? Are you happy I'm around, and just don't know how to admit it?"

"Mischa," I cackle, "I don't think we should let the weed talk like this."

"Do you feel like you've been waiting?"

My smile fades. "How would I know?"

"Did your soul already feel me, before your eyes had ever seen me? Did you feel it, when I pined for you? I get the feeling that I promised I'd never not touch you last time, even if nobody else would. Now you don't like to be touched."

"Everyone being too scared to touch me, now it's me who doesn't want to be? That's fucking apt. It would be ironic."

"I think the universe is turning us into a joke."

"And we have this new horrific life to wade through while the cosmos laughs at us," I agree.

"Well," Mischa sighs, "at least the twentieth century is over and we don't have to deal with any of that crap anymore."

"Never say never."

"I've really screwed up this new life already, by the way."

"Oh, but this life is still *young*," I tease him.

"*Yay*," Mischa says, sarcastically.

"There's been a lot of pain and bloodshed for both of us over the past twenty years, I think."

"You've had it bad too then? Slings and arrows?"

I shrug. "Pretty bad, yeah, despite appearances."

"I have serious problems that would probably ruin any relationship I could try to have," Mischa sighs. "I should have a caution sign above me. That's why I usually don't have relationships."

"I'm in a similar situation."

"We might not be able to pick up where we left off this time."

"There is no this-time or last-time," I tell him. "It's just a nice thought."

"Maybe, and I know I should be patient with you, but I think this trip is still probably all we'll get in this life. It was all I was really hoping for anyway."

I look at the fire. "No pressure then."

Mischa crosses his arms. "No, never."

"Maybe if we didn't screw up our lives so royally, we'd never have met either."

"Like some sick devil's bargain, huh? Maybe God hates us. This time's gonna be really bad. I can feel the chaos fidgeting to be unleashed by our passion, and I don't give a fuck. I want to caress your back. Can I?"

"Um... what?" I look at him.

"There's this nice spot on your back."

"My back, on me, specifically?"

"Uh-huh," Mischa nods. "Only you. Can I show you?"

"Alright."

He puts his hand under my shirt.

"I think it's right about..." he walks his fingers up my spine until he reaches a spot between my shoulder blades that feels like ecstasy, "*there.*"

I lift my head in recognition, and try not to let it show.

"Yeah," he clears his throat. "Now imagine if I did that for hours, while you were on top of me."

With that thought, his intense euphoric desire gets a vice-like hold on me, ensnaring me like an anaconda coiled around prey.

Mischa removes his hand from under my clothes. His eyes are welling, and I pretend not to notice.

"I should go," I say, after watching the fire for a while, but I can't move.

"It's late," Mischa says. "Don't wake him. Stay with me. There's enough room and bedding in my tent."

"Did you bring extra for me then?"

"It's best to be prepared. I have been waiting for twenty fucking years after all."

I smile at the thought. "You wouldn't try and force yourself on me?"

"Not *force*."

"That's the only way you are getting off tonight."

He thinks about it. "No, I may have a wet dream, not that I sleep much at the moment. I haven't been able to have sex since we met."

"Why not?" I ask.

"My dick only has eyes for you. You're giving me blue balls. I have touched myself several times thinking about you, but it only makes me want you more and..."

I laugh at the idea. "Jesus, want me *more*? As if your moon eyes aren't already bad enough."

"Exactly. And it makes me sad. But maybe it wouldn't if you're with me. Although I might not be able to stop if I started with you in the tent."

We are headed down a dangerous path, but there is this part of me burning from his touch and I let recklessness overrun me.

"You can jerk off if I stay," I blurt out, and my heart starts racing, so I throw in, "Anything to get you over me."

"Really?"

"Yeah. We're sorta friends, right? Besides, I'm *indifferent*, and I'm really trying to salvage this vacation. You said that reality plus fantasy equals nightmare, so maybe the nightmare will be a good reality check for you."

"Would you want to... jerk off with me?" he asks.

Impossible.

But if I could, would I?

Wait, why even *entertain* the fucking idea?

"Christ. Give you an inch and you take a mile. I'm not going to jerk off with you."

"But you don't mind if I do?"

"No, I don't mind. I asked you, remember? I mean, why would I care? I'll be asleep."

"What if I was spooning you?"

"That's fine. I might have an allergic reaction if you do get too handsy."

"Allergic reaction?"

"The seizures. It's a fucking curse."

"Why does that happen?"

"If I tell you, if they found out, they could use it against us."

"Who?" he frowns. "I won't tell anyone."

"Anyone who wants to exploit us," I shrug. "Only our most trusted people know what happened, and that does not include our dad. With rich people who have issues, you can do all kinds of fucked-up things to control them. We're not talking about me as a person. We are talking about an unfathomable fortune that influences everything and everyone. My brother has obvious issues, but his birthright can't be taken. Mine is not so certain so I have to be bulletproof, and protecting myself protects him. If he were considered incapable of looking after himself, they couldn't take his life over, because that would fall to me, and there's nothing they can pin on me. I don't even *want* my inheritance but anyone who does would have to take it from me and this could be the perfect way to do it."

"But can you give me some idea what it is?"

I remember the version that doesn't sound so brutal.

"A couple years ago, after our parents lost custody, someone attacked me and left me for dead. Luckily, my brother always knows how to find me," I clear my throat. "It sounds spooky, but he can hear me in his head sometimes, and I told him the way, but by the time he got to me I was half dead. It's a miracle I'm alive. Billy thinks that maybe our dad put someone up to it."

"Jesus Christ."

"I'm not so sure, though. I don't actually remember anything, but my body does."

"William remembers?"

"He just says I wasn't moving, and there was so much blood that at first he thought they had ripped my skin off. My injuries were severe, and the damage is done. It's always triggered by being touched, and it can be painful."

"You think we will be okay?"

"I just saw a healer so I'm very optimistic. If it goes wrong, lie on top of me till it gets better."

"Lie on you?"

"You know what? This is a terrible idea..."

"It's a great idea. Can I touch the rest of you?"

"Yes. Just don't touch my dick."

"Touch your ass?"

I roll my eyes. "Sure."

"So you are saying... just so I understand... you will get in my tent with me, let me jerk off, let me touch you, even your ass, just not on your *snook*..."

"Uh yeah I mean you're making this weird but yeah you can touch my skin, just don't inspect me. Besides, I only wear boxers and a tee to bed."

"Only wear boxers..." his breath shortens.

"You okay?" I ask.

"I'm fine," he coughs, and manages to inhale. "This is not usually my style, you know..."

"Don't be a pussy," I smile.

"Is this a trap? I don't know. It's a little rapey."

"Oh fuck off," I frown. "Don't use words you don't understand, *idiot.*"

"But.."

"You want absolution?" I do the sign of the cross over him. "Go with grace. Nut on me, just don't penetrate me."

"Why would you do that?"

"If I were awake, I'd probably have a seizure," I shrug, "but I want it for you."

"You want it for me? That's a good start. But why?"

"I don't know. Pity? This boy who went through a horrific war, for years and years. Who is alone in the world, desperate and love sick. That sucks. Who would I be to deny him one of life's simplest pleasures?" I shrug. "After this trip you'll never see me again and I don't want you to be sad when I'm gone. Also bringing the cooler on the walk was pretty neat."

"Pity? Nobody's ever... I was hoping you'd say it was a good kiss..." he trails off, clearly deflated.

I let out a frustrated sigh. "It was a good kiss." I don't need to look at him to know that got a smile out of him. "That doesn't change anything about what I can and can't do. I know it's not what you're used to and it makes me lame and weird." He goes to talk but I stall him with a hand motion. "But if you want this, and it will help you move past me, then yeah I want... I want it."

I spare him a glance, and he is nodding like I just said something important, sacred even, and he is absorbing every word, and then the spell breaks.

He blinks a few times. "Do you think you might want to continue this conversation lying down in the tent?"

I splutter with laughter. "Calm down, let me finish my drink."

I yawn a little while later.

"Time for bed?" he asks, still eager.

I nod. "It's been a long day."

❋ ❋ ❋

I have never seen someone brush their teeth so vigorously. It's a frenzy of foam and scrubbing while manically staring at me. It's so funny that I giggle at him as I do my back molars and spit out the toothpaste.

I feel... happy? That's a thing I haven't felt in years. That doctor healer lady really got me feeling like myself again. I know the feeling will fade but I want to enjoy it for now.

Mischa leads me by the hand to the small tent and pulls me inside.

"I need to take my clothes off," I tell him.

"Well, don't be shy," he says, encouraging me.

"I'm not taking my clothes off in front of you."

He turns around like a gentleman until I get into my sleeping bag.

"Good night." I kiss him on the cheek and roll over. "Have fun."

"Are you asleep now?" he asks the moment the flashlight is off.

"No," I say.

He goes quiet again.

"Austen," he whispers, a few moments later. "Are you asleep?"

"Almost," I laugh. "You keep waking me."

✻ ✻ ✻

I can't sleep. My trousers are folded beside me. I feel the syringe in the pocket, but I can't bring myself to take it. I know Mischa won't hurt me if I do, but just can't do it. I hadn't planned to be conscious. I don't know where to go from here.

We've been lying in silence for a while. Waiting. Mischa lies behind me and spoons me. It feels better than it has any right to. I can feel him shifting behind me. Mischa's hard cock is pressing up against my back. This is so foreign to me, but I feel so safe as well. I have a hard-on too. I take my hand off the pocket. I'm rocking gently as Mischa moves back and forth behind me. He unzips my sleeping bag. His hands are on my skin and moving up my chest. He reaches back down to hitch up my top until it catches under my armpits. He kisses my neck, then back, and squeezes my chest.

Mischa kisses hard on my collarbone and it feels good. His lips work down my spine to *that* spot. I arch my back and whimper involuntarily. Now he knows I'm awake, if he didn't before. His excitement crests and he starts sucking and biting my back in the spot making heavy noises.

I've never heard anyone moan my name before, *"Baby, Baby, Baby."*

The seam on my underwear pressing into me feels too good. I need to lie on my front to try and contain this stimulation. Mischa follows me and gets on top. Now my hardness is grinding into the ground with his movements. He kisses my neck in a spot that feels like white heat all over my body. I suppress a moan. His mouth is hot and eager over my shoulders. His hands reach mine above us and our fingers stitch together. I turn my head back and our mouths meet. I squeeze his fingers hard between mine. I can't catch my breath, and he starts groaning.

"You want me to fuck you Baby?" he asks.

I want him to. I want to.

I can't get the words out. They are stuck. Talking could set me off, so I don't want to say anything.

"Mmm," I squeak.

I turn over and pull him to me, and we kiss again. Our lips are firm when they press together, but somehow melt into soft pillows once they join. They know what to do, even if I don't. My legs know what to do too. They open and let him in so he can press against me fully.

"You want to?" he asks again.

I want to beg him to fuck me.

"Don't stop," I manage to say, finally.

He starts ripping all his clothes off. My hands touch him and his do the same. He cries out and I moan again. I want to take my clothes off too, but instead, I feel a sudden jolt, and know we've awakened the monster. Shit. I want to push it down, to feel this good a little longer, but I'm hit with another, bigger jolt. Goddamit.

Now Mischa's naked and in my sleeping bag. Beautiful Mischa. He kisses above and below my navel. I'm fighting as hard as I can to stop the spiral, but I'm losing. I try to relax every muscle one by one to calm my brain, but this is a high pressure situation. He nuzzles the nape of my neck, and nudges me like a dog trying to wake me.

"Baby, you okay?"

The jolts are coming faster now and I don't want him anywhere near them.

"Wait," I breathe.

He stops. The tent starts spinning and I get dizzy. I take a second to try to lift my foot and definitely can't. This is not good. Can't open my eyes either. My muscles have lead weights attached to them. Every minute it gets worse. It takes a lot of energy to stay with it.

"Did you say 'wait'?" Mischa asks, and puts his ear to my mouth.

"Yeah," I tell him. "Sorry."

"It's okay. Why are we whispering?"

"Can't... move," I say, spacing the words apart.

"Can't move?"

"Sort of paralyzed. It doesn't feel nice. Even to talk."

He lifts my hand and it flops back to the ground. It tingles so much it hurts.

"Pain," I wince.

He shines the light in my eyes and sees they've rolled up in my head.

"Oh *shit*," he gasps, sounding scared. "Should I get help?"

"Don't. He'll blackout and kill you, and stress makes it worse…"

"What should I do?"

"Do whatever you want."

"What do you mean?"

"It's not like I can stop it."

At the very least, having this guy ravish me will distract from the jolting flashes. Maybe.

"I'm not going to *assault* you."

"Is this a dream?"

"No."

"You can hear me?"

"Barely. You're hardly making noise."

"It's fine. I can't feel it."

"Yeah that's not the point."

"Just take what's left of me."

Mischa pauses. He thinks for a moment before he lines his head up with mine. He kisses the tip of my nose and I smile.

"I don't want to take what's left of you," he says.

"Is this really not a dream? Shit."

"I'm sorry someone took some of you to begin with. If you want them dead, just give me a name."

"My brother has it covered."

"I like William so much more all of a sudden."

"I should never have said that. Please don't repeat it."

"I already forgot what it was. Something about spaghetti?"

"Thank you," I breathe in relief. "Sorry I'm like this."

"Don't apologize. Shouldn't I apologize? I don't actually know if I gave you an allergic reaction or I put weight on an injury and broke you?"

"No, my brain's a naughty puppy. This is a psychogenic seizure. Not a bad one, but hard to speak when I'm this dizzy. I don't even know where I am. I only know I'm talking out loud because you're talking back. If I try move, it'll be very uncoordinated, and could put me in a sort of fit or coma."

"You said to lie on you?"

"If that's too weird, there's a syringe in the pocket of my jeans and you can knock me out."

"Right," he thinks about it. "Knocking you out would actually be weirder. I want to give you a good time, I just don't want to make it worse."

"You're sweet; this is my worst nightmare and you're making it nice."

"I'd really *love* to lie on you, or just like, hug you for a minute?"

"That might work. Please don't read into it."

He laughs, and cradles me in his warm arms. "I think we should probably have a safe-word."

"What?"

"You know when you're being tickled and you say *uncle* to get them to stop?"

I have no idea what he is talking about. "I don't have an uncle."

"That's fine. We can choose something else."

"Do we have to?"

"It would make me feel more comfortable," Mischa says.

"Sounds lame."

"My safe word can be *'Queenie'*. What's a name that makes you feel really safe?"

I can't remember why he wants a name.

"A *name*? Hmm. Honey?"

"That'll be confusing if you ever call me that."

"I *won't*. Bee?"

"Ugh," he gags. "Not that, because it's your brother's nick-name. What would you say if you were scared or uncomfort-able?"

It's so hard to think. I get so heavy that I sink out of my body and start spinning in the void and I can't remember where that nice boy is. Somewhere in the world, I guess. I can only think of the names of people I love.

"Kane... Marcella. Philippe. Mischa. Isobelle... *Sabrina.* Sabrina? She's my... erm... girlfriend.... *yeesh...*"

"Ugh. Absolutely not. Maybe like a pet or something you loved when you were little and made you feel safe."

"Oh, *Austen.* I can say Austen."

"Okay," he thinks about it. "Alright. Weird, but sure. If you ever don't like something, say your name and I'll stop."

I'm getting confused. "Austen's not *my* name, it was my *teddy bear's* name."

"Right."

"If I fit, I don't talk."

"How will I know you're having a fit?"

"You'll know. It's about to happen. Please get my inhaler, in my pocket."

He retrieves the canister and puts it to my lips. I suck on the narcotic dispenser and breathe it in. I feel the pain lifting off and I relax a little.

"Alright. What now?" he asks.

"You need to orgasm and get over that guy you're in love with."

"That's okay, I would rather spend a million days with you and I never get off, if it meant you were alright."

"Mischa. Your name is Mischa, as sickly sweet as Honey."

"Only for you baby. So why did you want me to lie on top of you?"

"Because the monster's almost here. Hurry."

"Sure."

He lowers himself down on me. I can tell he wants to protect me and his weight settles on me till it's like the only thing in the whole world. I get that creeping feeling. It attacks and my body short-circuits. The flashes crash into my brain and I jolt with image after image that I see behind my eyes. My breathing gets more and more restricted as my mind rushes off, and my muscles seize up, like they are being twisted and pulled. I whimper in pain. While I spasm, he strokes my hair, and I can actually feel it.

"Baby?" he whispers.

I'm so far away, but hear him over the sound. The horrible screams. I find me deep in the woods, by an ancient silent pond. A frog leaps in the water. The noise makes a splash. Maybe this could be Japan, but I have no idea where, or how to get back. I can't remember, that place where my body is, so I call to him.

"Where are you?" I ask.

"Right here," Mischa whispers to me on the rustle of leaves.

"I'm lost, but I can hear you a little."

"Come back to me," Mischa begins to chant quietly. *"Come back to me, come back to me."*

I follow the sound of his voice back to the tent in the desert far away. I watch the two of us in the tent as he kisses on my forehead, chin, cheeks and eyes, runs his thumbs along my eyebrows. It's soothing, and I'm back in my body in a few seconds. Not too bad, as these things go. Surprisingly short.

"Jesus Christ it's like being abducted by fucking aliens," I giggle.

I catch my breath, and thank him between his kisses.

"Oh God," he says, his breathing stressed. "I thought you died for a second there."

"Inhaler." I say.

He puts it to my mouth again. I pass out for a few seconds.

"You okay?" he asks.

"Try it," I tell him, when I come around.

Mischa breathes it in, and gets real high real fast.

"Oh," he says, in surprise. "Oh shit, what the hell…"

He sinks down next to me as the euphoria hits. He blisses out for a few minutes, but refuses a second hit, preferring to watch over me. He offers me more but I decide not to as well. I like just being here with him.

He doesn't really understand what's wrong with me, but he's cool about it. I pull my mouth towards his when I have the strength, I think. I'm not actually sure if we are kissing or not. I might be imagining it. I no longer know if my mouth is moving. It's more for comfort than anything else. I go somewhere between sleeping or seizure but it's hard to tell what's happening, but it's good. He lies his head on my chest and I feel better, and fall asleep.

❉ ❉ ❉

In the morning light I force my eyes open a peep. I can see the orange and green canvas of the tent walls. I'm still sick, but I can see and move. I rotate my hand.

"Thank *God*," I groan. "Oh thank fucking *God*."

Mischa is beside me, staring. He's wearing blue plaid pajamas. It's actually cute, and throws me a little.

"Are you okay?" I ask.

He sounds dazed. "Yeah. You?"

"Yeah. You get some rest?"

He sighs. "None, actually."

"What have you been doing?"

"Watching you sleep. I know you gave me permission, but it didn't feel right, after you were out. Just seeing you all peaceful made me feel like the happiest person alive."

"It doesn't sound like you're over me then?"

"Hell no," he says. "I love you so much baby," he makes a big sigh, "I'm gonna kill anyone else who ever tries to touch you ever again."

"Christ," I groan. "You sound like my *brother*."

"I really love William all of a sudden."

I shake my head. "I'm just gonna kill myself, so neither of you will have to worry anymore."

"That's no fun," he kisses my fingers. "How do you feel?"

I shrug. "Diabolical about sums it up."

Things feel awkward in the morning light. I'm acutely aware of how far we went, before it all fell apart.

He is watching me carefully, but then I notice his gaze roving over my body and lingering on the places he marked me last night when things were heating up. I can feel the sexual tension ramping up several notches. Unbelievable that after the most unsexy display imaginable, he can still look at me like he wants to devour me whole. Time to leave.

"Party's over, pervert. I just need a few more minutes and I'll be out of here."

"Yeah?"

"Yeah," I echo.

Mischa leans in and kisses me, and I let him. He's a good kisser, and it's a hot kiss. I lie back down, but I'm worried. I'm still exhausted and dizzy. He starts getting hard, and I'm right there with him, but realize this could spell disaster. The balance barely held last night is teetering again. It's all touch-and-go from here. If I let this continue I might have another fit and we could be stuck here for hours. If I try to stop this I might have a fit anyway. There are no good options. I'm going to traumatize this poor boy.

I'm not spiraling, but it's really weird. Everything that's happening is on the other side of a screen, or like a television, so I don't really get to be there. He doesn't really get to touch me. I don't really feel it properly. Should I just be happy to make this lovely boy happy? No. I'm too selfish for that. Now that I tried, now that I *want*, it all feels crueler than I ever imagined. It's yet another thing that has been stolen from me. I'm going to fucking kill myself. I just have to get this guy far away from me before I do.

I take my mouth away from his. He pulls his cock out and starts stroking himself. I sit up on the back of my elbows and lean back, glowering at him from heavy eyelids. Then, despite myself, I look at his cock. He has a good one, as these things go. He likes that I'm watching him, and suppresses a moan. I press my lips together and he begins to lose it. He kisses me again and I let him, and he ejaculates over my shirt. I'm surprised and relieved I made it the whole way through.

"Oh God," he pants. "That was great."

"That was *awkward*, but I really painted myself into a corner so I can't exactly protest too much now."

"What? You gotta say *'Austen'* if you want me to stop. I won't be annoyed!"

"You were past the point of no return."

Mischa looks confused. "Are you messing with me? Why did you lick your lips and bite them?"

"I only pressed my lips together because it was tense."

"Your bottom lip still has a mark because you were biting so hard."

He pulls my bottom lip down and rubs his thumb over it, then my top lip, then pushes it in my mouth along my tongue. I suck it, and wonder what the fuck I'm doing. I'm flying so close to the sun I feel like I've lost my mind. Mischa's hard again.

"Okay Jesus," he says. "I can't take it anymore. God Austen, I really need to fuck you."

I calmly remove his finger from my mouth. I gotta end this now, before I start wishing I did earlier.

"Okay, no. Nice experiment, thank you, but never again."

"Wait, what?"

"I'm revoking your privileges."

"Don't do that. Baby, I just have to get you out of my system, honestly maybe If you just let me get inside you..."

Did he just call me Baby *again*? Uncomfortable feelings squirm inside me.

"This isn't working. You're not getting past it and I'm having seizures." I try to get out of the bedding and it clings to itself, and me. I growl in frustration. "Our sleeping bags are stuck together, you *freak*."

"Yeah, you know I came a little the moment you kissed me? Wasn't even touching myself."

"Doesn't seem like a little."

"Honestly never happened before."

He presses the bridge of his nose and forehead to mine. His lips gravitate down and they connect with my own. I feel strange. I push him off me, and break the spell.

"I gotta get back to William before he wakes up."

"But…"

I pull at my sweat-rumpled shirt and boxers. "God. I have to get out of this. Turn around. I need to change my clothes."

"I hoped we were past that."

"Turn *around.*"

He does. I put my singlet and pants on, and hand him my top and underwear.

"You keep these," I tell him.

"Thank you," he says.

I look at him like he lost his damn mind. "They are *dirty*, Mischa. I don't want to walk back with them."

"Yes of course," he says, putting them in his backpack.

"They're safe with me."

I shake my head. "You are such a horn-dog."

"Yes, but you knew that already."

He tries to put his arm around me but I shrug him off.

"Yeah," I huff.

"Austen, are you angry at me?"

"No."

"You won't look me in the eye."

"I'm not angry at you, Mischa. I'm angry at me. I hate myself and want to die, but don't worry, it will pass. It always does."

"You're disappointed you had a seizure?"

The pain feels sharp. He's making me feel it, and I hate him for it. Such an asshole.

"It doesn't matter. Last night wasn't for me. I was just helping you out, and it wasn't as bad as it could have been. Small mercies."

"We could try again. Go slow. It was honestly the best night of my life."

"Glad you had fun, but no thanks. I just wanted to try it, and it's not my cup of tea."

"But it could be your cup of coffee?"

"No. Let's just forget about it. Thank you though." I sigh, and smell the air. "What is that smell? Perfume?"

"It's a luxury moisturizer," Mischa says and puts some on

my hands. "It's got oolong tea in it. I've got a whole carton I've been selling to the girls. I use a squirt to jerk off so... you know."

"You *moisturize* your dick before you touch yourself?"

He looks at me like I'm stupid. "I use it for lube—baby, haven't you ever rubbed one out?"

"No, and I don't plan to start now."

"Fucking Hell. Never?"

"Never ever."

"Let me—"

"No. I'm leaving."

"You should kiss me goodbye."

"Why?"

"You gave me last night to help me get over my lame and all-engrossing crush. Now give me *closure*."

"On one condition. Don't tell anyone I'm sick, and if anyone else ever sees me having a seizure, you gotta convince them that it's William, not me. This is literally a matter of life or death."

"Sure," he shrugs.

He moves on all-fours closer to me and brings his lips to mine. It's not aggressive, it's just a morning kiss from a satisfied guy. He's had his fill of me and now he's done.

"Please don't read too much into any of this. It was just an experiment."

"Yes." He kisses me again. "Of course."

"Bye Mischa."

* * *

Back at my own tent my brother is freshly showered and changing.

"Sorry I was out all night," he says. "I was getting laid."

"Why'd you kick me out then?"

"I was so tired after the exorcism thing I slept for a bit. *Then* I chased tail."

He moves his head to me and his brow furrows. "God you smell like girly-girl and... literally semen. That a *hickey* on your neck? Wait, Baby did you have *sex*?"

"Well... hands stuff..."

"That's good!" he flushes with joy. "Oh my God that's *great!* You let someone *touch* you. That's the most progress in eight bloody years... That healer is a bloody miracle worker! This is worth the whole trip!"

"Yeah well, I glitched before we could do it. Not much actually, but enough to make me stop."

"But you got off! Was it good?"

"Honestly... yeah, it's just that it was weird, when we were doing stuff the second time..."

"Second time? Nice."

"But I was sort of..."

"Behind a screen?" he interrupts.

"Yeah, exactly."

"That's normal. Did you explain that you are just a little traumatized from being kidnapped when you were younger, and beaten, stripped naked, and tortured half to death by Eastern European gangsters hired by your psycho father, because he was trying to steal your inheritance, and leave you for dead, and it turned into a total bloodbath, and the vision of your own mom getting assaulted and cut to pieces is permanently etched into your brain, and we literally killed a bunch of people?"

"I was saving that for the *second* date."

He snorts with laughter. "You should try it. They never believe it, and it's nice to get it off your chest, you know? Just don't tell them about the chopping block. That's a bit too icky. Totally kills the mood."

"I did kinda explain what might happen, kinda."

"And being branded on your chest, like cattle?"

"No, I kept my top on." I scratch my head. "It's just... I don't know... I felt really gross walking back here."

"Classic hallmark of a walk of shame, Baby. I always want to puke and cry after sex. That's normal too. You'll get used to it. You just have to power through. Which girl did you...?"

Oh God.

"I don't want to kiss and tell..."

"I don't want to accidentally go there if you have. I've had a few of these girls already."

I'm feeling the pressure now. "God, what *was* her name?"

"Was it Brittany?"

"No."

"Stefanie?"

"Who's that?"

"Hannah? Emily? Jessica? Kristen? Maddison? Taylor B? Taylor L? Vicky? Becca?"

"I think it was... Aim... Aimee...?"

His eyes shoot up. "Amelia?"

"That's it."

He pulls a change of clothes out of his bags. "Ah good I'll stay away. But isn't she from the Lake District?"

"I don't know, but she's British, yeah."

He frowns. "So she knows some shit went down?"

"She probably knows a little, maybe."

"It seems like she hasn't said anything to the others."

"No," I agree.

"She's a keeper then," he smiles. "I'll get her a gift; something nice."

"No," I say firmly, not wanting this lie to fall apart. "That's my responsibility."

"Alright."

"Thanks," I say. "I need a hug."

He hugs me and pats me on the back, and the spot he touches hurts a little.

"You're doing good, Baby," he tousles my hair. "I'm proud of you," he throws a towel at me, "but you need to shower. It'll help you feel better, and you're kinda gross right now."

In the shower block Mischa is—of course—there. Grabbing soap from the sinks because he probably forgot to bring anything like that or it didn't fit in his bag with all the dry ice and nonsense in there.

He freezes as I enter. I stop too, thoughts swelling inside me thinking of last night.

"You know, maybe we could..." he starts.

"The answer is no."

"You didn't even let me finish..."

"You can't shower with me."

"But..."

"Absolutely not."

I turn and he inhales sharply, like he's shocked at what he sees.

"Oh *shit*," Mischa gasps.

I check myself in the mirror and turn to see a large black spot just above my singlet, between my shoulder blades. He has left the world's most psychotic hickey on my back. Billy didn't see it, I'm pretty sure I backed out of the tent the way I came.

"Yeah," I sigh. "We are never doing *that* again."

I lock the door to my shower and turn it on. I hear the one beside me turn on too. The water is soothing. It makes the dry semen on me slick again. I wash my hair, then I lather myself inch by inch. My brother was right about the shower. I now fully understand his obsession with bathing. I'm so happy to get clean, I let out a satisfied sigh, and hear another one from the shower next to me. Mischa is next door, abusing himself again. I press my forehead into the side of the shower and fight the urge to bang it.

I turn off the water and dress in the cubicle. Mischa finishes and emerges about the same time as me, only he's naked. I must look so weary, trying not to see him, so he faces me and I look him up and down. He has cool tattoos. Very sexy. His limp cock is still half inflated, and pink from the night's activity. I need to look away.

"I'm tired," I say.

"Same," he agrees. "We should sleep together."

I laugh, and he smiles. Then we both turn silently and brush our teeth in separate sinks. He puts on some boxers and flip flops, kisses me on the cheek, and heads out.

On the bus, William sits with Kane and so I sit nearby.

Mischa comes over in shorts and a singlet and sits next to me. I ignore him until we're on the long stretch of highway and he gets drowsy. His head leans more and more towards my shoulder. When the two finally connect I push him off and he rouses a little, only to make his way back to my shoulder even faster. After a while I leave him there. He puts his arm around my waist and falls into a heavy sleep. I'm in a deep funk when William turns around and sees me. He chortles with glee at the sight. He laughs again when he sees my face an hour later. By then Mischa's drooling over my shirt and I look miserable. By the time we reach the Olgas, there's a large wet patch from his mouth down my shoulder.

Mischa wakes up and drinks water.

I look at my polo shirt. "Second time I've got drool on me today and this isn't even mine."

"Yes," Mischa smiles, "but at least this time it's really drool."

14 MISCHA

Austen is like a drug. I'm not satisfied by the night in the tent, it only makes me want him even more. It's like a taste without swallowing. Touching him was tectonic. It is almost certainly one of the pivotal moments of my life. I'm terrified just how significant the weight of it will be. I worry I might be stuck on an event horizon, circling this black hole of insatiable desire forever.

Austen had to twist his logic into a pretzel before he let himself sleep with me. I don't know if he'll bend that far again. He gives me no points for not crossing the line, either.

The fact he had a... something-something seizure also constantly plays on my mind. I loved what we did but I can't help but feel guilty for wanting. If I hadn't pushed, hadn't wanted it so much, he never would have reacted that way. He was sad that it went down like that, and the last thing I want is to *hurt* him. I'd rather never fucking come again if I could keep him happy.

It's more than sexual tension at this point. I love to be near him. I love mementos of him, like the pendant he gave me, photos with him in the background, the little bag of his dirty clothes. At a museum visit he sneaks an enamel pin of a cartoon puppy into my pocket. It's become my prize possession. He's my whole world.

He shares candy with me, without saying a word. Brushes past me, with a quick pat on the back along the way. I feel more emotions in these secret moments than I have ever had for any other lover.

His gay-as-fuck bodyguard Kane is loving every minute of it, and running interference for us with William, so he doesn't see anything.

We don't talk. We can't, because when we do, it's obvious we're into each other. When we do, we get lost in each other's eyes. When we do, I whisper the sweetest nothings into his ear. I tell him about the dreams I have about him that I'm only just recovering from, and my lips touch his lobe, hidden by my hands. It makes him blush. When we do, we stand too close to each other, I gaze at his mouth and eyes, entranced. The sound of his voice makes my breathing slowly get heavier, and I find myself in some euphoric, hypnotic state. His breathing slows like mine.

He bites his bottom lip involuntarily at me in the elevator on the first day in Sydney, and I lose my mind. My smoldering feelings possess the space in my chest, and I have to grip his arms, to hold myself back from him.

"Jesus *Christ*," I tell him. "Baby... You just... I need..."

"You okay?" he asks.

"You're turning me on too much. I'm *very* hard... I gotta go to my room for a while."

Thank god I've taken to wearing baggy flannel shirts. I run upstairs, and find Max in my room eating an apple.

"Get out!" I yell at him, and push him into the hallway, and pull the bar across the door.

"Hey!" he yells from outside.

It's only a few seconds, and it's intense. I feel light headed after, but clean up, and get out of there. I let Max back in like nothing happened. He's very confused. Austen watches me return downstairs with a cheeky grin on his face.

It feels so good just to look at Austen. I have taken to sitting in the back of the bus or plane or train everywhere we go. That way I can watch him and it isn't so obvious. Sometimes I sit near Kane, who keeps a distance but also never takes his eyes off his two principals.

One particular day in Sydney, in a hidden spot, alone at a bar near the hotel, we just stare at each other for far too long, and Athena comes across us.

"Just *do it* already," she says, and rolls her eyes as she passes us.

She's friendly with Will, so the comment throws Austen hard. We keep away from each other for a few days, but we're always in each other's orbit. Psychologically, we're in lock-step.

William plays piano with me. He's good and we're both show ponies for an audience, so it's free entertainment for everyone. We start duetting on every piano we can find. Sometimes we race each other for the right side of the piano seat. Sometimes we wrestle each other off the seat. Sometimes we play each other's parts. Austen is always there. When I catch his eye he freezes and looks back at me, it's like a deer in the headlights. It feels amazing. I'm certain this is driving us both insane.

* * *

With the tour ending and only a few days left in Sydney, two girls show up at the hotel, talking quietly in French. They are... you could say, sublime in their beauty. Angelic. Goddesses. Burn-your-fingers smoking hot too, actually. If you told me they are supermodels, I'd believe you. Both around nineteen or twenty, I guess. One is a blonde with shockingly green eyes, and the other a natural wavy redhead, a shade so deep and dark that I never knew red could come in that color. They are the kind of attractive that gives them a glowing aura. They make everyone's head turn.

They scan the lobby, as if they are looking for someone, and cast their eyes over me. The odd thing is, they don't notice me, and that's almost impossible... I burn fingers too. Not even a second glance or a lingering look. They aren't doing it on purpose either. They're not doing that stone cold, I'm-to-good-for-you thing. They just genuinely don't have eyes for me.

A man comes over to chat them up.

"Not interested," the redhead says before he can say anything.

"What about her?" he nods to the blonde.

"Don't fucking talk to her, don't even *look* at her."

I like this girl.

I think they must be a gay couple.

Will's bodyguard comes over and ushers the man away.

"Out of your league, buddy."

They spot William and Austen making their way out of the breakfast room and both the girls positively beam. It only makes them even more radiant. Austen sees them, and then, like a magnet, his gaze swings to me and with one look, I get a sinking feeling. William runs forward and noisily throws his arms around the girls, hollering and pulling them into a group hug.

"Baby come here," he yells, and grabs Austen and then they are all enmeshed in a tangle of limbs and pure joy.

It is not lost on me that these people can touch Austen, so I know they must be important. They break apart and William is smacking an enthusiastic kiss on the redhead.

She turns to Austen. "Hello, baby-bee," she says.

"Hello, angel," Austen says.

"*Frero!*" the blonde says to William, and throws her arms around him and he lifts her off the ground.

It's French for 'brother', and I realize the blonde girl is probably their sister, because she looks a lot like them.

Then they swap. More kisses.

"The navigators reunite," William says, and puts his hand around the redhead.

Then he begins to make introductions.

"This is my girlfriend Isobelle," William says, as he introduces the redhead to some of our tour group.

Not lesbians then.

"Girlfriend. *Girlfriend?* What a fucking asshole."

Brittany is furious, crossing her arms over her chest and glowering at William. She's a cute, curvy cheerleader with a high blonde ponytail that bobs around when she's mad. She turns to Isobelle.

"You know what's *funny?*" Brittany asks her. "He didn't *mention* he had a *girlfriend* when we were in Melbourne *together*."

"That *is* funny," Isobelle says, and gives William a hard look, then exhales with an air of loving the drama. "Hilarious."

Most of the other students dart away. The other boys all bolt to laugh about it, and most of the other girls remove themselves from the uncomfortable exchange.

"Yeah well, you can have him," Brittany says, unsure of herself.

She storms off with her girlfriends, and the lobby empties, and it's just me and them.

William looks at the ground, terrified. I think he's a little afraid of his girlfriend. I love this girl.

"And this is Sabrina," he continues. "Austen's fiancé."

Fiancé. My mind starts reeling. *Fiancé?* What a fucking asshole. I mean, I know he told me he was taken or whatever, but I was sure he was lying, and I am never wrong about that shit.

I look at her hand. She's twisting his signet ring on her finger. Austen and the blonde, ringleted Aphrodite stand next to each other like strangers. I can tell he wants to look at me, and when he does, I want to look as angry as possible. He steals a glance, and from the look on my face he knows he's fucked up.

"Nice to meet you," I say, and Sabrina ignores me.

"Hi," Isobelle smiles.

"We're heading to New Zealand for a little boat trip on Saturday," Austen explains sheepishly, and puts his arm around the girl he's engaged to be married to, like a complete and utter bastard.

"Last chance to relax before we start organizing the wedding of the year," Isobelle says.

I can actually feel my heart break. It really hurts. all the little broken shards stab at my chest and I try not to breathe too hard to stop the pain. This is what my brothers warned me about.

I take a moment to let the ground sink away from me while I try to stay afloat. They make small talk while William takes their bags up to their rooms. I feel Kane's hand stealthily pat my back. Maybe it's to give me sympathy, a little comfort while my world silently collapses, or maybe he's just doing his job as a bodyguard, warning me not to make a fuss, because he'll drop me if I mess with his client. My hand reaches behind my back and I grab his. Our fingers find each other and Kane quickly squeezes my hand, then lets go and rubs the back of my forearm.

I need to talk to this girl, and get evidence that this is not real.

"So Selina," I say.

"Sabrina," she corrects me.

"Right. How'd you meet Austen?"

I gesture to him in such a way that I touch his hand with the back of my fingers. It is just a second, and it's automatic, but Isobelle and Sabrina zone in on my hand as it returns to my side, fixated. They look at me and then they look at Austen, and Austen gives them an awkward face. They look at me again, then at each other. I think they know why I seem angry.

"Dance partners," Sabrina says finally, with a strange southern accent.

"He can dance?"

"I suppose," Sabrina says, all stony-eyed.

"He can," Isobelle nods.

"Where you from?"

"France," Sabrina says.

I don't need my superpower to tell that's a lie. She sounds like she's from Alabama or something.

Isobelle, William's redhead girlfriend, moves over to me. I can be intimidating, but this girl is an artist. She reminds me of a vampire. I want to laugh.

"William forgot to tell me your name," she says.

"This is Mischa," Austen offers. "He's friends with Bee."

I shoot Austen a look, then return to Isobelle.

"Are you studying in England?" I ask.

"We did a gap year with the boys," she smiles. "Last year, in France. Then instead of school, we got jobs in the city, realized that working sucks too, but luckily we have these two wonderful boys to take care of us."

Isobelle's eyes are soulless. Like Will's. She makes me slightly queasy.

"Sounds like you have a life others would kill for."

"Me included," she smirks. "Are you at university too?"

"I'm not graduating; I've learned what I need. I'm going to New York after this trip. I have a job."

"Really?" Austen asks.

I look at him and wonder if I should even bother to answer. Would he care? Do I want to tell him anything more about me?

"Yeah," I say and look away. "Nothing... keeping me in Amherst... right?"

"Kitten," Austen says to Sabrina, "Why don't you go unpack."

"You didn't even *warn* the poor child?" Sabrina says to Austen in French, like I wouldn't understand, rolls her eyes, and leaves with Kane.

I zone out watching her walk away. I feel helpless, every part of my soul fills with sadness.

"Can we talk for a second?" Isobelle asks Austen.

"Yes, my love," he says.

"Pleasure to meet you," she tells me, and pulls Austen away.

They go to the corner of the lobby and have a quick conversation. They are locked in to what one another is saying, like they're a sports team about to play the second half of a tied game. They're both excited. I try to read Isobelle's lips. Her eyes are wide, and she's whispering. Austen's *laughing*. Their hands knit together and she makes a little squeak. For a moment I imagine she knows there's something between me and Austen and is excited that I'm here, but that would only make sense if she didn't mind others in her territory, and she does. I just saw that.

The physical connection between her and Austen is strong. She starts hanging off him, he's holding her. She hugs and kisses him... intense hug... they are both really feeling it... his *brother's* girlfriend... and he *hates* being touched... she definitely says "I love you, baby," to him before she leaves. One last kiss. On the lips. I don't fucking like this.

"Sorry about that," Austen says, when he returns to me. "You okay?"

I'm fucking furious. "*Kitten?*"

"I *did* say they were coming."

"You should tell her," I say. "Your fiancé. You should tell her."

He laughs that uncomfortable, *a-ha-ha* laugh. "No I should *not.*"

"It's not fair on her, and we both know she picked up on it already."

"Sabrina's very happy with the deal."

"The *deal*? Baby..."

"Don't call me baby," he warns.

"Baby baby baby."

Austen cracks a smile and shakes it away. "Sabrina's very important to me."

"I'll bet. She looks *just* like you. I seriously thought she was your sister. She has your eyes, your face, how is she *not* your sister? Is she?"

"What?" he frowns, and thinks about it, like he's momentarily realizing something, or entertaining the idea. "No."

"You *sure*?"

He hesitates, tries to hide it with a frown, then dismisses the thought like it's ridiculous.

"I know you're upset, but please don't have a meltdown."

"Sorry if I'm freaking out, but the other triplet just got here wearing a blonde wig and you're expecting me to believe that you didn't share a womb? There's no way. I don't believe it! She's gotta be your sister *pretending* to be your wife so you can hide..."

"She was born in a different *country*. I didn't even *meet* her until I was eigh... *for Christ's sake*, I can get you her birth certificate if you like?"

"We won't need to if you just dump her."

"If you just want to get me out of your system like you say, why would you ask me to break up with her?"

"I have said *so much more* than that," I say, infuriated. "I actually fooled myself into thinking you were falling for me, but you're waiting for *her?* How could you do this to me? How could you do it to her?"

His mouth drops open. I head to my room to sulk. When I turn to walk up the main stairs, I see Isobelle at the top, leaning on the wall, watching us, with a giant smirk on her face. We lock eyes the whole way until I pass her, our faces getting more and more sour the closer we get, until she breaks into a maniacal laugh that seems to dare me to throw her head first over the railing.

A hot shower and an hour later I feel good enough to head outside and slide back into the lobby on the handrail.

Will is on the piano and Austen is on guitar serenading Isobelle with a song about her. It's really good. She's wiping away tears. Real tears. Deep ones.

Sabrina spots me and flashes her own perfectly round dimples, just like Austen's.

I go back up to my room.

✳ ✳ ✳

My adoptive father nicknamed me Lemon. It's sort of a Russian name for a grenade because of the shape. Grenades look like lemons. Sort of. It's because I have a special talent that makes me his secret weapon. I can't even tell my brothers about it.

Only he and Sofie know that I can read people like a book.

When my brothers play poker, I always see their bluffs. When we play blackjack, I can tell when Gregor and Maxim count cards. I don't have to count, because I know if I should take a card just by their body language.

Sofie and I spent a lot of our life around people who didn't speak our language. There were lots of languages in the city we were born in. After that we were refugees in Vienna, and had to learn German. Then Sivishni found us, and we had to learn Russian. He put us in a private French high school in Moscow, and when I graduated, he took us to America, where they speak Cartoon Language. Every time I master one language, I get stuck with another one. So I have become an expert in non-verbal communication, the same way deaf people become experts in lip-reading.

Contrary to popular belief, liars do not fidget. They all start out very still, and then they either stay rigid, or they over-compensate. Good ones return to their normal state fast, but they are rare. With them, you have to look at their fleeting, minuscule expressions. Most people also have "tells", the little things they do when they're not telling the truth, like putting their hand on their nose or something. By the way, all of these signals go haywire when violence comes into play, so I work best when people are not under duress, as distressed emotions cause most people to become rigid.

The truth speaks without words, without sounds, without a voice being heard, yet I hear its echo. The body is a window to the soul. It talks through mysterious signals, so subtle and profound, they can't be comprehended by reason alone.

Eventually Sivishni decided I had a sixth sense, and I guess I kind of do. I see through everyone. Who's nervous, who is secretly hated by the others, who will fold fastest, and who will break even faster. I'm never wrong.

He began to use my abilities to painlessly find the rats, cheats, and liars in the organization, exclusively for him, but I still reserve the right to use it for my own interests.

I have to fight this marrying-some-girl nonsense. I have a good baseline for Austen, and William, but I need to find their tells. Isobelle and Sabrina need closer scrutiny too.

I have one other talent. Cards. I need to see them lying. I need to get them to play a bluffing game.

I find them in the games lounge when it's raining, drinking coffee with Amelia.

"I need to do something, I'm bored to tears," I say, and jump onto one of the couches near them. "Do any of you know poker?"

I pull a deck out and start shuffling with one hand, and give a few elegant flourishes by doing a cascade and a riffle.

"You seem like a bit of a shark," Sabrina says, and stares at the cards with her piercing green eyes, just like William and Austen's. "We're about to get fleeced!"

Fucking hell her eyes really are exactly like theirs and the dimples for fuck's sake this shit is crazy how can I be the only one who sees this I am losing my mind here but I gotta push it down and screw a tight lid on this or I won't pull this thing off...

"Okay, no gambling," I laugh. "Have you ever played gambit?"

"Never heard of it," she shakes her head.

"It's a very cool game, and it's very easy," I tell her. "You'd be good, I think." I put a card in front of Sabrina and Isobelle. I look at Austen and William. "Are you in?"

"I guess," Austen says.

William shrugs. "Sure."

"Alright," Amelia says.

Perfect. The experiment has a control subject. I deal out the whole pack.

"This is a deck of playing cards, except the low cards, from two to six, have been removed, and there's double the amount of high cards. Eight kings, eight queens, and so on."

"I think I'm already confused," Amelia says.

I finish dealing.

"All that matters is that you don't get more than four of the same kind in front of you," I nod at Austen. "I'll start. I offer a card to you. I don't let anyone see it, but I'll tell you what it is." I put a card face down on the table. "This... is a *queen*." I slide a card over to Austen. "I'm either lying, or telling the truth. If you believe me, take the card, and turn it over. If you don't believe me, slide it back to me."

He looks at the back of the card for a moment, and then pushes it slowly with his finger back to my side of the table. I flip the card over to show the queen of hearts.

"You were telling the truth," Isobelle says, "so what happens to the card?"

"Austen gets it in front of him, if he gets three more queens, he's out. Now it's his turn."

"This is the King of Hearts," Austen sighs.

He presses his lips together for a split second, and slides the card in front of Sabrina.

"You don't need to say the suit," I tell him. "Just *king*."

Sabrina looks down at it. "I can't decide."

"So don't," I say. "Take a peek at it. Then slide it to someone else, and tell them what it is."

She carefully lifts it up to see and then pushes it toward Isobelle. "Do I tell her it's a king?" she asks.

"That card is anything you want it to be."

"I'm fine with king," her eyebrow twitches.

In the corner of my eye I see Austen wiping his hand over his mouth. That's not a king, and Austen has told on himself again.

"Can't I just look at it too?" Isobelle asks.

"Yeah," I smile. "Then give it to someone who hasn't seen it yet, and say what it is, or lie."

She slides it to Amelia "King indeed."

Amelia looks at it and slides it over to William.

"It's a queen!"

She's lying. Too enthusiastic.

"I still don't know what it is," I say. "If Will doesn't call the bluff, he could look at it too, and send it to me."

William takes it, looks at it, and slides it to me. "King."

William has a fake, masking smile, though not over the top. He'd be a good liar if he didn't try. Austen and Sabrina have stiff, wooden postures, trying to hold in the lie.

"Four people say king and one says queen," I say, and tap my hand over it. "I think I believe you," I tell Amelia.

"You do?" she frowns. "Why?"

"Because you said *queen* so enthusiastically."

Austen and Sabrina seem to deflate a little as their tension dissolves. They both saw the card, and know if I believe it's either a queen or a king, I will be wrong, and both ways I would lose the round.

I flip the card over to show the Jack of hearts to the surprise of nobody. The card goes in front of me.

I take a king of diamonds and tell Sabrina it's a ten. She looks at it and tells William it's a king. William believes her and turns it over, and the card goes in front of her. Pretty soon everyone has quite a few cards in front of them, and we're running out of cards to play. Amelia struggles, never grasping everyone's motivations enough to be good. Austen is good, but William and Isobelle make things interesting by conspiring against me. They send every Jack to each other, and then pass them on to me. I offload a couple, and end up with a three in front of me. Soon everyone is sending the last Jacks my way.

Halfway through the game there is something happening. Sabrina, Isobelle, William and Austen trust each other deeply, but it's all a little dry. Maybe it's a British thing, but it isn't even lukewarm in their corner. I already know Sabrina and Austen are dead in the water. They all want to help William win and they are all protecting Austen. People usually don't work together like this. Isobelle also looks out for Sabrina, even if it means losing. Sabrina is outgoing but submissive toward Isobelle, but not her boyfriend, or William, or me. Interesting. These people are not two couples with a gay bodyguard on the side. They are a squad. A well-oiled machine.

Austen spends the whole game acting as if I'm not here, as

if a single glance will hurt. I know the feeling. William and Austen are also off balance, but I knew that already. Once I have caught the drifts, I start looking under the surface.

"How long have you guys been dating?" I ask the group.

Sabrina's eyes shoot up in alarm, "What?"

"You and Austen?" I gesture toward them, "how long have you been together?"

Everybody is so stiff I have to squash the smile that wants to spread over my lips.

"Oh," Sabrina says, and looks at William, and he nods. "Since high school."

Why are they lying?

"You too?" I ask William, but he looks to Isobelle to answer.

"Same," Isobelle says, and brushes a strand of hair behind her ear.

Everyone has forgotten about the game.

"Did you go on the ski trip when they stole the plane?" I ask.

I said the wrong thing. The mood changes in an instant. Cold fury radiates from every pair of eyes. Kane, across the room, playing pool with Hayden, is at my full attention. Isobelle looks like she's deciding how to kill me, and William is murderous too. He has to sit on his hands to stop them from balling into fists. Austen looks very sad.

"No," Sabrina says. "I wasn't there."

"I was not there either," Isobelle says, but it seems like she's lying.

She nestles into William and suddenly they are touching each other like they really are lovers. Sabrina looks over for one split second like she's threatened. Blink and you'll miss it. Maybe her and Sabrina have a thing, and I'm watching some beard-on-beard action.

Sabrina leans into Austen. He caresses her midriff with one hand and her inner thigh with the other and it bothers me. She gives him butterfly kisses all round his fucking face, but at least it's not on the lips. Then they press their foreheads together like nobody else exists.

Sabrina and Austen whisper "*I love you, baby,*" in each other's ears and smile. They mean it. It's real, and it hurts. They really do love each other. Deeply. Fuck. Fuck. Fuck.

If it's fake, they are *really* committing to the performance. William stares at them and tries not to look uncomfortable. I'd be uncomfortable too, if my girlfriend's girlfriend was kissing my brother. It strikes me that they are all good at lying, because they believe their lies. People like that are often dangerous.

"Why is everyone acting so weird?" Amelia frowns, looking up from her cards. "Everyone knows you stole a plane from a ski field and crashed it into the snow. It's not a big fucking deal. The Harlow boys have done way worse, and Martin Henderson stole a boat and killed his best friend. Sorry if you thought you lived it down, but nobody cares anymore."

"Except our grandad," Will rolls his eyes.

Austen studies the carpet and sighs. "Not our finest moment."

William's mouth curls into a cheeky smile. "It's all true, the things they say. All the rumors."

Isobelle laughs. "One hundred percent *fact*."

"Really?" Amelia says. "People told me to stay away from you guys."

"And you should have listened to them," William tells her. "Our grandfather is a vampire, we ran away, we stole a plane, got disowned, have a drug problem, I impregnated a famous actress, the body of a stripper was floating in our pool after a wild party and our entourage covered it up, I'm violent, Austen's crazy, Isobelle's a lesbian, Sabrina drank so much semen at an orgy she had to go to hospital and get her stomach pumped, and all four of us sleep together and we're incestuous."

"Ugh," Austen groans. "Fucking gross."

"Hey," Will shrugs. "It's only right, because I am drop-dead gorgeous, so who would I be to throw another version of me out of bed?"

"*God,*" Austen throws his hands up. "Please kill me, then kill yourself too."

Sabrina looks horrified. "People don't really say I had *jizz* pumped from my tummy, do they?"

Everyone laughs, but Hayden's face gives something away. He believes some of those things. Probably the lesbian one.

Whatever secret Austen and William have, the girls know what it is. I think maybe Kane does too.

"Who's turn is it anyway?" I ask.

"Mine," Austen says, and slides a card over to me. "It's a perfect ten."

I take it. It's a jack; I'm out, and I'm surprised.

* * *

I wake up the next morning more heartbroken than I ever thought I could be. The sight of Austen pressing his forehead to that succubus kept me up all night. I see it behind my eyes. I want to die.

Fuck this. I need to let it go. One fucking day left and I never have to see these people again and look at Austen ever again and ever have to think about that asshole as long as I live. He tries to talk to me at breakfast so I put my bowl down and walk out.

We arrive at Taronga Zoo around nine-thirty in the morning. Koala interactions are limited to certain times and groups of just four, and tickets are first-come, first-serve. William, Is-obelle, Austen, and Sabrina plan to go as a group. I ask a few of the other students, and get Amelia, Taylor B and Kai and the Stupid Backwards Hat into a group with me. The only trouble is, by the time we all arrive, the koala experience is sold out. A gloom settles over everyone, and they head into the zoo.

"Are you sure we can't see them?" I ask the ticket attendant, after the others leave, and offer her some money.

"They might be able to fit you in. You can ask if there are any free spots at the plaza," she says, and points to the building opposite.

I walk past Austen and William. Austen seems a little upset and William seems angry.

"We'll stay in Australia another week if we have to," I hear William tell Austen.

I go to the small information desk and the assistant checks for me.

"One of the groups only has three people instead of four, so I can sneak you in that one," he tells me. "It's the last free spot for the day, and it starts in fifteen minutes, so you'll have to run down there."

I buy the ticket and pass William heading down the hill and grab his map.

"I need to find the koalas like, *now*," I explain. "I'm crashing on some other group and..."

"I need that ticket, Mischa," he interrupts. "What do you want for it? I'll give you literally anything. I'll give you my watch, my Maserati, I'll give you my fucking *house*."

"Is this some weird rich-boy flex?" I ask.

"If I have to beg you, I will."

I do hate William. He is an asshole. He did have a broken bottle to my jugular a week ago. He cheats on that girl and rubs it in her face. I want to say no. It's just hard because it's obvious he wants it a thousand times more than I do. And because he's devoted to Austen, and despite now hating him, I'm still madly in love with him.

"I'll give it to you," I say, "but you owe me a favor. Not one of these modern favors, an old-time, blood-oath, illogical, *dangerous* favor."

"The best kind," he smiles.

We shake on it, and he takes the ticket.

"You better run," I tell him. "It's in ten. *Andale andale, arriba!*"

He's delighted, and kisses me on the cheek with a loud *MWAH!* I laugh in surprise, and he runs off. He heads down to Austen and shows him the ticket. Austen jumps in his arms and William lifts him off the ground. I feel a slight twinge of envy that is about to explode into full-scale regret. Austen takes the ticket, and William's arm, and they run off as fast as they can to find the Australia section.

I head that way too, and pass the wallabies and wombats. The Koala experience is over in four artificial tree platforms, staffed by four koalas and their handlers. Each platform has a small walkway to get to it. Austen is waiting with William behind a group of three Chinese tourists.

Just before Austen's turn, he commits what could be described as a *'public display of affection'*. It's very brief and nobody is really around or watching them except Isobelle, Sabrina, and me, down below. For a moment, Austen is standing very *very* close to William, talking animatedly, like a child. They move into each other's arms. Long hug. Austen runs his hand through William's hair, and whispers something in his ear and kisses him. For someone who doesn't like being touched, that's a lot of touching. They break apart and William runs his hand up and down Austen's back, and I want to fucking scream.

Look, obviously Austen has got a big thing for koalas and he's excited. Obviously I've rubbed my sister's back and kissed her a bunch of times. I even slept at the base of her bed like a dog until last year. I'm not saying what I'm seeing is weird. It just pisses me off that William gets to be there instead of me. It enrages me that Sabrina will be there too and I will never be in the picture. I think Austen has already forgotten me.

At Luna Park they are inseparable too. In their own world. Happy for sure. But different. William is usually always so cold and aloof and Austen's always so withdrawn and shy. Now they are warm and present, fun and outgoing. It's beautiful, but so far from what I know of them. They're also hanging out with Amelia and a couple of the other students too. Before, Austen was furniture, and Will only talked to the girl he was trying to fuck that day.

Maybe it's having their girlfriends here.

Shit. That's probably it.

From time to time for the rest of the day, William rubs Austen's back, or tousles his hair. Every time he does I want to chop his fucking hand off. On the Ferris wheel they are with Sabrina and Isobelle. They reach the top and take photos and Austen kisses William on the forehead. Will throws his arms around Austen so he loses balance and their carriage teeters back and forth and they shriek with laughter. Later I watch them share a bowl of hot chips covered in ketchup and it may as well be another public display of affection.

There's only one thing making my superpower twinge. Austen keeps staring at William. It's only an affectionate look when William is looking back, but when he's not, Austen's expression is deathly. The kind smile, all the happiness, seems like it's just a performance for Will. I think Austen is not actually happy, just manipulating William for some reason. Yikes.

The whole UMass group decides to get a photo together. William and their girlfriends surround Austen, but someone suggests the girls move forward.

"The tallest should go at the back, and the rest of us at the front."

Kai stands on Austen's side, and is about to move closer when Isobelle and Sabrina pull me over and put me beside Austen.

"The three tallest should be in the middle," Sabrina explains.

We all move in closer for the photo. He puts his arm over my shoulders and I put mine around his waist. Will's arm is over Austen's shoulder too. We get the photo and then everyone breaks apart and wanders off. I am certain those two girls moved me over to Austen so he wouldn't have to touch anyone else. They know me and Austen have a thing and they are... I don't know... tolerating it?

I'm emotionally exhausted. I decide to leave, but as I head to the exit, Sabrina stops me.

"You're leaving?" she asks. "You want to get a photo in the booth with Austen before you go?"

"What?" I ask her.

"Baby," she grabs Austen's arm, "you don't have one to-gether with Mischa."

"Do you want to?" Austen asks me.

"I mean... I guess."

She pulls us into the photo booth and gets out, closing the curtain behind her. Austen pushes the buttons.

The first photo snaps and we're looking ahead.

"We should do a pose," he says, and the second flash takes us looking at each other.

There's a heavy pause. I never want to see him again, but I want to kiss him more than I want to breathe. It's all I've thought about for a week, that one by the campfire at Uluru. The one that made my hands shake and my knees wobbly. If the kiss in the tent was closure, would another kiss open it back up again?

Maybe he has read my mind, because he leans in at that moment. I don't even know it's going to happen until it does. His mask falls and a proper kiss takes its place. The camera flashes. I don't pull away; it's nice. The camera flashes again. He hears people outside, and pulls away and looks at me like he's surprised at what he just did.

"Sorry," he says.

The booth prints out two copies. I hand them both to Austen.

"You probably want to incinerate these," I say.

"I don't. I'm apparently a part of you so I don't think you are going to sell them to the tabloids."

"Thanks," I tell him. "Keep one."

"It was a lovely kiss," he says, and folds it together.

"Well, I can give you another one."

Isobelle is watching. Sabrina is pulling William towards a carnival game to win her a stuffed animal. I hear her call him *honey*, but I don't give it much thought in the moment. Austen wants to say something to me but doesn't. Instead he presses his lips together and rejoins his group. He hugs Sabrina, kisses her on the top of her head, and puts the incriminating photo in her purse. *WAIT, WHAT?* Then he walks with his arm over *Isobelle's* shoulder, and William holds Sabrina's hand.

What. The. Fuck?

It's like their girlfriends are interchangeable. I look at the photo. In the third photo his eyes are open, but in the fourth, they are not. I need to scrub my brain with a pineapple.

❉ ❉ ❉

I get on a fucking boat to the hotel, go to my room, drink the minibar dry, and lie on the floor until the heat of the day gets too much. Then I head to the hotel pools with a forty-ounce of zubrowka and get in the spa. The bottle has a spout-pour on the top so I can give myself shots straight from the bottle.

Do William and Austen show up? Yes. Yes they do. And they head straight for the spa and get in with me. Their insanely hot girlfriends arrive shortly after. I don't pay any attention to any of them. I don't even say hello. I stare at the bison on the drink label and pretend they don't exist.

"You got the grass vodka?" William asks. "I love that shit."

I don't want to share with him. I want to strangle him.

"Knock yourself out," I say, and hand it over.

William pours a shot in his mouth.

His redhead girlfriend, Isobelle, comes over and whispers in my ear, "Stop sulking or I'll kick you in the balls."

I am suddenly a lot more alert. Isobelle giggles and moves back over to Will. Creepy fucking bitch.

"No more," Austen says to Will and confiscates the bottle.

"Did you enjoy today?" Sabrina asks, sitting in Austen's lap.

"Delightful," I sigh. "And now I'm going to drink myself into a coma."

Sabrina and Isobelle take shots and comment on the taste. They like it, and have more. After a while it becomes too hot for the them, and they drag William into the main pool. Sabrina steals a quick glance over at me as they pull William from the spa. I glower back at her.

Austen stays behind. I do not look up or acknowledge him

at all. I sulk. Under the water he touches the top of my foot with his toes.

"I didn't say thank you."

"You gave Sabrina our photo," I frown. "What if she sees it?"

"I don't care if she sees it."

"Is she a gold-digger, a beard, or both?"

He shakes his head. "You just seemed upset so I kissed you, so what? Sabrina won't care."

"Both," I huff.

"We're sort of... in an open thing."

Nothing I could say or do will dislodge her. The idea needles my heart.

"You should have let me leave when we were in Melbourne."

"I know."

We sit in silence. I know I look distraught because I fucking am. He looks concerned.

"What's the big deal with Koalas anyway?"

"It's a sad story," Austen says. "We were trapped in a building..."

"You're talking about that condemned building? William was there?"

"Yeah," Austen nods. "He said if I didn't die, you know, freeze to death or something..."

I frown. "Or something? Are you talking about when you

were attacked? They are the same thing?"

"Yeah..." he sighs. "It's always the same thing, Mischa. I was injured bad. He... gave me his blood amongst other things. He watched me die twice. He said when we got out he would take me somewhere warm. Maybe Australia, and we could see some koalas. He promised me a lot, you know, to hang on, and that was the one my mind clung to as I was fading away."

"Well, don't I feel like an asshole..."

Austen laughs. "Yeah... the thing about it is, when he found me, he was walking into danger, and he got hurt protecting me."

"The firefight. Will shot them?"

"I don't know. You'd have to ask my brother, but I don't recommend it."

"How old were you?"

Austen grimaces. "Twelve? Actually I think about thirteen, almost, maybe."

"How'd you get out?"

"Isobelle's dad rescued us. It's not like I really give a fuck about koalas in that childish way, but it's this weird symbolic thing for us. We've kept our promises to each other. It's finally over. We can finally put it to rest."

"I'm sorry."

"No," he says. "You gave us more than you realize. I know he blagged that ticket off you and you seem a little jealous."

"I'm just jealous of how much fun you had today."

"Damn. That's fucked-up."

"I'm also annoyed that William got to be affectionate to you and I didn't."

"That's *really* fucked up."

"Isabella and Sabrina are just the cherry on top."

"Isobelle."

"Whatever. Singing to her and shit. *Fuck.*"

"You didn't like that huh?"

"It'll sound really good, once you learn to play your instruments."

Austen guffaws. "I guess you're kind of a jealous guy."

"I'm profoundly in love with you, and I'm certain you feel the same," I say, staring him down. "Our rooms are close to each other. I can feel you through the wall, you know? Sense you. Feel your heartbeat. Your heart is not exactly beating slow when I'm around," I shake my head.

Austen sighs. "Crush still crushing then?"

I smile a little, and rub his foot under the water. "Yeah, I guess I've fooled myself again. I gotta stop thinking this feeling will last forever. Or that I want it to. Eternal love is such a weird delusion. I must be near the end, almost. I hope so. Anyway, what are you doing tonight, baby?"

"It's been a long day," he says. "The girls are still pretty jet-lagged. We are turning in early, but please don't be sad."

"You're asking the impossible."

"Thanks again," he says.

The spa pool is very private. Austen looks around to check nobody can see us, and pecks me on the cheek. I press my face into his lips, and hold his arms under the water. He holds himself there, and I turn and put my lips to his, and steal a kiss. He doesn't stop me, it's only the briefest of moments. Then he stares at me, his eyelids low and entranced, and he blushes pink. My heart does a summersault.

"Don't read into this," he says, then steals another enthusiastic kiss.

That magnetism he described pulls us together, and it's strong. We latch together hard. I hear fucking music in my head. He knows he has to stop but can't break away from the embrace. He forces himself off and staggers.

"You know we'll never be together, right?" Austen asks. "I told you how it has to be, how it is."

Who's he trying to fucking convince?

He turns to leave. I follow and wrap my arms around his waist, and kiss him on the back of his neck.

"Come up to my room."

"Mmm, *stop*," he says, "before he comes back."

Then he's gone. I can't get out now; I have a raging boner.

I stay until everyone else has gone out, or gone to bed. The spa pool can only be seen by a few patios, but they're all empty. Austen comes outside his room, right above me. He can't sleep. He's watching me from his chair, drinking a bottle of something. I get out of the spa and the hot water comes off me in steam.

I'm still a little hard. I lie down on the deck chair and look up at him. He watches as I rub my groin and starts paying attention, and waits. I am completely sheltered by the planters and umbrellas, so I pull my cock out. He stares at me as the blood starts rushing to it, really gazing, as it gets bigger and harder. Soon I'm fully erect. I start stroking it. He looks around the courtyard and checks that all the windows are empty. I get more brazen, take my swimming shorts off and set my legs apart. I make long hard strokes and he leans over the edge to watch me. It excites me and I pleasure myself faster. He bites down on his bottom lip and chews it. I want to tell him to keep doing that, I want to call him baby, I want to say his name, make him bite down on his lip so hard he has to moan. Then I moan, and cum gushes from me. I see all the tension in his body leave him like it's him who's climaxing. His mouth is wide now. I release one more load and he squirms desperately as I do.

He doesn't know what to do. He considers finishing his drink but doesn't. He sits and slumps in his chair like the wind is knocked out of him. He wipes his hand down his face and neck, then goes back into his room with his stupid girlfriend.

I have to.

I have to have him.

Then maybe I can walk away from this obsession forever.

I have to fuck that guy.

I wipe myself down with the towel and put my shorts back on. The door inside creaks and I rush out, hoping for Austen, only to startle Maxim.

"Jesus!" he jumps.

"Shit. Sorry bro."

"Hurry," he says, in Russian. "You need to get clothes on before we go."

"Go where?"

"To do our *duty*..." he coaxes me, his eyebrows go right up, staring me down, "to our *family*..." I know what he's getting at but I am still not caught up, "the whole reason why we are *here*..."

"The reason why we're here?" I try to remember. "I promised to do some things..."

"And I've been doing it all for you, asshole. I can't go alone tonight. I'm going out to the middle of nowhere by myself. I can fill you in along the way."

"Yeah," I nod. "I'll be ready in five."

15 AUSTEN

I'm staring at the wall in my room. I've just watched Mischa touch himself, and I feel the most intoxicating desire to spend the night with him. I can still feel him on top of me from last time, and I can't take it anymore. I want him so much, I just don't want to have a stupid seizure, or to be behind a screen. I want to feel him touch me, but I can't.

I don't know what I should do. Someone has to tell me what to do. I know what they'll say, *"Go for it."* I just need to hear it. They need to know I'm choosing to try to have sex with someone, no matter if it makes me comatose for the rest of the bloody trip. I go to my brother's room, but he's not there. He's not in Isobelle and Sabrina's room either. They are sleeping.

"Come to bed Baby Bee," Isobelle croaks, when she starts to stir.

She pulls off the blanket to let me in and she's naked. It's her favorite and default setting.

I sit at the end of the bed. "I can't sleep."

"Mmm. Where's Honey Bee?"

"Don't know. He must have gone out."

"You think he's trying to make it up to that girl?"

"No," I say.

"Have you made it up to Mischa?"

"Not exactly."

"You should."

"I'm trying."

"Maybe it would help you sleep, if you did?"

"Yeah. I wanted to ask Honey advice, about sleeping with Mischa."

"Hmm. I am not sure he would take it well."

"Not specifically, just general advice. You're crazy too, so maybe you could do the pep talk."

She sighs. "You won't be pushed out of your body forever, you know, when you're doing it."

"How'd you know about that?" I ask.

"Honey told me. You've been busy on this trip."

She thinks I slept with Amelia too.

"Not really," I say.

"I've been worried that you might try kill yourself again."

"I feel different lately."

"Mischa's making you happy. You just need sex, Baby Bee. And to watch me bathe in the blood of our enemies. Then more sex. It really is that simple."

"That's kinda one of the hundred problems. I don't want him to find out we're homicidal maniacs."

"Fighting back is not homicide in the eyes of the law. They deserved it. Stop feeling guilty. Besides, it's none of his fucking business. When his mother dies in front of him, he can come talk to us."

I almost want to tell Isobelle about Mischa's life, but I don't.

"He thinks Sabrina looks like she could be my sister."

Isobelle splutters with laughter. "Well, that's a new one."

"But do you think…"

"Who cares? You're never going to fuck her anyway."

"I like him. I've already done a few things with him. It didn't go so well."

"Every time is different."

"Will I get my heart ripped out?"

"Absolutely," she smiles, her eyes still closed, "and it will totally be worth it. For me too, because I'll have the pleasure of ripping his heart out to avenge you."

"Please don't."

"And I'll show it to him while I drink his blood."

I smile at the thought. "Honey says he's always behind a screen and detached when he's with people."

"Not always. He's good now, sometimes. It will take you a little time."

"Yeah."

"Honey did it for you, you know? Pushed himself. Became a whore, to cover for your aversion to all of it. It's mostly smoke and mirrors," she grins. "A big song and dance. He just wants everyone to leave you alone. He thinks you need more time."

"Maybe I do."

"The problem is, he can't take much more of this. The little cracks in his spirit are starting to show, darling. He needs to rest."

"Yeah, I know," I sigh. "Stick to the solid plan."

"We're so close to the finish line."

"So close to having the life we never wanted."

"Oh Bubs." She opens her eyes. "We always knew it would be a hard road." She puts her hand on mine. "But at least we have each other, and soon I can finally kill James. I get wet just thinking about it."

"Can't wait," I say.

"I love you my Beebee."

I run my fingers through Isobelle's hair, over her little battle scar, the shiny white mark hidden above her hairline.

"I love you too, like you were my twin as well." I tell her. "Now, of my own free will, I'm now going to *try* to have consensual sex with a partner of my choosing. Fingers crossed I'm not catatonic by the end of it."

"That would be hilarious," she laughs.

"I want you to hold on to my alert bracelet. I don't want Mischa to press it if things go wrong, and have Lord Tyrannus to burst in and see who I'm with, and lose his fucking mind over it."

"Fair enough. Give Mischa my number instead," she says. "Good luck."

"Thank you," I say, and kiss her on the temple.

I close her door, and stare down the hallway. I have to be with Mischa. I need him, as much as he needs me. Tonight is the night to try again.

I go down to the spa, but he's gone. I go to his room and knock. He's not there.

I slide a note under the door, and go back to my room to wait, staring at the ceiling.

16 MISCHA

We slip out of the hotel in a rental car and Max drives us to the Blue Mountains. It's after midnight by the time we get there, but the bar in the country town is still open. Our contact hasn't arrived yet, so we play a game of pool with an attractive young girl with curly brown hair who seems quite drunk.

"You're cute," she tells Maxim. "We should fuck."

"No thank you," he says. "I'm taken."

When the contact does arrive it's obvious, because he looks exactly like Maxim, only younger. Just a boy. Maybe they share a Romanian look or something. Sexy vampires.

They talk quietly with each other, and I watch them from a distance. My superpower tingles. There's something about being close with someone. People ask if you are related even if you aren't and don't look alike. People don't ask that about close friends but always with the fuck-buddies and siblings, even adopted ones. Maxim's contact has this weird unspoken connection to the him, and Max is acknowledging that connection in his body language, and it isn't just that they are both from Transylvania or wherever the fuck. I am looking at his brother.

He can't be more than sixteen. Maxim has two brothers and he's trying to find them. The other contact in Melbourne must have been his older brother. No wonder he was so shaken at the restaurant.

The three of them were adopted to Australia when he was little, but the family ended up changing their mind and they went into a group home. Max went to juvenile detention soon after for running a huge fake I.D. ring through all the high schools and making absolute bank. It was epic. Soon after, Shivishni came knocking.

This is not a bad development. Maybe. Maxim's brother would be less likely to screw him over. Probably. Although, the two of them together just increased the chances of me getting screwed myself. Not very likely that Max would do it, because he's a good guy, and because our brother Ivan would chop him into pieces and leave him in a suitcase in Moscow Train Station.

We are setting this kid up with millions in product for pennies on the dollar. A small deposit to get a foothold in this almost unbreakable market. Even so, our small deposit is a lot of money for most people.

I keep watching, and they never look my way, which is good. If this deal was fine for Konstantin and Sivishni, I'm fine with it too.

The brunette girl we played pool with has passed out on the couch opposite us. I try to wake her but she's out cold. A creepy older man is observing us from the other side of the bar.

"It's time to leave," Maxim says.

"What about the girl?" I ask.

He shrugs. "Not my problem."

His contact-slash-brother looks at us. "You can't just leave her here with that guy eyeing her."

"I didn't drug her," Max insists.

Max's brother prods and shakes her but she only shifts a little. Then he checks her purse.

"She has a driver's license. She only turned eighteen a month ago," he says, and shows it to us. "It has her address on it, we could drop her back to her parent's house?"

"Blackheath is in the opposite direction," Maxim says.

"By how much?" I ask him.

"About twenty minutes."

"Yeah, fuck it," I nod to the Romanian brother. "We can drop you off first, and then swing by her house."

"Yeah," he says. "Cool."

I drive us to a quiet, forested lane and the contact-slash-brother follows in his car. He gets in the passenger seat and something feels off. I look at Maxim, and even he looks suspicious.

No. Max would never, but I want this over fast.

I hand the Romanian his product and he hands me a bag

full of money. He opens the case packed with three small glass vials. He turns off the car light and shakes one of the little bottles in the dark. It lights up with bright white zaps of electricity.

"Oh my God, oh my God, oh my God, it's so cool!" he yells, excited. "I never thought I'd get to see it."

"That's why they call it lightning in a bottle," I tell him.

"How much acid is in here?" he asks.

"That is one *million*, sixty-five thousand, one hundred and forty-*one* very fucking strong doses of LSD," I beam. "Enough to keep every space-cadet in this country happy for the next year. Dump it in the water reservoir and you'll have Sydney flying for the next *month*."

"Woah..."

"His father was a scientist," Max tells his little brother. "He taught him chemistry."

"But he didn't teach me how to make that," I tell him.

"My chemistry teacher taught me about indole alkaloids," the brother says, "and I've read all Professor Shulgin's books. What method do you use?"

"K-POP. Safest way."

"Nice."

I check the money fast. "That's a great payday."

The Romanian nods, and offers me his hand to shake. "You

know, I'd love to learn, if you want a prospect…"

Don't shake his hand.

"Yeah, we'd definitely…"

Shake his hand, and he'll kill you.

I freeze. My superpower is now blaring so loudly I cannot ignore it. Everything goes quiet and I hear a gun click.

Now the girl in the back seat is awake, and stone-cold sober. Her gun is touching me and I can feel it. I didn't imagine the weirdness a moment ago. The Romanian boy is suddenly very still, and Max looks at him then at me.

"Give me the money, and nobody gets hurt," the girl says.

I look at the Romanian and know he's in on it.

"Hurry up," she growls. "Don't be a hero."

They don't know what they're doing, but you do. Show them what it means to be an Abramov.

"Are you ready?" I ask Max, in Russian.

"What are you saying?" The girl barks at me.

The boy yells at Max in Romanian. I understand enough to know that this boy is telling Max to listen to him. I do not know which way Maxim's loyalty will fall, and I now have a bullet pointed at my fucking head.

"I need you now," I tell Max, my eyes pleading.

"Speak English!" the girl screams.

The Romanian little brother gets jumpy and pulls out his

own gun. He points it at Max.

"Stop," Max says, and puts his hands up in the air.

The Russian word for "safe word" is "stop-slovo". My brothers and I use it, or just "stop" three times if we are in trouble.

"Stop," I nod, and raise my arms as if we are trying to diffuse the situation.

"Stop!" Maxim yells and launches at the girl.

I take the Romanian's gun and break his fucking arm in one fluid motion. The gun thing I have practiced every day for *years* but the arm thing only once before. Maxim grabs the girl's wrists and pushes them up to the ceiling. She pulls the trigger and blasts a hole in the top of the rental car. I feel the bullet rip through the air just above my head and the sound ruptures my eardrum. I duck and she fires again. Maxim slams his forehead down onto her nose and breaks it. He grabs the gun and hits her face with it. He blood splashes on the window and she screams at him that it hurts.

For a moment everybody is too stunned to speak.

"That was actually *loaded*?" Max gasps.

"Okay," I yell, "new rule; no joyriders!"

"You broke my nose!" the girl screams, her shaking hands feeling the damage.

Max punches her just above the temple and knocks her out.

"Careful," I tell him. "That could actually kill her."

"No," he says. "I have done it to so many assholes, I know just how hard to hit."

He looks at her pistol. It's a compact.

"Cute. Looks like it matches yours."

I look at the Romanian's. Same brand, only bigger.

"Oh yeah," I say. "There must have been a Valentine's special."

The Romanian starts bargaining with Maxim in their language. It has not escaped my attention that Max hasn't knocked him out yet. I am still in danger, still holding the gun to this guy's face.

Maxim turns to me. "You should drive a couple miles out," he suggests. "We can leave them in the middle of nowhere."

I am silent long enough for him to know I don't like it.

"I could take her in their car," I suggest.

"Their car might be hot. We all go in this car."

I try to think but I can't. "I cannot drive this back to Sydney for obvious fucking reasons."

"It's only superficial damage," Max says.

I glower at him. "We can't return a rental with two bullets in it."

"It only has one bullet, and one hole. It's okay; I got the extra coverage, we just pay the excess."

"We can't drive around with cash and contraband in a bullet-ridden car," I huff.

"It's not bullet-*ridden*, it's just bullet-*sprinkled*."

I'm irritated now. "What if they have used this gun somewhere else? They could test that bullet and ask questions."

"We have an alibi. We don't live in Australia."

I take the safety off, and point the gun at Max.

"Maxim," I say calmly, "I am not taking my hands off this gun. But I'm also not going to shoot your baby brother unless I have to, okay? You are going to drive this car or I'll be eating two skull's worth of vampire fry for breakfast. Understood?"

His gun is still pointed at the passenger. He deflates a little, and hands it to me. I take both guns, get out of the driver's seat and swap with Max.

"We're all speaking English for the rest of the ride," I tell Maxim. "I don't wanna hear any Romanian."

He's quiet on the drive into the mountain valley. It's only been minutes when the girl starts to wake up. Seems a good time to let her out.

"You can't just leave me in the middle of nowhere," she whinges.

"I won't leave you alone with a man you don't know," Maxim says. "If you're together we can leave you together. So, what's the story?"

His brother nods. "We're together."

I groan in frustration. "You are a smart kid, but your girl is not, and she's a psychopath. Cut her loose."

"This is why you couldn't come with me," Max tells him. "You will always make the shitty choice and the whole thing turns to shit."

"At least give me the stuff I paid for," his brother says.

"It doesn't work like that."

"How will I get home? Give me my phone."

"Phones and wallets are *such* a pain to replace." Max looks up at the sky. "You were always a smart kid, but you need to learn wisdom. At least the next town is not far away. It's a beautiful moonlit night tonight, and this is a road. Follow the path home, wherever that is for you now. Maybe if you walk long enough, you might realize a thing or two."

Driving back Max is sullen.

"You can sell the product to our contacts in Sydney," I tell him, "or throw it in the drain; we got the money, it's all gravy."

"I was never afraid to die before tonight," he says, watching the road, "because I would rather die than let my family down. I forgot that my family is two different things. Sorry I made you doubt me."

"Maxim, I hope you know you are worth your weight in gold," I tell him. "If it was Sofie, I don't know if I could have done what you just did."

"That's different," Max smiles. "If it's down to her and you, I'm picking her every time."

I dial a number as we're driving away.

He answers.

"Who the fuck calls at two the morning?"

"William," I say. "I need that favor."

"My God," he groans. "*That* was quick."

* * *

Around three-thirty in the morning, Maxim and I are asleep in our seats by some forest park halfway to Sydney.

William bangs on the window.

"Wakey-wakey," he says.

We get out and grab our backpacks, William inspects the bullet damage as we do. We cleaned the blood pretty good so it doesn't look *too* bad. He's trying not to laugh and I'm trying to ignore it. Maxim can report the car stolen once we're in Sydney.

"Thanks," I say to Will, as we arrive back at the hotel.

"Hope we're even," he says.

"I do too."

At the hotel we get to our hallway and I wait for him to go into his room. He's waiting for me and Max to go into mine.

"I forgot the card," he says.

"What's the matter?" I ask. "Don't want to wake your girl-friend?"

He shakes his head. "No."

"You can sleep on the couch," I offer. "You'll owe me a mod-ern favor."

"The worst kind."

There are two small sofas in my room. Max takes one and Will takes the other. For some reason, maybe because his sofa doesn't convert to a bed like Max's does, William gets into bed beside me while I'm sleeping.

When I wake, Will's phone is ringing, and then the door knocks. I open it a crack.

"I know he's in here," Austen says. "I can hear his phone."

He pushes past me, and finds Will in the bed I've just come from. Will's not wearing much. Then he looks at me. I'm naked, wrapped in a sheet.

He looks hurt. "Nothing alike, huh?"

"This is not what it looks like."

"What does it look like?"

"Not what you think."

"Did you do this to get back at me for Sabrina?"

There are little bottles of alcohol strewn all over the floor and I kick them and they clink against each other.

"Since I last saw you," I tell Austen, "I have become hung-

over, seriously sleep deprived, and deaf in one ear," I point
to the small drop of blood that has leaked from my lobe and
smudged the side of my jaw, "and a little traumatized, but I did
not fuck your asshole brother. I jerked off at the pool last night
to an audience of *one*, and that was just enough."

He looks over to see Maxim asleep on the sofa.

Austen points to Max. "I remember that wet-cigarette-look-
ing man and his ridiculous horse penis from the sauna."

"Hard to forget, really. That's Max."

"Max? one you had dinner with in Melbourne?"

"...Yeah?"

"You know what? I don't actually care."

He bends down and inspects his brother.

"He smells sober," he says, and shoots a look at me. "Come
on buddy," he says to William.

"Baby?" William says as Austen rouses him from the bed.

He's barely conscious as Austen leads him back to his room.

❋ ❋ ❋

Things are frosty the next day. Austen won't even look at me.
It's sort of poetic justice that he feels scorned now too, but the
fact that it's blown up over Will is just as intolerable for me as
it is for him. I would never ever go with someone like Will. He
gives me the fucking creeps. Isobelle too. Psychopath vibes. She

also makes my superpower go a little haywire. The moment the puppetmaster's around it's hard to read everyone else. It makes me feel human. I hate it.

I find a note stuck to the bottom of my shoe. I don't know where it came from.

"You are my cup of coffee," it reads. *"Come wake me up."*

It plays on my mind all day. It's for me, from Austen. It has to be. So I ask him.

"I don't know what you're talking about," he says.

"It must have been slipped under my door."

"Maybe you didn't see it, when you went in your room late at night, to sleep with my brother."

I try to protest but he won't hear it, and storms off.

He left the note for me. I would have left him one too. He would have let me in his room the moment he heard me scratching at his door, pulled me into his bed, ripped my clothes off and kissed me all over my body. I would have tasted him and begged for more. I would have let him to tie me up, rub me down with massage oils, pleasure me, and maybe push himself deep inside me like I had never let anyone do before, harder and harder, until I drained him of all the cum in his body, and we would have had sex all night the way we have both been dying to do.

And now that's all off the table.

'*Thwarted*' is not an emotion, but it should be.

❊ ❊ ❊

Second to last day. The group is headed to the cave painting heritage site, I can't take it anymore. I move over to William in the back of the bus.

"Hey Will," I say.

William and Austen's eyes shoot up. I sit down in front of them and they both seem surprised.

"Morning," William says.

"So remember the other night when I called you when my rental car broke down and you picked me up? When you stayed in my room with Max because you said you didn't want to wake Isobelle up?"

"...Yeah?"

"Well, I know it sounds weird but at some point it felt like someone was sleeping next to me."

Sabrina and Isobelle look at each other. Kane looks over too.

"That was me," he says.

"Okay," I nod. "What the fuck?"

"Sleeping on a sofa was horrible," William scratches his head. "I'm too tall for that shit. I got up to piss, and when I came back, I thought: *I can't sleep on that, I'm getting in the fucking bed, I don't care anymore.*" He looks at me. "I mean, I was barely conscious, it's not like I'd ever do anything weird, if that's what you are worried about?"

"I'm just a little paranoid."

"I guess it was a crazy night for you." William smirks. "I figured what happened was, you were drinking in the pool, talked Max into going out to party. You were also probably high, and you fucked up the car. That's when you called me to come get you, because I owed you for the koalas. Am I in the ballpark?"

Austen's eyes look at me, expecting a reply.

"I mean," I sigh, "you make me sound like an *idiot*."

"Oh you *definitely* are," William smiles. Sabrina and Isobelle chortle. "You're also not my type."

My eyes bug. "You are one-hundred percent the opposite of *my type*."

"Sorry I made you nervous," William says. "Especially as, if the shoe was on the other foot, you'd be dead."

"I'll take your word for it. You've almost killed me once."

"Indeed," he offers me a fist-bump. "We good?"

We reach our destination. Austen and the others stomp off up the trail. William laughs to himself. He hangs back with me as everyone else gets out of the bus.

"Are you having deja-vu?" William asks me, as his face twists into an evil little grin like a cartoon villain.

"No," I say. "Should I?"

"Huh," he shrugs, trying to hide the enthusiasm that was making his eyes look crazy. "Must just be me."

We're in the parking lot at the start of the trail. William looks at me and bounces on his toes and looks away. He's radiating an energy he can barely contain. He stretches his arms, not because he's tired from the drive, but because he's masking something that's starting to spook me. I can feel him coming in for the kill.

"Am I about to be ambushed?" I ask.

"Apparently there are these natural little pools inside the forest park," he explains. "They're shaped like jelly beans."

Recognition of what he's saying is forming, but I push the thought back. *It can't be.*

"We should catch up," I say.

"Hey that car over there looks *familiar*," he says, smiling like a maniac.

He walks towards a black sedan and I follow in horror.

"Oh my god, is that a *bullet* hole?" His jaw drops in mock surprise. "*Someone* must have *dumped* it for some reason. Do you think *someone* should *report* it to the *police?* Don't worry, I'll put *your name* down too, so we can both claim the reward."

My mind stops working. "This is..." I stammer. "I don't... you... did you tell us to dump it here to mess with me?"

"It's mostly fun and games," he smiles.

"Mostly?"

"I did want a little leverage, but I hit gold. I knew that car was hot. I didn't think it would be *this hot*."

"I didn't *shoot* anyone, idiot. I got stood over buying drugs, and the asshole blew a hole in the roof of my car."

"Tell it to the cops."

"Okay, evil genius," I frown. "What do you want? Some old-time favor? Because I'm good at those."

"I can tell you'd be good for some biblical shit," he raises an eyebrow. "But a modern favor is all I want. I'll still owe you as well."

"Anything."

"I know you've got some little spark with Amelia. She seems in to you."

I glower at him, waiting for him to get to the point.

"Okay?"

"However, Austen likes her, they're seeing where it goes, and you should stay the fuck away so he can do his thing."

What the fuck is he talking about? Austen is engaged. To be married. To Sabrina. But loves me. Not Amelia.

"Your... brother Austen... has something going with... *Amelia*?"

"They hooked up when we were in the Northern Territories."

"You think they fucked in Alice Springs?"

"No, just you know, foreplay stuff. They got each other off. She gave him a hand-job."

"You know for sure? You were there?"

"Yes." He grimaces. "I wish I wasn't..."

You can't fake that level of disgust. He was not only told about it by Austen, but he saw some of it. So Austen's really trying to fuck around on me with all these girls, huh? I feel the gut-punch. I don't hide my reaction.

"Oh... that's... a pity..."

"Sorry, I know you were circling her, but don't worry; you're so goddamn good-looking," Will looks me up and down, "Jesus Mary mother of Christ, you could get with *anyone*."

Finally Will gives me credit where credit is due. Took him long enough.

"Austen told me he didn't like new people touching him. He said he has these seizures?"

"No. Austen misspoke. He never said that. He *does not* have seizures. *I have seizures.*"

"He has literally told me about five times not to fucking touch him because it might trigger some kind of seizure."

"Might, *might*, MIGHT. Never happened. Never will happen. He's just worried about that because of me. I'm okay when I get to know someone, but it's a risk. I have frightened a couple of girls, Isobelle included. I had an accident when I was younger, like a traumatic brain injury, but I'm on the mend."

"You black out, and beat people up?"

"Yeah, but not with *girls*. I have epilepsy, it's just the unusual kind."

"Frontal lobe epilepsy? I read it can make you violent."

"No. Sure. Whatever," he closes his eyes and shakes his head. "It doesn't *matter*. He's paranoid if people touch him unexpectedly it'll set him off, or if he fucks new girls he'll fit like I did for a while. That's why he's nervous about sewing a couple wild oats, so he only he finger-fucked Amelia and it was fine."

"Okay..." I frown, "but Austen has been dating Sabrina the *very hot* girl for apparently five years or something?"

"Yeah but don't worry about that. For the reasons I just explained, Sabrina's the only girl he hides the sausage with. And that's exactly the problem. I'm trying to fix him. I'm finally at the point where all girls blend together into anonymous blobs and I'm fine, and I want Austen to reach the promised land. That's why I'm hoping to get the ball rolling with him and Amelia, so he can fuck all the girls he wants."

"*Saaa-breee-naaa.*"

"*Diff-er-ent rulesssssss. Ru-ling fuck-ing class.*"

That sobers me. I'm a Russian citizen after all. Wealth and power really do taste like ashes in my mouth.

"They're getting fucking married," I say meekly.

"My friend," he puts his hand on my shoulder. "Every super-model knows a guy who's tired of fucking a supermodel."

"You're saying they're not into each other anymore?"

"I'm saying variety is the spice of life."

"But... I don't know. They're getting married..."

He closes his eyes and his brow furrows in frustration, and shakes his head emphatically, "Oh *jeez. That* does *not* matter *at all*, trust me."

"If he gets caught?"

"What's she gonna do?" he laughs, "*Not* marry the hand-some, young, and filthy rich guy?"

Such an asshole, but something deep down tells me William is wrong.

It can't be true. I don't care if he saw Austen physically inside of Amelia; there must be a reasonable explanation. Like he was just looking for his keys or something. More importantly, William sees what I see; Sabrina and Austen aren't right for each other, and their relationship is bullshit. We both want to intervene in this shit-show. This game is still fucking in play, motherfucker. Oh fucking hell to the fuck yes!

I do some fast calculations, and nod. "Sure, I mean, I guess I don't really give a fuck," I tell him. "Maybe I could get into Brittany's pants. I know she's been a bit hung up on you. Maybe we can all hang out in Bondi tomorrow before we head to the airport, and you invite Brittany and I invite Amelia, we could make it happen?"

William is pleased. "Two birds, one stone. I love the way you think; the best way to get over someone is to get under someone else."

* * *

Kai, with the Stupid Backwards Hat, tags along with Alissa and Taylor B, and another jock named Jordan.

"No bodyguards lately huh?" I ask Will. "At the zoo, Luna Park, not today either."

Will shakes his head. "Isobelle is here now."

Isobelle smiles at me.

"She's better than two big bodyguards?"

Will, Austen and his interloper girlfriend all nod automatically.

"They might take a bullet for us but she'd dish them out without a word."

Isobelle laughs, but her eyes are steely. "Fuck with my bee-bees and I'll murder you."

Amelia is very pale and has every kind of sunscreen on her. In Australia it comes in colored paint sticks, and Amelia draws designs on everyone except me, because I ask Brittany to get my back. Austen sits it all out because he is wearing a swim top... and doesn't like being touched. He certainly isn't trying very hard with the poor girl, that's for sure. He watches Brittany enthusiastically massage my shoulders. I get flirty and do her sunscreen too.

Kai and Jordan are on bodyboards and Brittany follows them into the surf. William, Sabrina, and Isobelle take off to the Iceberg Pools at the southern end, leaving me and Austen with Brittany and Amelia.

I put my feet in the water. It's a cool relief from the heat. Austen pushes the sand around with his feet. He seems lost. He doesn't know whether he should follow William, or talk to Amelia, or join me in the water. Slowly, he follows his brother to the pools.

I stand in the light blue sea up to my knees. I'm not ready to swim because I have two joints in the pocket of my shorts. Amelia organizes her bags on the sand and a Labrador walks up and sniffs her bikini. She squeaks when its moist nose touches her thigh. Then she joins me in the ankle-deep water, looking out at the Pacific Ocean in designer sunglasses.

"Hello, Miss Amelia," I say.

"Hello Sexy Mikhail," she replies in her London accent.

"Well..."

"Is that too forward?"

I weigh it up. "I mean, where's the lie?"

"Forgive me," she laughs, "but if I want any chance of getting my end away before the end of this, I need to be bold."

"Your end away? With me?"

She smiles smugly. "Oh yes."

"You don't like Austen then?"

She considers the idea. "He's a bit of alright; smoking hot actually. Also has lots of money, which helps."

"Ain't saying she a gold digger..."

She shakes her head. "It's just as much work to date a rich guy than a poor one, and sometimes it's much less work. That one is also much nicer than his brother. I mean..." she clears her throat, "sometimes."

"What do you mean; *sometimes*?"

"Oh... nothing."

I read her body.

"Oh shit," I frown. "you're sitting on something big, aren't you?"

"I mean..."

"Please tell me," I beg her.

"Don't say anything." Amelia pulls a small box out of her bag and shows me the diamond and sapphire bracelet. "I can't really explain it. Will pulled me aside yesterday coming back from Luna Park. He said it was from Austen. But... isn't Sabrina dating Austen?"

"Apparently."

"Perhaps he wants me to be his mistress."

"Does it actually look like he's really dating Sabrina?" I ask.

"He actually looks like he could be her *brother*," she laughs.

"Yeah. Right?" My eyes bug. "It's fucking *spooky*."

She nods. "But if *you're* offering, it's an automatic yes. I think you're a yes for Brittany too, if you want extra company. And it doesn't have to be before the flight. You can hit me up back home, or both of us."

"Good to know," I smile. "It's just awkward because William told me there's something between you and Austen and now with him giving you the bracelet, I'm not sure if I should get between you two."

"Interesting," she frowns. "I wouldn't mind riding that gravy train, but I don't know. Maybe those two are more trouble than they're worth. When people found out I was going to school with them they told me to be careful. When they heard Isobelle had joined them on this trip, they said to run as fast as I can, and not to talk to her."

"I'd love to find out why."

"Well," she thinks about it. "My cousin is at Oxford, with a girl who's dating a guy from their school, and he knows every-thing. I could always ask her to ask him?"

"I mean... if it's not too much trouble."

"My cousin actually mentioned there's a rumor they have a younger sister, but nobody can find the birth certificate or has ever seen even a bloody photo of the girl."

"*Sabrina?*" I swivel to Amelia and laugh.

"Sabrina!" she shrieks, and cackles with laughter.

"Okay, what else?" I ask, after we catch our breath.

"Apparently those girls had something to do with that aeroplane thing."

"Which girls?"

"Sabrina and Isobelle; their *girlfriends*," Amelia does quotation marks around her head.

"Oh... *more please.*"

"Sabrina's a nobody," Amelia shrugs.

"Not if she's their sister..."

Amelia snorts. "Isobelle's grandfather isn't, and he has an estate near theirs."

Amelia looks out to where the others had been.

"Um... is Brittany okay?" she asks, pointing out to the surf, "because she is much further out than a few minutes ago."

Jordan is coming in on a wave on his board and Kai's headed back out.

"Maybe go talk to a lifeguard," I tell Amelia, and hand her my wallet, weed, and sunglasses.

It doesn't take me long to get to Brittany. The water somehow drags me out to her. She's so exhausted from fighting the undertow she can't speak. When she grabs me she pulls us both beneath the surface. Water floods into my injured ear and the pain is like a hot poker being rammed inside it. I push her off and we come back up and we are both fighting for air. We are far closer to the big surf of the southern end than we should be. A cresting wave comes towards us. I wait for it to get close and dive underneath. Brittany tumbles with it and I lose sight of her. I surface and Kai's board cuts across my path and connects with my head.

In an instant everything goes black, and then... I'm floating... propelled out of my body in spirit form. I look down and see Austen climb the barrier from the Iceberg pool and leap into the water. William follows him in. They pull my body down there to the sand. Austen is trying to blow air into my mouth and William is doing chest compressions.

I can also see my dad.

My real dad, standing in a heavy winter suit, looking up at me. He is smiling. The Labrador looks up as well and gives a friendly wag. I do not understand anything that is happening. I do not know what to do, and I feel scared.

"It's okay," he says. "There's nothing to fear."

"Are you dead?" I ask, and he nods. "Am I dead?"

"Not yet," he says. "But I want you to know I love you, and I forgive you."

All at once, I feel extremely sad, but I can't cry, and memories I haven't thought of in forever come flooding back.

"I'm sorry," I say.

"Your mother forgives you too."

"I'm so sorry."

"It's okay," he says. "But you have to kill him."

I don't know who *him* was. I can feel myself fading away. The fear and pain we all run from in this life lifts off me. The desire we cling to leaves me also. Then even time and thoughts disappear, until nothing remains but my own consciousness. All the things that make me human are gone. I have left the beach, and I'm going somewhere far away, into a sea of light. The only thought I have left is of Austen and I don't want to let it go.

Then I feel the heat of a hot summer's day, and soft lips on mine, and I realize I'm not breathing and my chest is fighting to get air into itself and I convulse awake and cough up foamy water onto the wet sand beside me.

"He's okay!" Austen yells.

He slaps my back hard to get the water and mucus out. I collapse back into his lap and he holds me.

Kai is panicked, standing around holding his backwards hat

and feeling sorry for himself. Bondi lifeguards are assisting Brittany. When she is stable one of them runs over and drops down to look at me. He's blonde, but his skin is brown from the beating sun. He has three stripes of thick red, yellow and blue sunblock face paint across his cheeks and bridge of his nose. His face crinkles into a smile as he looks me over.

"British lads who can't fucking swim?" he scoffs. "Congratulations, you are officially a Bondi stereotype. I'm wondering how many more of you idiots plan on bloody carping out there today."

The sun is dazzling. My head feels like it's ablaze. Austen is holding me, shaking. He's really emotional, and Will is trying to smooth it all over.

"He's fine," William insists. "We should probably go. There are cameras... these guys have it under control..."

"You cannot be serious right now," Austen hisses back at him, and clings to me.

* * *

The hospital is a short ride. Austen holds on to me until we have to go. Brittany and I are in the same ambulance but we're too tired to speak. We are put on opposite sides of the ward. I call Maxim and tell him what happened. He tells me he'll bring the wallet we took from his brother for all the paperwork. I don't have insurance, so at least we won't have to worry about that. William walks in my room with Sabrina and Isobelle.

"Britt's fine," he says. "Austen and Amelia are getting drinks."

A few minutes later a nurse escorts Austen and Amelia to my bed. The monitor changes from the steady, rhythmic beat as my heart jumps, seeing Austen. It screams *beep beep beep!* The machine telling on me only makes my heart beat faster.

The nurse looks at me and looks behind me, bemused. "Relax," she says. "Try breathing slow."

Austen looks at the monitor, taking in the new evidence. William is amused at my growing discomfort.

"Hi," Amelia says.

"Hi," I say, and press my lips together, looking at the floor.

"Are you okay?" she asks.

"I have to stay for a little while longer."

She frowns. "You have to be at the airport in an hour."

The nurse scoffs. "He won't even be discharged in an hour."

Amelia is worried. "Shit, you're going to miss the flight."

"You should get going," I tell her.

"We want you and Amelia to come with us to New Zealand," Isobelle says.

The monitor jumps again. I look up at the ceiling and try to relax.

I take a deep breath. "Thank you Isobelle, but I can't impose on you."

"We won't leave until you agree to come."

"I'd like to have a word with Mischa," William tells everyone. "Why don't you all go check on Brittany?"

Austen looks nervous, and William shoos him out the room.

"That was entertaining," William sniggers, when he comes back to my bed.

I am mortified, and feel myself flush. I do not flush. I do not get mortified. People do not get under my skin. I'm fucking deadly. I'm a fucking gangster.

"Shut up," I say.

"Oh come on. I don't just mean that, I mean seeing you nearly die. This has been the most interesting day of the whole trip."

My heart starts pounding harder again, but this time it's because I want to kill this asshole.

"You actually don't need these anymore," the nurse says, touching the monitors taped to my chest.

"Fucking hell," I say, and rip them off. "Ouch."

"Well, that's one way to do it," she says, and walks off.

"I didn't realize the extent of your feelings for Amelia."

I frown at him. "Will, please fuck off."

"Look, if I had any idea you were in this deep, I wouldn't have played cupid."

I growl in frustration. "I'm sick of this. I want it to stop."

"Stop what?"

"This joyless, sexless fucking holiday. My life was perfect. I used to fuck whoever I wanted and didn't get attached. A lot. Now I'm all obsessed and the thought of fucking anyone else makes me sick. I didn't choose this, it just took over my body like a fucking demon but I feel like a creep and an awkward loser when I try make a move. The possibility of rejection haunts me. I worry that I'll ruin any chance of future happiness with one misstep. I have lost my common sense. I want it to be over, and back to lots of meaningless sex. Preferably anonymous too."

"Oh dear," Will laughs. "I can help you. Isobelle asked Amelia to go to Fiordland with us, Amelia said yes, and Austen is very unhappy about it. He's not as interested in her as I hoped. Now the girls want you there, to even it out, and Isobelle says she's gonna dump me if you don't come. We can help each other fix this."

I look at William like he's insane.

"Austen's taking Sabrina," I remind him. "His *fiancé*. How do you think this will end?"

"Sabrina is... stupid," William shrugs. "She's the one who

wants you and Amelia there. What's done is done. Please, keep Amelia company."

"And Sabrina and Isobelle think it's all totally cool and nor-mal to bring the side piece?"

"They'll think what I tell them to think."

I'm deeply confounded by Isobelle and Sabrina. They don't fit right. Perhaps observing them closely will explain what I'm seeing.

But there's something else. My superpower is sounding the alarm.

I search William's eyes. "You're lying."

"What?" he asks.

"Those girls think for themselves. You don't think Sabrina's stupid. It disgusted you to say that."

William's jaw drops open. "Damn, you're *good.*"

"How do you really feel about Sabrina?"

His face flashes pure love. *Holy shit.*

"She's okay, I guess..."

This is conflicting.

"I'm not gonna help you steal her from Austen if that's...."

He throws his head back and laughs. "Oh, bless your sweet heart! It's not like that! She's not my type."

"She's everyone's type."

"Not mine!" he splutters. "You got nothing to worry about

there. She's more like a sister to me than anything."

I can see that...

"Why do you really want me to come?"

"It's not like I have some sort of *agenda*, or something. Isobelle's the boss, and always gets her way, so please come with us."

I can feel his silken tendrils turning into a web.

"Jesus Christ, what are you planning?"

William holds up his hands like he's trying to stop me throwing a basketball into a hoop.

"It's nothing bad," he explains. "It's true about Amelia coming, but I want you there because I just want Austen to have a friend, that's all. He seems so comfortable with you. He even seemed upset when he thought you had drowned. I think he sees you as a friend, and that never happens. You have even touched him a few times and he hasn't flinched."

William shows an emotion that I've never seen in him before. Guilt.

"He trusts you and he needs someone in his life. Please be his friend."

"Okay," I say. "That was the truth. So that's the whole reason? Nothing else?"

"No. Nothing else."

I cross my arms. "Lying."

He closes his eyes and rolls them. "Okay," he sighs. "He ditches the bodyguards every chance he gets. He's sick of them. He even told me I was *suffocating* him—which is ridiculous. He needs someone who can handle himself, is mentally tough, obviously familiar with guns, will protect him, and who he'd never suspect. You tick every box on my wish list, to be honest. I also really like you as a person, by the way. You're a pretty cool guy."

I gag a little. "I have obligations. Shit I need to do back home, and I just did you a favor, and you fucked me over."

"But I'll still owe you that favor! And I'd pay you a hundred grand for the week. I mean, you work at a pizzeria, you *need* the money."

I blanch at him. "Will, I promise you, I don't need anything from you..."

William looks skeptical. "You're rejecting my offer?"

In a split second I realize I'm giving up the thing I want because Captain Dickhead wants it too.

"I didn't say that."

"Oh?" his eyebrows shoot up.

"Will, at that bar, in Alice Springs, when you almost slit my throat..."

"I'm fucking *sorry*, okay?"

"I'm just worried for you. You sort of are suffocating Austen. All the security in the world now won't help you deal with something that has already happened in the past. You need to talk to someone, get treatment..."

"Okay seriously, shut up, you don't know what you're talking about. I want to tell you something, so never repeat what I'm about to say, okay?"

I shrug. "Sure."

"Or I'll put a bullet in you, yes?"

"I won't tell anyone, so you don't need to threaten me."

"I'm not trying to deal with what happened, Mischa. I'm trying to stop something happening *again*."

"What?" I sit bolt upright. "You think Austen's in danger?"

"I can't be sure," he shakes his head. "My mind is playing tricks. It's been a nightmare. Someone was after him in France, so we left. There were these threatening letters. They knew stuff about us that only me, Austen and Isobelle know. Then it started again after a couple of months in America, I think, but my mind is a strange and terrifying place. You know I'm not well, you've seen it. I don't know anything anymore. I never used to be this bad. I'm dealing with it. I have been dealing with it. My therapist is expensive, believe me. Since we got to Australia I feel better. It's going to be okay, I just need to figure some things out."

"And that's why you want me?"

"Yes! You've made this trip so good! You're always around so I don't have to worry if Kane and Hayden aren't there. I don't want to give up that peace of mind just yet. I want to go hunting next week, alone. Please."

"Okay. I think you might be bi-polar."

"Really? I think I might be manic-depressive."

"Same thing, Will. I'm serious, I..."

"I'm joking," he huffs. "Maybe. I just need to relax, rest my brain for a few days, and not worry about my fucking stupid brother all the time."

"I won't do anything I think might hurt Sabrina and Austen, even if you want me to."

"Of course."

"If you make a move on her, I will tell on you."

"I won't." Will presses his palms together like he's praying. *"Please help me."*

He's handing me Austen, like a gift tied with a bow for me to unwrap. Must be careful now. Don't want to spook the scatterbrained brother.

"Maybe... yeah. Maybe I could. I could protect Austen. Take care of him."

"Yeah?"

William hugs me round my middle like I'm a life raft. I pat his crazy head.

"I mean... yeah, of course... hot girl... free holiday... on a boat... getting paid... fuck yeah I'm coming!"

17 AUSTEN

Max, the wet-cigarette man, is at Mischa's bedside when I return. I see him through the slit in the curtain. He gets up to leave and kisses Mischa on each cheek.

"Bye, Pumpkin," Mischa says.

"*Pumpkin?*" I say, when he's gone. Mischa's head shoots up. "Kinda nuts that you took your boyfriend to Australia to pursue me."

He pokes his neck around the curtain. "Where's everyone?"

"They went clubbing. Isobelle volunteered me to babysit you."

"No Kane?"

"We are in a hospital. I don't think any of the nurses want to kill me."

Mischa releases a tense breath. "He's not my boyfriend."

"I don't care if he is."

"I've just been throwing up seawater. It was very dramatic. He was upset, to say the least. He's also my brother, by the way."

"That's a disturbing kink, roll playing incest."

Mischa's brow furrows. "You need to stop talking about my actual brother as if I'm fucking him. Please."

"What's with all the sexual tension?"

"Ugh, you're killing me here. That's just *tension*. The last twenty minutes were awful. It's not sexual; he's Romanian. They're very passionate. You're misreading the culture. What if I accused you of the same thing with Will?"

I grimace. "Christ. I don't like to even think of William as having a sexuality. It'd be better if he didn't, actually. Half the girls on this trip wouldn't be so prickly towards me. But that's beside the point because Isobelle invited you on the boat, and I hope you will say no."

"I'm not with Max."

"I don't care..."

"But I do. A lot. You're giving me shit for sleeping with my *own* brother, and your own brother, despite knowing I don't even *like* him, and have too much fucking self-respect to sleep with someone who treats their intimate partners like dirt the way he does..."

"He doesn't..."

"...and probably Kane too when you know damn well I'm sex-starved and you've been fucking Sabrina for five years and Amelia now too, and have been since Alice Springs. William told me he was there and saw it."

What a ridiculous irony. "Oh that is just *perfect*."

He huffs. "I care about you more than you understand. You are not exchangeable. Max is my brother. Can't you just give me the benefit of the doubt? He's not my boyfriend."

"Why are you still hung up on Kane though? I promise that was just for show."

"He makes my gaydar go off, and I think he hit on me before Christmas and I think you'll give me shit for it eventually, so I'm shining a light on it right now so it won't bite me in the ass when you and I are just about to get married or something."

"I wouldn't worry about that. You have a tendency to read into things that aren't there, and be very optimistic about your chances."

"Certified closet-case," I shake my head. "Anyway, all this conversation is telling me is how hurt you'd be if I really did have someone else. Being a little brat about it tells me that you like me but don't trust me. I'm hurt that you hooked up with Amelia, but I don't own you. You're hurt because you don't be-lieve my brother is my brother, and that's on you."

"All right; I believe you," I say. "I don't care, but I believe you."

"Thank you."

"I wasn't with Amelia," I tell Mischa. "Billy saw me that morning at the campground, and knew I had been with *some-one*, so I lied to him. Now I'm spending a bloody week with her."

"Oh," he relaxes a little. "Well who cares, really? William's got some insane master-plan to fuck with me, just so you know."

"He's threatened," I smile a little. "Although to be fair, he helped me drag you out of the water. You owe him your life."

"I think you need to talk to him. He's got feelings for Sabrina."

"What?" I shake my head at the thought and push down a laugh trying to bubble up. "He loves her like a sister," I shrug, "but he's obsessed with Izzy."

"I'd be worried."

I want to howl with laughter but I force myself not to.

"I'll never worry about that."

"It seems quite intense though."

"I know him better than you. I'm his brother, does he seem intense with me?"

Mischa thinks about it.

"Point taken. Thanks for saving me. Again."

"There are better ways to get another kiss, you know?"

"Good, because I never want to do that again."

"Please don't."

I pat his head. He pulls me to him.

"You trying to give me a seizure?" I ask.

"Perfect place for it..."

"Good point," I say, and kiss his eyebrow.

He looks at me in wonder. "Every time your lips touch me I

feel like I might burst into flames."

"I think there's an ointment for that."

He snorts with laughter. "Anyway…"

Mischa pulls out his phone and brings up a photo of Maxim's passport. Close up on the name. Maxim Abramov. He zooms out to his photo again. Then back to the name. Closer. Abramov.

A smile infects me. "Already told you I don't care."

"Your eyes look at me in a way that says 'thank you'." He combs his fingers between mine. "So am I coming or what?"

❊ ❊ ❊

We use a private jet to fly south. This is a new experience for our two guests. Amelia and Mischa are wide-eyed getting inside it. Before we depart, the flight attendant asks which one of us is Mikhail Abramov, and we all look at him. He looks confused.

"Am I in trouble?" he asks.

"Your father arranged a gift for your trip," she says.

She shows him a box in the cargo hold, and he pulls out a bottle to show us.

"My dad sent us a case of wine," he explains.

Isobelle examines the bottle. "Fancy wine."

"A case of that costs a fortune," William says.

"Yeah," Mischa scratches his head. "My dad is one of those rich Russian guys who buys English football teams and superyachts and stuff. Owns a jet too, I've just never been allowed on it."

I look at the note that came with it.

"You are carrying precious cargo," it reads. *"My deepest love and admiration goes with you all. Thinking of you always, Victor Abramov."*

"Weird note," Mischa frowns. "He is not a touchy-feely man. He's never told me he loves me. I don't actually think he does love me, definitely doesn't admire me. Maybe he was drunk or something."

"What should we get to thank him?" I ask.

"Oh," Mischa's eyes shoot up. "Nothing. The man has everything."

* * *

New Zealand looks gorgeous from the air. It is every single green woven together, and the land is sculptural. We get in cars and drive inland. There are no other vehicles on the road. The sky is a deeper blue than anywhere else. After miles of flat grass fields a color so lurid they could be radioactive, the silvery lake and steep forested mountains of the fjord are a dramatic revelation. Waterfalls mist the sheer granite cliffs. The clear water laps a pebble shore.

We arrive at the tiny lakeside marina around midday. The yacht is pea green too, and called *The Runcible.* It's a mammoth double-hulled ketch, with polished wood and brass everywhere. We lock everyone's phones and cameras in a safe. William gets up on the bow and claps his hands.

"Right," he says to the audience. "Thank you all for signing the no-shit-talking-agreement and handing over your phones, because this is the only time we get to be normal. This is the one week of the year we get to act like nothing's wrong."

I hand out drinks to everyone. "And I don't have to have a bloody bodyguard for Christ's sake..."

Hayden shoots me a look. "Love you too, Austen."

"Yes," Billy agrees. "For one week, Kane and Hayden are not our bodyguards, they are only our friends and guests, so if you are attacked by a bear, you're shit out of luck."

"Just let it eat me," I tell them.

"No more egg white and broccoli dinners, working out, no fucking study, and no sobriety," William says.

"You're not getting wrecked though, Bee," I say.

"Any worry or care," he continues, "any fucks that you have, you better leave them on the dock of the lake. They are too heavy to carry, and could sink the ship. This is the only serious rule. Any fucks smuggled on board may result in you being left behind on a distant shore." He holds up his drink. "I propose a toast; to indifference!"

"To indifference!" everyone cheers.

"Where to first?" Kane asks, as we head out.

"Northwest until we hit the narrow channel, and just follow the shore," I tell him. "I'm not sure if we should try the north arm." I look to the others. "It really depends what you guys want to do? We can access parts of Fiordland most people can never reach."

"I wouldn't mind a fishing expedition," Mischa says.

I am surprised. "You like fishing?"

"I do," he smiles at me.

"Have you been trout fishing before?"

"I spend most summers at my dad's dacha in Russia."

"I'm going hunting," William says. "I really need to kill something."

It's almost time for dinner when we stop in a small cove. Mischa inspects boxes of fresh produce. He holds up a head of cauliflower and looks at it, confused.

"Who brought the *vegetables*?" he asks.

Isobelle rolls her eyes. "*Boys*."

"William and I did. We're cooking this week. We're trained chefs."

He eyes us incredulously. "Really?"

"Yes," I say, annoyed. "I asked you for a job, remember? Our dad's a chef in New York and we work for him every summer. We even went to cooking school in Paris."

"I thought you're dad's a CEO?" Amelia asks.

"Our *other* dad," I groan. "The one we *like*."

"What about Daddy?" Isobelle asks.

"Other-*other* dad," I smile at her. "You can call anyone our dad and we'll only get offended if you're talking about the animal who married our momma."

"I'd call *you* Daddy before I ever called James Blazey that," Billy tells Mischa.

"Please don't do that," Mischa says.

He laughs, juggles some onions and throws one to me. "Let's show off."

The sun is drowning in the evening's blood-red glow. We make Tuscan butter scallops and scampi ravioli from scratch. Billy and I race each other through everything. Lightning fast chopping and dicing, laughing and occasionally bumping each other. We argue about techniques. I call him a lazy shit and he calls me prissy. The girls talk with each other and drink champagne. The guys watch the lake and the food being made.

We put the seafood dish in front of our guests. Amelia looks at it with dread.

"That's okay," she says, and tries to hand it back. "I'm not hungry."

"What's wrong?" I ask.

"I'm actually allergic to shellfish," she says.

"You didn't tell us."

"We're on a *lake,* I didn't think it would come up."

"A lake on an island," William says.

"Oh my God though," Mischa says, offering her his second ravioli, "try it anyway, it's worth dying for."

This happens sometimes. People try too hard to fit in with us, and don't speak up when they should. The last hour must have been awful for her. William and I look at each other and get back up.

"You're not allergic to Cognac and steak?" I ask.

"No," Amelia says.

"Medium rare?"

She smiles. "Please."

"Coming right up."

"I am also not allergic to that either," Mischa says.

"Order for two," I smile.

"Anyone else?" William looks over at the others. "Hayden, three? Kane, four? Girls? Okay, let's fucking go!"

William is happy, because the few things he enjoys most are messing with people, feeding people, and killing things. Not a good combination if you think about it.

The girls politely wait and drink wine while we cook. Mischa eats his scallops and pasta while loudly exclaiming its virtues.

"This is like, that *good* good like, *crazy* good," he says between chews. "You two are like *artists*."

"I like you," William tells Mischa, and all eyes shoot between them.

Then Mischa takes Amelia's abandoned plate, and scoops up her ravioli. At the same time he starts eyeing Billy's. If my brother eats it, he might spiral.

"Have William's pasta, Mischa," I tell him.

"What?" William shrieks.

"Billy can't eat it," I explain. "He's lactose intolerant."

He scowls. "*You're* lactose intolerant."

Mischa grabs the plate and holds a large ravioli between his fingers.

"This is for your own good, Billy Boy!" he says and drops it in his mouth.

William narrows his eyes at Mischa. "I take it back; I don't like you."

We take the pan of steaks and drown it in Cognac and light it on fire. The vapors make a *vwoompf* sound as they ignite in blue flames.

We put the firework in front of our guests and Mischa lays

his head on the table like he's worshipping it.

Everyone has had a few more drinks than us, and it shows. They ooh and ahh and giggle and drink more. It's been a long day. I want to get them fed.

Mischa presses his cheek into the table and looks up to the flames, smiling coyly.

"I love you," he says to the flambé, as if nobody can hear him. The girls howl with laughter. "I love you so much, I think my heart might explode. You're all I'm ever gonna want. All I'm ever gonna think about for the rest of time. I don't know if I'll ever find love like this again in this life."

"You boys have a fan," Sabrina tells us.

William laughs. "Thanks buddy."

"I'm not talking to *you*," Mischa tells him.

"He's talking to the *steak!*" Isobelle interjects.

I pour the flaming cream sauce for Mischa. He accepts it with reverence. Everyone goes quiet as they try their first bite and fall into deep contemplation.

"Yeah," Mischa moans, and drunkenly holds up his steak. "We are getting the fuck married."

The laughter starts up again.

"You can't marry a cow," Amelia says, her skin red from all the wine.

"Or me," Billy says.

"Don't trivialize my love!" Mischa points his steak knife at Amelia.

He reaches down with his other hand and tickles her exposed midriff and she yelps.

Amelia is convulsing with laughter and cries, "Shellfish, your hands!"

The whole table starts caterwauling. Mischa drops the knife and puts his hands up, horrified.

"Oh no!" Sabrina gasps.

"Sorry!" he yells, holding his face.

"We have a couple of those emergency pens," I tell her.

Amelia checks her stomach.

"Yeah," she says and sits up again. "Good idea."

Isobelle punches Mischa's arm. "Your fishy fingers are attempted murder on my new best friend!"

"Smooth, Mischa," Billy taunts him. "Real fucking smooth."

Mischa runs to the first aid kit, grabs a syringe and takes it to her. Everyone's eyes go wide.

"Stop!" Isobelle growls at him. "What the fuck are you doing?"

"Giving her the shot."

"That is for William," she says, so shrill that she coughs, "and Austen."

He looks around in confusion.

"It's insulin," Sabrina explains gently. "For their hypogly-cemia. It will put her in a coma."

I'm not sure Mischa believes it. I'm pretty fucking sure insulin is refrigerated. It's the stuff I have to knock my brother out and vice-versa.

Mischa looks at the needle in his hand as Sabrina takes it. Hayden gets the antihistamine pen from a bag and gives it to Amelia.

There's a welt on her side but she can't quite see it. Everyone settles back down to their meals and pretends not to notice Amelia's neck and chest is turning bright red and lumpy. Sabrina and Isobelle make quiet humming noises while they eat and try not to laugh. Mischa doesn't know where to look.

"Let's get you another shot," Sabrina suggests.

Amelia checks her side and sees the growing rash.

"What's the matter, Mischa?" she asks and raises an eyebrow. "Has something come up?"

The laughter starts up again. Even Hayden cracks a smile. Amelia takes her antihistamines, but it's still bad. Her lips and eyes balloon like she's been beaten.

"I'll call the helicopter," Hayden says. "Amelia can go to the hospital tonight, and fly back here tomorrow."

"The medical bill for this trip is off the bloody chart," Kane shakes his head. "Pain in the ass getting all the medicine through customs too."

Isobelle shakes her head. "Could everybody please stop fucking dying all the time."

"This is why we never go anywhere," Billy sighs.

Amelia's eyes swell shut. Hayden feeds her yogurt and guides her to the loungers. He wraps ice packs for her and she presses them to her neck and eyes.

After dinner, Mischa still has room for dessert, which is also set on fire with a flaming sauce. He eats too much of it, chugs two more drinks and gets sleepy. He sits on the seat beside Amelia. Soon he's resting on my shoulder.

William is entertained. "He's always falling asleep on people."

I shunt over to give him room, but I don't give him enough.

"Move," he croaks in a husky, tired voice. In his drowsy state, he puts his head on my lap and gets comfortable. "This is fine."

At once, he goes into a deep slumber. I look around for help but everybody is amused.

"It's so cute," Sabrina coos.

"I can move him if you want," Hayden offers.

"No," I say. "It's okay. He's probably exhausted after partying all week, nearly drowning, a night in the hospital, an early flight, a long drive, and a whole lot of food and alcohol. He can sleep on me."

Sabrina looks at us. "It's... you know..."

I nod in fascination. "I really don't mind for some reason."

"He's kinda like a really big puppy," William says, and then adds, "or a sweet guard-dog."

"Yeah," I smile, and pat his dark curly locks.

It's nice to pat him. I scratch under his chin and he squirms a little and stretches his hands, adjusting so his head is on my forearm as a pillow and his big arms wrap around me.

"Adorable!" Sabrina squeals.

Isobelle is enthralled. "Oh my god, Austen has a friend!"

"I have friends," I frown. "I have you, Kane and Hayden."

"An unpaid friend!"

"Let me draw you," William decides.

"No Billy, please."

He pulls out his sketchpad, and begins the outline. "The day is almost over, and I haven't done one yet."

"I'm borrowing your lap, Kitten," Isobelle says.

She finishes her drink and lays down, putting her head in Sabrina's lap.

"Can I put my head in someone's lap too?" Amelia asks. "I know I'm a monster right now but I'm feeling really fragile."

"You are beautiful inside and out, my love," Sabrina tells her.

"But only inside at the moment," Billy says.

I pick up a piece of ice from the bucket and throw it at him. He ducks.

"I mean I'd still *fuck* you..." Billy smiles, and Kane throws more ice at him, "but it would *have* to be doggy style."

Isobelle picks up a whole handful of ice and throws it at him.

"Ow!" he laughs.

"Thanks," Isobelle says. "That's fucking great."

Hayden goes to Amelia and places his lap under her head.

After a few minutes of drawing, William sighs. "I wish I could lie in someone's lap and have them feed me grapes, while others fan me with palm fronds."

"Sounds like deep down you want to be worshipped as a pharaoh," Isobelle says.

"I'd love to," he says, "and not deep down."

"Ask your employee to do it," Isobelle says. "Besides, he's the last lap left."

William looks at Kane. "That might be considered work-place harassment. Anyway, he's off the clock."

Kane grabs a bunch of grapes and brings them to Billy's mouth. Billy wraps his lips around one and bites it off the stem.

"Thanks," he tells Kane. "I'll take a raincheck on the rest until I finish this."

Billy finishes the sketch and puts the book away. The nocturnal chill is setting in. Sabrina grabs blankets from the blanket box and places one over Amelia, another for Isobelle, Mischa, then me. Billy wraps himself in one and lies his head on Kane. He makes sweet, fluttering eyes, and Kane scoffs and gets the grapes again, slowly lowering them to William for him to eat.

The helicopter arrives and it is extremely noisy. Mischa wakes up for only as long as the racket continues. He's groggy and blocking his ears, and really disoriented. The moment Amelia and Hayden leave, Mischa pulls me back onto the sofa and puts his head back in my lap and falls asleep again. It's very sweet and natural and makes me laugh. I throw a blanket on him, pat his hair and he starts making truffly little snores.

"Are we gonna set up the rest of the tents?" I ask Billy.

"Ah fuck it," he says. "We'll manage tonight without."

Soon I am drowsy. I lean back and close my eyes. When I open them again, it is very quiet, and still. The deep fjord is a natural amphitheater. The hoot of an owl reverberates from miles away. It's only me and Mischa left. Everyone else is inside. It's cold, so I move down and lie on my side, tucked in behind him. My movements wake him.

"The fox and the hare bid each other good night," he whispers.

He wraps my arms under the blanket and kisses my hands.

* * *

In the pale dawn light a beautiful mist hangs thick on the lake. The native birds make a dawn chorus of bubbling, chattering, alien noises. Kane and Billy get into hunting gears and strap on rifles. He finds me behind Mischa and nudges me awake.

"Alright, see you cunts later," Billy whispers.

I lift up a little from my cosy spot with the sleeping Heffalump. "When are we picking you up?"

"We're going straight to The Wilderness. Back for afternoon tea tomorrow. We got a flare and a mountain radio. Just be good, unless you don't want to." He looks at Mischa. "Maybe you can try him out. I bet he swings both ways."

I frown at him. "Excuse me?"

"It's Owl Week. You can do whatever the fuck you want. Kill him, and I'll help you bury the body. But I mean, if I *were* going to experiment, it would definitely be with a sexy beast like him. He's *hot*."

I watch Kane roll his eyes. I can tell Billy is only fucking with me, so I run my fingers through Mischa's dark curls.

"Yeah, now that you mention it... I *have* been thinking about it... a *lot*... and I am comfortable with him. Maybe it would be good..."

"I'm down," Mischa croaks, and stretches awake. "It's a *fabulous* idea."

"Woah, wait," William says, horrified. "Okay... that's alright, but I mean I wasn't being serious, but maybe that's not such a good idea. I don't want you in over your head while I'm gone. I can stick around here today... I have other..."

"Holiday rules, Bee," I yawn.

"I promise to be gentle," Mischa chortles.

Kane starts to snigger too.

"You're fucking with me?" he asks.

"Yeah," I laugh.

"You fucking asshole," Mischa shakes his head.

"Thank *fuck*. See ya!" He bends down and pats my head and kisses my temple. "I love you so much, little-big baby brother."

I lie back down. "I know. Be careful."

"Keep him safe," he tells Mischa, clipping his ear.

"Ouch! From *what?*" Mischa groans, and jabs Billy just above his crotch so he buckles a little. "Fucking *foliage?*"

William looks at the dense treeline. "Everything."

I listen to Billy's footsteps disappear into the forest, and fall asleep again. When I wake, Mischa's looking at me. He has rolled on his back, and tucked me under his shoulder. I have a tendency to cling on in sleep like a baby monkey, and I have done it to him.

My eyes are at half-mast. I stretch a little and my knee and inner thigh slide past his hard dick. It's intimate and unexpected, and makes tingles spark across me so fast I think he must feel them too.

He smiles with eager eyes. His pupils are huge. He squeezes me as he stretches too. It pulls my erection into his hip, and again agitates his middle. He reaches under my shirt and touches my skin on the small of my back.

"Morning," I smile, and run my finger down the side of his face.

He puts his fingers between my fingers, and pulls my body to his. I crane my neck up and I gravitate to him slowly, inch by inch, until my lips finally connect with his in a slow and intoxicating kiss. A wave of incredible feelings floods into me.

I feel like I'm a different person.

I feel like myself.

We take our time. We could keep doing this the whole day, but I need more. I squeeze his hard cock over his clothes, and his breath hitches. He moves me up so I'm on top, my legs around his hips. My face is just above his.

"Is this okay?" Mischa whispers.

"Mmm," I smile, putting my hands on his shoulders.

"Will the girls hear us?"

"I don't care if they do," I say.

I kiss him, rocking on his hips while I do, until we're start-ing to make nice little noises. He's trying to keep his breathing quiet, but I'm not.

"This feels good," I tell him.

"This is heaven," he agrees.

Mischa makes a groaning-moaning sound and flips me on my back and gets on top, and between my legs. We kiss and he holds my wrists above my head.

I look up at my hands.

This doesn't feel good anymore.

I start convulsing like a fish pulled to the shore, and scream for my brother in a guttural and reflexive shout.

"What's wrong?" he asks, releasing me.

I push out from under him and move back fast until I'm up against the external wall of the cabins. We both cover our-selves with blankets. My mouth is hanging open, catching my breath.

I am on a boat. The boat is on a lake. Deep in a forest. With a startled and confused boy. Who I don't want to ever speak to again.

There's a crashing sound from inside. Isobelle bursts out to the deck completely naked except for a small gun holstered to her ankle. She has the most beautiful body imaginable. Her curly red hair is covering her face, but her stage fright is obvious. She's been thrust on to center stage without warning. She turns to us like her waiting audience, flips her hair and composes herself. She's bleary-eyed, as if she were asleep seconds ago. She puts her game face on, and smiles like a minx. She clears her throat and strikes a pose like a Greek statue.

"Hoo-hoo," she hoots, like an owl.

Mischa is totally bewildered. I want to curl up and die, but the hoot makes me smile. She goes to the side of the boat and throws up. Most of it goes into the water, but the trail down the side of the boat has steam coming off it, like hot breath in cold air. Her ass looks amazing from this view. Then she wipes her mouth, gets back into the middle of the deck and strikes another luxurious pose, and hoots again. I break into a snigger. At the same time, I also want to die.

She begins singing the first few bars of an Edith Piaf song, *Non, Je Ne Regrette Rien.*

"No, nothing at all," she sings in French. Her voice is raspy. "No, I regret nothing." Then she changes the lyrics seamlessly. "Does the innocent speak French?"

I shrug a fraction with one shoulder and reply also in French. "I love your beautiful voice."

She steals a glance at me. "Where are you at?"

How distressed am I? I consider it. Not much. Humiliated? Twenty out of ten. I hold up two fingers.

"It's not fair," I say.

"I know, Baby," she nods. "What about my tits, good?"

"Of course."

"I think they were money well spent," she says, and hoots like an owl again. "Can I smash them in your face?"

"Maybe later," I tell her. "You are still a *little* intoxicated, my love."

"Lucky for you. Your girlfriend's tits are also available just inside. She loves you too."

I'm so embarrassed I feel like gagging. I get up and set out the fishing gear. I can't look at Mischa, and carry on as if he's not there.

Isobelle throws up again. Normally Sabrina and Isobelle only drink as a social lubricant at big events so they can't exactly keep up with Amelia and Hayden.

"I am never drinking again," she heaves, and goes back inside.

I take the melted water from the ice bucket and clean Isobelle's mess.

"You okay?" Mischa asks me.

I nod. "You still want to go fishing?"

18 MISCHA

That was, by far, the strangest interaction I've ever experienced. I don't know what the fuck that was. I think I spooked Austen. He said the safe word, Isobelle came to his rescue and... tried to... hoo-hoo like an owl and... threw up, sang in French... and squeezed her tits and tried to... have emergency sex with him?

No, I don't get it, but I feel *awful*. He was shaking and looked terrified.

We set out into the forest. He assures me we are taking a shortcut. I am quiet through the thick jungle. We reach a mossy clearing around which only shorter, thinner trees grow. Here, I stumble upon one of the great moments of my life. I take it in with awe.

It's sheltered, with a thick, low canopy, so it feels like we are inside, somewhere cosy. The lime green moss and orange lichen are like a garish retro carpet, the tree trunks like pillars of an old church. The warm glow of the day filters through the green, and a single shaft of light does indeed glint in Austen's eyes. He does listen to the sounds of the forest. I watch him for a while, then step forward on to a twig, which snaps. It does echo.

This is the moment I predicted the first day I met him. The

moment that I told my brothers would scare him away forever. The moment I ask what the hell that was back there with Isobelle. Or try to touch him. Or tell him I love him. Or ask for more and more details just like the ones I always hated giving. Tell him I fucking *understand*, my fucking god, the exact thing I hate hearing the most. All of it will make him bolt.

He moves to leave.

"It's beautiful here," I tell him. "Thank you so much for bringing me."

He stops. "I'm sorry I'm like this," he says.

"No, I'm sorry. I swear, I was only going to kiss you. Maybe some grinding. I feel like a total idiot."

"Nah." He shakes his head. "It was my own anxiety that screwed it up. I'm overwhelmed by it all. I mean, the whole point is to make it happen, right? But I'm just one step forward, two steps back. I'm totally ridiculous."

I shake my head. "It doesn't have to happen."

"I think I'm kinda using you to explore maybe some growing interest in this, because I trust you, and I really do like you, but I'll never be who you want."

"You'll always be who I want." I hold the back of my neck. "I just forget that it's me in love with you, not you who's in love with me, and then stuff like that happens and I'm horrified at myself, again."

"You didn't do anything wrong. You can touch me a little without spooking me and it gives me hope, so I go with it, even though we'll never have a future. I know it's selfish, and I know you want me for real, but you need me out of your system desperately, so I'm trying to get you through this and not hurt you. It's just a lot to have on my shoulders, you know?"

"Eh," I smile. "That's my problem, you don't need to sacrifice yourself for my misery. If it's not meant to be, then it's not meant to be. We shouldn't force it. It's making me feel delusional, like you want this, but it sounds like you don't. So many people have done it to me. Not just lovers but even random people who decided we're fated to be. I've taken pity on them and let them have their way sometimes too. Fucked a few of them. It just adds fuel. Now I'm just like them, reading into every look you give me. Love makes you literally crazy. When someone's obsessed with you and you're not, it's just annoying."

He scratches his ear. "It's a little stressful, because I'm not capable of it, but I'm torn because I like you so much as a friend. I wish I could, I'm sorry, but I tried twice, and I can't."

"It's okay. I hate what happened this morning. I hate this version of me. I hate being so desperate and pathetic, and so out of control too. I want to be over this already. I want to be out of love with you. I want to stop harassing you to make it work. I want you to leave you in peace. I thought we could have a crack at it while we were away and get past it when we got home. I'm going to try to get past it now."

"Okay," he says. "Do you want to be my best friend?"

My eyes feel a hot mist, but I breathe in the cool forest air and let it go. "Yes. I'll take the friend-zone."

"Good," he sighs, "because I'd die if I lost you."

I have conceded defeat. "And I'd die for you," I tell him. "But you know... we're probably not compatible that way anyway."

He hugs me, and we continue on our journey, as friends.

We stop making noise when we hear water moving ahead. We get in our waders and arrange our gear. The fly hooks are little works of art. The box sparkles like a cabinet of small tropical creatures. Colorful bugs and feathery moths, all tied with silk to sharp little hooks. They are all made with such care and precision. I choose one the same color as Austen's eyes.

The eight-and-a-half foot fishing rods are as light as feathers. I hold mine out and it quakes ever so slightly from the motions of my muscles, and the blood pumping to my fingers. It's bendy, and bound in stripes of gold and red silk thread for strength along the pole.

The first stop is a canyon. It's ancient and silent and teeming with fish. There's nowhere to wade across to, so we work on the same side of the water. There are thick trees right behind us, so we can't throw the line back to get some distance for our casts. I think Austen is testing me. I work enough line above me in a long ribbon back and forward. Flinging it in a short arc. This way takes a lot of power in your arms. I have spent years practicing this, and picking up ballerinas, so I make it look effortless. The line shoots far across the river and the fly lands in the water without a splash.

I toss Austen a pointed look. His eyes are wide and his mouth presses tight to hide a smile, but I see he's thrilled. He makes a sideways cast, sending his fly under an overhanging beech tree opposite.

I want to enjoy this for hours but soon I hook something big, and so does Austen. We catch two magnificent rainbow trout and admire them. He unhooks them back into the creek. They shoot away and we move on.

"You're better than me," Austen says. "I'm impressed and depressed at the same time."

Around a bend we reach a wider gorge with a few water-holes and he passes me to reach the far one. I fire off my line, but I don't hear him cast his. I look behind and he is just watch-ing me. Looking at him, I know things I cannot know. My eyes tell me what I want to believe. I love looking at him, so I look at him, and he looks at me. My lying eyes tell me he loves looking at me too, but it's not true. Then it's just the bubbling sound of the cool water that runs between us. Between friends. Just friends. He owes me nothing. Nothing. I made this painful.

We catch some more fish and let them go. Sabrina and Isobelle don't like trout, Austen explains. We venture further up the valley and the river is different again. It has spread out over a wide braid of waterways and islands. We head to an elbow that backs up to a cliff, and is deep in parts.

Austen whips the line over his head, making it whistle back and forth. He pulls it back and snaps the little fly far off into an interesting pool. I follow further down and we wait. His line hooks and he starts reeling it in, but it's big. I get the net and lift a king salmon out of the water. It's huge, at least sixty pounds, but Austen looks sad.

"Do you eat fish?" he asks.

"Not so much now," I say. "My grandmother used to go down to the beach and a fisherman would come to the shore and all the women of her village would buy fish straight from the boat. Now it's not so fresh, so I don't. If you cook that, it'll be the first fish I've eaten in ages."

"The girls eat salmon. We should take it back for them."

Now I see why he's sad.

"I think it's undersized," I tell him, just before he takes the spike to iki the big bastard. "You can't take it. It's too small. It's illegal."

"Huh?"

"It's okay," I say, and unhook the fish. "I can tell you're not the best at this, but I will hook a decent sized one."

I throw it back in the water and we keep going. By the afternoon he catches a seventy pound monster.

"Pretty good," I say, "for you."

We hear the helicopter dropping Amelia and Hayden off. I gut and clean the fish and we call it a day. Back at the boat Hayden and the girls have been having a lot of fun without us. Drinking, swimming, playing, and bonding like functional people do. All three girls are completely naked, floating in the water like sirens. Hayden has on board shorts.

"Isobelle started it. She's been starkers all afternoon," Hayden tells us, with a cheeky grin. "I have been averting my eyes, I swear."

"It was our gift to the helicopter pilot," Isobelle says, making angel wings in the water.

Austen cooks the salmon, Amelia pours the wine. Hayden puts up the tents along the lakeside. They are far away from each other. He says they are far enough away so we won't have to hear each other having sex, if the occasion should arise.

"If you want to have a bonfire," he advises, "do it away from my tent, because I'm asthmatic."

"Don't you smoke weed?" Amelia frowns.

Hayden glares at her. "A joint is so much smaller than a bonfire."

Sabrina and Isobelle turn in early.

Amelia and Hayden do the dishes and leave for their tents. I play guitar quietly on the deck and Austen listens as the late summer sun sets. After a few songs I decide to turn in. I head down to my tent.

In my delusional mind, Austen seems surprised he will not be sleeping next to me.

* * *

We do yoga in the morning with the girls. Then Austen and I head out to fish again. It's a very hot day. We wade into a cool, tree-lined crevasse just off the main river. We hear an enormous boom in the distance, then another. The black darts vanish from the river as the noise spooks them.

"They must be close, Kane and William," I say.

Austen agrees. "They mustn't have caught anything. Billy doesn't quit until something is dead."

Twice more we find a spot and the shotguns go off. It seems almost like clockwork. Another hour goes by and BOOM!

"GODDAMMIT BEE!" Austen screams up the serene valley. "YOU ARE SCARING THE FISH!"

"Let's go spend time with the girls," I laugh.

We come back empty-handed and they boo us. Austen swims in the cool mountain lake with the others. I stay in the shallows because I have a burst eardrum, and the doctor said I can't.

"William and Kane are late," Austen says, near sunset. "They are returning from near the snowline," he frowns. "An alpine grass field called The Wilderness. Billy never comes back until he kills something."

He tries the radio and gets the cabin in the mountains. The hikers staying there go check the book for us, and Will and Kane left at dawn. They should be back by now.

We collect driftwood and pile it up far downwind from Hayden's tent. We light it after dark and Austen looks to the hills.

"They should have been back hours ago."

"They are less than a mile away," I insist. "Their gunshots stopped us fishing. If they had been on the shore we might have seen them, they were that close."

✳ ✳ ✳

At Midnight Austen tries the radio again with no luck. It's a beautiful clear night and we watch the mountains. Then I see it. A flare, over the peaks.

"There!" I point.

"What does that mean, though?" Amelia asks.

"It's a distress signal," Austen says. "They're up in the Alpine Pass. It's freezing up there."

"Why don't they use the radio?" Hayden asks.

"How far away are they?" I ask.

Hayden shrugs. "About twenty miles."

"How is that even possible?"

"They must have been so turned around, they've been walking *away* from us all day," Austen says.

"Well let's go!" I say, and grab a jacket.

"What? No," Hayden says. "It's too dark. We'll call it in for Air Rescue to deal with. I promise you, Billy is staying put, and knows we are too. We'll go at first light if we have to, and we're gonna need sleep for this."

Isobelle looks at him. "You're not supposed to give a fuck."

"This is different. I always give a shit about stupidity. We're in a forest bigger than Switzerland; I'd actually prefer my chances with a needle in a haystack. Everyone needs to go to bed."

"I can't *sleep*," Sabrina says.

"You should," Hayden tells her. "It'll be okay. We'll start early."

They girls see sense. Austen gets up and hugs Sabrina and Isobelle and the two head inside.

Hayden calls Search and Rescue and tells us to sit tight.

Then he and Amelia leave for the long walk to their tents further down the lake.

Austen grabs blankets and beds down on deck. I get up to leave and he grabs my wrist.

"Are you okay?" I ask.

Austen doesn't look at me. "Yes," he says. "I'm fine."

"I should go," I tell him.

"Stay," he says.

"I can't."

"Stay. You're my best friend. Stay."

Austen nestles into my arms and I hold him.

"Okay," I relent.

We make an impromptu bed on the lounge set. We lie down and watch the stars.

"Do you think he'll be okay?" Austen asks.

"He was just over the river a few hours ago. How much trouble could he be in?"

"Maybe it was someone else."

"He's part of you," I say. "Does he feel gone?"

"Not at all," he says. "I feel his heart beating close by. He's just around that bend, fast asleep, all cuddled up warm and content. I keep trying to wake him and he keeps saying he's tired, and telling me to fuck off."

"Sounds like him."

"But I'm probably imagining that and my life is about to be over."

We lie in silence. Then Austen looks at me.

"What?" I ask.

"How long do you think it's gonna take to get over me?"

I sigh. "Some days I'm more optimistic than others. Especially as I loved you even after I drowned and crossed over to the afterlife. But not in a *gay way*," I sneer. "As a *best friend*."

Austen guffaws and I do too.

"What if I kill myself, I mean, you know, if Billy dies?"

"Then I'll never get over you."

"I'm going to miss you," Austen says, "when you hate me. I'm going to miss you and I'll never admit it. But not in a *gay way*."

"Whatever it is, is it really that bad?"

"Depends who you ask."

"I won't then."

Austen scoffs. "*Yeah.*"

"Whatever you did."

"I didn't do anything, but if you ask I'll say I did."

"Why?"

"Because the truth is worse."

He turns on his side to me, and I turn to him. He curls into me and I put my arms around him and kiss the top of his head and rub his back. We stay like this for a long time and I know neither of us is getting any sleep. In the sheltered silence of the amphitheater, I hear a shifting sound that crunches more and more like footprints as it gets closer. We get up and look along the shore.

"Sabrina!" Austen calls. "Isobelle!"

There's a flashlight getting closer. When it gets close enough, Austen shines his torch and the light hits Hayden's face and he flinches, then shields his eyes.

"Look what I found," Hayden says.

"Hi baby," William says.

The light goes to him. He's carrying a deer on his back. Kane is behind him with a wild boar.

"Thank God," Sabrina sighs.

Austen wails and climbs over the side of the boat. He can't reach the rock, so he just drops from the boat into the water. He is talking and I can't understand a word of it.

"What is that?" I ask Isobelle.

"Creepy twin language," she shakes her head.

Austen is up to his armpits wading over. He falls on William. The weight of the pack, the deer, and Austen makes him stagger. Kane helps him take it all off while Austen sobs uncontrollably. Will tries to pull Austen back together as he comes undone.

"No no no, baby," William shushes him and says something indecipherable. "It's okay, it's okay, it's okay."

"Where did you find them?" Isobelle asks Hayden.

"My tent," Hayden says, a little too dryly.

Oh shit, I think he caught them.

"Honestly, we were only going to have a nap," Kane says. "We were so tired we never woke back up."

"The flair?" Sabrina asks.

"That wasn't us," Kane tells them. "I think it was the other hunters we passed. The chopper will be looking for them. You might have saved their lives."

A few minutes later the rescue helicopter roars past on its way to the mountain. Everyone at our camp is excited, nobody wants to go straight back to bed; there's a lot of conversation to be had.

Austen's still beside himself, relieved, but hysterical. Soaking wet too and refusing to be pulled away from William, so we smother him in blankets. It's William's job to calm him down while the rest of us have hot chocolate. He's gulping for air with a nose blocked with tears. William finally pulls him in like I had done. Austen curls up into him like he had with me, and spasms with sobs. Will kisses him on the head and Sabrina puts another blanket over him. Soon, Will holds up two fingers like a peace sign to Isobelle just like Austen did yesterday morning, but then swirls his index finger. She nods and goes inside and gets Austen a small juice. We all already have drinks, but Austen drinks it, and soon passes out. I'm going out on a limb here to assume she spiked the drink and Austen took it willingly.

The helicopter flies back overhead. After that everyone turns in for the night. I don't want to leave Austen alone, even though William is beside him. Kane beds down nearby, so his head is near theirs. I take the other couch.

Kane and William have a few words with one another after lights are off.

"I feel like such an idiot," I hear William say.

✻ ✻ ✻

I wake up in the middle of the night to pee. When I lie back down, I hear a soft scratching. I think it's like, an animal or something. I turn the torch on and point it to the noise. Kane is sleeping, Austen is sleeping, but where's William? The noise is gone. I move the light around and jump out of my skin when I see Will, sitting in the corner, holding a sketchbook and pencil.

"Jesus!" I jump. "Will?" I change to a whisper, "What are you doing?"

"Drawing," he says.

He's not looking at the paper, he's staring ahead. It was

fucking pitch black a minute ago. I wave my hand in front of his face. He's sleepwalking. Sleep-drawing. What a freak.

"What... what... what... are you drawing?"

"William."

"Can I see?"

He lets me take it from his hands. I look at the picture of Austen. In the picture he's with the Koala. I flip back. Some evil, hollowed-out eyes in heavy black and crimson pen... then an old building... there's one of Sabrina, naked, but tasteful. An artistic study of her. The next page is her too, naked again, lying down, looking up, biting her lip, and in the next one her mouth is open and screaming with her face in a pillow like oh my God William is fucking Sabrina.

The sketchbook is snapped away from me and I jump again. Kane closes it and puts it on the sofa.

"Time for bed," he tells Will, then lies him down on top of the pictures. "You never saw that," he tells me.

Jesus. I can never *unsee* that.

19 AUSTEN

My mouth tastes like metal in the morning and my head is throbbing. Honey is beside me. The top of Kane's head is butting the top of my head.

I don't have much energy, so I lie around and read books. The girls swim and lounge around too. Hayden has left camp for a long walk.

Amelia and Mischa are at the table with a pack of cards playing Speed. It's fun and boisterous and competitive. They are slamming cards down and laughing and arguing, occasionally tickling and wrestling. A lot of touching. They're frisky like kittens; their playfulness has them both in stitches.

I watch it with envy. It's far more amusing than anything I could provide, if Mischa was forced to keep my company. He doesn't look at me all day. He only looks at the girls, a lot. Sabrina the most. I think he's lost interest, at last. Maybe me crying like a little baby last night left him disgusted with me. I could understand if it did.

My brother makes me spar with him. I am angry, and I take it out on the boxing pads. My mind runs off somewhere else. We're dripping with sweat soon enough, I'm pummeling the life out of him so fast he can't keep up. Everyone starts watching. Mischa offers to go a few rounds and Kane steps in.

"Austen is kinda… scary good," Kane explains.

"I see that," Mischa says.

"He only spars with Will. It's a safety thing."

Hayden makes a bonfire. We spit-roast the boar. I can't eat. After dark we watch the flames like they are television.

Amelia and Mischa sit together. It seems like they are on the cusp of coupling up. I feel homicidal. My jealousy is selfish and hypocritical, but can't be helped. The wind changes and Hayden and I get a burst of smoke from the fire. He decides he needs his inhaler, and goes back to the boat. I get away from the plumes and move closer to Mischa.

Kane is exhausted, and says goodnight. He lays his blanket on me and Mischa before he goes. He puts it over our front and I move over. I'm now almost as close to Mischa as Amelia is. I shuffle over more, and now I am closer. I put my hand under the blankets, against his leg. He looks alarmed, then puts his hand on my tailbone. I try not to smile.

"I love star gazing," he says. "There was a night when I was younger I realized that I was so poor and so hungry that I had nothing but my sister and the stars in the night sky. Luckily they were the two most beautiful and precious things in the world."

"How were you poor?" Isobelle asks. "Aren't you a rich Russian guy's kid?"

"My dad found me when we were refugees in Austria."

"Where were you before that?" Billy asks.

Oh God, here we go.

"We're from Yugoslavia. There was a war that tore the place apart from the time I was a baby. It would die down in one place and ignite in another. We were sent to our aunt, but she was blown to pieces by a precision missile."

Isobelle and Sabrina look at me and William, but we don't give anything away. We listen quietly.

"So what are you?" Amelia asks. "I mean, where exactly are you from? What side were you on?"

"I never picked a side."

"No, but really though," she prods him.

"Does it matter?"

"What do you mean?"

"There's only one reason people ask that, to decide if I had it bad, if they like 'my side', to judge how much me and my people deserved it. I was eleven when I fled. Children don't get to choose sides, but they do get to be target practice."

"I..." she stutters. "I just..."

Mischa slides his other hand into mine and we weave our fingers together.

"When we get back to civilization, you'll do research, pick a side you feel was somehow the biggest victims, and if that's not what you think my side is..."

"No I..."

"And I can't say I wasn't on a side, because mixed people were targets of everyone and if that were really true I'd be dead like my friends. I saw dead kids from all *sides*. I just thought adults must be *insane*. My adopted dad was the first grownup I ever trusted except for my parents. I'm only on my own side."

William whispers to Sabrina and she nods. Then he decides to leave for bed with Isobelle. He's trying not to seem rattled, but he is.

"I don't mean to upset you, Will," Mischa tells him.

"Not at all," he shakes his head, but won't look at Mischa. "I'm just tired."

"I don't blame anyone; I'm not bitter. I can't live like that."

He doesn't know what to say in response. I can feel the girls shift into protective mode. Sabrina comes over and sits at my side.

Isobelle steps in front of Billy.

"That's a good way to look at things," she tells Mischa.

Isobelle leaves her blanket with Amelia, but doesn't take her eyes off Mischa.

My brother looks up at the sky. "I'm sorry about your aunt."

Mischa shrugs. "It's best not to feel guilty or angry, Will. Children do not share the guilt of their parents. I wouldn't want them to think that, no matter what their fathers did."

He quietly nods. "No."

Billy looks relieved. Mischa handled all of that beautifully. All of my fears and worries about him start to lift. I watch the worry lift off Sabrina and Isobelle too. If I did fall completely in love with Mischa, it would be right now. I won't, but if I did, I would be his, for life, from this moment on. It won't happen, but maybe we can actually get through this without a total meltdown from my brother.

Billy takes Isobelle's hand. "Your turn to get naked for me tonight?"

"You want to draw me like one of your French girls?" she asks.

"Amongst other things," he says.

It is tense and quiet after they leave.

"I'm sorry about asking," Amelia says. "I didn't mean to offend you."

"It's okay. I'm not angry with you. It's natural to look for answers for something you don't understand."

I rub the small of his back, under his shirt.

Sabrina is a quiet one, but a master in tact, and changes the subject.

"I'm going to wish on the next shooting star," she says and looks at Mischa, "and you can have the next one."

One blips past.

"Your turn, Mischa."

Another star shoots towards the horizon.

"Time for bed," Sabrina says.

She kisses me goodnight and mouths to me, asking if I'm okay. I nod. I'm fine.

"I love you," she tells me, then extends her hand to Amelia. "Come on, I'll walk you back."

Amelia takes her hand and turns in for the night.

"I think I just got my wish," Mischa says.

I sigh. "I think you know what I wished for."

We both laugh at the idea.

"All of that was very uncomfortable."

We laugh again.

"I know it's not her fault either," he says. "I try to remember that it's not easy to relate to."

"Be charitable to us running-dog capitalist Westerners. We're not as worldly as we think we are."

Mischa smiles. "I'm also in a weird mood too. I kind of wish you had let me die on Bondi."

"My apologies," I say flatly. "I'll try to remember that for next time."

"Like I said, weird mood."

"Why do you want to be dead?" I ask.

"I think my father's not alive."

"You think but don't know?"

"I didn't know he was dead until Friday. He was on the beach talking to me when I was unconscious. I asked him if he was dead and he said he was."

I pause a moment. "When you weren't breathing on the beach you saw him?"

"Yeah," Mischa says. "A disturbing jolt of news to receive when you are about to die."

"Maybe the fact that you were hallucinating is part of a near-death experience?"

"I thought about that, but it doesn't matter because it feels real. My father is either dead, or it was a delusion of my brain being starved of oxygen. Whether or not he is, sooner or later it will be true."

"I sometimes lose my connection to my surroundings when I get stressed," I explain. "It's usually only a few moments. My head flies away to other places. I know it's not healthy and definitely not wanted. The point is you went through something awful. I know how awful it is to be outside of your own body, in a dream, from a distance, and everything seems unreal."

"What had happened felt real, and like an incredible burden."

"One thing we all have to accept is the certainty of death."

"Some more than others," he says.

"True."

"I just don't think I can ever make this thing right again."

I look at his eyes, staring at the fire.

"What thing?" I ask.

"My life."

"You've had a rocky couple of years. Stability is not everything, but everything is nothing *without* stability. Give yourself time."

"Maybe," he smiles. "But you make solid ground feel a little impossible. I mean, why are you even letting me hold your hand?"

"I don't know," I say. "Maybe you wore me down, maybe it's a mind-trick, maybe it's the wine. I'm definitely jealous of Amelia getting closer to you, but maybe it's just because I wanted to remember what it's like to be touched."

"Do you like it?"

I shrug. "It's nice, I guess."

The fire is dying down.

"I never expected this," Mischa says. "Never expected my heart to break like a regular mortal. I've never had to hunt for affection. Most people show an interest in me, yet I've been hit so hard by some overwhelming force from outside of the physical world that now I'm drowning. Now I wish you could cut open my chest and tear out my heart to stop the pain. I told Amelia that I want to take it slow, but I think she wants it to be soon. I don't exactly want to follow you around like a lost puppy forever. I don't want to impose if it's really not what you want... I just think I should tell you, because I don't want all my desperate moves to sound like pressure, and I'm trying to be the only one that gets hurt in this."

I have a plummeting feeling in my stomach. "Same."

"But if there is any chance... literally any hope that you would... I don't mind waiting. I will wait or I'll go with Amelia tonight and you'll never hear from me again."

"Don't miss out on account of me—I'm not going to stop you. You owe me nothing. Go with her if you want."

"I don't want. I have known so little real want in my life. But the few things I have ever wanted, I want so much they torment me. It has all been eclipsed by the want for you. You burn me. It's charring my insides; I feel like any second it will burn through my skin and I will become nothing if I can't have you. I want you beyond words. What do *you* want?"

I stay quiet and stare at the fire, feeling for words in the darkness. He bared his soul to me, yet my soul does not reply.

"*Want* is a strange way to put it," I say, finally.

He huffs in frustration. "Need. Yearning. Pining. Aching.

Fucking aching. I ache for you and if I can't have you I will never be whole," there's pain in his voice. "Kiss me and I will never kiss anyone else. Hold me and I'll never hold anyone else."

I do not kiss him. I do not hold him. My soul remains silent. His face is frozen in the warm orange glow while he waits. He sighs and takes my hand off of his.

"You're going?" I ask.

"It's time to get some sleep; it's very late," he sighs.

He puts out the fire. The galaxy above us becomes bright and milky. We both stare at the brilliant night sky for a moment.

Not a word.

Can my soul be dead?

"Come on," he says.

He reaches his hand to me, and pulls me to my feet. I stand there, holding his hand until he drops it.

"You are going to Amelia?" I ask.

"I think I'm going... to bed... with her. For my own sanity. There's no privilege in having someone you don't want... wanting you. No matter how much I want you..." he sighs, defeated. "Good night, Austen."

My hand grabs the back of his top. I don't know why it's doing that.

He stops, but I don't have the courage to move. He steps around and I let him bring his face to mine. I put my lips on his mouth, slowly and softly until he breathes in sharply, and parts my lips with his own. He puts his hands in my hair and mine go to his face. Our tongues touch and I breathe in sharply again. It's like an earthquake is rumbling under my ribs. We press ourselves together and are enclosed in the warmth of our bodies.

His kisses become hungrier and harder, until we take a breath that we had both been holding. I can feel the flood of emotion welling inside me. I'm not fighting it. He's not holding back. His ache for me is being soothed. In the kiss is the promise that there is something there, that the ice will melt, and he will have me. I don't know why I am misleading him like this.

While we kiss I let him work his hands up my spine under my shirt, massaging the tension all the way down from the back of my neck. I let out a groan and push my pelvis harder into his, so I feel how hard he is under his pants. I look at his black silhouette in the dark. Even his outline is beautiful. My head nods automatically, but I don't know what it's agreeing to. In the heat of the moment he drops to his knees and nuzzles at my middle. It surprises me.

"What are you doing?" I ask.

"I need you in my mouth," he says.

"No no no..." I step back. "You're a little drunk. I don't want anything bad to happen."

"Alright," he agrees.

He gets up and kisses me once more, softly and sweetly.

"Sorry," I say. "I don't know what I'm doing. Why I did that, why I'm doing this. I'm so sorry, it's not..."

"No. Don't be sorry," Mischa sighs. "It's okay. I'm an idiot. Let's just forget about it. We should head back."

Then he takes my hand and leads me back to the boat, sleeps near me, but he won't speak another word.

20 MISCHA

We are only a day away from heading back to America. There are things bubbling away that don't seem right.

The big one is that I didn't notice Will and Sabrina, and I ALWAYS see that shit from a mile away. I *still* don't notice even the tiniest frisson between them. I just can't see it. I have seen some suggestive drawings, and a look of deep love from William for Sabrina; evidence going against my gut feeling. I should have seen more. I see way more tension between William and *Kane*, but apparently I am completely wrong; Kane's not having an orgasm in William's sketchbook, she is.

Something is weird today, and everyone is pretending it isn't. Firstly, Austen loves me, and I love him. I can hide my feelings, but Austen? Not so much. He's started staring at me, a little. I've barely looked at him the last two days, turning my attention strategically to the girls. Amelia in particular. When I even turn my head her way Austen fixates on us.

When Amelia goes to bathe, Austen sits beside me on the sofa. I am talking to his girlfriend, the one he's supposed to fucking marry or whatever, Sabrina, and he does that yawn-stretch thing where you casually put your arm over someone's shoulders. Sabrina stops talking mid-sentence. Kane is there too, with his coffee mug to his face, and he just freezes, watching. I look at Austen, and lean into it. He adjusts immediately to make it less intimate, then scratches his head, as I figured he would. I just laugh and return to my conversation with Sabrina, and she manages to brush it off like it didn't happen either. I offer him berries from the bowl, and then offer them to Sabrina too.

To the others, I must seem confused by his attention. Sabrina is not threatened, and Will is the only one who hasn't noticed jack shit.

Will's in his own world. That's the real weirdness. The guy is back to giving me the creeps. He won't speak to any of us all morning. His sudden change in personality is overshadowing whatever melodrama is happening around him.

Austen is off balance too. I think they've both stopped eating. Will only ate a little meat yesterday, and now it's just water and kick-boxing. We have not been over-indulging, but maybe they're just ultra healthy. I don't know. I don't understand what fuels this whole dynamic. I want to figure these people out before the holiday ends, and I want to win Austen. For real.

Isobelle pulls Austen outside when she thinks nobody is paying attention. I go stand by the closest window to listen in on them.

"Can you talk to him?" she asks Austen.

"I have been talking to him," Austen tells Isobelle.

"Where is he?"

"By the lake."

"Are you arguing?"

"No, he's not freaking out; just having a break so that he *doesn't* start freaking out."

"Can we all talk to him, together?"

"I guess, if we can get some privacy. Maybe we can wait till after we fly back. It's not like we can look into it right now."

They come back in, and I go out with the binoculars and search the shoreline, just in case they are talking about someone else. Just in case it's something even weirder than my imagination. There's nobody here but us.

Austen takes Amelia and Hayden down the river to skip stones after lunch. He wants me to come but I'm too busy observing his brother. After a while watching, go to Will and wave my hand in front of his face while he's organizing shelves. He doesn't notice.

I touch Will's arm and he stops.

"You okay hun?" I ask.

Isobelle, Sabrina and Kane stare at us, concerned.

"I'm fine, sugarplum."

I rub his back. "Yeah? You want to have a swim?"

His pupils are all black and wild-eyed. William looks at me with those far away eyes and shakes his head. He leans into me and I wrap my arms around him and pat his back.

"I don't want to hurt you," he whispers.

I recoil from him. I look to the others, momentarily frozen in fear. Kane taps Isobelle and she grabs a book from the shelf and takes Will away to "lie down". I look at Sabrina confused, and she fixes her eyes on her cup of tea.

When Austen comes back he already seems to know what happened. Like he's worried for me. Will snaps out of it by lunchtime, and is perfectly fine.

"I'm bored," Will says, acting normal, "let's shoot guns."

Kane sets up targets along the lake. We use them for practice. I don't know if I should show my gun skills or not, so I hang back. Hayden and Kane have military training, and they are very good with the weapons, but Austen and William are better than anything I've ever seen, and I'm in the motherfucking *mafia and* I was in a *war*. What the fuck? I don't hide how impressed I am. Austen suggests they show off their sniper skills.

"No," William shakes his head, and looks at me. "Let's not. Let's play paintball in the forest. Dragons against the innocents."

"You can't be on the same team as William," Isobelle tells William. "It's not fair. He should be on *their* team."

"*Austen*," I correct her. "You're *talking* to *William*."

Her eyes bug at him, and he stifles a smile.

"Sorry, *honey-bee*," she tells William, almost mockingly, giving him a sneering smile.

"Don't even recognize your own *boyfriend*..." he shakes his head.

"Whatever," she huffs. "Me, you, Sabrina, plus Kane, versus Amelia, our *lil baby-bee* Austen, Hayden, and Mischa."

Will laughs. "Still not balanced."

We get into camouflage and load up the paint rifles and designate the flat forest area on the near side of the lake as the paintball field. The other team heads off to the far end.

"Woodsball basics," Austen says when we get into a huddle. "Don't stay in one spot for too long. Paintballs tend to drop, so aim high. Never go after Will, that's my job. He's already coming for you, probably ditched the others already and is halfway here by now. Be quiet and hidden, and if you get past him, call out his position and coordinate together. I'll go this way, because I want to head him off. You two follow Hayden and go through the dense area around the back, set up an ambush."

Hayden and Austen lock eyes and my sixth sense wakes up. Hayden nods obediently, and Austen heads down to the wide uncovered area by the shoreline, like that doesn't make him an open target. Hayden leads me and Amelia through the thick underbrush and we start spreading out.

The moment my babysitter loses sight of me, I bolt. I hear Hayden call for me but I'm gone. I rush deep into the other team's territory and nobody is there to take me out. I see some old tracks and head to higher ground. I can't find them, until I hear one of the girls screaming. I go down the slope until it meets a sheer drop. I still can't see them but I hear them.

"Kitten stop!" I hear Will yell. "I'm sorry!"

I think there's a cave below, because she pops out of the granite wall. She turns and aims her paintball-gun at William. She's crying.

"Fuck off," Sabrina says, and fires a round at him.

I hear William go, *"Oof!"*

I don't know what happened, but this is so fucking funny. I am so happy to be here while this unfolds.

Sabrina puts her mask back on and sprints off. Isobelle runs after her, but then turns back to Will.

"Nice one, asshole," Isobelle spits. "You made it sound like she was the scum of the earth, and naturally evil, just for being *born*."

"It wasn't supposed to sound like that."

"Well it did," she says, and fires at him as well.

I hear Will take the hits. Kane comes out of the cave now too, looking pissed too. Seems like their huddle went bad.

"I didn't mean…" Will starts.

"Oh honey," Kane shakes his head, and fires at him, "you totally meant it."

He leaves, and Will staggers into view covered in paint, looking small after his whole team has turned on him. He slumps on to a rock. Austen follows behind.

Fraternizing with the enemy? What a traitor.

"You want to shoot me too?" Will asks Austen.

"I do, but I need to save the ammo for the game." Austen sits with Will and puts his arm around him. "I hated to hear you say it like that, but even though it all sounds ridiculous, I agree with you."

"Glad someone does," William shakes his head.

"I'm sorry," Austen says. "I should have said something, but the girls had arrived, and I was distracted. Do you think it could be possible?"

Will thinks about it. "Mischa seems like a good guy. Not malicious or anything. I think he's coming from a genuine place."

"Well," Austen shrugs, "we have terrible luck, and James *is* a total monster. I really hope it's not the case, but we don't know what we don't know. We should proceed with caution until we *do* know."

James, their father. Oh shit, I think Austen told Will my theory that Sabrina is their sister. They must be so fucking nervous. Austen is about to get out of a lifetime of misery for the cost of one

DNA test. He's lucky I said something.

"I'll be discreet," Will says. "No matter what the outcome, this stays between us."

"Thanks."

"But if it's true, I'm really going to kill James."

"It's not true," Austen huffs. "It's just a theory."

"I do think he's very sweet," Will says.

"Who?"

"Mischa," Will nods. "He's a sweetheart... quite good looking too. Ridiculously handsome, actually."

He's not wrong.

Austen is at a loss for words. "You find him attractive?"

"Yes," Will says gazing at the trees, and it's clear that he's just thinking out loud. "I mean, no. He just *is* attractive. Objectively speaking. From an unbiased perspective, he's very sexy. And very endearing. Surely you don't have to be gay to be attracted to him?"

Um what?

Austen takes his arm off Will and turns to look at him. "Okay..."

Will is getting uncomfortable. "I'm not attracted to guys, but if I *was* attracted to guys, he might be the kind of guy..."

Stop being weird, William.

"You're making it sound like you are."

DARK STARS IN THE SKY

"No, I'm not. He would just be my type, if I *was.* I mean someone *like me* would find him very tempting."

"Someone like you? What does that mean? You mean me?"

"Obviously not *you*," he scoffs.

"There's nobody more like you than me."

"It'd never even cross your mind," he rolls his eyes. "I mean a guy *like* me, but not me. Who would blame a guy *like* me for finding him hot? It's understandable. He's obviously very cute..."

"Cute?" Austen sneers.

I am so disgusted, I want to shower immediately.

"Empirically, I mean."

Austen looks horrified. "*Empirically* cute for a *guy like you*?"

William is going bright red, and starts to sound panicked.

"You're getting this all wrong; I promise, I'm not interested in him!"

"No," Austen frowns at his brother. "Of course not."

"Besides, you and me aren't into guys, right? We're totally straight. Like, so much so, that if one of us *did* fool around with a guy, it would just be curiosity, and not an actual persuasion, surely? If I *had* experimented with Mischa, it would only have been..."

"Jesus Christ!" Austen explodes. "Is this why you've been panicking all morning? You think he's *cute* and have a little crush on the guy? Do you have to fuck *everybody*?"

"No! I'm not saying that!" Will splutters.

I fucking hope not.

"I fucking hope not!" Austen growls.

"Why are you mad?"

"Because he's *my* friend! You're a fucking sex addict, you need actual help!"

Oh Austen, you do care about me.

"Okay, I'm sorry! It was just a thought!"

"I want to see your sketchbook."

It's not me who's in there, my love.

"What? No! Fucking hell, what's got into you? You don't seriously think I've *slept* with him?"

"You were in bed with him in Sydney."

Oh not this shit again.

"Jesus, calm down! Nothing happened! I swear on my mother's grave..."

"I want to see your fucking sketchbook!" Austen bellows, furious.

He looks so much more like William when he's mad like this.

Austen aims his paintball gun right at William's face, and William shields himself.

"Hey, you could give me an injury that close!"

"Good!" Austen spits.

This is jealous love right here.

"Pumpkin, pumpkin, *pumpkin!*"

Pumpkin?

Austen drops his aim, tries to calm down, and collects himself, fighting his rage.

Do they have a safe word?

The rest of the conversation is babble in their own language. It sounds like someone speaking Portuguese very fast with a Louisiana accent. Sounds *good.*

I can't understand their words, but I can listen to their bodies. Austen is thunderous, the fury twisting inside him. William is pushing away the air in front of him, trying to get away from whatever he did to anger Austen. He has no idea what that is, and looks very confused. Never seen Will cower before.

I don't think Austen has ever lost it like this, and that's why Will is so shocked.

Something stops Austen in his tracks. Soon, the discussion cools down, and Austen descends for his murderous energy, and seems amused. Will steps forward, on the verge of tears, and pats him on the head, apologetically.

"Mischa is off limits," Austen says, in English, "for all of us. Forever."

Wait, don't do that.

"Okay," William agrees. "Forever."

"You're an *idiot*."

And a fucking bastard.

William's stopwatch goes off.

"Sorry. Time's up. Go win."

"Should be easy with you out," Austen says. "And please stop upsetting Kitten. She's the love of my life."

The idea makes my blood feel colder.

"It's probably just her time of the month."

Austen smiles, shakes his head, then fires several rounds at Will's crotch, and Will keels over in pain. Austen keeps pummeling him with body-blows when he's down on the ground, then steals Will's unused gun, and heads into the green underbrush.

❊ ❊ ❊

I reach Hayden moments before Austen.

"I got William," Austen announces, when he arrives. "The others are in a group getting closer, so if we just spread out around here we can get all of them."

We embed ourselves in the flora and useful boulders.

Sabrina arrives first and walks through, between all of us. She's angry, distracted, and seems to have forgotten she's playing a game. While she's kicking the dirt Hayden hits her in the ass. It improves her mood. She stays to watch the action.

Isobelle and Kane are harder. Kane is a brilliant shot, and gets a round through the small slot in the hollow of the tree where Amelia is holed up, and hits her between the eyes. It turns into a shit-fight with me, Austen, Hayden against Isobelle and Kane.

Austen and I find ourselves hunting Isobelle near the spot where they all shot William. He shows me into the cave below. Inside it's dark, but lit up magically with glow worms. There's a boulder where someone has made a little shrine of candles. It's lovely and mysterious. We should be using the moment alone to get close, kiss maybe, but instead he's standing in front of the pagan altar, looking at me, waiting for me to make a move on him.

The fine line is getting thinner, in a damned-if-I-do, damned-if-I-don't kind of way. I can't look him in the eye. I try not to see him, the way he tries not to see me, and I want him to see my discomfort. He watches me struggle, trying to ignore his plausible denial and silent nudging. He doesn't move for me either. I'm off-limits now, I guess. Forever.

"This is cool," I say, and turn away from him. "We should get back."

I walk out. Austen follows reluctantly. A few minutes later I get Isobelle and Kane gets Hayden and then it's only me and Austen to take out Kane.

"There can be only one!" Kane yells, and it echoes around the dell.

I get bolder and sloppier. Kane gets more aggressive, and when he finally gets me, he momentarily forgets about Austen, who hits him in the back of the head. Game over.

It's so much fun we play another round, every man for himself. Everyone has it out for William. Sabrina, Kane, Isobelle and Austen especially. They go scorched-earth against him, and they don't come back for two hours. Austen wins again.

I want to know if you can swear on the graves of the living. Did William swear on the grave of his *undead* mother, or is their mother dead? I'm too cautious to ask, and I'm scared to know the answer.

❊ ❊ ❊

On the last day, there's a lot of laughter and fun, because everyone knows everything is about to end. The warm sunny days are about to be replaced by months of grey weeks.

Everyone is drinking and tipsy. Sabrina, Isobelle, Amelia and I share some blue meanies we found in the forest. None of us want to be too high so we put most of them in a strawberry daiquiri and share it out. Everyone only has a few sips. Amelia probably the most. The other half melts, untouched on the table. By the afternoon we are a little more irreverent than everyone else. I feel slightly queasy at first but then it's just my senses are heightened, and colors are brighter. Not much to write home about, so we pop a few more.

Hayden is very amusing when he's this drunk and loud, and finally out of his shell. He squeezes into a cocktail dress and mimes to opera. That's when he gets the idea to play spin the bottle. I think about it for a second. There are no good outcomes.

"I can't," I say, and sit on my hands.

"Why?" he asks.

I find an honest answer. "I'm a sex fiend that's gone cold-turkey for two months. I think if one of you touched me, I'd rip you to pieces."

One of you in particular.

"He's probably worried he'll have to kiss one of the boys," Sabrina teases.

"I don't think you understand," I tell her. "It's just not a good idea. I have a real problem; I'm really strung out. Man or woman doesn't mean shit. I'd fuck a goat at this point."

"Okay," Isobelle agrees. "Maybe don't poke the bear."

"I'm in," William says. "With a caveat that if it falls on Austen or Sabrina, I'm out. Also, by the way," he says to the crowd, "I'm the world's best kisser, but don't read into it. A kiss is not a contract."

Isobelle turns to Austen. "What about you baby? You want to give it a spin? You don't have to, if you don't want to."

"Yeah... yeah," Austen smiles. "I'm in."

They get in a circle and place a glass cola bottle in the center. I sit against the couch behind Amelia and watch.

Amelia clears her throat. "So the rules are, you spin the bottle and kiss the person it lands on, for a whole minute."

Isobelle's eyes narrow. "A minute? That's a bloody long time when you are kissing."

"And..." Amelia continues. "You have to do it straight away. Delays of more than seven seconds result in a penalty of a further thirty seconds. Any homophobia will not be tolerated and result in a piece of clothing being removed as punishment. If you've not kissed after thirty seconds you have to French kiss."

Isobelle sneers in disgust. "We have to NOT French kiss for a whole *minute*? What are we going to do? Peck each other to death? Are you actually mental?" She leans forward. "No, no, no. I'll show you how it's done."

Isobelle reaches for the bottle and gives it a robust spin. It goes for a long time before stopping on Amelia. Isobelle crawls to her like a big cat. She kisses her passionately, climbing on top of her and laying her down on the floor.

"Oh my God that was nice," Amelia breathes, when it's over.

Isobelle holds out a hand and pulls her back upright. The

next spin is Sabrina, which lands between Amelia and Isobelle.

"Kitten, go with Amelia," Isobelle says.

Sabrina laughs. "Well that's a no-brainer."

"Why?" Amelia asks.

"Oh..." she considers it. "Because you've just kissed Isobelle."

Sabrina locks lips with Amelia. It's sensual. She looks flushed by the end.

"I think I'm bisexual," Amelia says.

William lands on Kane.

"Okay ladies," William announces, "let *me* show you how it's really done."

"Oh *God*," Kane groans.

"Remember," William reminds him, "we're off the clock."

"Of course," Kane says. "I know you well enough to know it all means nothing."

Kane is on the floor, leaning back on his hands, with his legs folded. William adjusts to get into position, cracks his neck, and stretches like he's about to run a race. He's being dramatic, and enjoying every minute. He pauses to get a breath mint.

"Don't worry, buttercup; any feelings I inspire are perfectly natural I assure you. We should just change the music..."

"Penalty!" Amelia yells. "He's *stalling!* Take off a piece of clothing."

"I thought you'd never ask," William says.

He takes off his shirt, leaving a tight undershirt. It reveals a ripped physique, some welts from paintball, and some scars. Nothing alarming or unattractive. He's got a tattoo on his sternum; I can only see a little bit of it.

"Don't be fooled," Will says. "My kiss may make you think you're the only man in the world, but I'm just a fantastic kisser."

"I'm sure I will keep up," Kane laughs. "It's all fun and games."

"I'm giving you another penalty if you don't get on with it," Amelia scolds.

William does not hold back. He dives in with his usual confidence. He envelops Kane's hair with his hands, and they both give over to the moment. It's passionate and has a sense of deep connection, maybe because William is using a lot of tongue. William's hands move down Kane's body and when he reaches his hips he tries to pull him in closer. Kane has to move his legs out and William uses the opportunity to get between them. Now they are against the sofa with William on top.

If William were a sex worker, Kane would be getting something known as the "boyfriend experience." It pays well. He could make a lot of money doing this professionally.

I still think Kane is gay, and I think he likes this. Me and the girls find it amusing. Yeah, the longer it goes the more obvious these two are fucking on the downlow and Isobelle gives *zero* fucks. A minute is far too long for all this. The timer goes off on Amelia's phone and they separate. William looks in Kane's eyes and gives him a final smooch. Kane emerges dazed and rumpled. Will pulls him up off the floor.

"I'm pretty sure you just got Kane pregnant," Isobelle says.

Kane's eyes are wide. "I think I *feel* pregnant."

To Hayden's horror, he also gets William. Kane and Isobelle guffaw with laughter. William cracks his knuckles and flashes his smug, devilish smile.

"Round two! Pucker up, pretty boy."

"Homophobia!" Amelia yells. "Piece of clothing!"

William whips his jeans off. Hayden's arms are folded in front of him the entire time. William attacks him with just as much passion and confidence as Kane, but much less tongue than the first time.

"That was actually good," Hayden admits, when it's all over.

"Don't worry," William says. "I'll pay for the therapy."

Amelia lands on William and he's a gentleman. He doesn't lie her down or stick his tongue down her throat, he's respectful and sweet.

"He is actually good," Amelia says, "but my lips are getting chapped."

Kane lands on Amelia. Amelia kisses him, but the stress is starting to show in her.

"I can't take a fifth one," Amelia says. "I'm out."

I brace myself as Austen takes his turn. No matter what, I have to watch him kiss someone else, and not let my face give the game away.

As the bottle slows down, Amelia winds up tight. At the final moment, she knows it's going to fall on her, and she rolls out of the way. Now the bottle is pointing behind her. At me.

"Your turn, Mischa," she says.

My heart begins to pound.

"No," I frown. "Fuck no. I'm not playing."

She lowers her eyes. "Be a fucking gentleman and take one on the chin." She turns to Austen. "I think you're sexy, Austen, but I'm on shrooms, and doing some deep work on myself right now. Besides, I want to see *you two* kiss."

"Don't let Amelia bully you," Isobelle laughs.

"All good, I can kiss him..." Austen says. "If that's okay, Kitten?"

Sabrina looks around and shrugs. "If it's alright with you, it's alright with me."

"It's not alright with me," William tells Austen. "We're identical; you're an extension of me, so if you kiss him I'm basically kissing him. We don't want to do that."

"Oh for Christ sake, Honey," Isobelle frowns at William. "This is not about you. Let baby-bee decide."

"I don't want to disappoint," Austen says. He turns to me. "Unless you think I should kiss Amelia?"

"No!" I yelp, without thinking.

"Well then you have to kiss me! That's how this works!"

I can smell alcohol on his breath. Maybe he's had too much to drink. I feel my heart race. He's not thinking straight. I'm a little high and definitely not thinking straight.

I backtrack. "Okay, kiss Amelia." Then I bargain with him. "Or how about *I kiss Amelia* like I'm *supposed* to?"

"But it's *my* turn!" Austen says.

"I'm good, thanks," Amelia waves us away and downs a glass of wine. "I have too many self-esteem issues for this shit."

"I'm on a hair-trigger," I tell Austen, between gritted teeth. "When shit pops off, *which it will*, I might actually have a shot with her and I don't want to ruin our *friendship, Austen.*"

"You *had* a shot with me," Amelia says. "*Had* a shot."

"True," he nods. "Look, no pressure. Let's forget about it. I can spin again."

"Nope!" Amelia grabs the bottle away. "You have to kiss Mischa! We've all had multiple gay kisses and you have to do it as well. It'll be really hot!"

"Do you ever go for guys?" Isobelle asks me, a cheeky little smile on her face.

"Well," I huff, uncomfortable with the question. "I'm usually up to my ears in girls—but you know... *addict*... *goddamn guys*—you're throwing a starving man *food*."

Amelia squints her eyes. "There's a lot of homophobia around this table, I think. You both have to undress!"

"No," I whimper.

"And you're both stalling! Four pieces of clothing! Two extra minutes!"

"Jesus Christ!" I squeak. "I only *have* four pieces of clothing!"

"You don't have to do this," William tells me.

"You know honey, a kiss is not a contract," Austen says.

He just called me honey. He is drunk.

"This is not a good idea," I warn him.

"Ugh," Austen groans and moves across to me. "I know that, but don't be *weird* about it. You've probably tortured a ton of people like this. It's karma."

He mounts my lap. I feel the warmth of him. My poker face is good, because it's always been a matter of life or death, but Austen is testing my limits. The mushrooms are not helping. It feels like the volume of reality has been turned up loud, and like it's been a thousand years since our last kiss, two nights ago. I thought that might be the last one. Maybe this will be.

He runs his fingers through my hair and gently guides my

face closer to his. My skin prickles. I swallow, feeling my heart thud in my chest. Butterflies erupt in my stomach. From the surface to the depths, the feelings have an intensity that I never imagined possible. Yearning sparks inside my ears like electricity, meets at the tip of my nose, and runs down my body in a flash, and finds my cock, racing to the head of it. This is about to make me hard. I have to focus.

I look up at him. "Listen to me, *Queenie*," I whisper, "listen to me, listen to me; sitting on my lap isn't the *greatest* idea. I'm going to think about chess and you should probably only give me some chaste pecks, alright?"

"Okay," he says. "I'll go slow."

He doesn't get off. Instead, he kisses me. I cooperate. It's on the mouth, and very brief. He pulls away and looks in my face, amused. The room is dead quiet. All eyes on us. We look at each other and neither of us make a move.

He stares at me. His eyes are like dinner plates. His lips hover over mine. I watch him bite the bottom one. His beautiful features take my breath away. His emerald eyes are luminous from the evening sun slanting through the window. He holds me captive with his glance. His finger touches my neck, as he moves away a lock of hair. It gives me the chills. I'm beyond logic now.

"This was such a bad idea," William mutters.

"You guys are stalling," Amelia says.

"No," I say, and caress his cheek. "We're not."

Amelia huffs. "Well I'm not starting the timer until you go for it, and I'm adding another thirty second penalty."

He kisses the tip of my nose like I did to him in the tent. I smile. He slides in tight. I hold his waist. I feel safe. I'm pretty sure he feels safe too, because we are encircled by five people who would kill me to protect him without question.

We are so close together. The sweet peach and honey scent of his body overwhelms my senses. His strong, tanned arms tuck themselves under my body. His warm lips touch my throat. The exhale from the lips of the man above me sends shivers of pleasure down my body right through my heart. He nuzzles where my neck meets my collarbone. I squirm and quake under his touch, fighting to not make any noise, but a soft moan escapes me.

"I'm giving you four minutes. Hurry up. Do you want to go for five?"

Leaning in, our lips meet in a sweet, lingering kiss, soft and unhurried, as if we were tasting the very essence of love.

Amelia starts the timer.

The truth speaks inside our bodies, without the noise of words. The kiss flaunts our shared secret. It thunders in my racing heartbeat. It whispers in the smile pulling at his lips.

"That okay?" he asks, as he stops.

My heart is about to beat out of my chest and I open my eyes and take a deep breath out. He nuzzles my neck again. My back arches involuntarily as I fight the feelings ballooning inside me.

"Yes," I say, gasping for air, and surrendering to Austen.

He looks at me again. He's silent, and gives butterfly kisses. His hands run down the sides of my head to my neck, out to my shoulders and down to my hands. He grabs them, soft yet firm, puts them in front of me and pauses. We have all the time. We look in each other's eyes again and smile as our lips touch. He lays a kiss on my forehead, my chin, then cheeks and eyes, like I did to him that night in the Outback.

I'm feeling the shrooms, tripping a little. We are surrounded by strings of color, shimmering like water. I feel them swirling through us. We look at them in amazement.

Some of the ribbons go out to the others and they share them between each other too. William is covered in so many from everyone, it's like he's wrapped in an enormous rainbow cocoon.

"One?" I mouth to Austen without noise.

"One," he agrees silently.

Amelia calls a minute and it intrudes upon an eternity of togetherness.

"You're stalling again."

We kiss again and it's sensual. Nothing about this moment feels ordinary. He lies me down and gets on top. Our legs tangle. He stitches our fingers together like puzzle pieces and puts our hands above our heads. Our soft inner arms press together along the length of them. I'm in total submission to him.

He kisses me again and again, more deeply and passionately each time. As we do, Austen moves above me, moving ever so gently. Where we are connected, an intense desire spreads. From my heart to my chest and belly to my inner thigh, it's as if a heavenly glue is sticking us together.

I tilt my head and after his deep breath out he bites my lip gently. It doesn't hurt, it only makes me want more. I bite his top lip back, then our tongues connect again.

I feel us ascending. I open my eyes and see that we are in a different world that glistens and sparkles in a fresh light, newly created. Now I realize we drowned on Bondi, and are already in Heaven, together.

Our past lives stretch out behind us; all the strange but familiar vessels that were once ourselves. I've always known him. All lives are quietly profound, unmistakably beautiful, from a distance. William is sewn into the cosmic mix every time. I've met Isobelle before too, and often not in happy circumstances. She is a formidable opponent, and an even more terrifying friend.

Epochs pass, and empires rise and fall as we make out. We only come up for air one more time. We break apart and our eyes are bleary now. I smile and he lets go of my hands, and starts exploring my body. I kiss his neck, reach under his shirt, and make my way up his spine. I find the spot that made him moan in the tent in the desert. He moans again, as quietly as he can. I can feel his muscles straining. Poor Austen. The pressure has been building in him this whole time, and it's time to release it.

"Time's almost up!" Amelia warns.

"*Don't stop*," Austen whispers, as he puts my earlobe in his mouth.

I let out a gasp like I sprinted a long way and look around wildly. Everyone looks hypnotized, watching us, except William. Isobelle and Sabrina are covering his eyes. I have to get back to Austen. He needs me. I kiss his bottom lip on his open mouth.

"Ten seconds!" Amelia announces. "Nine, eight!"

After weeks of torturous holding back from each other, the build up of sexual energy explodes. I grab Amelia's timer and throw it against a porthole where it smashes to pieces. She squeaks.

"You want a show?" I ask the others. "Four bits of clothing?"

I pull my shirt off, then turn to Austen. "You like it baby?" I ask him between kisses.

"Yes," he smiles.

"You want to keep going?" I ask.

"I do."

"You hands, running down my body. I need it. You want it?"

"Yes."

"Yes?"

"*Yes yes yes.*"

"Is he *drunk*?" William asks Isobelle, taking her hands off his eyes.

I shower Austen in kisses and kick my shoes off, telling him how much I need him, adore him, that I love the way he tastes. I want to go down on him for hours. I want to be inside him. He shushes me.

William stands up, and the strings that connect Kane and the girls to him pull them up too. Hayden rises to his feet as well, but his strings are different.

"Beebee," William says to Austen softly, in his ear, pulling on his arm.

"I'm busy," he says, pushing him away.

"Oh God baby," I whisper as I kiss Austen's neck. "I can't wait to fuck you. You want me?"

"*You know I do,*" he whispers back.

The spirit of lust overruns me completely, like black magic taking hold, casting me out of my own soul. I rip off his muslin overshirt and the buttons ping around the cabin.

"That's enough," William tells us.

The ribbons of color start whipping around like a hurricane. There's some strange unmoving black water between the twins and their girlfriends. It's thick, like oil, or blood. My hand on the back of Austen's neck, I pull him on to me tighter. He rests his arms on my shoulders. I press my mouth against his. Another moan escapes me as I part my lips. Austen seems entranced by the kissing. I take off my belt.

William pulls him off me. I get up and grab Austen's hands. Nobody seems to know what to do. What can they do? Austen is an adult. I pull him outside and find his lips, steering him with his hips backwards onto a lounger and get on him. The boys pull me off him again. I throw them off with force and the girls yelp.

Again and again the boys intervene, but I keep pushing them away and coming back. Austen lies back on the sofa and I lower my hips between his legs. As I kiss I move down, lifting his shirt over his belly-button and kiss just above it, then just below it, while I unbuckle his belt. William is incandescent.

"Get the fuck off him," he growls.

Finally the boys pin me down to the deck and the girls pull

Austen away inside. Sabrina locks the cabin.

"Get the fuck off me!" I yell.

I writhe around like I am possessed, and kick Kane and bite Hayden.

"Jesus!" Hayden yelps, as I chomp the side of his hand.

I get away from them, and William punches me in the eye. It's like running into a brick wall. You do actually see stars when someone hits you hard enough.

I am in shock. It sobers me a little. I can't open the door. I'm shaking all over. I clamber to the table and grab my drink. My hand tremors so much as I put it to my mouth that the liquid splashes everywhere.

"Are you okay?" Kane asks me.

"N-no," I stutter. "I need Austen. I need *sex*. I can't take it anymore. I have to have him or I'm gonna go insane."

"Oh God," Kane says. "He literally warned us, we should have *listened*."

I rub my temples hard. "Austen, baby, listen!" I yell to him from outside, pressing my face to the crack in the door. "What happens on holiday stays on holiday. We obviously need to have sex with each other." I start banging my head on the door in time to what I'm saying. "Let's go in one of the tents! It's gonna be great, I can tell! It's gonna be amazing! I promise to be gentle, I'll let you do what you want to me. I want you to be in charge. Whatever you want me to do to you, I'll do it. You can tie me up and do whatever, I just *need* to fuck you, okay? After *that* kiss, I have to know what it's like!"

"Stop bashing your head!" Kane yells.

While I ramble, Austen unlocks the door and locks lips with me. They pull us apart again.

"Let me go," Austen barks at Kane and Hayden. "Don't fucking touch me."

He pushes off his bodyguards and menaces them. They wisely back right off. They don't want to catch a punch from this absolutely lethal fighter.

"Come here baby," I tell him.

"Touch him again, and you fucking die," William warns me.

I go straight to Austen. "I've died before."

Austen holds up my hand and looks at the back of it. He moves it around in the air while I kiss his neck.

"It's okay Bee," Austen tells William. "It's *beautiful*."

"What are you doing?" William frowns.

"There are little rainbows coming off his skin," Austen says.

"Baby?" Isobelle whimpers, alarmed. "What cup have you been drinking from?"

"I've got the jug of blueberry," he says and points to it.

Looks like he's eaten a lot of the blue meanies out of the pitcher. Awesome.

"That has magic mushrooms in it!" she yells.

"I know!" he giggles. "That's why I tried it! I like it. I like kissing too. It's really nice."

He cups my face and kisses me over and over and I accept each one eagerly, faster and faster until they become one long kiss. I moan as he pushes me up against the wall. A whole new panic sets in, as everyone tries to figure out how much he's taken.

"He's totally out of it," William says, pulling him away again. "He has no idea what he's doing."

The recriminations fly. Isobelle and Sabrina blame Amelia and she's outraged. The blame shifts to me and they all agree it's my fault for supplying it, and now I'm taking *advantage* of him.

"Fuck me baby, *please*," I howl, and the others go quiet. "The thought of you naked is driving me crazy. I think I'm going to die if I don't have you soon. I need you. I need your body. God Austen, please, *please* fuck me."

"Okay," Austen says. "Yeah, okay. I think I want to."

William is searing with rage. He wants Austen the fuck away from me. Isobelle tells him to let her deal with it but he doesn't want to listen.

"You're gonna have to share your fucking binky for a few more minutes," she snarls at William.

She grabs two juice boxes and runs to me.

"I need you to drink this," Isobelle says, offering me a sip.

"I need Austen," I say, defiantly.

"You can kiss as much as you want, but you both have to drink this."

Her sleepy-sleepy-night-night juice won't do shit to me. I'm an ox. I take a gulp. It's warm. She gives Austen some too.

Our bodies start glowing gold. I grab Austen's arm to lead him inside, and Will grabs the other arm in a tug-of-war, until Austen yanks himself free of his shadow, and locks his brother outside.

We jump in one of the beds. I pull his shoes and socks off and throw them over my shoulder. He lets me get on top of him and grind. We kiss and kiss and *kiss*. He scratches his nails down my back and my moan gets louder.

"*Mmmnnm Austen,*" I gasp. "*Oh baby... fuck me fuck me fuck me...*"

He shushes me, but the sound sets Will off outside again. He pounds the door. We can hear everyone screaming at him, and it makes us both laugh.

I get down to my boxers. Austen takes his jeans off, giggling. Things are going good, only I feel heavier and heavier. He gets drowsy too. I can't hold my head up, so I put it down the cushion next to his.

He kisses my ear. "Every atom of me is drawn to every atom of you," he whispers. "We crossed an ocean of pain to find each other."

"I'll never let you go," I breathe in his ear. "Never let you go. *Volim te... volim te... volim te...*"

"*Volim te*," he repeats.

I think he knows it means *I love you*.

Before I pass out, I see William come over and pull Austen's light into the dark water.

❋ ❋ ❋

I wake up in the jet, forty thousand feet over the Pacific Ocean. My burst ear is excruciating. I lurch upright. William is sketching me from across the table. He's very good. He's captured my likeness. He has a black eye and I don't know why.

"Hi Sugarplum," he smiles.

"What... the... fuck?"

"We thought it was best to start traveling home, and got you on the plane while you were asleep."

Austen is trapped between Kane and Hayden. The two of them look angry at Will, but not me. Really fucking angry. Amelia is sleeping.

I decide to play stupid. I pushed my luck way too far. It might be easy to convince them I don't remember much, because I really don't feel any shame, or care. And because I don't care, it doesn't have to be the performance of my life, either.

I look around and wipe the sleep from my eyes. "What happened?"

Isobelle looks between me and William. "Do you remember how we played spin the bottle?"

"Yeah. It was amazing. I was *really* high and I saw the most amazing waves of color," I yawn. "William got down to his boxers and stuck his tongue down their throats," I tilt my head to Kane and Hayden. "Amelia kissed you, I think, or maybe Kane? It gets a bit fuzzy. I wasn't playing. I'm a sex addict, and two weeks away from my sixty-day chip from my Twelve-Step program. I *need* that chip."

Everyone shifts uncomfortably.

"We forced you," Isobelle admits.

"Bullshit. I'd *never*. I want that gold chip on my keychain so bad."

"It was mostly Amelia," Sabrina says.

"It was horrible," Isobelle sighs.

"You went totally nuts," Sabrina tells me.

"I'll bet I did. I can't control myself."

"That's for sure," Isobelle says.

"Jesus Christ. Did I punch you?" I ask Will. "I'm so sorry. I don't remember it!"

"No," he looks away. "This wasn't you. I gave you that, though."

I touch my eye. It hurts, and I wince.

I look at the girls. "I would never force myself on you, I promise."

Sabrina shakes her head. "You didn't... not us."

"You kissed Austen," Isobelle says.

"Oh yeah..." I frown. "Whatever. I actually kissed all of you, but only in spirit form," I pretend to relax. "He was all golden and like, glowing."

"You really kissed," she insists.

"Yeah but that's not *so* bad. He's not a little girl. I didn't tell him I loved him or wanted to marry him, did I? I do that sometimes when I get carried away. It never ends well."

"No."

"Oh, great. Not so bad then."

"Well it was still *a lot*."

"It's just a stupid kiss. I'm sure he can handle himself..."

I close my eyes and tilt my chair back. I can still feel everyone's eyes on me, so I wrap up this performance. I furrow my brow with absolute humiliation, and shrink myself, holding my breath so my face goes bright red like it needs to, and slide down the seat as far as I can.

"Oh..." I clear my throat. "Oh I... remember..." I put my head in my hands and rub my face with feigned stress, staring at the floor. "Not just a stupid kiss. Me and Austen... we didn't?"

"No," Isobelle says, "but nearly."

"Yeah... good. Good. Thank god," I nod, pretending it's all coming back to me, and fidget in my seat. "That was not good," I wince, and cover my mouth. "I remember." I look at the bite mark on Hayden's arm. "Sorry I bit you."

"I'll need a tetanus shot," he shrugs, "but we're good. You didn't light the fuse," he says, and looks at Amelia.

I work through all the imaginary anger that I must totally be feeling at this moment. Everyone watches me with trepidation. They must feel awful. I am flipping the script, because they all know they let their chaste, struggling, vulnerable addict friend down completely. Motherfuckers pushed me off the wagon and into Will's fist.

I turn to William. "It's a good thing you stayed sober, Will. I'm embarrassed, but without you there, it could have been way worse. I owe you one. Or maybe we're even."

"You and I share a particular issue," he tells me.

"Sex mania? Not that it matters, but technically I *didn't* have sex, so I can still get my chip, right? I just think it's a cool thing to have."

"Yeah," he laughs, joyless. "I can see you're really powerless in the face of addiction. I just hope there's no... unfinished business."

I frown. "There is, until someone fucks me. There's nothing subtle about this. I thought I could try for a while, fooled myself that I could actually rein it in, but it just made me even more out of control. I'm so *over* sobriety... or serenity... abnegation..."

"Celibacy?"

"That too. Sucks. But not the good suck. I realized tripping on the mushrooms that sex is life, the reason why we're here, and without it we all die, and I don't want to die. I want to have a lot of sex. I'm going straight home to fire off *lots* of texts. Not now though. *After* I get the chip."

Kane starts to laugh.

Will pulls a fake, rigid smile. "Fair enough."

It's terrifying how unmoving Will is. He's hiding his rage. I pretend not to notice. Isobelle looks weary too. Austen catches my eye. He's intimidated. I look at him with sympathy.

"I'm sorry," Austen says.

"No... I'm sorry. I feel terrible."

"You still wanna be my friend?" he asks, and flicks his eyes up at me.

"Yeah, *of course*," I say. "You still want to be mine?"

"Uh-huh," he nods.

"We're back in the friend-zone?"

"Friend-zone," he nods.

I sigh with relief. "Thank God."

"How was your first... boy kiss?" Sabrina asks Austen.

"It was very interesting," Austen smiles, tilts his head and looks at my hands, fascinated. "No rainbows," he says.

I look at my hand. "No."

"Am I good?"

"What?" I ask.

He looks timid, with an embarrassed smile, and scratches his head.

"You are objective, because you are a guy. I'm just curious, was it a good kiss?"

"I mean..." I swallow, my throat dry and sore. I turn the question back at him. "Wouldn't you put it in your top five?"

He looks around, unsure what to say, and then darts his eyes back to me.

"I guess," he shrugs.

"Well, there you go."

"So... not terrible?" he asks, hopefully.

Isobelle and William drill their eyes into me and wait. Sabrina is clinging to the arm of her chair so tight her knuckles are white.

I look at Austen, and smile like a devil. "I mean we... might have to do it *again* before I can say for *sure*..." I point to Sabrina,

"You guys ever do threesomes? You're definitely..."

William shakes his head at me. "I will murder you in your sleep..."

I chuckle. "No, but seriously," I say, and raise my eyebrows. "You are a really good kisser, Austen. I have kissed hundreds of people, and that was one of the best kisses I ever had. If you ever want to kiss me again, I'd be happy to oblige."

"But not in a *gay* way," he smiles and bites his lip.

"No!" I laugh, "but I reserve the right to tease Will about this forever. He's obviously hung up about it."

Austen looks relieved. So does Isobelle. Sabrina's knuckles get their color back. Will returns to drawing.

❋ ❋ ❋

I wait until everyone else on the plane is asleep. Austen and I don't need any more rest because we have both just woken from an eight hour coma.

He stands up and gestures for me to go to the bar out the back. I push him into the bathroom and lock the door.

I plant a kiss on his neck. "It seems like I no longer trigger your naughty puppy syndrome."

His hand goes to my chest and pushes gently.

"I just wanna talk," he says.

I part his legs and push my hips in between, and put my

mouth to his ear. "We can talk and do this too."

"I'm sorry I kissed you," he says. "Not at spin the bottle. I was fucking tripping *balls.*"

"I know, sorry, I was too. I think I'm still high now. Those little suckers are *strong.* I'm on the fence about whether this is all real. Like, I'd expect my psycho family to smuggle someone on a plane, not *yours*, even if it is just a little landing strip like that. Or is this actually real?"

Austen shakes his head. "I'm still feeling it too, but I'm just sorry I kissed you by the lake. I shouldn't have done that."

"Why?" I ask, and kiss his neck. "I loved it."

He drops his hands down and sighs. "I had a few drinks and I manipulated you, so you wouldn't sleep with Amelia. She's young, and she doesn't deserve to be…"

I recoil from him. "I'm *younger!* Are you trying to say you did it to *save* her from me?"

He nods in a way that wasn't just up-and-down, but side-to-side as well. "It was terrible of me to do that to you."

I flash my fury. "It's terrible that you are trying to manipulate me right now. Are you always going to say the opposite to what you do? Who are you trying to convince; yourself? You kissed me because you want me. You. Want. Me. *Sooooo* bad. That night in Uluru wasn't pity. I'm not insane; this is *real.*"

He looks down. "I'm not like that. I don't know what came

over me. Maybe I wanted to know what it was like. I think I just got swept up in your passionate advances."

"Austen..." I say, as calmly as possible, trying to quell my molten anger, "your hands are around my waist."

He drops his hands to his sides, and then puts them behind his back.

I gag with disgust. "Well, *now* I'm convinced..."

"Look..."

"*Volim te*," I interrupt, and he freezes. "Every atom," I kiss him. "Every proton," I kiss him again. "Every neutron," and again. "Every electron," and again. "Everything that is me is drawn to everything that is you. Tell me you don't love me. I can't stop this and you can't either. We have to go through it. I don't mind keeping it a secret. I don't mind being completely different people when we're out there. Either I'm with you, or I'm recovering *from* you; so tell me which one it is. Tell me you don't love me; tell me, tell me, *tell me*. I need to *know*."

He shakes his head in that ridiculous circle. "Mischa, I'm not gay. I'm not going to have sex with you."

"Okay, okay..." I say, "Let's go on body language. Maybe your body will tell the truth if you are going to lie to my face."

"I cannot do this," he says.

"Jesus, what happened while I was asleep?" I ask. "Why does he have a black eye? What do you think he's gonna do, exactly?

DARK STARS IN THE SKY

You think he's gonna like, try kill me or something? Fuck that stupid asshole. I can protect myself, Austen."

Austen looks at the wall and thinks about it.

"You don't know what you're talking about. You have no idea."

"Yes, I do. My third eye isn't closed yet. The doors of perception are still wide open, and I know some monstrous thing is about to devour you, and I'm never going to see you again after this. I've always known it. I understand now. I can already feel myself losing you."

Austen reaches for the door and unlocks it. It opens an inch and I slam it shut again, push him against the sink and press into him.

"Say *Austen*," I tell him. "You are slipping away somewhere dark and I am not letting you go without a fight. Say Austen. I will stop. Say it."

He doesn't say anything. I put my face to his. He turns his cheek to the side to stop a kiss, so I run my lips up his jawline, and press his earlobe between my lips. His breath hitches, and I kiss down his neck and he lets out a little, "ahhhmn."

I look at him, his mouth open, breathing heavily. "You like that? Or you want to say '*Austen*'?"

"We shouldn't," he whispers so silently that I have to read his lips.

I kiss him and he stops talking. We look down and his hands are on my waist again. He swallows hard and looks away.

"I'm going to touch you like airport security, and your body can tell me if it's not interested."

"We can't..." he swallows hard.

I look into his eyes and run my hands down his body.

"We can't stop? That's my whole theory. We've been interrupted, held back, held down, and prevented and stopped and ripped apart, punched in the fucking eye, and died a hundred awful tragic deaths, even condemned to infernal storms, but we *always* find ourselves back here. I promised I'd never not touch you, that I'd follow you anywhere. We're not supposed to be separate."

Austen closes his eyes. "You're mythologizing everything because reality is just too painful."

"You know what? Fuck the psychoanalysis."

I rub his crotch and his penis pushes up from the top of his pants, so I unbutton him to release it. He breathes in sharp. He is hard, and big and gorgeous. I can feel the head of my own cock aching to be touched.

He summons some fight and looks at me defiantly. "Anyone would get hard if you touched it like that. It's just a sensation."

"Okay," I throw my hands up. "I won't touch you."

He watches as I take his hand and put it to my crotch. I am

hard. Really hard. I've had a semi since he kissed me by the lake, days ago. I rub his hand up and down my zipper. He bites his lip and I take my hand off his. I unzip. He does not move his hand away. his breath is jagged. I put it down my pants and he closes his eyes as he touches the base of my penis. He breathes deep. Precum starts to drip out of him, and me.

"How are you doing there?" I ask.

His eyes half close for a second and fix themselves on the head of my cock. He's so aroused he looks like he's in a trance. He licks his bottom lip and I want to kiss it desperately. I move his hand up and down my shaft, in long slow strokes. I don't have to push his hand much at all, as he starts to move all by himself. I watch him work me and he gets faster, and I get closer.

"You want me?" I whisper.

I want him so much I can barely get the words out. His breaths are heavy and labored. I want his open mouth on my mouth. His tongue I want on my tongue.

I can't take it anymore. I'm about to come and I press my lips to the corner of his lips and explode into his hand. As I do, with that single touch of my lips kissing the side of his mouth, he comes too; and a *lot*. I touch his shaft again and the feeling of his delicate skin and its hardness sends me over the top. With my hand pumping him, his knees buckle a little, and the cum keeps coming from both of us. His hand and shirt are absolutely covered in me. My mouth is stuck to the corner of his, not wanting it to stop. He turns his head to touch more of my lips as he pants into me. As our tongues finally connect, I pump down on him again and he shoots one last huge squirt. I feel some of the warm goo hit my chin.

We pant together, pressing into one another until we catch our breath, and kiss again. Then as we come back down to earth we remember ourselves. I'm amazed how much liquid I deposited on his hand and stomach. We both slowly look up to the low ceiling of the bathroom, which now has a splatter of goop across it.

"You hit the roof," I smirk. "That's impressive."

"I'm sorry."

"Don't be."

I'm shocked at what just happened. Shocked at myself. Intense feelings start rushing over me. Maybe because I have lost people before, I can't lose him, but I still don't really have him.

"I love you," I say, the moment I start to break, as it all hits me harder. "Don't leave me."

He is surprised by my words, and his mouth drops open. The feelings are raw, for both of us. He tries to shake them away. I feel like it's a desperate grief only he can soothe. And he does. He kisses my temple and strokes my cheek.

I push it all back down and so does he. Then he looks at the door, and fills with terror too. He knows we have to go back out there, and is scared of what's waiting for him. He turns the faucet on and washes the mess off himself.

I can see the cogs in his brain moving. He's thinking we went too far, he shouldn't be in here. He needs to sort out this bathroom, and make a quick getaway without anyone seeing us together. Like it never happened.

He zips his pants and then goes for some wipes to clean the ceiling. I take them out of his hands.

"I'll do it," I tell him. "Go back to your seat. I'll wait five minutes, and then I'll come out."

He doesn't look at me, but nods and looks at the floor.

"Sorry," he says again.

I kiss him on the forehead. "Stop saying sorry. Go."

A few minutes later as I come out of the bathroom, Austen pushes past me as he runs to the small cabin where the flight attendants prepare food. There, he crumples to the ground and throws up in a trash can.

I put my hand on his back as he tries to gather himself.

"I can't do this," he says. "I'm sorry."

I'm confused, and don't say anything.

Back in his seat, he curls into the fetal position, throws a blanket over his head, and pretends to sleep through meals.

He only "wakes up" when we land.

21 AUSTEN

When I wake at the airport, before we fly back to America, it's messy. We're alone in the car with the monster. Everyone else is getting luggage up the stairs to the jet. My brother is an angry, scary, shaking mess. He has a black eye too, so I guess he glitched at some point. His rage is different from the blackouts. New to me.

"What would he do if he found out about us?" he asks me.

Poor Bee. He's terrified. I'm worried too. I embrace him and tell him it was a one time thing. I know it has to be.

"There's nothing to find out," I tell him. "Nothing happened, so there's nothing to know. It was just a bit of fun. I didn't mean it. I'm sorry."

"They never stop coming," he sobs.

"Mischa's not here to hurt us, I promise. If he's a problem, we can deal with him."

"I do like him," he says. "He's sweet. I don't want to hurt him."

"I didn't mean you. I meant me and the girls. We'll take care of it. I'll always choose you. I'll always protect you."

Then he cries. He *never* cries. He begs for forgiveness.

"You did nothing wrong," I say, and wipe his tears. "I had so much fun, It's all going to be okay. I feel really good now."

We say sorry and I love you to each other and I give him lots of pats. I say he needs to rest, and he agrees that he can't be here much longer. I tell him he did really good, that I'll miss him, and I'll come find him soon, and we say goodbye to one another. Then we get on the plane together, eat popcorn and watch a movie. Then Mischa wakes up.

Mischa takes me to the bathroom. I like it too much. I like him too much. It's almost a need. My beautiful Mischa. I want to protect him from mess that could destroy everything. From me. He makes me climax so hard that my ears are ringing and it feels like I have an icepick in my skull. It should have never gone this far. Pain and revulsion run through me. I start to sweat. I feel so unwell it's like my body has been poisoned.

I tried to fix it and I just dug the hole deeper. What would Billy do if he found out? He would kill Mischa just as a starter. He can never know. I have to protect him or else... I feel like I am starting to panic. The air around me feels thick and my throat feels like it's being strangled. Pretty soon I am violently ill. Mischa sees the whole thing.

"I can't do this," I say. "I'm sorry."

I can't look at him. It almost feels like it's out of my control, and I have to go along with this thing with Mischa. My mind wants to stop but my body's weak. Like his willpower is over-running my own. I try to remind myself that nothing is set in stone, and that calms me a little. I don't belong to him, I belong to Bee. I said the thing I needed to say. I can leave Mischa in the dust once we land. It's already decided. I never have to see him again. I shut my eyes tight.

❋ ❋ ❋

After landing the girls are talking to Mischa. They come over to me as I head for the exit. I hold my hand up to Sabrina before she tries to say anything.

"I need to get out of here," I tell her.

"Mischa's too tired to drive all that way," she says. "And Amelia's staying with her friends in Boston. Can you drive his car?"

"I cannot drive him home, Kitten. For fuck's sake. Can everyone just stop trying to play matchmaker? Get Hayden."

"Honey said Hayden had to ride with you."

"Honey can drive Mischa then."

"He left with Kane already, and you know he's not well anyway. He can't drive like that. So..." Sabrina thinks about it, "I'll get Izzy to do it?"

Isobelle stares at me silently.

"No!" I say, feeling the panic rise. "That'll look weird. I'll do it, but you gotta come."

❋ ❋ ❋

Mischa even likes the kind of cars I like. He has an old British off-roader. I ask him if he drove it through a swamp before he left.

"More-or-less," he shrugs.

We both stare straight ahead as I drive the mud-covered truck down the freeway. Hayden is with Sabrina in the back seat. I look at his gas meter and realize we're running on fumes.

"We need to fill up," I sigh, trying to hide my frustration.

"I'm hungry," Sabrina says, as we take the offramp to a service centre. "Can we grab food from the diner? You could go through the carwash while I get something?"

I fight the urge to scowl at her. "Order something for us too."

She turns to Hayden and waves her purse. "My shout."

Hayden looks at me. "Is that cool?"

I nod. They leave and I'm alone with Mischa.

"Thank you," he says, as we pull in behind another car waiting for the drive-through car wash. "I'm so jet-lagged, I can't even imagine driving."

"Did you plan this?" I ask him.

"I didn't even ask for this," he says. "The girls said *you* offered."

"I think that was a misunderstanding."

"It's just the fates, Austen."

"Yeah," I say, and look away.

"It was wrong what I did, on the plane. I don't know what the hell I was thinking," he shakes his head and looks distraught. "Touching me made you sick."

"No, Mischa," I say. "I wanted you to, but the problems this causes made me sick. You are right, I say one thing and do another. Lying to myself. It must be driving you insane. It was the most honest moment of my life; I'll treasure it forever."

"Why are you talking like it's over?"

"It's just not allowed."

"Not allowed?"

"I want you, but can't have you," I say.

"...Okay," he frowns. "Why?"

"I have lost everyone but the people with me on that boat. If I choose you, it all falls apart, and I'll lose them. I just can't do this anymore, it has to end."

He takes it in, with a somber, tired acceptance. "That was the deal, I guess. Not like we can be friends anymore," he sighs. "Don't want to make your life more difficult than it already is. It's fine. Totally fine."

Wait.

This feels so *wrong.* Deep deep down in my soul, I am shaken. Mischa would never let me go. That's what he said. He'd *never* let me go. What am I even doing? I have to reject him, because I have to, so I did. I've done my duty. Mischa has to ignore what I say, and do the opposite, so it'll all be his own fault. He has to scream and cry, start yelling, telling me I belong to him, grab my hair, and force a kiss on me. But he doesn't do anything. He just accepts it, like a fucking asshole.

I don't know what to do. I panic in silence and stare ahead.

Is he really going to break up with me like this? That's cold. If I call his bluff, I might be calling my own bluff at the same time. That will make me look like such a bastard. He'll never trust me again. God I hate myself, I'm so disgusting. Why would he even want me? How could we ever even be together? I've screwed it up now anyway. Should I call my therapist right now? Would she even answer? How do I even explain this? She would have a lot of catching up to do...

Mischa looks at me, and it seems like he's thought of a narrow way forward. Hope leaps inside me.

"What?" I ask.

"Want to say goodbye properly? Then I'll get away from you forever and you won't hear from me again."

"Alright," I reply, hesitantly.

He grabs my collar and pulls me to him, kisses me hard and I feel myself heating up. His hands run up and down my back, knowing exactly where it feels good. He starts taking off his clothes.

"Stop," I hiss.

In seconds he's down to his underwear.

"I need to get you the fuck out of my system," he says. "You know the safe word."

"We *cannot*," I start.

"Yes we fucking can. The guy in front is putting in his little code for the carwash, and he'll be inside there in a minute. The guy behind can't see us. Give me this carwash and I'll leave you alone. Forever."

His boxers are tenting. I swallow. I want to... and this is goodbye... it is extremely cold, but his body doesn't seem to know it, so I turn up the heater for him.

"How thoughtful," he says, and gives me a kiss on the cheek, "but I'm burning up."

"This is a *terrible* idea..." I start.

I watch the garage door close the car in front of us inside the cleaning apparatus. Mischa's hand is at my crotch and he releases my cock from my pants.

"Are you gonna let me deal with this situation, or are we going to have a very awkward ride home?" he asks. "The others might have questions about why your dick is halfway to the ceiling..." the corner of his mouth curls into a smirk. "Might as well get the most out of our farewell."

He strokes me slowly. I check outside. It's out of view of everything. Just a concrete wall. This is our last time. My only fucking time. We ought to make the most of it.

I lean back into my seat and he kisses my neck. I let the warm heat of his touch flow through me. I kiss him like the first time. His hands are slow and delicate, and pure ecstasy. I moan as I get close and he slows down.

"Baby," he says, "I want you in my mouth."

The automatic door in front of us starts lifting up. He leans over me and presses the button to put the window down, and then goes back to rubbing my cock. I lean out and put the code in the machine and I see my breath in the cold air coming out in hard pants. A green light comes on and I drive the car forward until a red light comes on to tell me to stop.

"Have you ever played Seven Minutes in Heaven?" he asks, giving me butterfly kisses.

"What?"

The roller doors close and we are alone.

"Get in the back seat," he says. "Now."

I jump in the back and so does he. He kisses me hard and growls with pleasure. Then he's on his knees.

"I just..." I say. His lips are already around the head of my dick and I can't get any more words out, except, "*Oh fuck.*"

Foamy detergent covers the car and colored fairy lights twinkle through it. He tries to get my pants off me as he's sucking me off. I lift up to help him get them down and I slam into the back of his throat.

"Sorry," I say.

My cock makes a popping sound out of his mouth as he comes up for air.

"Stop saying *sorry*, Jesus."

The tip of his tongue works down to my balls and he laps at them.

"Oh my God..." I breathe hard.

The brushes are pummeling the car outside. I have never felt this before. Every caress makes me hungry for more. He starts working his tongue just at the cleft at the head of my cock while his soft hands caresses the rest. I run my fingers through his black curly hair. We are both already moaning, but I'm loud, it feels good to make noise. It also feels impossible *not* to make noise. He was right about one thing; I love screaming his name.

"*Mischa, Mischa. Oh god Mischa,*" I gasp, between my loud sweet primal *"ahs"* that automatically follow his movements.

My muscles are straining. From the way I'm screaming we both know I'm going to lose control soon. He speeds up and I let go. Cum squirts against the back of his throat and he drinks it down.

"Good boy," he says.

We kiss again and our tongues connect and I taste myself.

My legs are on either side of his hips. He starts to touch his cock, so I take it and start working it for him.

"Oh God baby," he pants. "I want to fuck you so hard…"

The car wash starts blow-drying the car. Our time is almost up. I stroke him faster.

"Oh fuck," he says.

The air-dryer stops. The car wash beeps three times. The truck is clean. I feel a slight alarm.

"You gotta come," I tell him.

"I don't want to."

"You have to."

He grabs my hands and puts them to his throat. He starts jerking himself and I don't understand. I hold his neck and kiss him tenderly.

"Choke me," he says.

I'm not sure if I can. The doors start rolling up slowly. I grip his throat a little, while his eyes bore into mine. I squeeze a little more. He flushes red and squirts on me. Thank God. He dives down and licks the warm cum off me.

I look behind to check the next customer. The windows are steamy.

"Shit," I say. "We fogged up the glass."

He finishes licking my length and reaches up to leave a handprint on the window.

I look at the watery imprint. "No! Don't do that!"

He laughs and puts his pants back on.

The car behind us beeps as he jumps in the front. He grabs his shirt and throws it on. The car behind beeps again.

"Keep your pants on!" he moans. "Some of us are trying to have *sex*."

I'm on the floor of the backseat desperately trying to dress myself as he drives out.

"What about the windows?" I ask.

He winds them down, and turns the aircon on full. Then he sprays cologne, and pops a breath mint, and throws wipes at me.

He has such an evil smile. "The perfect crime."

I look at him. "You're not supposed to be driving!"

"Oh *whoops*," he starts laughing. "Not the perfect crime. Why are you still in the back?"

I get my belt on and look at the diner. Hayden and Sabrina are exiting.

"Shit, shit, shit!" I groan.

"Jump back in the front," he tells me.

"You're such an asshole!"

He howls with laughter. "But you knew that already."

"It's not fucking funny!"

"It's all good," Mischa beams with levity. "We took a minute out of someone's day. They'll live."

I hook my belt just in time. Sabrina opens the door next to me and hops in, confused.

"Hi *boys*," she beams.

Mischa is laughing so hard he can hardly catch his breath. "Hey."

"Why were you beeping?" she asks.

"Mischa's just being an idiot," I splutter.

"Everything okay?"

"Just…" I say. "I'm in the back."

"Okay… Why?" Sabrina frowns.

"I just am."

Hayden looks between me and Mischa.

"Ride shotgun," I tell him.

Sabrina turns to me quietly. "What's…"

"Later, Kitten," I say.

We reach the leafy road outside of Amherst where the long driveway to my house starts. Sabrina, queen of tact, wraps her scarf around Mischa's neck from behind him. God, she is such a blessing.

"A goodbye present," she tells him.

The gate opens for us automatically.

"How does it recognize my car?" Mischa asks. "Do you have a remote?"

I cough uncomfortably. "William must have buzzed us in."

We pull up to the front door and get our luggage out. Our foster-parents are watching from the rooftop terrace. They lean over and say hello, but I don't introduce Mischa, and just keep unpacking the car with my head down. Isobelle arrives in the sports car next, and runs in the entranceway, into our foster mother's arms. After a few moments William pulls up behind us with bags of take-out.

"We got dinner for everyone," William explains.

I lied about William buzzing me in. Mischa caught that. Shit. He looks at me with curiosity. I don't want to give any more away to this mind reader. I am also still mad at him, so I grab my bags and throw them inside.

"You want to come in?" Sabrina asks him.

"Nah, I better get back," he says. "I need to go murder my brother."

"Ooh!" Isobelle coos, "I'd love to join you. I get hot for bloodshed."

"I believe you."

"I hope we'll see you again," Sabrina tells him.

"Maybe," he says. "I hope so."

Isobelle smiles, and she and Sabrina hug him.

"Thanks for the holiday," Mischa tells William.

"We're cool, right?" he says, apologetically.

"I didn't mean anything by it, with the kiss and everything."

"I know."

Mischa looks at him shyly, "Please don't actually kill me."

"No," he scratches the back of his head. "I just get really psycho when it comes to um... Austen... I'm sorry."

"I wish I had a brother like you," Mischa smiles, and throws his arms around him.

He looks touched by Mischa's gesture, and I watch him brighten in a way that disarms me for a moment.

"You are a brother like me," he tells Mischa, and hugs him back.

Mischa sure does have people skills. He's turned a murderous lion into a kitten. Once everyone is through the door, I grab the last bag, and Mischa's arm.

"I hope you're satisfied now," I tell him.

He shrugs with one shoulder. "I guess."

"See you later."

He searches my face. "Tell me you don't want to see me anymore."

"I don't want to see you anymore," I say, automatically.

That hurts him. He looks at the ground, mouth open.

Why did I say that?

Because he told me to say it. My exhaustion and annoyance is putting words in my mouth. Shit. I can't backtrack and smooth this one right in the driveway. I just stand there, frozen. I am such an asshole. Such a coward.

"I... I didn't think you'd say that," he says, and thinks for a moment. He reaches out and shakes my hand. "We never know how much time we have. Thanks... for the holiday... and thank you... for everything else," he clears his throat. "Have a nice life. I hope I see you in the next one."

It feels unreal. He turns away, and I let him.

He stops and turns back, and pulls me into a hug. I'm rigid at first, but then hug him back. I still don't know what to say.

"I need you to keep going," he whispers in my ear, and holds me tight. "Even when it's painful, when you think you can't, even when you want it to stop, keep pushing forward. Don't give up. You'll make it, and I will never not love you."

I let my lips secretly find his collarbone, a tiny spot between scarf and jersey, and kiss him there. His body tenses up, and he recoils from me. I let go, and see the look of pain on his face. He darts away to his car without looking at me again. I watch him zoom down the drive.

I didn't leave him in the dust. He left me. I don't even know his number. I stare into the void, and feel Sabrina's hand pat my back.

"Should we watch Brideshead?" she teases, and sips her soda through a pink straw. "Or is it too soon?"

"You cheeky blighter!" I laugh, and grab her around the waist.

Isobelle and Kane are watching us from the door.

Sabrina sniffs my collar. "He smells really nice. You're allowed to be with him, you know?"

"No," I say. "I'm not."

"He's good for you. I could help you hide it?"

I shake my head. "I can't risk it. Honey's already insane and paranoid, and it will tip him over the edge. I'll regret it for the rest of my life either way, but this way protects us all from anything that could happen. Stops James from getting to him too. Besides, he's just infatuated. He'll grow to hate me. Find ways to hurt us. Then we'll hurt him before he gets a chance. I either break his heart, or break his faith in humanity, and I don't know which one is which."

"Nothing lasts, trust nobody," she nods in agreement, and kisses my lips. "You gonna be okay?"

"I'll be fine."

I kiss her forehead and rub her back, and stand in the driveway holding each other and saying how much we love each other for an unhealthy, but desperately needed length of time.

I don't know if I'm rid of Mischa for real. If past behavior indicates future actions, I'll be seeing him every day for the rest of my damn life, but all at once, I am not so sure.

I watch movies with Honey Bee and Kane and the girls. Afterwards I go up to my wing of the house and hear the silence tingle in my ears like a weird background static. I call the dogs, Rufus, a Rottweiler, and Rex, a Doberman, up to my room. I throw a ball around with them to simply make noise. That night they sleep on the floor inside the shrine with me so I can listen to the sound of them breathing. I wake in the morning and find Isobelle and Sabrina have joined us, and are asleep on the shrine floor too, wrapped around me. I can smell our foster parents cooking breakfast. Things are getting back to normal.

✻ ✻ ✻

Can't sleep, can't eat. I start classes on Monday, and have band practice three days a week. I have some study to catch up on and so does my brother. We power through assignments between lectures. It's all a blur of things to get done and study.

Mischa is nowhere. Not at the pizzeria on Tuesday, so I pass by Wednesday and Thursday, and every other day of the week. The freezer gets full with pepperoni. I ask Billy if he's been training with him on Friday, and he says he hasn't heard from him yet. That night I play a gig in Springfield and he doesn't show. Saturday I hit every spot in town and come up empty.

Sunday is cold. The girls are staying with us but they're off on their own a lot. I have to stop trying to find him. I dread bumping into him by accident, so why am I seeking him out? I don't know why I'm doing this. I don't know why he's hiding. Both things are pissing me off. I take it out on my drums for hours at a time, until I'm a sweaty mess. I have to replace my sticks, a cymbal and two drum skins this week.

Perhaps I was just flattered to have someone's attention, and losing it makes me feel invisible again. I need to get the fuck over that. This is what I wanted. Obviously he wanted it too.

I need to get over it. The next Monday is just as grey as the last. I need to get my affairs in order. I need to donate my stuff to goodwill. I need to get on with things.

* * *

"Baby, why are you not ready?" Honey Bee asks on Saturday afternoon.

He's standing in the kitchen, in a tuxedo. Isobelle and Sabrina are behind him in ballgowns looking stunning. I'm in my pajamas, and have been for two days, now scooping a bowl of pudding, marshmallows, and popcorn for dinner.

"Oh God," I groan. "Where are we supposed to be going?"

"The fundraiser," Brina says. "In New York."

I have no idea what she is talking about.

"Can I skip?" I ask.

"Granddad is coming," Honey says. "He wants to see you, and he spent fifty grand on our tickets so get fucking dressed."

"Oh jeez..."

"What's wrong with you?" he scowls. "Shower, dress, and we'll go in thirty."

"Bee..." I start whinging.

"NOW!" Isobelle bellows, and we both jump.

I scamper upstairs, wash and put on a suit. I am obviously coming down with a cold, because it is painful to do all three. At least we're flying there. Moments before we arrive at the country club I remember why we are there.

"Jesus," I say. "A *charity* auction?"

"What did you think it was?" Sabrina asks.

"I thought it was a bad fucking dream."

Billy sighs. "The bad dream started years ago."

"Easy for you, Bee. Let's go to the Hamptons and hide out," I suggest.

"Can't go around it," Isobelle says.

Billy pats me. "We gotta pay the soul tax."

Inside the club it's festive and beautiful. One of the organizers grabs me and William and bustles us between other important guests. Billy turns on the charm and is warm and attentive.

Grandpa cuts a lonely figure as his limo door opens. He's taller than most people, and has retained his thick head of hair, now white with age. Everyone turns around and watches him. They all speak quietly amongst themselves as we both fly to his side like we are still small children. He lifts his cane so as to block our affection.

"I see you boys managed to pull yourselves together tonight," he says coldly, stepping between us to meet Isobelle and Sabrina. "My beautiful girls, it has been too long."

They both greet him, and catch up like he's *their* grandfather. There's nothing we can do. Grandpa has to keep up the appearance of frostiness. We can hear the faint whispers from the other attendees of *"Disowned... Delinquent... Bratty... Estranged... Bullies... Violent..."*

As he walks away I flush a dark shade of beetroot. Billy watches the old man ignoring us and tries to stifle a chuckle. He doesn't care about all the hearsay. I want the Earth to swallow me. William makes his way over to the waiter carrying the drinks and takes one.

A middle-aged woman with a bright floral dress comes over to save me from my humiliation. She says her name is Nancy.

"Why don't we meet some of the other boys on the chopping block tonight?" Nancy says.

She grabs my hand and pulls me to the corner of the room.

"What do you mean?" I ask, feeling uneasy. "Chopping block?"

"The other men we're auctioning."

"Auctioning guys?"

"This is the Date Night auction, you know, a bachelor auction? You'll be our first victim."

"Oh *God*."

Isobelle finds her way over to me and gestures across the hall with her head.

"Well," she grins, "look who it is."

On the other side of the room, I see Mischa, and my heart goes crazy. I wonder if I'm seeing things. He's standing in the corner with a beautiful young woman on his arm with the same black curly hair like his. I imagine her to be his sister. He looks sharp in a suit, with Sabrina's cashmere scarf draped over his shoulders. He looks a little thinner. His cheekbones are really popping. I think of everything that happened between us and my body gets wobbly. It feels like some invisible force is trying to lift me off my feet and pull me towards him. I'm fighting it, because I don't want the other guests to see me floating through the air.

I want to run to him. I want to knock everyone over as I do, but I move casually, nonchalant, calm. *Indifferent.* I grab a drink and weave through hundreds of glittering people like a sunflower field.

He's talking to a very attractive guy. Light hair, athletic, chiseled, *gorgeous*. Gravity centers back in the pit of my stomach and falls to the floor. I want to kill him just for standing next to Mischa. Things between them look... close... personal... intimate. That is his real date, no doubt. I shouldn't be surprised he moved on so fast, but a little part of me is.

"Oh *shit*," Mischa says, when he sees me.

He looks surprised. Horrified, in fact. His jaw drops as I approach, and he just stares.

"You look good in a suit," I say.

He's a little lost for words. "Thanks...." he looks at my tie. "So do you."

The beautiful girl looks at me and back at Mischa.

"This is Sofie," he says. "My heart, this is Austen."

"Austen?" she looks back at Mischa. "You spent Christmas Eve together?"

"Yes," he nods, a little sheepish.

She is delighted, and embraces me. "Mischa's told me so much about you!"

I'm charmed. It feels like we're already good friends.

"I have heard all about you too."

"Thank you for the car, it's wonderful."

I feel my cheeks flush. "Not me," I tell her. "No matter what he has said."

She looks quizzically at Mischa. "He thinks he can lie to us?"

Mischa lowers his gaze to his glass and swirls it. "Don't lie to my sister, Austen."

I shift uncomfortably.

"I'm sure you deserve it," I whisper.

Mischa spits out the sip he's just taken, and laughs at me, loud and brash. I'm sure I'm turning purple.

"I don't deserve it," Sofie says, "but I will take good care of it."

"I would love to spend some more time with you... and um, and Mischa..."

"You would?" Mischa asks.

"Maybe I could take you both to dinner?"

The attractive man steps forward, expecting an introduction. Confirmation perhaps, that he means something to Mischa, and Mischa means something to him.

"And this is Sebastian," Mischa says. "He's from Paris. This is William and Austen. They're the brothers I visited Fiordland with."

The beautiful man shakes my hand. "*Enchanté*."

I look behind me and my brother is indeed shadowing me.

"Hey Sugarplum," he says to Mischa, and hugs him.

"Will, so good to see you," Mischa says, and pats him on the back. "This is Sofie. Our other sister Natasha is here too, and she keeps saying she wants to meet you, but um... please don't hit on her. Please. She's fucking crazy and you'll regret it."

Sofie nods in agreement.

Billy splutters with laughter. "Okay. I promise. It's only fair that I stay away from your sisters too, I guess. Are you getting auctioned?"

"Unfortunately we are," Mischa says.

"Bugger." Billy grabs another glass of champagne from a waiter and knocks it back. "We can do introductions later. I'm going to need a few more drinks before the shit-show. Excuse me."

"Please don't get drunk," I say.

He follows the waiter out into the middle of the hall to Sabrina, who is also trying to get a few drinks in, and I'm alone with Mischa and Sebastian.

"You study?" Sebastian asks.

"I do," I say. "Law. And you?"

"I am Étoile with the ballet. I'm hoping Mischa and Sofie will dance with me soon." He turns to Mischa. "Is it not, *mon grand?*"

Mon grand. *My big boy.* Something a hundred-year-old Frenchman might call his son, or a young Parisian might call his lover. Mischa is flushing bright red. It turns me to stone in an instant.

"That sounds wonderful," I tell Sebastian.

I excuse myself from the group, and try to find my brother. I stop at the first tray of drinks and chug as much as I can before the auction starts. Mischa approaches and we are face to face again.

"I'm so sorry, I didn't know you'd be here," Mischa says. "They're raising money for the ballet, and I don't understand why they requested me personally, I'm not even a professional yet, they just said some patron wanted me to come and..."

I cut him off. "You have as much a right to be here as anyone. Sebastian is a dreamboat, by the way. I get why you're avoiding me now. I'm glad you're over it."

"I'm not, Austen; it's torture." He looks at me with those smoky eyes, and shows me his shaky hands. "My palms are sweating, my heart's racing just seeing you. I can't stop looking at your photo, for *hours*. It's fucking nuts. I worry this thing has tipped over into insanity. I can't eat, I barely sleep, and when I do, I dream of you. You're also my every waking thought. Nothing else could ever come close. Every single moment of my day I feel a cold abyss trying to separate us forever. It won't give me any peace. I hope it's the darkness before dawn, because I can't take much more of this."

He's beyond adorable, I can't stand it. I wonder if my mother chose him, and has been guiding him to me, whispering in his ear this whole time.

"Poor thing. I'm still willing to help, if you'd like?"

His eyes shoot up. "You want to?"

"Terrible idea," I smile, "but we *are* friends... and I would like to... a lot."

"There you are!" Nancy says from behind me.

I jump in surprise. "Hey."

Nancy grabs my arm again. "It's showtime."

22 MISCHA

Austen appears on stage. His grandfather smiles up at him warmly, and he smiles back. I guess they are sort of on good terms, and things aren't as bad as they say.

Me, Sebastian, and Sofie have seats at a table next to William and the girls, right at the front. Everyone else in the hall finds their tables.

Our sister Natasha is here with us. Tonight she looks like Russia personified; almond eyes, round face, slicked back blonde hair, wearing white fur, sparkling diamonds, and incredibly polished. She has been working the room, but has her sights set on both of the twins, and I am quietly terrified.

The hostess dings her glass into the microphone, and the crowd quietens.

"I hope you all have your paddles ready," she says. "We're starting off strong tonight! For our first bachelor of the evening, we have everyone's favorite rowing and polo athlete, *William* Blazey!"

My mind doesn't register for a second that Austen has been mistaken for his brother. It only clicks when Kane and I look at each other. We both are slightly confused. Austen looks embarrassed.

The hostess continues to dig his grave. "William can fly

helicopters and planes, and can arrange the date of your dreams anywhere on the Eastern Seaboard. He has a yacht in the Hamptons, and would be delighted to take his date sailing. Shall we start the bidding off at a thousand dollars?"

I'm amused at the turn of events. This means Austen will be auctioned for a date he won't even be going on. Or will he? The bidding starts and heats up. We are up to eight-thousand.

Wait, can I just buy Austen right now?

I grab Natasha's elbow and force her paddle up in the air. Her eyes bug at me in surprise. Sofie is giggling. She knows what's up.

"We've got *nine*-thousand!" the auctioneer says, ecstatic. "Ten!"

The guests make a little "Oooh!" sound.

William is offended. He forces Isobelle's hand in the air and she scowls at him.

"Stop bidding on me," Will hisses. "You can't, I'm off limits."

Austen is staring into my eyes. He's desperate to break into a huge smile but presses his lips together and tries to stay neutral. My face morphs into a mischievous grin. Natasha is now up to speed and fully on board.

"But I *love* helicopters," she tells William, and bids again.

"Hey, knock it off," he says, and forces Isobelle's arm again while she looks annoyed.

"No," Natasha says, and goes again.

William is scandalized, and tries to take Isobelle's paddle but she won't give it up. He snatches it away and outbids Natasha. Now it's a battle between the two of them. He's so angry that he doesn't even notice when I switch my wine glass with his. Then Austen can't help but laugh.

"You know I don't have forty-thousand dollars?" Isobelle asks William as things get intense.

"Alright," William says to our table. "Fuck this." He stands up and takes Isobelle with him. "One-hundred thousand."

The crowd gasps and claps. Isobelle gags in disgust, Sabrina looks at the floor. Kane slaps his hand to his head, and Hayden is trying to hide his giggles.

"William," I chide him. "You are spoiling our fun."

"Good," he says.

Natasha gives him a death stare. She's fired up, and stands up too. I grab her wrist and paddle, pulling her down, shaking my head at her not to bid again.

"I got a better idea," I whisper in Russian.

"Going once!" the auctioneer yells, jumping in her high heels. "Twice! Sold to table two for one hundred thousand dollars! Mister William Blazey! We reached our goal! This is amazing!"

She is bouncing with excitement like she is on a pogo-stick.

Austen gets off stage and Sebastian gets on. The crowd is animated. A healthy bidding war for him carries on between two ancient women. Austen makes his way to table two, and his grandfather makes his way there also.

"That was not good sportsmanship, son," his grandpa tells William, "but it was entertaining."

Will introduces his grandfather to us. The old man is polite, but sours immediately. He gives William a disapproving look and walks off. William finds it funny.

As Austen sits down, I introduce him to Natasha.

"That was hilarious," he tells her.

One of the other organizers approaches with a checklist.

"We have Austen Blazey up soon," she says.

William looks at Austen and he scowls.

"I'm not getting up there again," Austen says. "No way! You can be Austen for once!"

Isobelle laughs at Will. He sighs, and goes with the woman.

"Kiss me," Sabrina tells Austen. "Please."

He looks around the table and then nods to her. She holds her purse up to cover their faces so nobody can see if they use their tongues or not, but I assume they absolutely did not.

Sabrina brings her purse away. I give her the side-eye. She laughs at me.

"Austen Blazey" is introduced and Will steps out.

"Your eyes are not deceiving you," the hostess says. "There are two of them."

I watch the stage, and whisper in Natasha's ear, and she nods. Then she whispers in Sofie's ear, and she steals a knowing glance my way.

The bidding starts and William can do nothing but watch from the stage as Sofie and Natasha stand up, and push the bids up to nine thousand dollars. Some other girls join the fun and soon we're at sixty grand.

"Maybe lightning will strike twice," the hostess says. "If we could have an identical set of one hundred thousand dollar donations for our identical twins, I think we'd make everyone's night!"

I detect a small smile, and an even smaller cough. Natasha pushes Sofie's arm, and her paddle goes up in the air. The whole crowd gasps at her and conversations break out around the hall.

Natasha puts her own paddle back on the table, sits down, and crosses her arms.

"One hundred thousand dollars?" the auctioneer asks.

Sofie looks terrified. "Yes, please."

William's brain is working overtime but he tries to hide it. There's nothing he can do.

"One hundred thousand from table number two. Going

once, twice, sold!"

Our table erupts in laughter. The ovation starts and Sofie is red with embarrassment. Natasha does a little wave to the crowd. The hostess is giddy with delight by this point and can barely concentrate as William gets off stage.

The hostess heaves excited breaths from her chest. "What a great night!"

Back at the table, everybody has got the giggles, Hayden is in stitches, desperately trying to pass it off as coughing. William stomps over, absolutely raging at me.

"I can't believe you bid on me again," he says, "like *seriously*, I will not humiliate myself by taking you on some goofy date for your own sick entertainment..."

"We didn't bid on you," Natasha interrupts, her fierce eyes drilling into his.

"What?" he asks.

"We bid on *Austen*."

"Excuse me?"

"As a gesture to Austen and his fiancé."

"To make up for my horrid behavior on your boat," I explain.

"It's *romantic*," Sofie shrugs.

Sabrina is hanging off Austen's neck and kissing his cheek.

"How *sweet!*" She gives him a big smile. "I can't wait!"

"Really?" William frowns.

"I'll borrow your helicopter if you're offering," Natasha raises an eyebrow, "and you could take me to dinner too, unless you think you're too good for me?"

"N... no no," William stutters, and looks to me for help.

Hayden loses it and walks away crying with laughter. Austen looks at me and his smile is infectious. Soon I'm taken away to be sold to the highest bidder.

As a Slav myself, an indentured one no less, I find a human auction all very distasteful, but I'm purchased for a good price anyway. When I look down at our table from the stage, I see Ausen is gone, and I head backstage. Kane finds me at the exit, and stops me.

"I think Austen was looking for you," he says, in a hushed tone. "Near the farthest lounge. Check inside the washroom maybe."

I pass my table, and the girls have already left to mingle, and I can't see him anywhere, so I go to the back lounge.

23 AUSTEN

I wait a thousand pounding heartbeats for Mischa to come through the door. He walks in timidly, looking around. I check my stopwatch.

"Kane said you were around here, and want to talk to me?"

I go to him and put my hands to his face.

"We don't have long," I say, and touch my lips lightly to his.

He looks at me wide-eyed. "Can I read into this?"

"Yes," I smile.

He lets out all the tension he is carrying in his body, and meets my lips. We heat up fast. In a cubical he slams me against the wall and kisses me passionately. Our cold and rigid stalemate dissolves, and we breathe in relief.

"Hi," Mischa says sweetly, and wipes away a tear.

We hug tightly.

"I'm sorry."

"Stop saying that."

He unzips my fly and moves his hand inside my pants, while I run my hand through his curls. I'm already hard, and he starts to stroke me slow.

"God I've missed you," I say, between kisses.

He sucks my earlobe. "I can tell."

"I looked everywhere for you," I say.

"I've been here, working, really busy."

"I guess this means I owe you a night out?"

"Or a night in," he kisses me again.

"You wouldn't like to spend it with Sebastian?"

"That'd be exchanging gold for brass. Besides, I'm not fucking Sebastian. He's just trying to persuade me to wear a tutu full-time. That's all."

I'm not convinced. "He hit on you right in front of me."

He scoffs. "I'm a hot guy, Austen, and I'm approachable. *Everybody* hits on me. You could use the date with your girlfriend if you really want?"

"I can take Sabrina out anytime," I tell him.

"Well, I guess it's you and me then," he says.

"*Mmmmh,*" I moan, as his hand gets faster. "Thanks for buying me."

"Best hundred grand I ever spent. Also the *only* hundred grand I ever spent."

"It's a *lot.*"

"William gave it to me."

"*What?*"

"To watch over you in Fiordland," he says and kisses down my neck. "He's *crazy* overprotective. Paranoid you're in danger, even in a remote forest at the farthest edge of the world."

"Yeah," I sigh. "We have to be stealthy or else..."

"He'll kill me..." he scoffs, and gets down on his knees in front of me. "I know, I know."

* * *

Kane knocks after five very short minutes. Mischa waits so nobody sees us together, but we cross paths again out front, where he's with Natasha, talking to Billy.

"Hey man," he pats me on the back as he passes me and Sabrina. "Come for a gym session with Will next week."

I nod as he walks off without looking back.

"That was a very interesting young man," Grandpa frowns, as we are saying goodbye. "The one hugging your brother earlier. What's his name?"

"That's our friend Mischa," Sabrina says for me, "Mischa Abramov. He's studying with William. They work out together sometimes, and he came with us to Australia, and Izzy and I asked him to tag along on your boat afterwards."

"Abramov? A relation of Victor Abramov, no doubt?"

We both shrug.

"Oh, I think he is actually, yeah," I tell him, trying not to flush. "He sent some wine for us. He owns a football club or something. Is he a friend of yours?"

"No. We should talk about this later, in private."

"He and William are not close," I assure him. "I wouldn't

worry. Mischa missed his flight, and only came to New Zealand because the girls took pity on him."

"How convenient. I'm glad you are more careful of the company you keep, dear boy," he says, and leaves.

24 MISCHA

February 14, 2008, 3.49 p.m (Valentine's Day).

Nobody's around when I arrive at Austen's place. I know he's home alone today, so I pick the lock to an empty security booth, disarm the sensors, jump the wall and run along the tree line, then dart over the lawn to the house. It's my way of saying nothing will stop me.

They really are hillbillies, they have a blue bottle tree. I can't walk straight in, because some lady with dark hair is cleaning inside. Two dogs, a large Rottweiler, followed by a Doberman, see me and bolt towards the door outside. There's ivy growing all over the brickwork. Brilliant.

I start ascending the vines that cling to the old place. The dogs bark, but they can't get me as I climb higher. I scare a bird and it scares me. There's a window open at a balcony on the third floor and I climb to it and peek in. It's a bedroom and beyond is an open bathroom door. Austen is in there, shaving. I watch him check his phone, and hear a pitter-patter sound loafing in from the hall. The dogs have found me and are now going feral. I duck down and they growl and bark at the window. Austen calls them off and shuts them out of the room, but they are still howling. I hear a clacking sound and he comes to the balcony with a loaded crossbow in his hands. He sees me and puts down his weapon. He gives me a hand up, and I sit on the ledge.

"Impressive."

He waves to the empty garden.

I look down three stories. "Who are you waving to?"

He shows me the red dot of a laser sight pointed at my chest.

"Kane."

"Oh right."

"You're here for your date," Austen says.

"Our date," I correct him.

He runs his hands through his hair. "Well, you might as well meet the dogs before they break down the door."

He yells at the dogs to be calm and they obey, then he lets them in and stands between us. The two growl like they have a serious problem with me. Austen chides them and they quieten. He lets them approach and they sniff my shoes. They recognize my scent, look back at Austen, and chill out a little. I kiss Austen on the lips and they growl again. The look on his face makes it worth it.

"You got reservations?" I ask. "I hope you're not taking me to the local pizza place everyone raves about?"

He shakes his head. "I'm taking you to New York."

My mind does not compute. "What do you mean?"

"It's a city a few hours away; you might like it."

"Oh man. I just drove all the way from there! It'll take *forever.*"

"Helicopter," he says, and puts a jacket on.

"Can I fly it?"

"Do you know how?"

I pull out my helicopter license. "Yeah, but I know you've been in a crash, and I don't want to put you on edge."

"That was a plane crash, not a helicopter, and I enjoyed it immensely."

"You didn't think you were going to die?"

Austen rolls his eyes. "That was kinda the point."

"Okay so you should definitely not fly..."

Austen laughs. "Leave it to the pilot. It'd be embarrassing to crash on a first date."

"You should have more faith in me."

"Hey, what does your father do?" he asks, as he opens a suitcase. "My grandfather was asking the other week."

Don't tell him.

"Oh," I say, feeling my toes curl. "Business. He bought companies during the Russian collapse. It was a crazy time, but he became the last man standing, and so the companies ballooned. The businesses have done well over the past couple years, especially in the mining boom."

"Oh right," Austen nods. "Mining. Mexico?"

DARK STARS IN THE SKY

"Yeah."

He adds a few pieces of clothing to his baggage.

"That explains how they know each other."

They know each other?

The air gets heavy around me. The skies are supposed to be clear tonight, but I hear a clap of thunder.

It can't be.

"They know each other?" I ask.

"Seems like they are business rivals," Austen nods, folding a shirt. "Grandpa was a little prickly about it."

No no no.

The sudden realization that this could become the agent of our destruction flashes in my head. It all clicks.

Don't think about it.

I don't even know if I'll get more than this date, and if Austen loves me even a fraction of how much I love him, he wouldn't hold it against me.

Don't think about it.

Besides, what can I do?

Don't think about it.

He might never find out anyway.

Austen said his favorite food is Italian. Anything Italian.

It's a fucking coincidence.

Sivishni was shifty about moving to Amherst. It was sudden. He wanted the two best *Italian* restaurants... got all the best ingredients imported from Italy, and some fancy chef... spent all that money... in this tiny town... made all his devoted children move here...

No. It doesn't prove anything.

Our only act of rebellion was putting the wrong phone number on the flyers. Sivishni was not happy when he found out the number didn't work. Apparently he was so angry he even scared Ivan. The shop phone has been ringing a lot lately.

No. Don't fucking think about it.

"I was even worried your father was some sort of Russian crime boss who got offside with my grandpa or something insane like that, and you'd try kill me," Austen giggles, as he zips up all the compartments of his luggage. "I have terrible luck, so I'm paranoid, and imagine anything could happen sometimes."

I don't want to hear this.

Don't tell him. Austen's fragile, don't even entertain the idea.

It's not likely... but not impossible.

IT'S IMPOSSIBLE.

There are some weird things. Like how Sofie and Natasha have to come in to work on the weekends. Sivishni pays for them to get their hair styled before they arrive. All my brothers have to show their sexy faces at the fights in Springfield every month. It's mandatory. Defying a king is treason.

Just stop thinking.

Who convinced me to go to the bathhouse?

Who convinced Austen?

Who was it this mysterious person Natasha said invited us to the charity auction, at ten grand a fucking ticket?

It doesn't matter.

My brothers and sisters. All good-looking. By design. Chosen for their charm, intelligence, and beauty. Then the dentists, dermatologists, even a little cosmetic surgery for any-one that needed it. Bought and paid for. Is the only reason we are here in this life, in this country, in this *family* even, is just to be bait for Austen and William?

Stop, just stop.

It's true. I can feel it.

Just the way he kept *smiling* at me the other day...

Russians don't smile.

Fuck fuck fuck. I'm just some fucking honey trap?

He's your father. He's your hero. Your king. Your savior. He's your fucking God

He never cared. I'm an appliance, a piece of meat, a sex toy.

That part is true.

Even if it's true. What would even Sivishni want them for? Why, WHY, WHY would...

FUCKING STOP!

STOP STOP STOP!

Him. That's who *him* is.

To run the world, you have to take it from the one who already has it. Whatever it takes. I swore an oath to do whatever it takes.

I may have pledged myself to that man for life, but he doesn't know that I swore eternity to Austen, in every lifetime. For a hundred generations, across space and time, I have kept my promise. I'll bring down the whole damn Abramov family before they even realize I've turned on them.

"You're overthinking," I clear my throat, as I stand beside myself like a ghost, barely holding on to my own body. "Are we ready?"

❋ ❋ ❋

I've always been good at separating from the difficult parts of my life. The helicopter ride makes me completely forget the metaphorical curveball that just smashed me in the fucking face so hard it made my soul leave my body for at least ten minutes.

The thing is, I shouldn't really care if we win the war or not. We'll be remade, and will try again, and again, and again. Even if I die tomorrow, I'll have this time with Austen, forever.

That's all I'm going to think about tonight. I'll figure out everything else later.

We arrive at a fancy hotel restaurant in uptown Manhattan. There's starchy white tablecloths and fine bone china. It's more uptight than I was hoping for, but Austen pushes through the door to the kitchen like he owns the place. Which may be the case, now I think of it.

"We're eating at the chef's table," he explains.

He takes my hand. I feel victorious. The cooks slaving away on the line greet Austen like an old friend. We pass the prep and storage area. A short, older man in a beautiful white chef's uniform is retrieving a second uniform from a locker.

"Mon petit chou!" he says to Austen. French for my *little cabbage*.

They kiss on both cheeks and chatter in French. He introduces me and the man is delighted.

"This is Philippe; my papa."

I know this man is not Austen's father, or related at all, but I'm not bothered. He's lovely, and the fondness between them is obvious.

"Bonsoir," I greet him.

"You speak a little French?" he asks.

"Yes," I reply. "I went to the Lycee in Moscow."

"Then you probably speak better than me!" Philippe laughs.

He hands Austen a chef's uniform and he puts it on. "Tonight you do us the honor of eating a meal we prepare for you."

"I might be a little rusty," Austen warns Philippe.

"No," he smiles. "You are an artist, I know it."

Philippe seats me at a table in the back of the restaurant kitchen, where I watch them cook. Austen is all, *"Oui, Chef! Non, Chef!"* They are in perfect synchronicity, and fast. Philippe plates and Austen decorates.

"Such a pity your brother is not here," Philippe tells Austen.

"Next time," Austen says.

"He's coming Wednesday for his *own* date."

"Auction date?"

Philippe's mouth curls at the edges into a smile. "Perhaps."

Austen brings the caviar over, and offers it to me. I put a dollop on the back of my hand and hold it back out to him. It's almost a dare. He licks it off my skin and his cheeks turn pink. Then he brings the first dish over, a savory pastry. It's delicious, but watching them work is fascinating. Austen is so happy. I'm falling in love with him all over again, just when I thought the pain might ease. I'm entranced watching his beautiful body move. He shoots glances back at me. When he catches me watching, I'm transfixed, and it makes him laugh. It makes him light up from within, and everything in my imaginings tells me again that he's looking at me the way I look at him.

After the third incredible dish I beg him to eat with me.

"You have to eat too," I tell him.

He reluctantly sits while Philippe makes the main course, and feeds me from the fork.

"I don't understand how broccoli and mashed potatoes can taste this good," I say. "Like seriously, what the fuck?"

A couple of the chefs who know Austen come over to say hello and present dishes. Austen introduces all of them to me. There's a lot of warmth. They all touch him, and he touches them, and he's totally unbothered.

"So you like the guys, niño?" the sous-chef with a neck tattoo, Carlos, asks in a thick Latin accent when he brings the main. "Jack owes me twenty bucks."

"I think a lot of people made money tonight," Austen nods.

"The big money is on your *brother*."

Austen scoffs. "I'm in for a grand then. He's a womanizer."

A black girl on the line near us bursts into laughter, really loud and really hard, an infectious sound sets off the others around her.

"*Child*," she says, "I'll take that bet."

Carlos shakes his head, amused. "Abuela's out of hospital. She wants a visit soon."

"Definitely," Austen says.

"Good to see you doing good, man," he says, and hugs Austen and Austen hugs him back. Then he turns to me. "I owe niño my life," he says, and taps my cheek. "We've known each other since we were kids, man. He's taken care of me and my brothers, cousins, my mom. If you hurt him, nobody's ever gonna find like even your finger or nothing."

He gets up and rushes back to his station. By the time dessert rolls out Philippe is fixing a screw-up on the line, and we watch the action while eating a chocolate parfait. It is so good that if I could have sex with it, I absolutely would.

"I never want to eat again," I say, "unless I can eat this."

"I guess I'll have to be your personal chef," Austen says.

I stop, and narrow my eyes at him. "That was very smooth. How many people have you brought here? How many dinners have you whipped up? How many people have you offered your cooking services to?"

"I've actually never..."

"Oh yeah, you have never taken anyone else here?"

"I've never been on a date before."

"What?"

Austen shrugs. "How am I doing?"

"You're definitely nailing it. How long have you been working here?"

"My parents spent the summer at this hotel for the first time when we were eleven."

"You worked here when you were eleven?"

"And twelve," he nods. "It's a messy thing. I don't know if you'd believe it."

"Try me."

"Okay," he sighs. "Mom fired our beloved French nanny that summer—literally the only adult on Earth who could tell us apart. We were supposed to go back to school in autumn, but my parents were feuding, and stormed out on each other. In the morning everyone had left the hotel. Mom must have taken our little sister back to start school. My um... father, who I mostly just call James, had left separately. He forgot to drop us off at our new boarding school, so we just sort of... stayed here."

"What in the *Home Alone*?"

"To be fair, we called both of them. Their assistants said they'd call back."

"They never did?"

Austen shakes his head, and seems resigned to the fact.

"Life was better without them anyway. We'd always been invisible. At first we'd stay in bed with room service and watch cable television. We had already been alone most of the time since we arrived, so the staff were used to us, and knew we were some guest's kids."

"You never got in trouble?"

"Never," Austen's eyes are wide. "We'd get bored and visit

the chef, Philippe. We would hide in the pantry and watch him until he got us working in the kitchen. It felt good. Like the PBJ summer in Appalachia, you know? At first we washed a lot of dishes, chopped onions, but soon we were junior chefs working on the line. He'd train us what to do, and we did it over and over a hundred times. I was on pastries and William was the roast chef. When we got bored we'd swap and everyone would pretend they didn't notice, and help fix mistakes while Philippe wasn't looking."

"Did he know you were alone?"

"Not at first. He'd pay us a little money each night, and we'd go around the city and visit the parks or the library or museums during the day. We became real city rats. Isobelle even visited us during her school holidays. Then one day we got sick. Philippe went to our rooms to fetch our parents but we told him they left in September and he was furious, but it was midnight. Philippe's wife Marcella showed up and took us to their house in Brooklyn. She was from Seychelles, couldn't have kids, and here were two adorable French-speaking twins thrust upon her. She kept asking us who we were and we told her 'we're the Twins' and she loved Peter Pan so we won her over with the Lost Boys thing. We begged her to let us stay."

"Did she?"

"Yeah, she basically stitched it up with Meemaw to share us.

Things were uncomfortable at first. I don't think Meemaw had never met a black person before, or been to a city, and she was struggling to understand almost everything. She was a fast learner though, and saw the good in Marcella immediately, and vice-versa. So that was our life until we were discovered by our other Grandma."

"She tracked you down?"

"No. She just bumped into us. We were in the restaur-ant before work one day, and there was a table of old la-dies laughing away. One particular lady kept looking over at us eating our club sandwiches. She looked more and more alarmed and finally came over and said, *'Boys?'* It was our dad's mother. She asked what we were doing there. We said, *'We live here.'* She asked where our parents were, and we said they were gone. Grandpa's company had just been paying the bill. My grandfather arrived and Grandma was going *mental.* She kept screaming *'FOURTEEN MONTHS VINCENT! FOURTEEN MONTHS!'* She paced around the penthouse. Grandma did not believe Meemaw when she said that she was our meemaw and had physical custody because she was so young. We just visited her for her fifty-third birthday last summer, so I guess Meemaw would have been like, maybe forty-four then, so we think she must have had Mom when she was like, thirteen or twelve maybe? Grandma kept screaming *'Who is she?'* and

Meemaw explained that we were not leaving her care. We'd stay in America, and there was nothing they could do. Then Grandma said that she was going to kill our mother and father."

"Understandable really."

"Grandpa was more chill. He asked where we had been for Christmas, and we told him we took our paychecks and bought each other presents from Macy's, and went ice-skating. He asked where we had paychecks from, and we said we had jobs. He laughed, and said he was so proud of us. Grandma started screaming that she was going to call the police on whoever used her grandchildren as slave labor. We stopped saying any-thing after that."

"It sounds like a dream."

"It all feels unreal now. It became some wonderful timeless pocket of space we were hiding in. Turned out my Mom had taken off and everyone thought we were with her but she'd vanished."

"Where was she?"

"They don't know. Meemaw agreed to share custody if she got our school breaks and holidays, and lots of hush money. *Millions.* Anything James would have got, Meemaw has it now. Now her town is a hillbilly fortress, and a great comfort to me. James went full psycho about losing that fortune, threatening everyone, trying to get us back. Then Meemaw shot a robber trying to break in and everyone got all paranoid and teamed up to keep us out of sight."

"Is James still after you?"

"Probably not, I don't think he ever really was. All bark, no bite, plus a coincidence involving a dead burglar. We never even saw James again, or Mom," he shrugs.

My gut-instinct tingles, so I know he has somehow "seen" his parents again, but I'm guessing only in the society pages of magazines and tabloids.

"So where'd you go?"

"Grandma sent us to a boarding school. They're pretty regimented places. From the moment we got up till the moment we went to bed there was somewhere we were meant to be, from horse riding at five in the morning till we brushed our teeth at nine. Every minute was written down. Obviously we rebelled to start off with. Hid in the traveller camp down the road. We promised Grandma we'd behave if we could see Phillipe and Marcella, and we got chef training. And we have behaved ever since."

"But you stole the plane? You were disowned."

He shoots a look at me. "I try not to think about it."

"Sorry," I say.

"Actually, you're right. Grandad wanted us away from

everything, and safe, so Philippe and Marcella fostered us and Isobelle fulltime after we were emancipated. We lived with them until last year."

"Why was Isobelle there?"

"To be with us. She's our best friend. The point is, this kitchen represents the happiest time of my life, this is my family, and those were all my favorite dishes."

"The happiest time of my life was in the hospital in Sydney, when you were massaging my head, and spin the bottle."

"You poor sad bastard," he frowns. "Please tell me that's not true?"

"It really is."

"Pathetic."

"I *know*."

"We have to fix that," he says.

We say goodnight to the kitchen and Philippe hugs and kisses Austen. Then he embraces me. He tells me to take good care of his boy, that Austen is a delicate creature. I tell him I will, and thank him for an amazing night.

Austen takes me up to the penthouse. It's huge. It's like a house up there. I have to look in every room. My family has money, but me and my brothers have our boots on the ground. We never have perks like this.

He's sitting on the couch watching me take it in. I've noticed it a lot tonight. Him watching me. In the car, the chopper, eating, and now. I take control of the sound system and music comes on. Sexy music. I've already decided.

I kick my shoes off. "I'm gonna give you a lapdance."

He accepts. I loosen my tie and take my shirt off. I kneel in front of him and push his legs apart. I move up between them and take his hand, and run it down my middle, to my navel. He inhales sharply. I run my hands down his body. I rip his shirt open and the buttons go flying. He likes it.

"You seem to want to destroy every shirt I own."

"Oh yes."

Then I sit on him and start grinding. He smells sweet like summer fruits.

"I'm going to pull the shirt behind you and bind your hands together. Is that alright?"

"I think so," he says, his breathing hard.

I bring his shirt up. I don't know why, but I can't bring myself to knot his wrists with it, even though it'd be very sexy, so I leave it loose hanging off him. I'm looking in his eyes and gyrating so he's a little distracted. There's this moment of rocking on him where we both give over to it. The faint sounds of the city and music and low hum of the building are left behind.

His hands lace with mine and we kiss. It's slow and sweet, and against all odds, it's even better than the other times. It's the kiss of two people who are past the point of no return. Where return is nowhere even in sight. I'm hard, he's hard, and I'm rubbing right along his length. I can feel the heat from his body and his blood pumping in his chest.

"Oh God," he breathes hard. "That feels *too* good."

"Impossible."

I'm surprised by his enthusiasm, and have to remember this is not a dream. I'm turning Austen on and he's letting me know it. He's with me, and nothing else matters. Nothing means more. It's the most beautiful moment of my life, and I'm having it right now. Sooner or later it'll end and I will return to the slow, burning, hopeless addiction. Tonight I am a wildfire.

"Oh fuck," he pants. "I'm going to come like this."

My movement gets faster, "Good boy; come for me baby."

We kiss frantically. I try to philosophize about what we are and what we mean to each other but I can't think and do this at the same time. I realize that what makes us "us" is primitive and natural. I don't feel anything but him and me. No pasts. No futures. He moans and then screams into my mouth, and explodes beneath me.

He catches his breath. I need to be as close to him as possible. We just need to get off the clothes that separate us. I reach down to pull up his singlet, and he stops me.

"I don't want to take this off," Austen says.

DARK STARS IN THE SKY

"Naked or not," I say, "I need you."

"I'm supposed to be spoiling you," he says.

He pushes me onto the sofa and takes my pants off. He wraps his hand around my shaft. I gasp as his hot breath lands my cock head. He kisses it a little and I moan, but he hesitates.

"Are you sure you want to do this?" I ask him. "You worried you'll seizure?"

"More worried I'll do it wrong and fuck it up."

"The best advice is do things you like," I say. "You know, from your girlfriend, and don't do what you hate. Sabrina spit or swallow?"

He looks disgusted. "I... I don't know."

"Does she do it toothy or not?"

He thinks for a moment. "Yeah. It's not *bad.*"

I laugh a little. "Is that a joke?" I ask but he doesn't answer. "Has she never sucked you off?"

He raises an eyebrow. "Not much."

"Or not at all? You fuck?"

"Of course."

He looks at me like I'm an idiot, but I know when people are lying to me.

"Austen, is this your first time? Are you a virgin?"

"Of course not," he says, like it's an obvious answer to a stupid question. "I'm literally having sex with you right now, and on the plane."

"I jerked you off... I sucked your dick... that was a lapdance; I'm talking *sex*."

He's extremely uncomfortable and choking on his words. "I think it goes without saying I have never been any further with a guy."

This is very hard for him to talk about. He's distressed and fidgety and his discomfort makes him hard to read.

"Have you had sex with a woman?"

"Yes," he says.

"With who?"

"Sabrina. And it's none of your... look... okay... we're waiting."

"Waiting for what? You said you let me touch you maybe just because you wanted to see what it felt like, then you said that about what it was like to be kissed. You said this was your first date. Ipso facto..."

"No ipso facto."

"Ergo..."

"No ergo. It's..."

"Therefore!" I interrupt. "You have not been touched, except for by me."

He huffs in defeat. "I haven't gone all the way with a girl, no. Happy?"

"What have you done?" I ask.

"This."

"This? With me?"

"Yes," he frowns.

"And nobody else?"

"Not yet."

"Not *yet*?" I flinch. "What does that mean?"

"Sabrina and I were planning to swap virginities when..."

"I will slit her fucking throat."

"Please don't. None of this is her fault."

"I disagree; she's no virgin."

"Yes, she really is."

"She's fucking William."

"No she isn't," Austen rolls his eyes.

"Yes."

"No."

"How are you so sure?" I frown.

"Because William loves her."

"He can't fuck people he loves?"

"Absolutely not. He's the yin to my yang."

"Hold on, so you mean you really haven't been capable of intimacy *at all*? What's the deal with Sabrina then? She your sister?"

"No! Stop saying that."

"Austen, you *need* to get a DNA test." He doesn't speak, but his body language agrees with me. "Or have you... gone and done one already? You're waiting to find out?"

"Stop, stop, stop," he growls. "I don't want you to ever bring it up again. It's not your concern, and it's dangerous for her. Besides, we are just together so people don't ask questions or speculate about me."

"That is literally the definition of a *beard*, baby."

"No, my stupid brother's just worried people might think I'm *gay*."

"You are gay! That's a beard! That is what a beard is for!"

"Don't tell Billy; he'll kill himself."

"Better him than you."

"Never say that."

"I have seen that asshole chug a glass of milk, you're not the same fucking person."

"That actually made him sick..."

I put the new information together in my mind.

"Sabrina is not your girlfriend."

"No. She's my *fiancé*."

"But you don't want to marry her."

"I don't have a choice."

"You've only ever let *me* touch you. I thought it was just

guys but... Wait, wait, *wait...* was I your first *kiss? Romantic* kiss? With tongue? You asked me if you were good like you'd never..."

He breathes in sharply. "This is mortifying," he says, and hides his face behind a cushion. "Let's forget this. I ruined the mood. Let's go back to Amherst and..."

"What? No!" I wail. "You're killing me here! I'll get on my knees and beg if I have to. I'm just surprised someone as sexy as you didn't... become like me or Will."

"Ugh. I wish I could. So yes, I'm new to this, so can we just... start slow?" Austen asks. "I never thought I'd ever do any of this so... maybe... teach me how?"

"Okay," I say. "Alright. We don't have to do everything tonight. We should maybe go slow."

"I don't know what 'toothy' is. You may actually have to spell it out."

"Of course," I nod, and stand up. "Put your lips around the head and make sure you don't get your teeth on my skin. Use your lips to cover them because they hurt when they scrape up and down, you know?" My cock goes in his mouth. I feel his warm tongue. It's wildly exhilarating. "Hit that spot underneath where the head meets. Easy. Just like that. That's good, *ahm...* it's good," I swallow hard. *This is ecstasy.* "Really good. You don't have to suck hard or deepthroat or caress the balls to be... good. It just adds variety and you get better with time. Just stick to the head. That's really nice. You can lick up the shaft too. Yeah. Like that. Run your lips and tongue down it but always hit that spot I told you. This is... *oh*... you're a really fast learner..."

All the love that poured inside me in the bathhouse is now bubbling in my veins. Austen's making little sounds. Little rhythmic hums of pleasure, losing concentration as he goes deeper. His teeth are halfway down my shaft and he tries to take more. He scrapes a little as he gets further to the base. While not usually a pleasant feeling, I'm so aroused it barely registers. Austen's growing excitement is intoxicating.

He stops a moment and breathes. "You have a really big dick huh?"

I don't dare look down. My whole body is in this moment. Not just my cock, but my skin and every organ of my body seems to vibrate a good feeling into me, even my brain has hit some divine frequency.

"If I look at you," I tell him, "I'm gonna come... I should probably... not do that."

I go quiet and he begins working my head again, slower this time, but I still get close and take it out of his mouth. I take a beat, until I think I'm okay to go again and he pops it back in.

I run my hands through his hair. It's thick and soft. I feel like I'm throbbing. My cock definitely is throbbing. I can usually cope with a guy edging me but I'm not coping now. He's barely edging me. We only just *started.* I feel high, like on drugs. Really good ones. Of all the sex I've had, I've never truly known it until now.

He becomes absorbed in his task and I know I'm getting close. I look down at him. We lock eyes and I'm overwhelmed with love for him. The wave crashes over me, and I can't hold on any more, and shoot in his mouth with a loud cry. He doesn't move and inch and lets me ram right to the back of his throat and that just makes me come more. Then I carefully remove my still hard cock from his mouth. He sucks all the cum off it as it comes out, and swallows.

He looks at me with his big doe eyes. "Was that okay?" he asks, catching his breath.

I look at this extraordinary creature and nod. "You did really good."

I remove what's left of my clothes and we move to a bedroom. Austen's still almost fully dressed. I unbuckle his belt carefully, take down his pants, and remove his boxers. When I get to his singlet he crosses his arms over his chest. There are some small scars on his forearms. He might be a cutter, but they don't look like that. Something might have happened, the assault, the plane accident, I don't know. I imagine there are some on his body that he's not ready to show me. They are all a part of his attractiveness. It reminds me of things about the war, but those thoughts can't bother me here.

"You still want to leave this on?" I ask him.

"If that's okay? I'm not ready to have that conversation."

A chill goes down my spine, as my imagination and childhood memories make muffled noises in the locked basement in my mind.

"Of course it's okay. You don't have to show me your body if you don't want to. You could tie me up if it..."

"No," he says firmly, as he gets on the bed.

He is not entirely naked but he's more vulnerable than me. His body's colder than mine, he's shivering. He fumbles as he lays down and I lie on top of him. I see him as he is; eager, frightened, and hopeful. I think of all the weeks of terrible shame, hunger, desperation, and most of all, danger, to allow ourselves this night.

"The wolf lies down with the lamb," he whispers.

"I'm nervous," I say. "I haven't been scared for myself since I was a kid."

"You're lucky." He runs his finger over a star on my collarbone. "I like your tattoos."

"I was worried you wouldn't."

He kisses each of them. His hands reach behind me to caress

my back as he draws me in.

"Thank you," I tell him. "For letting me have this with you tonight."

"And tomorrow, and Sunday. It's only right; it cost you a pretty penny."

"It's worth it," I smile. "But you don't have to sleep with me, do you? Because of the auction?"

"No, we're not obliged to sleep with the winning bidder."

"Oh, good," I say, and breathe a sigh of relief. "The old lady who won me looked like a *real* man-eater."

He cackles at the thought. He rubs his hands down my spine and holds me at the small of my back. I run my hands through his hair and trace the geography of his face with my finger. His skin is as soft as it looks. As we kiss, I slide against his body. There's so much precum. His hips rock gently with me.

In chemistry, if there is any reaction between two substances, both are transformed. In our blooming intimacy, I feel his anxiety unravel. Moving together, he follows his pleasure away from fear and ascends with me to a warm stillness. He holds us together, stroking up and down. My whole body is vibrating again. The ticker-tape of thoughts in endless languages running through my head stops as the bliss rises.

Most people cannot recognize true love when it is in front of them, even when they are in its power. It's a creation of their soul they somehow discover. It can't be controlled or willed into being, or driven out when it's not ideal or convenient. It either is, or is not.

Tonight, it is.

Austen and I are in a deep alignment. It's a silent dance, an unrehearsed choreography. We are weightless, speechless, thoughtless creatures. No longer human, just animals, flowing through eternity.

He makes a sound I have been waiting a lifetime to hear. A moan in my ear. The one I love loving me back. I want to make him moan like this for the rest of our lives, together.

"I don't want to ever sleep or eat again," he says after, and kisses me. "I don't want to talk to anyone else. I don't want any other touch but yours. I wish I could hide inside this moment for the rest of time."

"You're mine," I tell him. "Stay here. Be mine forever."

'I almost had you,' William chokes.
I squeeze harder so his face goes red and his veins pop up. He's coughing up more and more breathless laughter. I look in his green eyes as I strangle the life out of him. They are so beautiful; just like Austen's, only there's no soul behind these ones. A capillary bursts in the white of his eye and it fills with blood. I have to stop, for this psychopath's brother; for Austen. I don't want to, and it takes everything I have, but I do.
I let William go.
He sucks in air and heaves with mirth. 'I bet you want to break every bone in my body.'

Only the deepest of loves could cause the most shocking betrayals.

Obsession, secrets and lies could turn star-crossed lovers into enemies locked in a blood feud that will destroy both their families. Even if they discover the truth, can they fix the damage once it's been done?

What could be so terrible about the love of your life, that knowing it might kill you both? In the sequel to Dark Sky Full of Stars, Mischa Abramov, younger brother of a fearful Russian mafia dynasty, navigates unknown waters when his unrequited love for the troubled and elusive young billionaire Austen Blazey blossoms into a dangerous clandestine affair. The path forward is rocky, and both are hiding dangerous secrets about their identities, but knowing the truth could get them killed, if they don't kill each other first.
Will Mischa discover the dark secret before it's too late? And what will he confront about his own dark and tragic past along the way?

A provocative story of high passion and emotion.

* This is a full-length novel with explicit scenes

IF YOU LIKE THE BOOK,
PLEASE LEAVE A REVIEW

https://www.goodreads.com/book/
show/230432180-dark-sky-full-of-stars

ABOUT THE AUTHOR

Roman Schreiber

https://www.bookbub.com/authors/roman-schreiber

To me, love has always contained a quiet kind of magic. Not fireballs and spellbooks, but that soft, disorienting feeling that the world has tilted a few degrees. Colours seem brighter. Time goes strange. Ordinary gestures—making tea, sitting on a porch at dusk, folding laundry side by side—suddenly feel sacred. Something in you insists: this matters, even if you can't explain why.

Modern romance is brilliant at attraction—at banter, chemistry, aesthetics, and heat—but I'm more interested in the weird, luminous feeling underneath. The way love makes the ordinary world feel slightly enchanted, even when nothing out of the ordinary is happening.

My stories are about that: character-driven, real-world romances with a soft, dreamlike shimmer around the edges where love makes ordinary life feel quietly magic. My characters stumble into something that feels quietly impossible and choosing it anyway. Not into fantasy, but into a kind of childlike wonder—like the world might be deeper and kinder than it first appeared.

BOOKS IN THIS SERIES

The Red and the Black Series
Only the deepest of loves could cause the most shocking betrayals. Obsession, secrets and lies could turn star-crossed lovers into enemies locked in a blood feud that will destroy both their families. Even if they discover the truth, can they fix the damage once it's been done? What could be so terrible about the love of your life, that knowing it might kill you both?

A provocative DARK MM romance story of high passion and emotion.

* This is a full-length novel with explicit scenes,

* Rated Mature for foul language, scenes of a sexual nature, sexual activity between adults, and mature themes.
Reader Discretion Advised

Part 2: The Moon In Daylight (2026)

"Show me the letters," I tell him.
William shakes his head. "I've burnt all of them."
"Right."
He looks at the count on his fingers. "You have about three questions left, Kane."
"Does Austen know this man?"
He does not deduct the question from his fingers. "Yes. You already asked this. That's a waste of a question. Try again."

"Are you afraid of this man?"

"That's irrelevant."

"Is Austen afraid of this man?"

"Maybe. I've never asked him that."

"Did something happen to Austen?"

"I can't tell you that."

"Does anyone else know?"

Will puts a finger down. "Isobelle and Sabrina."

"Can I ask them about it?"

He puts another finger down. "No. They can't know something's up. They can't know anything about you knowing, or the letters. That wouldn't end well. Imagine kicking a beehive; it would be like that. Last question. I hope it's the right one."

"Is this situation the reason why you are... sometimes... fucking... unhinged and terrifying?"

Will sighs, and puts his last finger down. "Yes. It's the only reason."

I let it sink in. "Okay, yes. I'll work for you."

Part 3; Dark Stars (2027)

Time is the only thing that always goes the wrong way.
Despite knowing William Blazey since childhood, Kane Kingsland is sure of one thing; William is not who he says he is. But no matter how far Kane runs to get away from him, he's always right back where he started.

William Blazey has to always be in control. Too many people depend on him, and too many secrets need to stay buried. But if he were to ever tell anyone the truth, it would be Kane. Kingsland. That's why Kane needs to be gotten rid of, and soon too.

Part 4: Scarlet And Black (2028)